Mariette Lindstein was born and [raised on the] west coast of Sweden. At the age of 2[0 she joined] Scientology and worked for the next 25 years at all levels of the organization, including at its international headquarters outside Los Angeles. Mariette left the Church in 2004 and is now married to Dan Koon, an author and artist. They live in a forest outside Halmstad with their three dogs. *Fog Island* is her debut novel and was first published in Sweden where it won the Best Crime Debut at the Specsavers CrimeTime Awards. Mariette now dedicates her life to writing and lecturing to warn others about the dangers of cults and cult mentality.

Fog Island

Mariette Lindstein

Translation by Rachel Willson-Broyles

ONE PLACE. MANY STORIES

This novel is entirely a work of fiction. The names, characters and incidents portrayed in it are the work of the author's imagination. Any resemblance to actual persons, living or dead, events or localities is entirely coincidental.

HQ
An imprint of HarperCollins*Publishers* Ltd
1 London Bridge Street
London SE1 9GF

This paperback edition 2019

1
First published in Great Britain by
HQ, an imprint of HarperCollins*Publishers* Ltd 2019

English translation © Rachel Willson-Broyles

Mariette Lindstein asserts the moral right to be identified as the author of this work.
A catalogue record for this book is available from the British Library.

Rachel Willson-Broyles hereby asserts the moral right to be identified as the author of the Translation.

ISBN: 978-0-00-824534-4

MIX
Paper from
responsible sources
FSC™ C007454

This book is produced from independently certified FSC paper to ensure responsible forest management.

For more information visit: www.harpercollins.co.uk/green

Printed and bound in Great Britain by
CPI Group (UK) Ltd, Croydon, CR0 4YY

Fog Island

Prologue

She has been lying awake in the dark for ages, marking the time by counting her breaths. One breath in takes three seconds. One breath out, another three. Seconds become minutes. And soon, an hour.

The darkness is dense. There are no shadows, outlines, no numbers on a clock radio. She feels weightless lying there, as if she's floating. But the counting keeps her awake, and anyway, she is far too tense to fall asleep now. Doubt gnaws in the back of her mind. The fear of failure makes her nerves whine like the strings on an untuned violin as a blurry veil of anxiety settles over all her thoughts. Best just to breathe, not think, just *be* until the right moment.

She hears a faint tapping against the window; it grows into a persistent patter. Rain, despite the forecast. She curses the weather service and thinks about how hard it will be to run through the forest.

Then it's time. She cautiously slides out from under the blanket and kneels on the floor. Her hands fumble under the bed, finding the bundle of her backpack. It contains everything she needs — and yet, almost nothing. Her tennis shoes are there too, the kind you just stick your feet into, no time for tying shoes. She carefully pulls on her jacket, which had been wrapped around the backpack, and puts on the shoes. Tiny, cautious steps across the floor. Her body feels dreamlike and heavy.

There's a murmur from one of the beds and she stiffens. Someone turns over, making bedsprings creak. She waits until she hears deep breathing again. The last few steps. She fumbles for the door handle and finds it. A gust of cool air rushes in from the corridor as the door swings open. The night-time lighting paints the white walls a pale yellow. It feels like she's gliding down the hallway. She pushes open the heavy iron door to the basement stairs, where the main breaker is. This is it. Sink or swim. She only has ten minutes, fifteen at the most. After that they'll notice she's missing. She knows the routines all too well. Once the first wave of confusion has settled down, they will gather and count the personnel. Then the manhunt will begin.

I am not afraid, I am not afraid.

She repeats the words silently to herself, like a mantra, and takes a couple of deep breaths. She can still change her mind. Turn around. Crawl back into her warm bed. But if she doesn't escape now, she never will, and that thought is so unbearable that it blows the spark of her courage back into a flame.

As she pulls down the handle of the breaker, there's a snap and a crackle and suddenly it is so dark that she feels dizzy and sways a bit in the black void. She grabs the wall, feels her way to the emergency exit, and opens the door. Cold, humid air hits her. The rain falls over the courtyard like a thick curtain; it has already drenched the grass, which eagerly sucks at her foot.

She splashes through puddles at a run, completely vulnerable to chance now. If her luck runs out, someone will spot her from the window of the manor house. But nothing happens. All she can hear is the drumming of the rain against the roof, the water pouring out of the drainpipes, and her own thudding steps.

The ladder is leaning against the wall. Thank God.

She has to make it over quickly, because soon the backup generator will be turned on, the courtyard will be bathed in light, and the barbed wire at the top of the wall will be capable of delivering a serious shock.

She climbs up the ladder, fumbles for a foothold between the razor-sharp barbs of the electric wire, and stands up on the slippery wall.

This is the moment she has been dreaming of, with longing and terror both. Down there, on the other side, there is no return. A burst of exhilaration runs through her mind, but then the fear grabs hold of her again.

She tosses her backpack down first, then jumps with all her might. Over the barbed wire, away from the danger behind her, into the darkness. Pain shoots through her foot when she lands. She brushes her hand over it and the pain abates. Her eyes search for the head of the path. And find it. She runs down it like a madwoman. Sometimes she misses a turn and almost darts into a bush, but she always makes it back to the path. She is riding high on adrenaline now. Forward. Forward is all that matters.

I am not afraid, I am not afraid.

She tries to make out the terrain, jumping over winding roots and rocks that criss-cross the narrow path. Her heart is pounding, her chest burning. The alarm begins to sound at the manor, behind her. The sweeping beam of the searchlight glints off the leaves. Things are going to get chaotic for a while. Then it will be all hands on deck, chasing her down.

Her clothing is wet and heavy and the backpack is digging into her shoulders. At last, she can see a light through the trees. She is close to her hiding place now. So very close.

She slows down. Stops.

Her eyes search for the end of the path. A sudden creak in the forest.

Her heart jumps into her throat; her muscles lock in panic.

He emerges from between the trees and stops not far away from her. She doesn't have a chance; there is nowhere to run. The terrain is rough, either side of the path overgrown.

Her disappointment is overwhelming. Her insides tighten into one big, hard knot.

It is impossible.

And still, it has happened.

And still, he is standing there.

Somewhere, a dog barks.

The alarm sounds.

The last thing she thinks of is a voice. A faded memory returning to her.

You will never, ever get out of here. Just so you know.

The blood pounds at her temples.

Flickering sparks shower onto the curtains of her eyelids.

Then come the violent waves of dizziness and everything begins to go black.

I let the bumblebee fly around in the small aquarium for a while. It tries to get out, buzzing angrily, but all it can do is bounce off the walls.

Then it gives up for a moment and lands on the cork mat at the bottom.

I lift the glass lid off, slowly and cautiously. I hold my breath as I lower my hand, which holds a pin. It only takes a millisecond, and then the bumblebee is stuck to the mat. It hums furiously, spinning on the pin in a crazy, futile dance. Its wings work frantically, but it goes nowhere. Then I lift the cork mat out of the aquarium, place it before me, and pick up the tweezers.

Lily looks at me, her mouth agape. She runs her tongue over her lower lip. I search for something in her eyes, fear or hatred, but all I find is a great emptiness, a dark abyss that sucks me in.

But first, the bumblebee.

I pull off the wings first, then the legs. Taking my time, lining them up on the table in front of her. The stupid bumblebee never stops buzzing, moving around on the pin, just a body now, as if it ever had a chance.

'Why are you doing that?' she asks.

'Because it's amusing,' I say.

'What? To watch it suffer?'

'No, your face when you watch.'

I almost can't breathe when I realize she's trembling a bit.

That's how it all begins. With a tiny bumblebee.

1

The small ferry bobbed in the swells on the dark water. They were close now, but couldn't see the island; the morning fog was a heavy blanket on the sea. The horizon was invisible.

Sofia felt relief as the mainland, on the other side, vanished behind the curtain of fog. She was putting distance between herself and Ellis. It was nice to get away from him, if only for a while.

There had always been something hectic and wild about her relationship with Ellis, an intensity that could lead to nothing but disaster. His terrible temper should have set off warning bells, but at first she just thought it made him exciting. They had argued about absolutely everything and it ended with him getting his revenge online. She had been so distracted that she almost bombed her last exam at college. She passed in the end, but just barely.

It was in the midst of this catastrophe that the invitation to the lecture by Franz Oswald popped up in her email. And it was because of that lecture that she was sitting here on a ferry, on her way to a strange island way out in the archipelago.

Wilma, Sofia's best friend, was there too, staring into the fog. There was a hint of excitement between them. A vague sense of apprehension about what awaited them on the island.

On the morning she received the lecture invitation, Sofia had been on the computer, Googling phrases like 'planning for the future' and 'career choices,' realizing in the end that her search was not at all helpful. When she read the email, her first thought was to wonder why it hadn't ended up in the spam folder.

A lecture on ViaTerra by Franz Oswald. For those who wish to walk the way of the earth, it read.

How the heck did a person do that? She thought it sounded strange, but she had heard of Franz Oswald before. There was some chatter about him around the university. He'd showed up out of the blue, giving talks about his philosophies of clean living, which he called ViaTerra. Among the young women, the talk about Oswald mostly revolved around the fact that he was attractive and a little mysterious.

She read the email again. Made sure that the event was free of charge. She figured it couldn't hurt to listen to what this Oswald had to say, so she sent a text to Wilma, who didn't take much convincing. They did nearly everything together by that time.

They had arrived late to the talk and sat in the front row of a full lecture hall. A big banner was hung above the stage; it said 'ViaTerra: We Walk the Way of the Earth!' in huge, green letters. The lecture hall was otherwise bare and sterile and had a strong smell of cleaning agents.

A buzz of surprise ran through the audience when Oswald walked onstage with a wheelbarrow full to the brim with something white. Flour or sugar. She couldn't tell what it was, because the lights were focused on the podium; the spot where he was standing was much dimmer. The woman sitting next to Sofia groaned. Someone behind her whispered, 'What on earth?'

He set down the wheelbarrow and stood still for a moment before coming forward and gripping the edges of the podium.

'Sugar,' he said. 'This is what the average family goes through in three months.'

Sofia suddenly regretted coming, and she felt the urge to get up and leave. The feeling was so strong that her legs twitched. She really should have been looking for a job, not listening to a lecture. And Oswald made her nervous.

He was tall and well-built, wearing a grey blazer over a black T-shirt. His dark hair was combed back into a ponytail. The tan couldn't be real, but it suited him. He gave the impression of being trim and sophisticated while also radiating something primitive, almost animalistic. But above all, it was his strong stage presence that made the air tremble with anticipation.

He stood in silence for a moment. A calmer, more expectant mood spread through the audience. Then he launched into a dizzying tempo that only increased throughout the lecture. His voice went on like a machine gun. He showed the crowd a PowerPoint full of brains, nervous systems, lungs, and flabby bodies that had fallen victim to toxins and stress.

Sofia began to catch on to what he believed in. A sort of back-to-Mother-Earth philosophy where anything artificial was the root of all evil.

'Now we'll take a break,' he suddenly said, 'and afterwards I'll tell you about the solution.'

During the second half, his elocution was calm and controlled. He spoke of things like sleeping in total darkness, drinking clean water, and eating organic food. Nothing new or sensational. Yet he made it all sound absolutely ground-breaking.

'Our program also contains a spiritual element,' he said. 'But it's not like you think, so listen carefully.'

He paused, and it seemed to Sofia that he was staring at her; she squirmed in her seat. He fixed his eyes on her as he continued.

'Aren't you tired of hearing that you have to be present and live in the now? We must stop listening to all these religious wackos who preach that the present is what matters. Buying their books and courses so we can learn to sit with your eyes closed and breathe deeply. In ViaTerra, we do not deny the past. We draw power from it.'

Sofia's hand flew up of its own accord.

'But how do you do that?'

Oswald put on a measured smile.

'Your name?'

'Sofia.'

'Sofia, I'm glad you asked; the answer is in our theses. The physical program takes care of the body. The theses are for the spiritual side. But the short version is, you learn to draw power from everything that has happened in your life. Even your negative memories.'

'But how?'

'You have to read the theses to understand. It has to do with intuition. When a person stops denying the past, a whole lot of inhibitions disappear. One's abilities are set free and one can rely on intuition again.'

'Are your theses available to read?'

'Of course, but only if you undergo the whole program. We have a centre on West Fog Island, off the coast of Bohuslän, a sanctuary where we help our guests find the correct balance in life. One can only make use of the theses in a setting free of all distractions. That's why our centre is on an island.'

A man behind Sofia raised his hand.

'Are you a religion?'

'No, we're actually the first anti-religion.'

'Anti-religion? What's that?'

'That means that whatever you hate about religion, we're the exact opposite,' Oswald replied.

'I hate that you have to pray to God in most religions,' said the man.

'In ViaTerra, we don't pray to God. We're realists, with our feet planted firmly on the ground.'

A stout, red-haired woman in the first row stood up.

'I hate all these damn books and writings you're supposed to read. And then you're supposed to believe all that crap too.'

By now, almost everyone was laughing.

'We don't have any books in ViaTerra. Just a couple of simple theses we use, but that's all voluntary.'

It went on like this for a while. Oswald handled each question deftly. He was really on a roll.

Then a man wearing a neat, black suit and round glasses stood up.

'Do you have scientific evidence for all of this? Is this an accepted science, or just a cult?'

'Everything we do is based on sound reason. It has nothing to do with science or religion. The important thing is that it works, right?'

'So how do we know that your gimmick works?'

'Come and see for yourself. Or don't.'

'Nah, I think I'll pass.'

The man made his way through the rows of seats and left the hall.

'There you go,' Oswald said with a shrug. 'Let's move on, with those of you who are truly interested.'

★

When the lecture was over, they were ushered out of the hall by young people in grey suits and led to a large coatroom where several tables had been lined up along the walls. Pens and forms were handed out. A thin young man with slicked-back hair and a goatee loomed over Sofia and Wilma until they had filled out their forms; then, when they were finished, he greedily yanked the papers from their hands. They mingled for a bit, chatting with a few young women their own age.

Then, suddenly, there he was. He popped up behind Sofia. Wilma was the first to notice him, and she was startled. When Sofia turned around, he was right next to her. Only now that they were face to face did she notice how young he really was. Twenty-five, thirty at the most. His skin was smooth, except for the hint of a few wrinkles on his forehead. His jaw was wide, and a five o'clock shadow lent a hint of manliness to his soft features. That, and his thick, dark eyebrows. But what she noticed first was his eyes. His gaze was so intense that it made her uncomfortable. And then there was the noticeable scent of his aftershave: pine and citrus. He was something totally out of the ordinary — there was no standing this close to him without noticing it.

At first he said nothing, and the lengthy silence became awkward. She noticed his hands. Long, thin fingers with nails cut short. No ring. The expression in his eyes was unreadable. She swallowed and tried to think of something to say but realized that she was tongue-tied.

'Sofia, I got the impression that you had more questions?' he said at last, putting the emphasis on her name.

'Not really. We're just curious.' Her voice sounded rough and hoarse.

He raised and lowered his eyebrows and drew up the corners of his lips, as if there were a secret between them. He was well aware, irritatingly so, of how good-looking he was.

'Come and visit. I'd be happy to show you our centre. No commitment, just a tour of the property.'

He handed her a business card. Green and white, with embossed letters.

'This number goes to Madeleine, my secretary. Call her and book a time.'

He held onto the card for a moment so she couldn't take it from his hand. His eyes flashed and then he let go. Sofia was about to respond, but he had already turned around and was on his way into the crowd. Wilma tugged at Sofia's sleeve.

'Stop staring at him. Why don't we visit that island and take a look? What harm can it do?'

She clears her throat a few times. Doesn't quite know how to say it.

I just stare at her. I know it makes her uncomfortable, and I enjoy that.

'We can't go too far,' she says. 'I mean, it could be dangerous . . .'

'Isn't that the point?'

'Yes, but . . . you know what I mean.'

'Nope, not really. Tell me.'

'I don't want it to leave bruises.'

I snort.

'So wear a turtleneck. Stop being such a wuss. You like it, don't you?'

She lowers her eyes, all innocent. This is something new. Her fear.

It seeps out of her and turns me on; I get incredibly excited.

Have to take a few deep breaths, hold myself back, to keep from grabbing her and shaking her hard.

I own this person; I have her completely under my power.

She bends to my will like the grass in the wind. I turn my back on her.

Feel her drawn into the vacuum.

I think of how this night will be.

2

'Are you dreaming, Miss?'

This was the man who captained the ferry, Edwin Björk. He was slightly overweight, with sideburns and a wind-chapped face; he smelled like diesel and seaweed. Sofia and Wilma had made friends with him on the journey over. Sofia tore herself from her memories of the lecture and looked at Björk.

'Not really, just wondering if it's usually so foggy here in the summer.'

'It's not unusual,' Björk said. 'She's not called Fog Island for nothing. But it's worst in the fall. The fog sometimes gets so thick that I can't bring the ferry in. What are you two up to on the island?'

'We're going to visit a group at the manor, ViaTerra.'

Björn wrinkled his nose.

'Then be careful. That place is cursed.'

'Seriously? You're joking, right?' Wilma asked.

'Nope, I'm certainly not. It's haunted by the Countess. I've seen her with my own two eyes.'

'Tell us.'

So he told them, with such feeling and conviction that Sofia began to shiver. The fog slipped in under her clothes and settled on her skin like a cold blanket. Images flickered through her mind as he spoke. Creepy images she couldn't shake off.

'The manor house was built in the early 1900s. You don't often see estates like it out in the archipelago because the islands were home mostly to fishermen and boatbuilders. Count von Bärensten was determined to live here, though, so he had that wretched place built. But you see, his wife, the Countess, grew restless out here. She took frequent trips to the mainland, where she fell in love with a sea captain she met in secret. One night when the fog was thick, the captain's ship ran aground and sank just off the island. It was winter; the water was cold and everyone on board perished. A great tragedy, it was.'

'Is that true, or just a tall tale?' Wilma interrupted.

'Every word is the truth. But listen now, because we're almost to the island and I'll have to dock the ferry.'

Wilma fell silent and they listened breathlessly as Björk went on.

'When the Countess realized what had happened to the captain, she went out to a cliff we call Devil's Rock and threw herself to her death in the icy water.'

Björk straightened his cap and shook his head in reflection.

'And when the Count found out . . . something in his mind must have snapped, because he set fire to the manor house and shot himself in the head. If not for the servants, the whole mess probably would have burned down. They managed to save the house and the children, but the Count was dead as a doornail.

'After the tragedy with the ship, they installed a foghorn at the lighthouse. Whenever it sounded, the superstitious islanders said the Countess was standing on Devil's Rock, calling for her lover. And then people began to spot the Countess on the cliff. Always in a fog. She continued to appear for many years.'

'It must have been their imaginations,' Sofia said.

'Hardly,' replied Björk. 'She was real, believe me. Meanwhile, the Count's children, who still lived there, fell ill and the barns burned down. The curse went on for years, until the Count's son was fed up and moved abroad. The estate sat abandoned for several years.'

'And then?'

'The misery continued. A doctor bought the manor in the late 1990s. Lived there with his daughter. Big plans for the place — he wanted to turn it into some sort of rest home. But his daughter died in a fire, in one of the barns. An accident, they said, but I wasn't fooled. The place is cursed.' Björk held up one finger. 'I'm not done yet — around the same time, a boy jumped from Devil's Rock, hit his head, and drowned. The current took him. Since then, diving from the cliff has been forbidden.'

Sofia wondered if the old man was just making this up, but there wasn't the slightest hint of teasing in his expression. Why would Oswald want to establish his centre in such a place? It seemed incredible.

'So you can go look at all that, the lighthouse and the cliff?' Wilma asked.

'Yes, the lighthouse is still there, but the foghorn is no longer in use. Otherwise it's all the same. And now the manor is being run by lunatics again, as you'll soon discover.' At last a booming laugh welled from his throat.

'Do you know Oswald?' Wilma asked.

'Nah, he's far too uppity to spend time with us islanders. He always stays in his car when he takes the ferry over.'

Sofia gazed into the fog. She thought she could see a faint outline where the horizon should be.

'Here she is now!' Björk cried.

Slowly, majestically, the island took shape. The contours of the

17

firs on the hills, small boats at rest in the harbour, and shadows of houses here and there. The shrieking of the gulls reached the ferry. The fog was lifting. A pale sun, which couldn't quite pierce the clouds, hung like a yellow blob in the grey sky.

'See you on the evening ferry, then,' Björk said as he guided the boat toward the pier. 'There are two ferry departures each day. The morning ferry at eight and the evening ferry at five.'

When they stepped off, they immediately found themselves in the village, which was like a summer paradise. Small cottages with turrets and gingerbread; cobblestone streets and boutiques. Children were playing along the quay. Summer visitors drank coffee at an outdoor café. It was only early June, but vacation life was in full swing here.

Barely fifty metres from the ferry pier was a cobblestone square with a fountain in the middle. A woman in a grey uniform was waiting for them. She was thin and almost as short as Sofia. Her blonde hair was up in a bun and her face was pale, with delicate features. Her eyes were large and almost colourless; her eyebrows were white.

'Sofia and Wilma? I'm Madeleine, Franz Oswald's secretary. I'll be showing you around today. First we'll have a quick look around the island and then we'll go up to the manor.'

She led them to a station wagon that was parked on one side of the square and opened the car door for them.

'There are roads along the coast on both sides of the island,' she explained. 'Farther inland it's mostly forest and heath, but I thought I would show you the landscape before we head to ViaTerra. There's a lookout point on the northern tip of the island where you can look out over the Skagerrak Sound.'

'Where's the manor?' Sofia asked.

'On the north end. Just a short walk from the lookout.'

The western coast was flat, with sandy beaches and grass lawns full of picnic tables and grills. A couple of jetties extended like bridges into the hazy heat of the sea. Small boats were moored on the jetties and the shore was lined with boathouses. The eastern coast was barren and wild. The cliffs plunged to the sea just past the edge of the road.

They drove to the end of the island and parked the car, then walked across an expanse of heath to the lookout point, where the cliffs sloped to the water.

The fog had lifted and the sun was high in the sky. It was glittering blue as far as the eye could see, aside from the white flash of a lighthouse on an islet. Right away Sofia's eyes were drawn to a rocky cliff that jutted out over the sea. It looked like a trampoline.

'Is that the cliff you call Devil's Rock?'

Madeleine gave a snort.

'We don't, but I guess the superstitious villagers do. As you can see, though, it's only a cliff.'

'We were given a warning on the way here. The ferry man, Björk, told us some creepy stories about the manor.'

Madeleine shook her head.

'Oh, he's not all there. He only does that to scare off our guests. The islanders have been so bloody suspicious since we moved here. They're allergic to change. But we don't care. Come on, let's go see ViaTerra!'

They travelled back along the coast road for a bit and turned off at a wide gravel drive that was lined with huge oaks whose foliage loomed over them like a cupola. And suddenly they were at the manor house gate, which was at least three metres high, made of wrought iron, and adorned with winding curlicues, angels and devils, and an enormous keyhole.

'Do you open it with a huge key?' Wilma joked.

Madeleine just shook her head.

'No, no; there's a guard, of course.'

Only then did Sofia notice him. He was in a sentry box built into the wall. He waved them in, and the gate gave a creak and slowly swung open.

She didn't know quite what she'd been expecting to find within the gate. Maybe an eerie, tumbledown mansion full of towers and crenellations. Instead, what spread before them was a palace. The property had to be half a kilometre square. The manor house in the centre looked like a castle and had three storeys. The façade must have been recently sandblasted; it was brilliantly white. There was a large pond in the middle of the lawn before the grand house, with ducks and a pair of swans swimming in it. There was a flagpole beside the motor court, but instead of a Swedish flag it was flying a green-and-white one.

Along the west side of the wall was a row of several long annexe buildings tucked into the edge of the woods. The roof of another long building was visible behind the manor house, and in the distance there was a pasture full of grazing sheep. Only a few people were visible: a couple drinking coffee in the yard outside the annexes and two people in uniform moving rapidly across the drive.

Sofia looked up at the manor again and discovered that something was carved into the upper part of the façade in large letters.

We walk the way of the earth, it read.

She stood there as if she had just fallen from the sky and took in all the splendour. She exchanged meaningful glances with Wilma and turned to Madeleine.

'What a place!'

'Yes, isn't it fantastic? We've put a lot of work into it. Franz had a vision, and I think you could say we brought it to fruition.'

Sofia felt instinctively that there was something there. Something worth having. It wasn't just beautiful; there was more to this estate, an unusual tranquillity. It felt as if they had been transported to a parallel universe where every television, cell phone, computer, and tablet had been simultaneously switched off. As if the endless buzz of the world had gone silent within these thick walls. At the same time, an inexplicable and vaguely forbidding atmosphere seemed to have settled there. She couldn't quite put her finger on it. *This is so beautiful it takes my breath away, and yet it gives me the creeps*, she thought.

But she pushed that feeling away, deciding it must be Björk's ghost stories lingering in her mind.

'First I'll show you the manor house, where we work,' said Madeleine. 'Then I'll show you the annexes, where our guests work through our program.'

Sofia wondered whether Oswald was there. She stared up at the many windows of the manor and it occurred to her that he might be looking down on them from up there. She found herself wishing she could meet him again.

The fire has almost gone out.

The last glowing coals tremble at the bottom of the charred wood.

We're enveloped in darkness. I can barely make out her features.

She tosses on a little more wood, pokes it, and gets a nice fire going again.

In the glow of the flames she looks like a witch with her thick red hair and cat eyes.

'What does he do to you?' I ask.

'You know what he does,' she says, turning away.

'I don't want that bastard touching you.'

'Oh, he's just a dirty old man. He only gropes me. He gives me whatever I want as long as I let him. That's the way it is, when you're adopted. They think they own you. You know?'

'He doesn't go all the way?'

'Jesus, no. He's not like that.'

'I thought he and my mom were messing around,' I say.

'That's not a bad idea. They'd be a good pair.'

A sudden image appears in my mind: his head on the body of a mosquito. A stupid mosquito that flies into the fire and burns up.

'You'll long to go back to him once I'm finished with you,' I say.

And she finally laughs.

3

The view from the large windows afforded a glimpse of the sea beyond the forest. The waves rolled in, crashing against the cliffs and tossing up foam.

They were on the third floor of the manor house, where the staff worked. Madeleine had herded them quickly up the stairs, explaining that the first and second floors were still being renovated into living areas for the staff. It smelled like wet concrete and sawdust down there. They could hear a table saw, and they had to climb over a large roll of insulation near the landing.

Nothing was in need of renovation up here. Everything — walls, ceilings, and furniture — was a glistening white or pale grey. There were no interior walls, just an open-plan office with desks and computers scattered here and there. The staff seemed to sit wherever they liked; everyone appeared to be in high spirits, offering smiles and friendly nods. There were two doors on the other side of the large room. Madeleine noticed that Sofia's gaze was drawn to them.

'Those are offices for Franz and the staff manager,' she said. 'Otherwise everyone works in this area. Aside from those who take care of the guests and the farm, of course.'

Sofia looked back at the doors, wondering if Oswald would emerge and whether he was even in his office, but she didn't want to ask.

'So it's a working farm?' Wilma asked.

'Yes, we're almost completely self-sufficient,' Madeleine stated with pride. 'We grow all our own vegetables and fruit here, and we make our own milk and butter. We've even got some sheep. And the manor house is heated with solar and geothermal energy. But those of us who work up here are actually Franz's staff. We take care of personnel matters, mail, purchasing, and that sort of thing, so Franz can focus on his lectures and research.'

'Could you tell us a little about Franz Oswald?' Sofia said. 'Where he's from, things he's done?'

'It doesn't matter,' Madeleine said brusquely, sounding slightly annoyed. 'Franz wants us to focus on the guests and the program, not on him. He is what he is. Our leader.'

Sofia considered Madeleine's profile. She looked anxious and a bit distracted.

'But you don't pray to Oswald, or worship him?'

'No, of course not! We're not a bunch of fanatics, if that's what you're thinking.' Madeleine's voice had risen into a falsetto. Their conversation was about to go off the rails, but Wilma took over. She guided them back to the right track so skilfully that Madeleine probably wasn't even aware of how her tense features smoothed out again. They went back to polite questions and mild flattery.

Fifty people on staff? Wow. What kind of work do they do? What a fantastic job you've done with this place! Wilma could butter anyone up.

Sofia listened with half an ear as she gazed out at the cubicles again. She wondered if the staff were as happy as they seemed and found herself thinking that if everything Madeleine had told them was true, this place would definitely count as an environmental organization.

A woman in a chef uniform suddenly popped up beside them. 'Lunch is served in the guest dining room!' she said.

'Okay,' said Madeleine. 'Time for you two to get a little taste of what we grow around here.'

The dining room was large and bright, with tall, rectangular windows. The hardwood floor was highly polished and almost completely covered with sheepskin rugs. The chairs and tables were white. The room didn't have the usual food smells; instead a faint whiff of seaweed and fish emanated from the kitchen. Muted classical music streamed from the walls. There were guests seated at most of the tables, yet it was surprisingly quiet. The mood was serene, like that of a temple or of a sleepy bar in the early morning hours. Sofia found herself whispering when they spoke.

Her gaze was repeatedly drawn to the other tables, to see if she recognized anyone. Madeleine had mentioned that many of the guests were celebrities. But the other tables weren't very close by, and she didn't want to stare.

Lunch was tomato soup and fish with vegetables and herbs. When she was finished eating, she felt a gentle clap on her shoulder. She turned around and there was Oswald, his hands on the back of her chair. He looked angry — even furious.

'How long have you been here?' He turned to Madeleine without waiting for a response. 'I'm the one who invited them, and I wanted to show them around myself.'

His voice was restrained and calm, yet his displeasure settled over them like a heavy blanket. He had no uniform; instead he wore black jeans and a fitted white T-shirt that showed off his muscles and tan. They shook hands and he offered a smile, but its warmth quickly faded.

Madeleine's cheeks went a deep red. Her head sank so low that her chin nearly rested on her chest.

'I just thought you had so much to do, and I wanted to help. I figured you had more important things on your schedule,' she said, nearly whispering.

'You can go now. I'll take over,' he said, waving his hand at her as if she were a pesky fly.

Madeleine slowly slunk out of her chair and disappeared down the aisle with tiny, mincing steps.

Oswald turned to Sofia and smiled again, but irritation lingered in his eyes.

'I did want to meet with you, but I didn't know you were coming today and now, as you heard, my schedule is jam-packed. But we can have a look at the guest houses, at least. Did you find the ferry ride agreeable?'

'Yes, we learned all about the ghosts at the manor,' Sofia said before she could stop herself. She never could hold her tongue.

But Oswald only laughed.

'Yes, that Björk is such good advert for us. People end up totally fascinated by the miserable history of the manor. *Come meet the evil Countess!* But surely you don't believe all that stuff.'

'Of course not,' Wilma said quickly, pinching Sofia's pinkie finger.

'Good,' Oswald said. 'Then let's get on with the tour!'

He held the dining room door for them and led them to the annexes. He walked close to Sofia, holding a gentle hand under her elbow as if to guide her. He was hardly touching her, but it was very purposeful and made her shiver with pleasure.

She wasn't the sort of person who turned heads in the street, yet Oswald had chosen to be close to her — even though Wilma was right there, with her busty figure and confident gait.

Before they reached the buildings, his hand brushed the area between hip and back where all the nerves meet, and the contact almost took her breath away.

The guest-house annexes looked like barracks with a row of numbered doors on the front side, but the solid timber and massive iron door handles hinted at the good quality of the construction. An expensive renovation, just like the manor house.

'Let's see!' Oswald said, taking a key from his pocket. 'Number five should be empty right now. This is a typical room. They're all nearly identical.'

The room was actually a suite, made up of a living room, bedroom, and bathroom. It still smelled new, like lumber and plastic.

They poked around, curious, but all Oswald was interested in was describing the lighting and ventilation, which he said was absolutely revolutionary.

'The ceiling light emits ultraviolet rays, to counteract reactions to the lack of sunlight in the winter. The ventilation system constantly lets in fresh air, and if the air is cold it is automatically warmed. All the walls are completely soundproofed, so you're never disturbed in your sleep. As you can see, there's no TV or computer. The guests don't use their phones while they're here either. We have a computer in the common room, for emergencies. But tranquillity is the goal here. You have to dare to leave behind what you *think* is essential to discover what is *truly* essential.'

He paused to make sure they were still with him.

'But the most important part is the bedroom. Come here, I'll show you.'

He herded them into the room, closed the door, and pressed

a button, and black curtains unfurled to cover the windows. It was pitch black.

'Now there's not a speck of light,' he said. 'You won't even be able to see the outlines of the furniture. This is how you must sleep for the body to get true rest. Fascinating, isn't it?'

Sofia shuddered and held tight to Wilma's shirtsleeve. This reminded her of the first time she had slept out in the country when she was little. She had woken up in the middle of the night, in the dark, and thought she had gone blind. She had screamed her head off until her mother turned the lights on and off probably a hundred times to show her that she hadn't lost her sight. Yet she had been incurably afraid of the dark ever since.

At last, Oswald put the lights back on and led them back into daylight. Then they headed for the recreational area, which had a sauna, saltwater pool, and gym. In one corner of the gym was a contraption three metres high; it looked like a metal egg.

'What's that?' Sofia asked.

'You can go in there and train your perception. Sound, light, colours, smells, temperatures — all the impressions that are thrown at you in a holy mess in your daily life. In "the egg", as we call it, you can experience them all separately. It's an important part of our program.'

They passed a large classroom full of people studying. Some were reading; others were sitting still on chairs, their eyes closed.

'This is where we study the theses,' Oswald said.

Sofia had comments and questions on the tip of her tongue, but Oswald looked at his watch and suddenly seemed to be in a rush.

'You can see the farm and the greenhouse next time,' he said. 'But there is something I'd like to show you before you head home.'

He took them to a freestanding building alongside the guesthouses — a wooden structure with a porch; it might have originally been a servants' quarters. Sofia was expecting more hypermodern design inside, but this house was completely empty: just floors, walls, and endless bookshelves. It smelled pleasantly of wood and polish, and the afternoon sun had just found its way through the windows to form a golden streak on the floor.

'This is going to be our library,' Oswald said, giving her a meaningful look.

'I see . . .' she said hesitantly.

'I've heard you're a whiz at literature, that you love books.'

'Where'd you hear that?'

'It said on the form you filled out after the lecture that you just received your bachelor's degree in literature.' He was giving her that significant look again. 'I need someone who can create a real library here. With books that fit in with our philosophy. There are no limits, financially. All that matters is that it's done right.'

'So you need a librarian?'

'No, what I don't need is a librarian, with old-fashioned ideas about what *should* be in a library. I need someone who can think independently. So when I saw your form, I thought of you. And then I noticed that Wilma studied literature too, and I thought maybe I had found the right people for the job.'

Sofia was astounded. He had just offered them a job.

'What's the catch?'

'You'd have to become part of the staff, of course. We work on contract. Two years at a time. And I'm not sure whether you two have boyfriends . . .'

'We don't have boyfriends, but I'm not signing any contract,' Sofia said firmly. 'No matter how interesting it sounds.'

Wilma cleared her throat. A small warning, to let Sofia know she was about to cross a line into rudeness again. But Oswald didn't look defeated; if anything, he was amused.

'I thought as much. But I have a suggestion. Come for two weeks and go through the program, like our guests do. No cost to you, no commitment. If you still don't want to take over the library when you're done, you can go right back home again.'

Sofia and Wilma looked at each other, speechless. Wilma was just about to open her mouth, and Sofia knew what would come out. The trip to Rhodes with her mother, the internship she'd arranged at a newspaper, blah blah blah. But Wilma closed her mouth again and smiled at Oswald.

'Can we talk it over in private and let you know?'

'Of course! It was nice to have you here. Let me know when you decide. I'll tell Madde to meet you in the dining room for afternoon coffee before you leave.'

He was already walking off, but then he turned around and looked directly at Sofia.

'You seem clear-sighted. I'm sure you can tell that this place is something very special.'

Then he winked at her, turned on his heel, and vanished.

★

Everything was silent on the ferry home. She hardly heard the shrieking of the gulls, the lapping of the waves, or the pleasant hum of the engine. Her thoughts were torn, bouncing around inside her head like tiny demons. The peaceful, well-organized atmosphere of the manor clashed with her own chaotic life. And the thought of working with books was a tempting one.

Wilma was also noticeably quiet; she was staring down at the foam where the keel of the ferry broke the surface.

'Jesus, what a place!' she said.

Sofia laughed.

'Like a different universe, right?'

'I think you should try out the program.'

'Without you?'

'I promised to go to Rhodes with my mom, and I can't blow off this new job. And you were obviously the one he was into. The air practically crackled when he looked at you.'

Sofia's cheeks grew warm.

'Oh, quit it. But who knows, maybe I'll do it. No way I'm signing any contract, though.'

'Of course not,' Wilma said.

Sofia was dragged back into the roiling sea of thoughts in her mind. But then the mainland came into sight on the horizon and the sound of the sea and the ferry engine returned. It was as if the sea was a bridge between two worlds — the real world, where they were headed, and the strange, dreamlike world they had just left.

She didn't know whether this new world, the one she had just discovered, was a new adventure awaiting her, or just a creepy illusion.

I'm practically right next to him before he notices me.

He's fixing the chicken wire, on his knees in the dirt. He has put his garden gloves on the ground and is holding the barbed wire with his bare hands.

His entire being disgusts me. The start of a bald patch on the top of his head, the sweat gathering in beads on his neck, and the pungent odour of grime, earth, and grass pouring off him.

I lean down, place my mouth near his ear, and say 'Hello, Doctor!'
Loudly.

He jumps and seems relieved once he realizes it's me. He looks like a little piglet, lying there in the dirt.

'Well hello there, Fredrik! Nice to see you.'

'Not that nice,' I say.

'What do you mean?'

'I mean it's not so nice, what you do to Lily.'

Sudden, naked fear appears on his face and he readies his fat, protruding lips. But I cut him off before he can say a word.

'You don't need to say anything. I know everything, do you understand me? She told me the whole damn thing, but I'm not going to tattle. Why would I?'

He starts to speak again but I put up my hand, and then I feel the rush, that intoxicating mixture of power and strength.

He squints up at me; the sun is at my back. I want him to see me like this, like a backlit angel of justice.

'All I want is for you to leave us alone,' I say. 'And I want access to the attic. I need to look for something there.'

'Of course you can go in the attic, Fredrik. But what on earth did Lily tell you?' He makes an attempt to get up. I just turn my back on him.

'You know perfectly well what she told me,' I say as I walk away.

I'm so pleased that I have to repress the urge to do a little victory dance there in the sunlight. Now I'll have Lily to myself and free run of the estate.

For as long as I can remember, I've had a plan. A grand plan.

He is only a tiny, flimsy part of it. And anyway, it's all for his own good.

4

It was unusually dark when she woke. She felt rested, but something was wrong. Her eyes searched for her digital alarm clock, but there was only blackness. Her fear of the dark strangled her for a moment, until she realized where she was. Far from home, out on the island. That was the way of things here — no light at all when you were sleeping. Although she had left a tiny crack at the bottom of the roller blind, in spite of the ban.

She fumbled for the button on the bed frame, and as she pressed it the room was slowly bathed in a warm, gentle light. The clock became visible: quarter past ten! She had overslept again. 'Use your mental clock,' they had told her. 'Decide when you will wake up, and it will happen.' But so far that wasn't working for her.

Breakfast was only served until ten, but that didn't matter. She would take a walk around the island before lunch.

She had been there for three days, and completed the first step, which was called 'unwinding'. It really just meant that you ate, slept, and took walks. And did a few hours of what they called 'altruistic work' — in other words, free labour for them, because it involved working in the fields or pottering in the gardens. It didn't matter, though; it was pleasant to weed flowerbeds. Today she would meet with a personal advisor and receive her program plan, and she was curiou... ...

was curious about Oswald's ...

Outside it was cloudy and ca... ...

aside from some bleating sheep. S... ...

lookout point and gaze out at the sea for a ...

from the manor, but this time she walked thr... ...

wanted to test her ability to navigate the terrain.

Most of the trees were pine or birch, lined up in ... ...n-

metrical patterns. Here and there an oak or spruce compe... ...d for

sunlight, but they remained short and straggly in the shadow of

the majestic pines. It had rained during the night and the forest

smelled like wet moss and earth. The trees were heavy with

raindrops that clung to the leaves.

She got lost straight away, but then she heard water burbling

in a small brook between the trees. The water was rushing so fast

that it had to be coming from somewhere higher up.

She followed the brook and found herself in a clearing. She

stopped, inhaling the moist air, enjoying the sensation. Suddenly

she felt observed. When she looked up, she spotted a bird sitting

before her, perched on a pine branch and staring with keen

eyes. A buzzard or sea eagle. It wouldn't look away. She cursed

ViaTerra's ban on phones, which had just cost her an incredible

photo op. But then something creaked in the woods and the spell

was broken. The bird flapped its wings and soared up to the grey

sky with a mewing, plaintive call. She kept walking, and soon

she could see the lookout point through the trees.

Beyond the large heath and just before the cliffs plunged to the

sea, there was a bench. She sat down and looked out at the water.

The sky was clearing. Behind the wall of cloud on the horizon

rose more clouds, fat and fluffy, like giants on their way to the

...her gaze on them and began to daydream. ...ike that, perfectly still, for a long time.

Her rumbling stomach finally brought her back down to earth.

She jogged back to the manor, and by the time she stepped into the dining room it was half past noon. As she waited to be served, she noticed a new guest: Ellen Vingås, the opera star, was sitting alone in front of a large portion of food. Just as Sofia's plate arrived at the table she was interrupted by an 'ahem.' An unnaturally thin guy was standing before her, smiling. She immediately recognized him from Oswald's lecture in Lund. It was the guy who had insisted that she and Wilma fill out forms.

'Sofia, my name is Olof Hurtig and I'll be your personal advisor. Enjoy your lunch, and then I want to see you in my office. We'll plan your program.'

His small goatee bobbed as he spoke.

'Sure, is your office in the main building?'

Sofia had hoped to run into Oswald there. She hadn't seen him yet.

'No, all guest service takes place here in the annexes. The offices are right next to the gym. There's a small room there, and that's where I'll be waiting for you.'

She ate up her food, ravenous.

Hurtig was waiting at a desk in a little room just behind the gym. The visitor's chair was so low to the floor that whoever sat behind the desk was transformed into a lofty god.

'Let's see now, Sofia. I've got your file here.'

He opened the folder before him.

'A file? I didn't know I had a file here.'

'Don't worry. Everything you say here is confidential. We are bound by professional secrecy.'

'But I only got here three days ago. How could I have a file?'

'It's just your form and a few notes from the interview when you first came to the island.'

The folder contained a whole stack of paper, not just a few sheets, but he went on before she could point this out.

'I see a pattern here,' he said thoughtfully. 'Someone who has caused you pain and anxiety. A great betrayal. Maybe a failed relationship, could that be right?'

Her head was spinning. Had he Googled her? How could he know about all of that?

'Maybe, I guess, but how did you know . . .'

Hurtig shifted in his chair. He seemed incapable of sitting still: he leaned across the desk, clearly delighted at her reaction.

'Don't look so surprised. It's our job to read people. Let's talk about your program instead, how we're going to help you take control of your life.'

He scribbled furiously, nodding now and again. He held up the paper when he was finished.

8:00–10:00: workout and breathing exercises
10:00–12:00: altruistic work . . .

The schedule went on, noting mealtimes, time in the egg, thesis study in the evening. She wondered how this could possibly be different from everyone else's programs, but before she could ask, Hurtig stood up and put out his hand.

'Sofia, it's been a pleasure. Good luck with the program!'

The only time he had taken his eyes from her was when he was writing her schedule. He was still staring at her, confident that she would turn around and leave. And so she did. Her legs just stood up, and her body followed. Then she felt the urge to go back and demand to see everything in her file. But did it really matter? The things he'd said could be true of anyone. Were there any women who *weren't* carrying the baggage of a failed relationship or two?

A few days later, she made a discovery in the woods. Her schedule was stricter, but there was still time for morning walks. Sure, they were expected to be brisk walks, to stimulate the circulation, but Sofia was only out for a stroll that day.

She had returned to the clearing. Her iPhone was in her pocket, in case the eagle showed up again. Naturally, the tree it had been in was empty, but then she caught a glimpse of something red through the foliage. Just twenty metres from the clearing was a summer cottage, in the middle of the forest. It was small, and the overgrown lot it sat on was only a few hundred metres square.

Out front was a wind-torn hammock and some shabby outdoor furniture. Inside, the blinds were down.

She walked into the yard. Someone must have been there recently, because at one end of the house stood a rusty wheelbarrow half full of last year's leaves. Behind the cottage she found a watering can, empty pots, and a bag of potting soil. She returned to the front and tried the door handle. The door swung open. *I'm really intruding now*, she thought, but she stepped inside anyway. The front room was both kitchen and living room, with a gas stove, a table, and a kitchen bench. The curtains were crocheted in white lace that had yellowed with cooking fumes and become dotted with fly droppings. It smelled a little musty, thanks to the raw, damp air, but it didn't seem mouldy. And there was a fireplace with newspapers in a neat pile next to a stack of wood.

She picked up one paper and looked at the date. It was almost a year old.

There was one more room, a bedroom with a single bed and a dresser. The wallpaper was white and patterned with beach balls and snails. The bedspread was crocheted in the same white lace as the kitchen curtains.

She searched for the bathroom. There was only a toilet and a sink, no shower. She wondered if the water was on and tried the faucet, which sputtered and released a thin stream of water. *Incredible, out here in the middle of the forest*, she thought. She knew she had to leave now to get back before the program started, but she couldn't tear herself away.

There was a dusty bureau in the living room. The top drawer was full of newspaper clippings. She picked up a scrap of paper on the rag rug before the bureau; it was a ferry ticket bearing yesterday's date. She suddenly felt like someone was watching her and whirled around. The front door banged in the breeze, creaking on its hinges, but the cottage was empty. She let the ticket flutter to the floor and went outside. The sun had found a crack between the trees and was shining on the lawn in front of the house.

There was no one there.

*

That evening she ate dinner with a man and woman in their fifties. The man introduced himself as Wilgot Östling, chief of the county police; his wife, Elsa, was an accountant. Ellen Vingås joined them as well. She was a large woman with lively brown eyes and dark skin. Her laugh was burbling and infectious, and she kept the conversation going with stories about life in the opera world. It was impossible not to enjoy her company. The Östlings talked about how wonderful the program was, dropping words like *down-to-earth*, *peacefulness*, and *vitality*.

'How are things going for you, Sofia?' Ellen asked.

'Oh, fine — I just got my program.'

'Me too. The guy who planned it for me must be a mind-reader. That, or he Googled all my online biographies. Oh well, a little relaxation can't hurt.'

'It's a lot more than that for me,' said Elsa Östling. 'It feels like I've finally come down from the stress of my job. I feel as cool as a cucumber, in fact.'

Her husband nodded in agreement.

'I've known Franz since he started ViaTerra. If there's anyone that can put a dent in the level of stress we have in this damn country, it's Franz. He's created a real oasis here.'

'But what happens when you go back to real life?' Ellen asked. 'How can you be sure you won't go right back to eating McDonald's and sneaking alcohol?'

She laughed so shrilly that the guests at the next table turned around.

Elsa looked at Ellen in alarm. Wilgot looked offended.

'I think it's up to each individual to change his own life. To keep making use of everything we learn here,' he said.

Ellen turned to Sofia.

'We'll see how it goes. If it all goes to hell, we can always find some other nutso self-improvement group somewhere. There are plenty of them.'

Sofia laughed. She hoped she would get to talk to Ellen again.

★

After dinner she looked in on what would eventually become the library. The door was open, and the building was even more beautiful now that the sun was setting and casting an orange glow across the spacious room. She imagined what it would look like with books everywhere, large sofas, a modern computer system.

At last she went to the common room next to the dining room to use the shared computer. She wrote an email to her parents and promised to come home for a visit in a few weeks.

Her thoughts wandered to Ellis. He had completely flipped out when she broke up with him, throwing things and screaming like a madman. Then came the blog: posts and comments about her that popped up all over the internet. It had all culminated in a few pornographic images with Sofia's face pasted in. Anyone could tell that the pictures had been Photoshopped, but it didn't matter. They made her feel awful.

Her thoughts of Ellis caused her to shudder as she worried about what he might do next.

She peered over her shoulder to make sure no one was looking, then fished out her phone and placed it next to the keyboard. She texted Wilma a summary of the first couple of days and ended by writing, *Have you heard from Ellis? Feels like he's haunting my brain again.*

Was it the book, the cape, or the cave that came first?

Right, it was the cave, it must have been. Definitely the cave.

The sun is setting. We've climbed all the way down the cliffs to catch the crabs that get stuck in the little cavities between the rocks. I show her how you can crush them with your shoe and throw them out to the crying gulls. She's wearing a short denim skirt. Her legs are so tan; smooth, long, and delicious. She turns to me and the sun catches in her tangled hair so it glows like a flame. It looks like someone is holding a match to her head.

I think about taking her with me after all, but I don't know what role she could play in my plan. How I would use her.

She squints up at the cliffs, pointing.

'Look, Fredrik!'

I look up and see it: an opening in the rock that gapes like a missing tooth.

We climb up. The hole is tall and deep, but the entrance is blocked with driftwood and rocks, probably deposited by the most recent storm. We pull and tug, clearing and overturning, tossing rocks and wood down to the water, until the opening is free.

Then we crawl in and sit down on the cave floor.

'I bet you can get in from above,' she said. 'Just climb down the cliff rocks.'

I nod, pulling her closer. I press her onto the cold floor. We wrestle for a bit and I get my hands under her shirt.

'Not here,' she says. 'It's too cold on my bum.' She sits up and looks around the cave. 'This place is awesome!' she says with a grin.

We sit there for a while, quiet, watching through the cave opening as the sun sinks into the sea.

5

She continued to think of Ellis now and then, but she still felt unusually at ease. The fresh air, healthy food, and good sleep had put her body into a pleasant torpor. Then came the theses, which shook her right out of it.

Although it didn't start off on such a good note.

'This is a blank piece of paper!' she said, looking at Olof Hurtig, who was standing before her with an expectant gaze.

'I know, Sofia. Maybe you should read the first thesis again.' He placed it in front of her, on top of the blank sheet of paper.

Thesis #1: Your inner self knows everything.

There is a voice inside you that isn't really a voice. If you learn to listen to it, you, the dreamer, will awaken from your dream. This voice has many names: a sixth sense, clairvoyance, vibes, or ESP. But we call it intuition.

This voice is like the sun on a cloudy day. Even when the clouds cover the sky, and even during the darkest night, the sun is shining. The clouds and the darkness are your mental distractions, which keep you from reaching your inner self.

Exercise: Your advisor will give you a portal into your mind. Observe it and search for your inner self.

'I already read that,' she said. 'Why should I sit here staring at a blank piece of paper?'

'Do as it says in the exercise,' said Olof.

She felt disappointed and duped, and resentment was buzzing in her head like a bee, so she just stared sulkily at him.

'Why is the text so short? I thought the theses were real essays.'

'The truth is always simple, Sofia.'

'Yes, but isn't staring at a piece of paper taking it a little far?'

He gave her a sympathetic smile.

'Let's say that this paper is your mind. It's perfectly blank, and you can do whatever you want with it. That's why we call it a portal. What do you see on this paper, Sofia?'

'Nothing!'

'Exactly. Try to find the empty space in your mind, and you'll find your self.'

I'm glad I didn't have to pay for this, she thought, fixing her eyes on the white sheet. Her boiling anger gradually cooled and she let her eyes relax until the paper grew blurry. She sat staring for a long time. Time seemed to disappear, until finally she felt something: weightlessness and relief. Some mass around her head seemed to disperse.

She took her eyes from the paper and looked up at Olof.

'I feel lighter. Weightless.'

His face split into a broad smile. He nodded eagerly and put a hand on her shoulder.

'Good! What you felt was your inner self. It's that simple. We'll move on to thesis number two tomorrow.'

Her disappointment ebbed away later that night. Her spirits really did feel lighter. Colours were brighter, sounds sharper, and her laugh a little warmer. She noticed it all and felt pleasantly surprised.

The next evening, she went to the classroom with low expectations. Olof was already wound up, rubbing his hands and beaming at her with that smile that almost distorted his narrow face. She looked around, wondering if everyone else in the room had also found the first thesis peculiar. They looked so unconcerned, as if staring at a piece of paper was the most natural thing in the world. Ellen Vingås was there too, laughing so loudly that her advisor shushed her. The only decoration on the white walls was a poster with the English phrase *Simplicity is power.*

Sofia wondered why it wasn't in Swedish, but maybe the Swedish didn't sound as nice.

'Thesis number two!' Olof said. 'Are you ready?'

She nodded and sat down in front of him.

Thesis #2. You are your past.

  What you are right now is a culmination of everything you've ever thought or done, and everything that has been done to you. You are the sum of your subjective and objective experiences. Thus you can change yourself through the thousands of choices you face each day. All the power you will ever find already exists within you, in your past.

  Exercise: Your advisor will teach you to draw strength and energy from your memories.

'We'll be doing this exercise in my office,' Olof said. 'So we can work undisturbed.'

He closed the blinds halfway when they entered his small office, making everything look pale and grey. She sank into the puffy visitor's chair while he fished a small piece of paper from the desk drawer.

'Now close your eyes. I'm going to give you a few simple commands, and you should tell me what you're seeing and thinking.'

The commands were brief, but he dragged out the words in a deep voice that was almost a whisper.

Remember a time when you felt strong.
Remember a time when you felt triumphant.
Remember a time when life was easy.
Recall your first achievement.

There seemed to be endless variations on the question, and he always had the next command on the tip of his tongue. She had a hard time recalling at first, but then incidents began to pop up. Hidden memories. Lovely images.

'What do I do if a bad memory pops up?' she asked, because she had been reminded of a bike accident when she had broken her arm.

'Did you feel strong that time? Superior?'

'Not exactly.'

'Then we'll ignore it. Just find another memory.'

They went on like that for a few hours, until Olof's voice began to fade out and she felt warm inside, a little fuzzy — almost giggly. She sank into a warm darkness where she was alone with her images, and Olof's voice was way off in the distance.

Then came an image that was extra clear and colourful. A pair of tiny feet tottering across a lawn, viewed from above. At first she pushed the image aside, because it seemed so unbelievable. But it returned, and she could feel the dew under her feet and her inner joy at the ability to walk. *It's strange that my feet have gotten so big*, she thought with a shudder, because all at once she knew the memory was real.

'I had no idea,' she heard herself say, but her voice came from far beyond her body.

'I'm sorry?' Olof said.

She forced herself to open her eyes, and there he was, looking at her curiously.

'You said something.'

'I was thinking out loud, about how I had no idea I could remember so far back. I remembered taking my first steps. It seems incredible, but I know it was real.'

'And . . .?' he leaned forward, eager, encouraging her to go on.

'And I was thinking that the past really is the key to existence.'

Bingo! Olof slapped his hand against the desk.

'That's it! That's it! The exercise is over. We'll do thesis number three tomorrow.'

★

She was a little nervous as she entered the classroom on the third evening. She wasn't quite sure why; she only knew that it had to do with losing control, losing herself in the exercises.

'How many theses are there?' she asked Olof as soon as they sat down.

'Five, but you'll do one through four first and then spend some time practising your new abilities.'

'Have you read the fifth thesis?'

'No, no one has yet. Franz is going to release it as soon as five hundred guests have completed the first four. He says the fifth is

48

so powerful that it will take a team, sort of. But right now, for you, let's focus on number three.'

> *Thesis #3: One person's dusk is another's dawn.*
>
> *Your true self can only exist free of constant fear of causing offence, wounding, or hurting others. The desire for approval is a scourge on humanity.*
>
> *Exercise: The process for Thesis 3 is done in the classroom with an advisor who uses this repeated command: 'Remember a time when you could have helped someone by hurting them.'*

She shivered as she finished reading. 'That sounds brutal.'

'That's the point. Your desire for approval is protesting now, not your true self. Now let's do the exercise.'

But she couldn't come up with an answer. She squirmed in her chair, distracted by everything that was going on in the classroom as her irritation at the idiotic exercise grew.

'I can't think of an answer to your question,' she stated at last.

'Then that's what we'll say.'

'What? What do you mean?'

'Franz says thesis number three isn't for everyone. There are those who are dominant and those who are submissive. This thesis doesn't work for the submissive ones.'

'I'm not submissive, damn it! What are you talking about?'

'Sofia, it's not a bad thing. The whole universe is built on dominance and submissiveness. It's just as natural as how the seagulls in the bay eat herring. Take the rest of the night off and we'll get started on the fourth thesis tomorrow.'

She was stewing as she left the classroom — that scrawny jerk didn't know a damn thing about her. Submissive? The very idea was idiotic, ridiculous, and, above all, one hundred percent wrong. And comparing her to a fucking herring! She walked around the yard for a while, then sat by the pond and watched the swans while yanking at the grass.

At last she stood up and walked briskly back to the classroom. Olof Hurtig was still there.

'Okay, I'll do the damn exercise.'

His face broke into a smile.

'I thought so.'

So they started over, and she came up with a few answers to the question, which made her feel a little better. Good enough to Hurtig to let her go for the night.

*

'This thesis is so simple that it's best if you don't use your brain when you answer it, but your heart,' Hurtig said as he placed the fourth thesis before her.

'How do I do that?'

'Just try.'

She read the short text.

Thesis #4: Darkness is the root of light.

A millimetre below the surface of the earth, darkness rules completely. Within your body it is perfectly dark, and yet you are alive and are radiant with energy. The DNA in your cells have no light, yet it is the blueprint for what you are. Darkness is the root of light.

Exercise: Your advisor will show you to a room that is perfectly dark. This is all you have to do: sit in compete darkness until you can see.

50

'I can't do this exercise,' she said at once.

'Not this again, Sofia.'

'You don't understand. I'm afraid of the dark. I can't handle being closed up in a pitch black room.'

'But you sleep in total darkness here.'

'It's different when I'm asleep,' she lied, because she always left a little gap under the blind.

'I'll be right outside the room the whole time,' Hurtig promised. 'If you panic, all you have to do is knock on the door and I'll open it. You can at least try, can't you?'

★

The room was at the far end of the building. The atmosphere there was very different from the classrooms. The air was raw and stale and there was a heavy smell of body odour from someone who must have sat there for a while. There was a chair in the middle of the room, which was otherwise empty.

'It's creepy in here.'

'It's not meant to be comfortable.'

She walked in slowly and sat down on the chair.

'The room is soundproofed,' he said. 'But I'll hear you if you knock on the door.'

The door closed with a heavy thud.

At first, she was paralyzed by the silence rather than the darkness. It was so quiet that the whole world seemed to have disappeared. She could hear her pulse and a strange, gurgling buzz in her ears. *That's the blood flowing through my veins*, she thought. *My hearing has moved into my body.*

Then the darkness crept in under her clothes and found every last nook and cranny of her body, settling in her armpits and groin, tightening over her larynx until she could hardly breathe. Then came the familiar waves of sweat, starting with nausea and spreading heat to her chest, hands, and forehead until she was drenched.

I can't handle this. I need out, out!

And just then, it happened. She found herself outside. Not just outside her body; that didn't exist anymore, but outside the whole island. She was floating way up in the sky.

Everything was bright colours. There were the lookout point and the cliffs plunging into the sea; the big woods and the harbour, where the boats looked like little toys.

The wall curled around the manor like a white snake. The swans in the pond were two tiny white dots. The air was thin and she herself was ethereal and warm. Everything was moving in slow motion. The crowns of the trees blew gently in the wind and the sun was like a golden rain falling all over the landscape. She didn't know how long it lasted. When she asked Olof later, he only shrugged. But when she returned to her room, her fear was gone. The darkness was gentle and comforting, like a warm bath.

I saw! I saw without using my eyes!

She knocked on the door.

The light blinded her when Hurtig opened up, but she was only grateful that she didn't have to look at his smile when she told him what had happened. She only heard him clapping his hands together and rubbing them, and laughing.

'There you go, Sofia! You're ready! You've achieved the final phenomenon of the fourth thesis.'

★

In the days that followed, everything felt different: a peculiar new calmness in her body. Harmony. Tranquillity. The very sensation she'd come to the island to find. *To think that I'm always so worried*, she thought. Consciously or unconsciously, it was always something she fretted about. The vague sense of panic that had been her constant companion had gone up in smoke.

She completed the final phase of the program, a second winding-down, where you just sat in the classroom with your eyes closed for a little while each day. You were expected to practise drawing power from your memories, but she mostly sat there enjoying how good it all felt.

On the third day, Hurtig approached and shook her shoulder, waking her from her reverie.

'Franz wants to see you. Right away!'

It sounded as if God Himself had called her to a summit.

She knew where Oswald's office was, but no one answered after a few knocks so she stepped inside. Entering his office was like stepping into a spaceship. There were no pictures on the walls, no flowers, not even a single photograph — there were only white walls with enormous windows that looked out over the sea. She could see the lookout point in the distance. The office was otherwise full of electronics: computers, printers, screens, and gadgets she didn't even know the names of. It occurred to her that this was odd, given that computers were forbidden at ViaTerra, but perhaps computers were indispensable when you were the boss.

Oswald himself was sitting at a large desk, absorbed in reading something on a computer. He didn't look up when she came in. Madeleine, who was sitting at a much smaller desk in the far corner of the office, put a finger to her lips and gave Sofia a sharp look. *Don't disturb him*, the look plainly said. Sofia cautiously took a seat in the visitor's chair before Oswald.

He was wearing a T-shirt again. She noticed that the muscles of his back were taut and wondered if he was tensing them on purpose. There was a strange gleam in his eyes when he swung around in his chair, as if he expected her to say something. But she didn't know what. His presence was so strong that she lost her composure and couldn't speak.

'Sofia, congratulations! I heard you finished the program. I hope it all went well.'

'It was fantastic. Better than I expected.'

He drummed his fingers on the desk good-naturedly.

'So, can I have your answer about the library now?'

'Well, hmm, I'm interested, I just have to talk to everyone at home first.'

He leaned forward, placing his hand over hers on the desk. It was dry and warm. Hers jumped at his touch, but she didn't pull it away.

'No, you don't get time to think it over, Sofia.'

'Why not?'

'The thing is, I think you've already made up your mind,' he said, pressing her hand ever so slightly.

It was as if someone else were speaking through her. The words just fell from her mouth. She could see herself in profile, from outside her body as her mouth opened and the words slipped from her tongue.

'Then I guess my answer is yes.'

Her voice echoed back at her as if from a void.

Oh my god. What have I gotten myself into?

'You won't regret it,' he said, letting go of her hand and leaning back in his chair. 'I'm sure you have things to take care of before you return, so just call Madeleine and let her know when you'll be back.'

Then he spun around in his chair and went back to reading.

Madeleine shooed her from the office.

She stood outside his door for a long time, at a loss, shaken over what had just happened.

*

There would be innumerable times, later in life, when she would search her mind. *Why on earth? What got into me? How could I?* She always came to the same conclusion: it was a combination of factors. A seductive, irresistible blend. The beautiful island, the breadth of luxury, the food, the sleep, the feelings left behind after the theses; but above all, and she would be ashamed of this and have trouble admitting it to herself, it was Oswald and his power of attraction. This wasn't a sect or a cult; it was something completely different. Almost like a new world — a microscopic vision of the future, brought to life.

ViaTerra was different.

But hindsight is twenty-twenty.

At the time, despite being disconcerted and sweaty all over, she still knew she had to come back to the island. Otherwise she would continue to be drawn there, like a moth to a flame.

And as she stood there in the corridor, alternately kicking herself and feeling bursts of dizzying euphoria, she found that she had a ridiculous smile on her lips.

We return to the cave several times.

We watch the rain move in over the bay and whip at the sea.

At night, we see the moon make a glittering path across the surface.

The cave is my special place. I can think clearly here. I think about my plan almost constantly. I examine it from every angle, picking at its seams; it's as if I'm spinning a net that will one day cover the whole island.

Sometimes I'm so deep in thought that she shakes me for answers to her meaningless chatter. Then I wrestled her to the floor and grab her by the throat until her legs kick like crazy. A sign of her submission.

I know now that I can't take her with me. She's too flighty, and besides I've already explored every corner of her body and she's starting to feel like a milk carton, once the milk is gone.

Although I will miss the cave.

The power in its hard walls.

You can see the whole universe from here.

You can even see the future, like a mirage on the horizon.

6

Her light-heartedness remained.

The constant worry in the back of her head was gone. She'd heard of people who didn't even know they had a headache until it went away, and that was exactly what this felt like. *This is my real self*, she thought. *A week on this program and I feel like a new person.*

What's more, she had become aware of an exciting mystique that affected the whole island but especially the manor. When she gazed up at the main building, she felt a jolt of excitement in her belly. She was already looking forward to her return.

On her last day, she rented a bicycle and pedalled around the island. She had gotten a ride to the village and left her luggage in a locker near the ferry. She spent the morning sunning herself on the beach and enjoying the scents brought out by the sun: the smell of tar from the fishing shacks and the pungent odour of the seaweed bobbing at the shore. She ate lunch at an outdoor café on a pier. The restaurant was packed with tourists. It really was high summer now.

There were so many people in the village that the narrow cobblestone streets were crowded. Most of the buildings were clustered around the square, where the ferry docked, but the village had climbed up the cliffs and some cottages rested high above the sea. She wondered what it would be like to live up there in the fall, when the storms drew in over the island.

There was a small souvenir shop on the square, and she went in to look for something for Wilma and her parents. Suddenly, Ellen Vingås appeared, tan and wearing a colourful summer dress that showed off the better part of her large bust.

'Sofia, it's so nice to run into you!'

'Same to you. It's my last day here.'

'Mine too. So how did it go?'

'Oh, it was great. I'm coming back. I'm going to help out with the library.'

She didn't want to say that she would be joining the staff. That would seem too hasty, and she didn't want the famous singer to think she was so easily taken in.

'How did the theses go?' she asked Vingås.

'Well, I liked number one and number three. I didn't get four; nothing much happened when I did it. But overall I think it went well.'

'Funny. It was the other way around for me. I liked number four best.'

'Imagine that. But now I'm headed home, back to the daily grind. We'll see if this good feeling lasts. It sure as hell did make a dent in the old finances!' she said with a shrill laugh.

A couple of women who were inspecting some porcelain shot her a look of alarm.

She dug through her large handbag and pulled out a small card, which she handed to Sofia. 'My card — let me know if you happen to be in Stockholm sometime and I'll get you some opera tickets.'

Sofia watched as Vingås left the shop, her hips swaying. She really wanted to meet her again.

At last she found a set of mugs with island motifs for her parents, and a little brochure of nature photography for Wilma.

She decided to bike to the north end of the island. It was as if the lookout point were calling her to it one last time.

The wind was coming from the east for a change and waves crashed persistently against the cliffs to her right. The wind whipped at her hair and whined in the spokes. Gulls sailed freely on the breeze.

She parked the bike at the end of the road and began to cross the heath toward the lookout point. When she gazed out at the sea, she saw someone standing on Devil's Rock and looking down at the water. She squinted, trying to make out the figure, but the cliff was too far away. The figure climbed down and vanished from sight, but didn't show up on the heath. She approached the rock, but there was no one in sight on the cliffs. She toyed with the thought that she had seen the old Count searching for his Countess in the depths. Yet all she could see from the edge of the cliff was the clear, dark water that seemed never to end; at least, the bottom wasn't visible.

She sat down on the cliff and dangled her legs over the edge. You could almost see the curve of the earth at the horizon. *From here you can see the beginning and end of the world,* she thought. *You can see all the way to eternity.*

She wanted to visit the cottage one last time, so she left the bike at the edge of the road and set off through the forest.

As soon as she stepped inside, everything seemed different. The rag rug in the entryway was mussed and there was a key ring on the kitchen table. The bedroom door was open and there was someone in the bed. Her first impulse was to turn around and go. But curiosity got the better of her and she sneaked over to the bedroom.

Stretched out on the bedspread, deep in sleep with his mouth open, lay a young man in a grey suit. At first she wanted to wake him up, but that would be embarrassing for both of them. Just as she was about to sneak back out, he opened his eyes.

'Busted,' he mumbled, sitting up in the bed and rubbing his eyes.

He had bright, lively eyes. His chin jutted out a bit and his whole face, aside from the very top of his forehead, was covered in freckles. His hair was red, shaggy, and uncombed. Despite his large mane, his head seemed too small for his torso, which was broad and muscular. When he stood up she realized how tall he was — he had to be six foot three, a giant compared to her five-two.

'Benjamin Frisk,' he said, putting out his hand. His shirtsleeve slid up, revealing an arm covered in red fuzz. He tried in vain to smooth his wrinkled blazer with the other hand.

She had a few cutting remarks on the tip of her tongue, but she refrained since she didn't want to contribute to his embarrassment.

'What are you doing here?' she asked instead.

He smiled, showing a big gap between his front teeth.

'Shit! I can't believe you found me like this. Well, maybe you've heard that we're renovating the staff quarters. I'm in charge of shipping and purchasing and stuff, so I'm really busy. I hardly get any sleep.'

'So you steal a nap here and there?'

'Yes, that's about it.'

'My name is Sofia.'

'I know who you are. I've been spying on you; I've seen you come to the cottage and I noticed you in the guest dining room. I was hoping we would run into each other. But not like this.'

'So how come I've never seen you?'

'I guess I've kept my distance. Until now. But have a seat, by all means.'

He pointed at the kitchen table as if he owned the place.

'I want to know more about this cottage,' she said once they had sat down. 'Do you know who owns it, and why it's always empty?'

'An old lady owns it. She comes in the summer. That's all I know.'

'There's something special about it. Like, I was drawn here.'

'It's in a funny spot. In the middle of the woods.'

They didn't speak for a moment as they looked at each other. A lone ray of sunlight cut through the gap in the curtains and set fire to the dust, which whirled up to the ceiling like a tiny tornado. There was so much life in his eyes. When she gazed into them she felt a pleasant sort of rush, a stream of warmth trickling through her body.

'Don't they miss you when you disappear?'

'Nah, an hour here and there doesn't matter. It's so chaotic down on the first floor.'

'I have to run to catch the ferry.'

'When are you coming back?'

'I have no idea, but it will be soon — I'm going to work in the library.'

'I know that too. Rumours spread fast in our little group. Can't you take the morning ferry instead? I know every nook and cranny of this island; I can show you around and —'

'Not today. But maybe when I come back.'

She glanced at her watch. It was almost four-thirty.

'Shit! I have to hurry!' she said, dashing through the front door.

She ran into the woods and toward the heath, but she turned around one last time before she disappeared into the trees.

He was standing on the lawn and gazing after her.

Benjamin Frisk, she thought. *Another reason to come back.*

She pedalled frantically all the way to the village.

The sun glittered off everything: the asphalt, the bike, the sea, and the cliffs.

We search for the book and find the cape instead.

We sit in the hot, stuffy attic, poring through books that smell like sun-warmed dust and mothballs. Sometimes they fall apart when we pick them up.

'What are we looking for?' she asks.

'A book of family history. It's supposed to be bound in leather and I'm sure it's handwritten.'

'How do you know it's here?'

'Mom saw it once. When she was cleaning. She put it up here with the other books.'

She is impatient. She gets up and starts snooping through the attic, getting farther and farther away from me.

Then I hear her voice, far off in the darkness.

'Fredrik, look at this!'

At first I can't see her, so I have to stop looking through the books to get up. The interruption infuriates me, but then I see what she's holding up. A hanger with a big, black velvet cape, hood and all. I recognize it immediately.

'That belonged to the Countess! The one who killed herself,' I say.

'How do you know that?'

'I saw it in a picture. She's on a horse, wearing it.'

'Oh my god, it's beautiful!' she says.

'Put it on!' I order her.

'What?'

'I said, put it on. But take off your clothes first. You have to be naked underneath.'

'No way. Why?'

'Just do as I say!'

She obeys, pulling off her skirt and sweater. I shoot a meaningful look at her panties, so she takes those off too. She stands there naked on the attic floor, grinning. Then she sweeps the cape around herself with a dramatic flourish.

Her hair falls across the black velvet like gold.

'Open the cape and show yourself,' I say.

She does as I order. The effect is magnificent.

'Awesome! You have to wear it tonight in the barn,' I say.

Her only response is a nod, but I can tell that she likes the thought.

I take in the vision of her again. And that's when the idea comes to me. Like a lightning bolt out of the blue.

7

'And your cell phone, laptop, tablet, and anything else like that.'

'Are you joking?'

'Do I look like I'm joking?'

No, Bosse — *in charge of personnel*, as he had introduced himself — didn't look like he was joking in the least. Like most of the staff, he was young, and he had a blond crew cut and eyes that were so intensely blue that they looked unreal. His presence suggested that he was used to being in charge.

When she stepped into his office, he had looked at her with mild distaste, like she was vermin or an animal that had to be tamed. She immediately found him irritating and put up a mental wall between them, so he would see that he didn't have any power over her. No sir.

'Sofia, you'll have your own locker here. Your belongings will be safe, and of course you can use them on your time off. It's just that it doesn't look good when our staff run around with cell phones and tablets. A crucial part of our program is helping our guests free themselves from the need for gadgets. There's a computer in the staff dining room where you can email your family and friends, or surf the web on your time off.'

Sofia reluctantly placed her iPhone on the desk in front of him. She thought of her laptop, which was in one of her suitcases, but she quickly decided it was none of his business.

'Computer?'

'No, I left it at home.'

'Good choice. You can keep your watch, of course. It's important to be on time around here.'

He seemed to be examining her, especially her unruly hair, which was probably one big rat's nest after the ferry ride through the humid air.

'Maybe you should think about putting your hair up in a bun,' he suggested.

'Oh, maybe.'

'What size skirt and blazer do you wear? For your uniform.'

'Thirty-four.'

'And your shoes?'

She had known it was coming.

'Eight and a half.'

'Pardon?'

'I said eight and a half. We have small bodies and big feet in my family. We are firmly planted on the ground.'

The joke was lost on him. He only nodded and made a note. Suddenly she felt uneasy, being there. It was not at all as she had imagined. Her doubt had begun to surface even on the ferry ride over. But by now it was too late to get out of this.

'Then it's time to sign your contract,' Bosse said.

He was well prepared. The contract was in the centre of the desk, under a large, black pen. He handed it to her and she read carefully as her discomfort rose.

'"I agree to work under temporarily difficult conditions," what does that mean?'

'Just that you're prepared to work hard. It's necessary sometimes.'

'And what does "I waive the right to bring action against the organization and its personnel" mean?'

'Yikes! Surely you're not planning to sue us? Sofia, you have to sign a contract to be hired at just about any job. It's nothing new. Confidentiality and all that.'

'What happens if I change my mind?'

'You don't think we'd try to keep you here, do you? We don't need to force anyone. There are plenty of people who want to work at ViaTerra.'

'So then why do I need to sign a contract?'

'Like I said, most jobs require a contract. I don't understand why you're being so difficult. Didn't you know there would be a contract?'

'Yes, but I hadn't read it.'

Bosse sighed.

'Shall we sign now, so I can show you your room?'

★

Together they walked down the stairs to the second floor. Bosse carried one of her big suitcases, and Sofia pulled the other; it bounced loudly down the stairs. A terrible aftertaste still lingered in her mouth after their conversation. She was kicking herself for handing over her iPhone; she couldn't help but picture inmates subjected to cavity searches in a prison. *Maybe he's right*, she thought later. It probably would be wrong for the staff to tweet and text in front of the guests.

'The first floor is still undergoing renovation,' Bosse told her. 'But up here, everything is finished.'

He held open the door to the second floor. The corridor was

quiet and still, with new flooring. There were ten neatly numbered doors on either side. Bosse opened number seven. The first thing she noticed was the three beds. So she would be sleeping in a dormitory. Next to each bed was a wardrobe, bureau, and chair. The room was otherwise bare of furniture. The windows didn't face the sea; instead the view was of the long building behind the manor and the animals grazing in the pasture.

'As you can see, you have your own wardrobe and bureau,' Bosse said, with a look at her large suitcases. 'You won't need much in the way of clothes here; your uniform will arrive in a few days and in your free time you'll mostly just need jeans and so forth. You might want to keep some of your things in our storage area in the basement. Just let me know and I'll show you where it is.'

She peeked into the bathroom. White and bare, with a large medicine cabinet over a sink. Small name labels over each of the three white bath towels. A shower, but no bathtub. An air freshener gave off the uninspiring scent of lavender.

'Who else lives here?'

'You'll be sharing a room with Elvira, who's here with her parents, and Madeleine, who I believe you've already met.'

Sofia's heart sank. It didn't seem like she would have anyone to talk to. She suddenly missed Wilma so much it hurt. Wilma, who wouldn't be there to stop her if she spiralled out of control. If that was even possible in a place like this — everything seemed so minutely planned and disciplined.

'Well, I'll leave you alone so you can unpack,' Bosse said. 'Dinner is served at seven. The staff dining room is on the first floor; it's easy to find. Once you've eaten, Madeleine will give you instructions for the library. You can always come to me if you have questions. As I said, I'm in charge of all personnel.'

He left the room and his quick steps vanished down the corridor. She went to the window and looked down at the farm. It looked so peaceful, cows and sheep grazing in the pasture. Why did she feel so uneasy? It must happen to everyone who came to the manor, a reaction to leaving everything back home.

She began to unpack her suitcases and arranged her clothes in the wardrobe and bureau. She sang to herself, but it just sounded dull in the soundproofed room.

Under her clothes was the black leather journal Wilma had given her as a farewell present. She placed it in the top drawer. Then there was the laptop. She had brought a set of sheets, but she saw that the bed was already neatly made, so she stuffed the laptop into the pillowcase and wound a sheet around it, then stashed the bundle in the bottom drawer. She shoved her suitcases and everything that didn't fit in the bureau under the bed. She wasn't about to let her belongings out of her sight.

Dinner was already in full swing in the staff dining room. All the tables seemed to be full, and she lingered hesitantly in the doorway until Madeleine spotted her and came over.

'You can sit at our table.'

Madeleine tried to make small talk during the meal, but her chatter turned to a buzz in Sofia's mind. Thoughts of regret wandered in and out of her head. It was impossible to control them, so she let them carry on.

'Is that okay?' Madeleine suddenly asked.

'Sorry?'

'I asked if it's okay if we head to the library now. Franz has written a project description for the library. He wants you to read it.'

'Sure, that's fine.'

It was cold and quiet in the library, not at all like when the sun had warmed the small building. Madeleine turned on the overhead lights.

'Okay, so it's up to you to start creating something here.' She eagerly handed a thick document to Sofia. 'Read this and tell me what you think.'

Sofia sat down on the only chair and left Madeleine to stand.

'I need a desk here. The kind a librarian would have, and a chair for visitors. And I need a computer if I'm going to do research.'

'They're already on order,' said Madeleine. 'Arriving tomorrow.'

Sofia began to read the project description, which was ten pages long and contained over one hundred bullet points. She couldn't focus; Madeleine was standing over her like a hawk. Words and letters melted into one another. Her eyes jumped back and forth, searching for the freaking end of all the things she was expected to do. *I can't handle this today*, she thought. *I'll read it more closely tomorrow.*

'It looks good,' she said.

'Great! Then I'll tell Franz you like it.'

'Sure, go right ahead.'

'Okay, we go to bed at ten o'clock and lights out is at eleven. So you have a few hours until then. You're welcome to take a walk, if you like.'

★

The island was as beautiful as she remembered. It was the middle of August now, and the evening air smelled faintly of autumn. But everything was still green, and the paths were overgrown by leafy grasses.

70

She went up to the lookout point and sat down to gaze out at the sea. The sun was setting; the sky was slowly draining of colour and the muted blue of the sea paled to turquoise, with a shimmer of pink from the sun. Darkness fell quickly, and black, empty space hung over her. But she stayed put, releasing her worries and her scattered thoughts and letting them float up to the sky. A faint breeze raised gooseflesh on her arms and legs. She pulled on her cardigan and began to wander slowly back to the manor.

When she returned to the dorm, it was almost time for bed. Madeleine was already there, in the process of undressing. A girl who couldn't be more than twelve was sitting on the other bed. She had pale blonde hair that was so long it was resting in her lap. Her skin was snow white and she had enormous eyes, like those of a manga character. She giggled and twirled a lock of hair, smiling hesitantly at Sofia.

'This is Elvira,' said Madeleine. 'She lives with us too.'

Sofia said hello, thinking that Elvira looked like she belonged in a John Bauer painting, or at least in school on the mainland — anywhere but here.

Sofia had expected to spend some time chatting, but as soon as she'd put on her nightgown Madeleine turned out the lights and the room descended into total darkness.

'Oh, I forgot. How do we wake up in the morning?' Sofia called.

'I'll wake you,' said Madeleine.

So they would still be using mental clocks.

It was impossible to fall asleep. The sensation of being in a military camp or a prison returned, and it wouldn't go away. The others' breathing slowed as they dozed off. She thought about her parents, who had said goodbye as if they would never see her

71

again. Her mother's nervous tendencies had been dialled up to new levels; she had spouted words like 'sect,' 'cult,' and 'bloody trickery,' only to regret her words and say she was only worried about Sofia. Worried, as usual. Worried about everything. But now Sofia missed her until her chest ached.

Then came the silent tears. She let them flow until they ran out.

And then, finally, came blessed sleep.

'Someone's coming! Go!' I say, giving her a shove.

It's a perfect day. The fog is so thick that you can hardly see the cliff from where we're hiding in a small grove of trees.

We've been waiting for a long time. She spent the time whining, nagging me to let her go home.

'No one's going to come, Fredrik. I'm freezing.'

But I won't give in. The fog is perfect and I'm not about to squander this opportunity. And someone really is coming. A man, slowly making his way across the heath.

'Go,' I hiss. 'And stick out your arms, like a ghost.'

She glides out into the fog, otherworldly in the black cloak and hood; she seems to be floating.

The man stops when he catches sight of her.

She walks to the farthest point of the cliff and reaches for the sea.

And then she howls like a lonely wolf.

The man is petrified; he doesn't believe his eyes.

She does as I've told her and drops down from the cliff. Into the cave, of course, but it happens so fast that she seems to dissolve into the fog.

The man walks all the way out to the edge of the cliff point. I hold my breath as he looks down. He can't see her, of course, so he is terrified. He turns around and dashes across the heath like a madman.

I can hear the twigs of heather being crushed under his feet and his heavy panting — the only sounds that reach me through the thick fog.

I wait until he's out of sight and crawl down to her. She's sitting on the cave floor, giggling. We laugh until we're gasping for breath.

'We'll show them who's in charge on this island, dammit!' I say at last.

8

The routines she had hated so much at first turned out to be what made her enjoy life on the island. They had the same schedule every day; all was so minutely planned that there was no time to think about anything but work, food, and sleep. It was easy to fit in. Each person was there on equal terms. Everyone took part in the same routines.

They woke at seven — at least, those who had mastered their internal clocks did. Sofia was dependent on Madeleine. There were no worries about how to dress; all you had to do was shower, put on your uniform, and head for the dining room, where breakfast was served. Always the same breakfast: poached eggs, whole-grain bread, and organic marmalade.

Then it was time to go to the courtyard in front of the manor and fall in line for morning assembly.

Bosse always led the assembly. He took roll call and talked about situations and priorities. Madeleine and Sofia formed one line together, as they were Oswald's personal staff and worked directly under him. The other lines were for the household staff, the guest services crew, those who worked on the farm, and the administrative staff.

Each day, she kept an eye out for Benjamin Frisk but to no avail. She stared at each line, hoping to catch a glimpse of him, but was disappointed time and again.

A few weeks after Sofia's arrival, a faint but growing unrest began to spread through the ranks. Bosse became stiff and distant. The staff seemed restless. Madeleine had stopped attending assembly.

One night, Sofia asked Elvira what was going on.

'It's the renovation of the staff quarters,' Elvira said. 'No one has wanted to ask you to help out, because Franz created your project himself, but the rest of us have been working a couple hours a day on the first floor. Haven't you seen us?'

She supposed she had. You had to walk through a cloud of sawdust and piles of boards and tools to get to the dining room. But she hadn't made the connection between the work and the morale of the group until now.

'But what's so difficult about doing renovations?' Sofia asked.

Elvira laughed. Sofia wondered if she'd misjudged her — she suddenly seemed so pleasant.

'Well, on the second floor, where we live now, Franz had to hire a contractor to get it all done. But now he says we have to finish the first floor on our own. It's a type of test, you know?'

Sofia was sincerely grateful that Oswald had drawn up that library project. She was in charge of her own day and could work at her own pace.

*

One day Oswald showed up at morning assembly. He appeared without warning behind Bosse, who was once again droning on about how important the renovation project was. It was a comical sight, because everyone but Bosse could see Oswald. Once Bosse realized why each staff member's gaze had frozen on a point behind him, Oswald just smiled and said, 'Go on. Don't mind me. I'm only listening.'

It continued for a few days. Oswald would come to the assembly and just stand there with an amused smile on his lips. This made Bosse anxious. He began to stutter, trip over his words, and lose his train of thought as he spoke. He started bringing notes with him. An awkward silence descended upon the staff, who were swept along in Bosse's despair and suffered with him.

Then one day, Oswald took over. He waved dismissively at Bosse, who immediately ducked into line like a dog afraid of being beaten.

'You are all an incredible resource,' said Oswald. 'You just haven't realized it yet.'

Murmurs of agreement cropped up here and there.

'I only want you to finish renovating your new living quarters. Can you manage that?'

Their positive response came in unison, as if with military precision.

'Well there you go!' Oswald said. 'Bosse can stop nagging you now, and you can stop pretending that you don't know what to do!'

They looked at him with great anticipation; they wanted him to keep talking because a sudden sense of solidarity had arisen. But he was done with them.

Sofia stayed behind as the staff scattered, hoping he would notice her. He did, and waved her over.

'What do you say, Sofia? Do you believe, too, that people have more potential than they realize?'

'Definitely, I'm sure they do.'

'Good, because that's my life's motto. I hate mediocrity.'

She didn't quite know what he expected her to say, and she felt that anxiety that came from standing before Oswald in silence. Later on she would learn that she didn't need to say anything at all. Oswald didn't speak with his staff. He spoke *to* his staff.

When he spoke to you, you were only supposed to make eye contact, and, when fitting, nod or express agreement. But she hadn't come to this realization yet, so she nervously scraped one foot through the gravel.

'Are you working on my library program?' he asked.

'That's all I do.'

'And what do you think of it?'

'It's fantastic,' she lied. Or, rather, exaggerated.

His face brightened a bit.

'Good, good. Keep at it. I want to see everything — the layouts, the computer systems, your list of books to purchase, the whole lot.'

Then he took a quick step forward, so he was standing very close to her.

'Your hair,' he said. 'It's nice when you put it up like that.'

He looked at the bun she had, with great effort, gathered on the very top of her head.

'Thanks.'

'Although I like it better down.'

'Oh, but Bosse said —'

This was as far as she got before he ran a finger down the back of her neck.

'Wear it loose tomorrow. Bosse's an idiot.'

'Okay, I will.'

He smiled at her, but the warmth in his eyes was gone.

'You're new here, but you should know that I don't have a boss. Least of all Bosse. You can get back to work now.'

His touch was still burning her skin as she hurried across the courtyard.

*

One night in September, she became fully aware of the coming autumn for the first time.

She was on her way back to the library after the evening assembly. A cold wind swept across the courtyard, tugging at her blazer and finding its way under her clothes, to her body. As she looked up, she realized that the aspens and birches were almost completely yellow. There was a fresh tension in the nature around her. Those migratory birds that were left seemed restless, as if they knew what awaited in their long journey south. The trees bent in the wind, full of nervous creaks and rustles. She was struck by the fact that she would be spending the entire winter on this island. The trees would lose their leaves. The whole island would become bare and bleak. The autumn fog everyone talked about would move in from the sea.

Shivering, she slipped through the library door, hoping to find a bit of warmth, but the cold wind had found the cracks in the draughty old building. She turned on the radiator, then decided to check her email, even though it was against the rules. She was one of the few staff with computer access; it was strictly for research purposes. But she had written a long email to her parents and had been waiting for a response for several days.

An answer was waiting, but it wasn't from her parents. Instead, a message in large type had appeared at the top of her own email. A rejection of sorts.

INFORMATION ABOUT THE INTERNAL PLANS OF THE ORGANIZATION IS CONFIDENTIAL AND MAY NOT BE SHARED WITH OUTSIDERS.

Someone had censored her email. She had no idea that anyone had been reading what she wrote to her family. She hadn't even known it was possible to censor email. An uncontrollable wave of fury welled up inside her. She immediately knew who was behind this.

In a rage, she put on her jacket and shoes and headed back into the wind. She found Bosse bent over a folder in the staff office.

The door was open, so she stepped in and stood before him, her hands on her hips.

'Have you been reading my email?'

'Sure! I read everything the staff sends out.'

'What's wrong with you? Those are private; you have no right to read them.' Her voice had risen into a shrill falsetto.

'Sofia, it's okay. I don't care what you say in them. I only care about the security of the group.'

'The security of the group? I was writing to my family.'

'You were writing about your plans for the library, down to the tiniest detail. That doesn't concern them.'

She was just about to start shouting, but it was obvious that he wouldn't give in. He'd done this before — gone along with some idiotic rule he probably hadn't even come up with himself. Besides, Sofia's emphatic tone had brought all the work in the big room outside to a grinding halt, and many watchful eyes were on them now. A few colleagues had stood up and were aiming looks of disapproval at her.

She stormed out of the room, determined to declare war as soon as she had gathered her thoughts.

It was impossible to concentrate on her job once she returned to the library. The wind was even stronger now; it whistled in the eaves. The windows were even rattling.

She turned on her computer and decided to surf the net, mostly just to defy Bosse. She Googled her name. It had been a long time, but her rage made her feel brave and she wanted to make sure that Ellis had stopped blogging about her.

Up popped a new page called 'Sofia Bauman's Blog,' and she clicked on it right away.

At first she thought it must be a mistake, that the face staring back at her belonged to someone else. Or that it was an old entry. But then she began to read the text and realized at once that Ellis hadn't vanished from her life after all.

Save Sofia Bauman from the cult! the headline read, and the text underneath continued along the same lines. There was even a picture of Franz Oswald in the corner, horns drawn onto his forehead.

She sat perfectly still for a long time, trying to calm herself as a burning chill spread along her nerves.

She didn't even want to know how many people had read the blog; she only wanted it to go away. She wanted something to happen to Ellis, a terrible accident, *anything*, as long as it would put a stop to him from here on out. It was inconceivable that he could still make her feel so awful even when she was on an island out in the archipelago.

How can he even get at me out here? she thought, then decided that in fact, he couldn't.

But then she thought about the blog again and wondered what would happen if Oswald got wind of it.

We've spent a whole day looking for the diary, the family history — whatever the hell it is.

Lily is tired and whiny, and I feel like I might smack her at any moment.

'I don't want to be here, Fredrik. It's too warm and icky and it smells nasty. Can't we do something fun instead? Please?'

'We have to find the book,' I say, gritting my teeth.

'But why is it so important to find some old book?'

'There's stuff in it I'm going to use.'

'For what?'

'To prove who I am.'

'Oh, come on. Hey, can't we go now? Take a swim or something?'

I stand up, take her by the arms, and give her a firm shake.

'Who is in charge here, huh? Stop nagging me, or else . . .'

She is frightened and recoils. And at that moment I figure out what happened and I let go of her.

'She hid it, of course,' I say. 'That bitch hid it away.'

'What bitch?'

'Mom. She doesn't want me to find it.' I decide to switch tactics on Lily. 'Listen, if you find the book I'll take you down to the village and buy you some ice cream, and then we can go for a swim at the cliff.'

Her whole face lights up.

'Promise?'

'I said it, didn't I?'

She's suddenly full of energy. She darts around until the dust swirls up, pulling out drawers, yanking things off the shelves. And then the unthinkable happens. Suddenly she's standing there with a book in her hands, wrinkling her nose as she tries to make out what it says inside.

'Give it here!' I shout. Because I know, I just know, that she's found it.

I yank it from her hands and sink to the floor, flipping pages and looking for the part that just has to be there. And when I find it, it's like the doors of heaven open, revealing angels, strings, harps, the whole nine yards. Adrenaline surges through my body like a rising flood.

That's when I see a little corner poking out from the back cover of the diary — something is hidden there.

I pull the envelope out and open it. Photographs fall into the book.

I moan when I see what they are.

The girl in the picture can't be more than twelve or thirteen. She's standing against a wall, naked, her hands bound high over her head. She's in profile, but I recognize the man pressed up against her body, a whip in his hand. He's younger in the picture, but it's definitely him.

This is so huge, so timely, that I almost forget to breathe.

I just stand there, listening to Lily's gasping breaths behind me.

Whoever left the pictures there was careless, idiotic.

But they're a windfall for me.

9

There was a hard rap on the door. The room was pitch black, as usual, but she could tell instinctively that it was still night-time. The lights came on gradually and Madeleine, who was sitting up in bed, became visible. The clock on the wall read twenty past four. There was another rap, impatient and frantic.

'Assembly in the dining room in ten minutes! Wear jeans!'

It was Bosse's voice. Angry and harsh. Sofia thought something must have happened — an accident or emergency of some sort. She didn't know how long she'd been asleep, but it couldn't have been more than a couple of hours — she had lain awake for a long time brooding about Ellis and the blog.

Elvira was also awake by that point, and she looked terrified, the blanket drawn up to her chin.

'What's going on?'

'I don't know,' Madeleine said. 'But we have to get dressed and run down to the dining room.'

They staggered around the room, pulling on jeans and whatever they could find in the dresser drawers.

'Do you have any idea what it might be?' Sofia tried again.

'No, but Franz was up late. I probably shouldn't have gone to bed.'

Just about everyone else was already there when they arrived in the dining room. They were lined up in their usual way, with tired, pale faces, messy hair, and anxious eyes. The dining room was cold and damp. They could hear rain pattering against the windowpanes.

Oswald was standing before them. He was wearing his usual outfit: black jeans and a T-shirt, and he had almost certainly not been to bed. But he didn't look tired, only terribly angry.

He read the blog!

The thought hit her like the flick of a whip. It had to be. He had been surfing online; he had come across the disgusting blog and read the whole thing. She couldn't think of any other reason he might gather them at four in the morning.

A few stragglers came through the door and Oswald stared at them in annoyance.

'Is everyone here?' Bosse asked.

Bosse walked around, inspecting the lines, counting and mumbling until he could declare that everyone was present except Katarina, the gardener.

'She's sick; she has a fever,' he said. 'So I didn't wake her up.'

'I said I wanted to speak to the *entire* staff,' Oswald said. 'So I'll wait for her.'

He crossed his arms over his chest.

Bosse hurried off and an awkward silence followed. No one wanted to talk. Everyone stared straight ahead, avoiding each other's eyes and, above all, trying not to stare at Oswald. The silence was cold as ice.

At last a panting Bosse returned with Katarina in tow. She looked terrible: she was sweaty, her eyes were feverish, and she was so pale that her skin took on a green tinge in the cold light. She was still wearing her nightgown and slippers.

'I was working late tonight while the rest of you were snoozing,' Oswald began. 'And on my way home I peeked in here to see how the renovations are coming along. Come on, I'll show you how it looks.'

He marched out of the dining room with the staff trailing him, and they headed down the corridor to the part of the building being renovated. The shorter staff members tried to crane their necks to see over the crowd, and there were bottlenecks at the doorways. Oswald didn't say anything; he only walked around pointing at various boards, tools strewn about, piles of sawdust, safety glasses on the floor, and cans of paint that hadn't even been sealed up for the night. Then he walked around, showing them the rooms. All twenty of them. There wasn't a single finished room in sight. Sofia was flooded with relief even in the midst of her misery. It wasn't the blog after all. Plus, she wasn't responsible for this mess.

'You have been working on this bloody project for three months,' said Oswald. 'Now I'm going to show you what happens when you make such a mess of things.'

He strode out into the courtyard and everyone followed. They were almost immediately drenched by the cold, incessant rain. Sofia snuck an anxious glance at Katarina, who was coughing behind her. Oswald led them past the small barn to a wooded area.

Anchored to the moss under a few pines was a large white tent. Oswald pulled the zipper down and showed them inside. There were sleeping bags, pillows, and blankets all in a pile, as well as several suitcases. Sofia, who had stuck close to Oswald, managed to poke her head through the opening. A heavy odour of mould and sweaty feet struck her.

'This is where your household unit lives,' Oswald said. 'There is no room for them in the main building. Pleasant, isn't it? This is how they are living, like pigs, on my property.'

He didn't say anything for a long time. The situation was absurd, bordering on comical. The rain fell harder, trickling into Oswald's eyes and mouth and forcing him to blink and swallow again and again. The only sound that could be heard through the roaring downpour was Katarina's rattling cough.

Maybe he felt ridiculous, drenched as he was and with his voice drowned out by the rain, because he just shook his head and said, 'I don't want anything more to do with you. Not a single one of you bastards. Go back to the mainland, run home to mommy and daddy. Get a job you can handle. You don't belong here.'

Then he marched back into the main building.

The whole staff stood there, at a loss, terrified and soaking wet.

Bosse broke the silence: 'Assembly in the dining room!'

★

Back inside, a small group congregated in one corner, whispering to each other: Bosse, Madeleine, and Benny and Sten, who were two peas in a pod. The pair could often be spotted riding around the property on their motorcycles or sitting in the booth at the front gate. They were large and obstinate but quite dull; they matched her idea of a typical guard perfectly. At first she thought they were cut out for the job, but now she wondered if it was such a good idea for them to be involved in decision-making.

She considered joining the little group to prove that she cared, but decided to hold off. She wanted to avoid taking responsibility for the renovation project at all costs.

Bosse hopped up onto a chair.

'Now we're going to shift into high gear,' he said. 'We'll show Franz we're a team. Everyone must pitch in and work on the renovation until it's complete. No exceptions. Those of you who take care of the guests will just have to make sure that they have food and stuff. But otherwise we'll work until it's done.'

Her hope of sneaking back to her warm bed was immediately extinguished. This didn't look good. At all.

Bosse divided them into groups that were to work on different parts of the renovation. She ended up in the painting group along with Elvira.

And so began the craziest, most chaotic and sleepless period in her life thus far. Days and nights flowed together into the sort of mishmash that can only arise from a large group of people who have no plan or idea what to do. They sawed, swept, polished, sandpapered, and painted. Bosse and his new henchmen ran around trying to make everyone move faster by shouting things like 'Faster!' and 'You have fifteen minutes to finish that!' and since all these commands were perfectly meaningless, no one listened.

They slept for a few hours each night; sometimes not even that much. After several sleepless nights, staff were dozing off here and there and had to be shaken into consciousness to get going again.

Sofia tried to stay awake as best she could. She painted and painted. Her hands, arms, legs, feet, and hair were covered in white paint.

What have I gotten myself into? What am I doing here?

The thought returned to her daily, but she kept painting with Elvira. They became friends there among the cans, brushes, and turpentine. They shared water bottles and gum. They kept watch for each other when one slipped into the storage room to take a nap on the hard floor behind the shelves, when they simply couldn't manage any longer. If someone in the leader group, as they called Bosse's gang, headed for the storage room, all the person keeping watch could do was rush over and distract them. She would cough three times to wake the sleeper, to give her time to rub the sleep from her eyes. That was all it took — it was impossible to sleep deeply on the ice-cold floor. The three coughs broke through slumber like it was the first thin layer of ice on a pond; the alert brought the sleeper to her feet and she would dart out of the storeroom and go right back to painting.

Each time it seemed they were done, something else popped up. The wrong colour paint somewhere; baseboards that weren't high enough; mismatched furniture. And every time something went wrong, the group experienced new, greater levels of hysteria and frenzy.

She was swallowed by exhaustion; it got worse each day. Her eyelids were leaden and the brush felt huge in her hand.

But she gritted her teeth and kept painting.

Then one day, all of a sudden, they were finished.

They looked at each other in wonder, dumbfounded, almost positive that it couldn't be true. There had to be something else that needed fixing. But after several checks, the leader group determined that the job was done.

They hadn't seen Oswald a single time since that horrible night in the rain, but now he had to be called to inspect their work.

He made them wait for two days. They spent the time cleaning and polishing, moving furniture back and forth, burnishing door handles. They didn't dare leave the floor out of fear that he might suddenly show up.

When he arrived, he walked around the rooms three times.

He didn't utter a word. At last he nodded.

The nightmare was over.

★

Oswald allowed them to celebrate with a party in the dining room. Food, wine, music, and dancing — it was like stepping into a new world. He attended the party too. He spoke with the staff, joking, laughing, and back-slapping.

When he caught sight of Sofia, he made a sort of apology.

'I know you're new here,' he said. 'But sometimes it's necessary to take off the kid gloves. I'm sure you understand.'

'Of course!' she said cheerfully, hoping he wouldn't notice the white paint she hadn't been able to get out of her hair.

But his fingers took hold of a matted clump near her cheek, then slid down her face to the tip of her chin.

'Look how hard you've been working! Sofia, I'm so glad to have you here.'

A jolt zinged from her cheek to her groin. She tried to keep a poker face and shrugged. But he noticed. He gave her a meaningful smile and raised his eyebrows before moving on.

She was still feeling drained from the lack of sleep and couldn't quite let herself sink into the joyful mood. She kept thinking about how her dorm room was empty and she could sneak off, pull out her laptop, and send an email home. Make contact after two weeks of silence.

The party music was loud, throbbing. The sounds of renovation, blows of the hammer and the whine of the circular saw were still echoing through her head. She decided to make herself invisible and sneak out the front door.

That's where she ran into him.

He must have been coming from outside, because he brought with him a gust of cold autumn wind and the scent of leather from his jacket. His eyes were just as she recalled, happy and lively. The wind had blown his hair back, making it look like a funny toupee. His mouth was half open, revealing the gap between his front teeth.

'God, I'm so glad you're here!' he said, taking her hands. Suddenly she wasn't tired in the least.

A few weeks have passed since I found the book.

A thought has been with me ever since.

It's insane and dizzying, but genius.

I've been snooping for more evidence hidden away by my idiotic mother — she thinks she's so clever.

At the moment she's sitting at the kitchen table, gazing out the window. Grumpy and grim. Her jaw is clenched as if she has taken a vow of eternal silence. I sit down on the chair across from her.

'I hate you more than anyone else ever could,' I say.

She doesn't say 'Oh, no!' or 'You can't say that!' or anything a normal mother would have said.

She just sits there staring, stiff and silent as a dead fish. And it's all her fault — especially the fact that we're sitting here in a fucking summer cottage, poor and insignificant. All because she had to have a quickie with the count. And yet, to my great chagrin, I see myself in her as she sits there.

We are strong, bull-headed, stubborn. There is not a pitiful bone in our bodies.

Not like that cowardly bastard who fled the island for some stupid place in France.

No, I know that I take after her, and that makes me hate her even more.

'I wrote to him,' I say, holding the letter up for her to see. Close enough

*for her to read the name on the envelope. At last her eyes go cloudy with
worry and she opens her mouth to say something.*

But I'm already on my way out of the cottage.

*When I turn around on the lawn, I see that she has stood up and
come to the window.*

Go ahead and stare, *I think*. Stare all you want — but it's too
late.

10

The fog took hold of the island in early October, and by mid-month it had an iron grip on the place. It crept in at night and each morning it was so thick that Sofia couldn't see the outbuildings from the window in her dormitory. The brightly coloured leaves had faded and the landscape had turned shades of golden-brown. It was steadily growing colder. Normally she would have felt a little gloomy thanks to all the fog. But not now — she spent almost all her time thinking about Benjamin. It was as if the fog transformed the island into a fairy-tale world with infinite curtains a person could pass through and discover fresh views.

Benjamin showed up in the library every day. She never knew when he would appear, so she remained in a state of constant expectation and excitement. He always had a good excuse to visit. Oswald had instructed him to help with all the purchasing. But most of the time he came by with trivial questions and errands. He had that eager way about him as if he were always on the go. He could fill an entire room with his energy just by stepping across the threshold. He would forget to remove his boots, tramping around and leaving marks on the rugs without noticing. His body was always in motion — he walked around looking out of windows, picking up objects, putting them down again — even as he spoke with her. But when he sat down in front of her he became perfectly still. He could move in and out of these states, from wound up to absolutely relaxed, in an instant.

She had a constant internal dialogue about whether it was right to start a new relationship so soon after the disaster with Ellis; her brain went back and forth, over and over. This nervous droning was like background music as she worked. But when Benjamin entered the room, the voices stopped. And then it started up again until Sunday, when he showed her the cave.

It was their day off and the whole island was blanketed in a thick fog. Everything was wet: the trees, the bushes, and the earth, which smelled like mushrooms and decaying leaves. He showed her a new path through the woods; they had to climb over huge, moss-covered stones to move forward.

From the top of the highest boulder, they got a glimpse of the grey, foamy sea between the trees. It was windy out there, but not in the woods.

Sofia stayed on the boulder for a while as Benjamin climbed down.

'Here it is!' she heard Benjamin's voice from below.

She slid down from the rock and saw that he had found a patch of chanterelles in the moss.

'This is my secret chanterelle spot. Come on, let's pick them.'

He had brought a backpack, and they gently placed the small mushrooms inside.

'I'll show you something you've never seen by the outlook point,' he said.

'How do you know the island so well?'

'We had a summer cottage here when I was little.'

'Is it still here?'

His eyes darted away a little too quickly.

'No, we had to sell it. Mom left us when I was twelve. Dad died in a car accident soon after that. Now it's just me and my sister.'

'I'm sorry, I mean, I didn't know . . .'

'It's okay. It was a long time ago.'

'Why did your mom leave?'

'It's hard to say. One day she was just gone. I couldn't help but blame myself a little bit, though. It was like, I wondered what I had done wrong.'

He seemed to have sunk into himself; he looked smaller.

'But you always seem so happy!'

She could tell right away how wrong it sounded, as if he had renounced his right to happiness.

He stood up and slung the backpack over his shoulders.

'Well, what can you do? The future is what's important. And I have my ViaTerra family, of course.'

The outlook point was windy. The fog had lifted from the sea, but the sky was still grey. Waves crashed in hard enough to make foam fly from the rocks.

'That's Devil's Rock,' Benjamin said, pointing. 'Have you heard about it?'

'Yes, Björk — the guy who runs the ferry — told me the whole story. Do you really believe all that?'

'Sure, some of it. Once when I was younger, it was foggy and I thought I saw the Countess on the Rock. It was scary as hell. Someone was standing out there, dressed all in black. And then she vanished into the fog. It was like she dissolved.'

'I saw someone there when I first came to the island. But it looked like a regular person. At least I think it did.'

'We used to jump off Devil's Rock when I was little,' he said.

'But then there was an accident. One guy who jumped died. The current dragged him out to sea.'

'Did you know him?'

'A little, he was a few years older than me. But I remember how scared we were when we found out. His mom worked at the manor. A doctor lived there back then. I don't remember him, but I do remember his daughter, Lily. She was older than us too. Pretty girl — she had long red hair and she was thin as a rail. We used to spy on her when she was sunbathing. But she died in a fire in the barn. It all happened around the same time. It was awful.'

'Maybe it's true, then, about the curse on the manor?'

'No, I don't believe in ghosts like that. But I do believe some souls have trouble finding peace. That they can stick around, sort of.'

She looked out at the cliff and could almost see a figure there.

'Ooh, now you're scaring me.'

He laughed and put his arm around her shoulders.

'Let's climb down the rocks,' he said, looking at her rubber boots with concern. 'Be careful so you don't slip.'

They cautiously made their way down the steep rock face. Sofia did lose her footing a few times, but managed to steady herself and tried to keep up with Benjamin.

They came to a small grassy slope between the boulders, and he stopped there. They were directly underneath Devil's Rock, and the cliff hung over them like a huge ceiling. The waves crashed, roaring and splashing. Benjamin pointed up at the ledge. At first she couldn't tell what he was pointing at, but then she saw a big dark spot among all the rocks. It could have been a black rock, but she realized it was a hole.

He came over to her and took her lightly by the shoulders.

'You have to swear not to tell anyone about the cave. Promise?'

'Of course.'

'Good, let's go in.'

The cave was about four metres deep and one and a half metres in height. It was cool and damp inside, but the floor was dry. She had the strange sensation as she gazed out at the waves, as if she were in a house floating above the sea.

Benjamin emptied his backpack. Some kindling, a frying pan, and matches, as well as some cheese, bread, and fruit he'd begged from the kitchen. They got a fire going and grilled chanterelle sandwiches over the fire. They had to eat with their fingers — he'd forgotten cutlery. They chatted nonstop, then sat quietly for a while and gazed out at the sea and the sky, which still hadn't cleared. Then the fire died out and the cave grew chilly.

'Now we're going to eat dinner in the village,' he said. 'We're going to Fritjof's. It's crab season, and theirs is the best.'

It was starting to get dark, so they went to the village by the road.

For a while, they didn't say anything as they walked. She could hardly make out his face in the dim twilight, but she got the sense that he was brooding about something. His arm had been around her, but he let it slide off her shoulders. She was just about to ask what was on his mind when they arrived at the pub.

Inside, in the warm light, he seemed normal again. He laughed at her cold, blue fingers and warmed them for her. He joked with the waitress and ordered so much crab and so many sides that there was hardly room on the table. His hair glowed in the light from the candle; it almost looked like it had caught fire.

She asked about the renovations and their lack of sleep, what he thought of it all.

'We wouldn't have completed the renovations if Franz hadn't put his foot down,' he said firmly.

'So you're a fanatical follower?'

'Maybe. I mean, ViaTerra is my family. The only family I have.'

'But that doesn't mean everything about it is perfect, does it?'

'You're so new, Sofia. You'll get used to it. The purpose is what matters.'

That same shadow fell across his face again.

'What are you thinking about?'

'Nothing.'

'Come on, out with it. I can tell something's up.'

He cleared his throat, looking embarrassed.

'Well, it's just, you know . . . if you're a couple, at ViaTerra, the expectation is that you'll, um, move in together.'

'Move in together?'

'I just want to make sure you know the rules before we start anything. It seems like no one explained them to you.'

'What rules?'

'You can only have sex if you live together or you're married.'

'Who said anything about sex?'

'Don't make this even harder for me.'

'What kind of moron thought up that rule?'

Benjamin laughed.

'Franz, probably. But don't you see what it would be like in such a small group, if everyone was sleeping with everyone else all the time?'

She considered it for a moment. This was all so exciting. It was new and unusual and a little titillating, and for some strange reason she liked it.

'But just because there are rules doesn't mean you can't bend them a little sometimes, right?'

He nodded in agreement as if they had just made a pact.

★

It was totally dark when they left the pub. A half-moon shined down on them from the clear sky. They could see their breath, and the chilly air nipped at their cheeks. She flipped up her collar and buried her hands in her jacket pockets. Benjamin put his arm around her shoulders again.

The walk to ViaTerra was long, but it passed quickly. She leaned against him, snuggling into his chest now and then.

Sten was on guard at the gate, and he waved them in distractedly. The wind was still beyond the thick walls.

The windows of the manor house were bright in the darkness. When Sofia looked up, she thought she could see a light on in the attic — then she remembered that the attic was unfit for use. A moment later the light had vanished and she decided she must have been seeing things.

★

They bent the rules just a few weeks later. They never discussed it, but the tension between them had risen until his visits to the library became unbearable.

It was their day off, and he met her by the gate. They didn't even talk about where to go — their feet just carried them to the cottage and their hands were linked as if frozen by a constant electric current. She moved right up next to him for the last little bit of the journey and noticed that his breathing was already faintly erratic and heavy.

She'd had good and bad sex before, but never forbidden sex, so this was something new. She walked ahead of him into the cottage and right away he grabbed her from behind, lifting her loose hair and kissing her tenderly on the back of the neck. He nibbled at her earlobe and tried to get his hands in under her clothes, but one hand got stuck between the buttons. She pulled him to the kitchen bench and they collapsed onto it, eager but awkward in all their outerwear. They rolled onto the rag rug on the floor. On the way down she accidentally grabbed hold of the lace tablecloth and a candlestick came flying by, narrowly missing Benjamin's head. They burst into laughter but managed to pull off each other's clothing: jackets, boots, gloves, pants, and sweaters ended up in one big pile that grew as they gasped and howled in amusement.

This is how it should be the first time, she thought. *Wild and joyful*. Then she thought about what would happen if someone came into the cottage and discovered them on the floor — but it wouldn't have mattered, not even if it was Oswald himself. It was like they were a runaway train, and no one could stop them.

Afterwards, as they lay twined together on the rag rug, she decided that forbidden sex blew everything else out of the water.

She rested her head against his shoulder and they lay like that for a long time. Completely devoid of energy, drained.

'What's the punishment?' she asked.

'The punishment?'

'Yes, for what we did.'

'What do you mean, what we did?'

'Stop messing with me!'

'Well, it's pretty bad. I mean, you get shunned from the group. Dismissed. Sent back to the mainland.'

'No way! Just for having sex without living together?'

'That's right. But we don't have to tell anyone, do we? It's between us.'

She thought of the library, her dream for the future. How would it feel to tell her family and friends that she couldn't hack it? That she had been fired?

'Exactly. It has nothing to do with anyone else.'

I'm sitting on the cliff and staring into the fog.

It seems strange that the fog lingers even though spring is here. Maybe it's a sign, calling me to leave.

You can hardly see the water, only hear the waves crashing against the rocks. A few ducks fly down and land on the surface, where they turn into little brown balls of feathers. Too bad I left my rifle at home. I toss a rock at them and they flap their wings and fly off.

The wind is picking up and the fog is scattering farther out at sea; I can see the lighthouse out there, a dot floating in the mist. It's a peculiar sight. Not beautiful — because beauty is a concept I never make use of, an expression used by the weak to show how sensitive they are.

But it's calm here by the sea, maybe even peaceful.

I haven't received a response to my letter, but it doesn't matter. Now he knows.

Everything is ready. I've pawned my mother's jewellery, things she won't miss until I'm long gone from the island.

The ticket is safely tucked in my trouser pocket. My backpack is under my bed, the diary and other important documents inside. I think about my exodus. How I will disappear. How it will feel when I come back once it's all done.

One last night with Lily is all I need now, a ceremony and an acknowledgement.

Then I hear a sound. It floats in from the sea and echoes off the rocks. A dull, monotonous bellow from the old lighthouse.

The foghorn.

My first thought is that it can't be true. That the message is for someone else, an old person in the village or some suicidal idiot roving through the forest.

Because I know what that howl means.

It's a warning to someone who's about to die.

11

A storm followed on the heels of the fog in early November. The weather service had issued a Class 3 warning, so everyone scrambled to prepare the property. They secured anything loose, brought the animals into the barns, piled sandbags where the water might rise, and tested the generator.

Sofia looked online to see what the warning meant. 'Considerable damage to property, considerable disruption to crucial public services, danger to the public.' She had never experienced a big storm on an island before. Bosse told her about last fall's storm, how the water level had risen over a metre, and how no one could go outside — the trees had fallen like bowling pins. They'd been without power for a whole week.

'They were too busy fixing the electric lines on the mainland, so we had to wait. But now we have our own backup generator,' he said proudly.

The wind began to whine and howl late in the afternoon. Sofia sat in the library, putting the finishing touches to her list of books. She'd poured her heart and soul into that list. Oswald had said he wanted to see it, but she was well prepared. She knew exactly how many shelves the books would take up, how they should be categorized, and why she had chosen each one.

She also had another, shorter list of books with controversial or erotic contents, which Oswald probably wouldn't approve of if he'd read them. But he hadn't read them — she was almost certain of it. She would put the two lists together once she was finished, letting the controversial books mix in with the others. This project had taken up all her attention and she often thought about how good it would look on her CV when she was done.

But now the storm was raging. It was already dark; it was five o'clock and the wind was supposed to peak around midnight. The aspens behind her building bent in the gusts that rattled the windows. The gale had found every crack in the old building, making it raw and cold inside. She turned up the thermostat before she headed over for dinner. As she crossed the yard, the wind tore at her down jacket and she had to stop and catch her balance to keep from being tossed forward. A branch came flying through the air and landed on the ground as a flowerpot rolled across the yard. She hunched over against the whipping wind.

Bosse stood up during dinner to give a speech about the rules for the night. Everyone had to stay indoors and be prepared to lend a hand if anything happened. No going on walks. Sofia snorted. As if someone would get the bright idea to go out in the dark and risk being crushed to death by a falling tree.

By bedtime the gale was even stronger, and it was so dark that nothing could be seen; they could only hear the terrible noise. A few small branches flew by, striking the window. The air was so full of static that it made her skin tingle. She began to feel uneasy. She chatted with Madeleine and Elvira a bit, but everything felt wrong when it was time for lights out.

'We can't just lie here in the dark, listening to this miserable weather, can we? Do we really have to pull the blinds? What if something happens?'

Disagreement was on the tip of Madeleine's tongue, but Elvira agreed with Sofia.

'I don't want to listen to the wind in the dark either; that's just terrifying,' she said.

So for once, they left the blinds up.

She had trouble falling asleep in the roar of the storm. The wind brought objects smashing and crashing into the yard, but at last she slipped into a sleep-like state. She drifted in and out for a long time, until she was suddenly yanked out of her dozing: the whole room lit up for an instant and the flash was followed by a loud rumble of thunder.

She sat up with a start. There was another round of lightning and thunder, but this time it was so loud that she leapt out of bed and ran to the window. Down in the yard she could see a piece of the flagpole, which had broken in half. A couple of figures were fighting the wind on their way to the barns.

What happened next would be imprinted in her mind in slow motion, even though it was all over in a fraction of a second. A bolt of lightning shot down, accompanied by a deafening clap of thunder. The lightning struck a tall pine behind the barn; the tree seemed to split in two as it crashed onto the annexe behind the manor, taking an electrical wire with it. Great flames leapt from the thatched roof.

Madeleine and Elvira had woken up too and were sitting up ramrod straight in their beds.

'Shit! It's on fire!' Sofia shrieked.

Suddenly she remembered the fire drills they'd practised with Bosse late last summer — exercises she'd found annoying at the time. They were supposed to wake everyone up and shout 'Fire!' and give the location. She pulled her boots on without socks and swept her down jacket over her nightgown.

'Didn't you hear me? A fire!' she shouted at Madeleine and Elvira, so loudly that they flew out of bed and started looking for their clothes.

She dashed from the room and started knocking on doors in the hallway.

'Fire in the barn! Fire in the barn!' she shouted, running from door to door.

Elvira popped up behind her as she headed for the first floor.

'Make sure everyone wakes up and comes down!' Sofia shouted.

It was pitch dark in the yard, aside from the flames shooting out of the barn roof. The broken electrical wire must have taken out all the power. But then she heard the generator kick in and the outdoor lights came back on. She could see Bosse and Sten manoeuvring the fire hose toward the barn. The wind had let up a bit, but the thunder was still constant. She saw lightning and heard thunder at the same time, and realized it must be very dangerous to be outside.

Moos, bleats, and hysterical clucking echoed from the barn.

'I'll let the animals out!' she called to Bosse.

'No, they'll trample you!' he shouted back as he aimed the hose at the fire. A cascade of water jetted toward the roof, but the flames only grew higher, up towards the treetops.

The shrieking from the barn was unbearable.

The thought came over her quickly, but her body was even faster. It was like she was a remotely-guided character in a computer game, always acting before her mind caught up. She had already opened the barn doors by the time it occurred to her that she would rather be trampled than let the animals burn alive inside.

It was absolute chaos inside the barn. The fire was crackling in the ceiling of the far corner, where the chickens were caged. It smelled like smoke and burnt wood. The animals sensed the danger instinctively; they were stamping and shrieking, their eyes rolled back in fear.

She opened the gate to the sheep enclosure first, and they immediately ran for the door and pinned her against the wall, but she managed to shoo them out. The cows had begun to throw themselves at the doors of their stalls, wild with fear.

She climbed up on one of the stall walls to leave the aisle free. One by one she let the cows out and they immediately set off down the aisle and vanished through the door.

The fire had burned through the ceiling by now and flames were licking at the chicken coop. Thick smoke began to pour in and fill the aisle. She fought with the coop door, but when it finally opened the hens just flapped around at random, squawking and cackling.

She grabbed a pitchfork from the aisle and started shoving them toward the door.

'Get out, for god's sake, fly out!'

At last they caught on and started flapping down the aisle, but a couple of confused hens turned around and went right into the fire, where they flew around like torches, uttering ghastly noises. At the same time, she heard the dreadful creak of a beam falling on the far side of the barn.

By now the smoke was thick in the aisle and it hurt to breathe. Then suddenly she couldn't get any air at all and her eyes were swimming, about to go dark. It was crackling behind her, and the heat of the fire licked at her back, just enough to give her one last shot of adrenaline that sent her out of the barn on staggering legs. Once she was out, she collapsed, lying supine on the ground, and sucked in the cold air. She lay there for a moment, staring up at the clouds moving across the black sky.

'Sofia, are you okay?'

It was Benjamin. He sank down beside her and grasped her hand so hard it hurt.

'Breathe, Sofia, breathe!' he urged her.

'Thanks for the reminder,' she said, trying to laugh. All that came out was a rattle deep in her lungs.

'We have to get to a doctor.'

'No, I'll be fine.'

Her voice already felt steadier.

Bosse had arrived with a few other staff members in tow.

'Jesus, Sofia, you should have listened to me!'

'But I didn't, and that's why most of the animals are still alive,' she said, sitting up.

The yard was full of people. Staff and guests, all mixed up. Some were fighting the fire; others were herding the animals into an empty barn nearby. They seemed so strangely organized: everyone was in motion; everyone had something to do.

At that moment, the rain came, a heavy downpour that joined the cascades of the fire hoses and put out the fire until all that was left was the smoke and the acrid smell. The back of the barn was destroyed, and thick, grey smoke billowed from its charred skeleton. A few animals were still running around in the yard. It was freezing cold, but it didn't matter. They kept working.

When they were all done and the fire hoses were rolled up, they just stood there looking at each other in the rain. The relief on their faces was beautiful. It was a sight she thought she'd never forget.

She searched for Oswald but realized he wasn't there. There were guests in soaked clothing, even some in pyjamas and nightgowns, but no Oswald. She looked up at the manor house and saw a figure standing on the balcony: the silhouette of a man gazing down at them with his arms crossed over his chest. It looked as if he was nodding.

An onlooker on the outside, peering in.

★

She couldn't stop whining about Oswald to Benjamin in the days after the fire.

'What the hell was he doing on the balcony?'

'I don't know, Sofia. He probably wanted to see how we would manage.'

'The whole barn was burning down, animals and all.'

'Quit complaining. Franz likes to keep a little distance.'

'Even the guests were out there, in their pyjamas.'

'Listen, if I didn't know better I'd say you were a little fixated on Franz.'

'Fixated? Everyone is, around here.'

'No, not me. He's really just a regular guy — it's best to take everything he says with a pinch of salt. Instead of expecting him to be some sort of god.'

They went on like that for a few days until Oswald came to an assembly and rewarded Sofia with a bonus and two days off for her actions during the fire. He said that the county police chief, Wilgot Östling, had been on the island that day and had seen her rescue the animals.

★

She swallowed her annoyance and accepted her time off and bonus, using it to travel home to Lund for a few days to see her parents and spend some time with Wilma.

Her mother was more anxious than ever. It took almost a whole day of repeated assurances that Sofia was happy on the island, and felt just fine, to calm her down. Sofia didn't mention the fire.

It felt strange to be back home again. She found herself going back and forth between several different moods: at times she felt so melancholy that she wanted to remain in Lund, but other times she felt restless and wanted to get her visit over with so she could go back to the island.

There was something strained about Wilma's mannerisms, as if she were trying to keep from mentioning something.

'What's wrong, Wilma?'

'Nothing.'

'Oh for god's sake, I can tell something's up.'

'I don't want to worry you.'

'Out with it.'

'Ellis emailed me. I don't even know how that creep got my address, I've changed it so many times. He asked where you were.'

'What did you say? You didn't tell him, did you?'

'Are you nuts? I told him you got a job in France.'

'What did he say?'

'He wrote back: "you're such a lying bitch".'

'Was that all?'

'That was all.'

'What a fucking jerk.' Tears welled up in Sofia's eyes, and then came that familiar feeling of discomfort and panic that Ellis always brought on. 'What am I supposed to do? He's going to haunt me forever.'

'Oh, you've got guards and a wall and all of that on the island. What can he do? He'll just keep writing about you online, and he'll get sick of it eventually, once he doesn't hear anything back from you.'

★

The same day she returned to the island, the first snow fell. Thick flakes drifted down, forming a speckled curtain of fog in front of the ferry. The pines on the highest point of the island were already white; the harbour looked like it was made of spun cotton.

It felt like she was coming home.

Something goes wrong.

Something totally unexpected, inexplicable, and so goddamn wrong.

But she's the one who messes up.

The rules of our game are clear and plain. She doesn't follow them. So what happens happens.

We have planned the evening down to the tiniest detail.

She lies in the straw, on the cloak. Her hands are up over her head, her hair spread out like burning fire. And the candles are in front of her, their flames flickering.

I stand there looking at her until I'm totally hard, and then I take out the belt.

She's used to it by now and doesn't look frightened, which is too bad because I enjoyed that look in her eyes.

There's a trick, something I've learned — thrusting into her as I pull on the belt. It's best that way. Maximum pleasure.

I am careful to get it right this time. The last time.

I place the belt around her neck and lean over her. I thrust and pull at the same time, and she gasps and whimpers. It feels so good that I almost lose myself for a moment, but then she resists and starts kicking wildly.

She cries out — a shrill, piercing scream that has nothing to do with our game.

Someone might hear her. She has to stop.

I pull a little harder, just to make her be quiet.

Her eyes roll back in their sockets in such an odd way; all I can see are the whites and she goes strangely limp in the straw.

I loosen the belt and try to jostle her back to life. But it's as if she's made of jelly, soft and lifeless.

A hellish pain flares up in my foot and when I turn around I realize she must have kicked a candle over, because the straw behind me is on fire and big flames are licking at my feet.

I give a shout, then stand up and grab my trousers.

I toss them over the fire, trying to smother it, but it only gets worse.

My trousers are on fire now and the flames are crackling and spreading through the straw. I realize I'm naked and pull on my briefs, the first thing I find.

My mind is working incredibly fast. I've got to fix this. I've got to make it out.

I place her hands over her chest and cover her body with the cloak. It's all I can do.

Got to hurry, the fire's spreading. It's at her feet now.

I run out of the barn.

I run like a madman.

12

She felt guilty, and the guilt only got worse the more she worried that they would be discovered. They had grown careless. A quickie in the library bathroom, his hand on her bum in the food line — lust was making them take risks. And now she couldn't concentrate on anything at all. She felt like the staff were staring at her with suspicion. She couldn't bring herself to look Oswald in the eye when he came to assembly. At last she found herself wishing Benjamin would go to the mainland for a while, just so she could work in peace.

'We have to stop.'

'What do you mean?'

'That we have to stop. I can't handle it anymore.'

'Sofia, come on. Let's just move in together.'

'Never. Or at least, not right now. I have to finish the library.'

'But it's no big deal to live together. And that way we don't have to sleep in the dorms.'

'Later, maybe, but for now we need to take a break.'

'What do you mean, a break?'

'No more sex until the library is done.'

'That's going to be hard.'

'Then we'll just have to deal with it.'

She gazed out the window as he reluctantly left the library, in a sour mood. He dragged his feet as he crossed the yard. Pointedly — he knew she could see him. She sighed; she knew it really would be hard.

It was the second Sunday of Advent. It seemed they would have a white Christmas; there were several inches of snow on the ground, which meant an endless amount of shovelling every day. The sky would clear now and then, but clouds would gather again almost right away, ready for the next snowfall.

She had decided to go home to her parents for Christmas. Benjamin had tried to convince her to remain on the island, telling her about last Christmas, when the staff had four days off and celebrated together.

But she refused to give in. She was going home.

Dusk was just falling and the big spruce in the middle of the courtyard was all lit up. Someone went around lighting lanterns and torches. It was so beautiful that a shiver ran through her.

The speaker on the wall crackled. Madeleine's voice echoed through the empty building: 'Come up to Franz's office. Immediately!'

The message sounded rushed and urgent as usual, but Sofia had learned to take Madeleine with a grain of salt. Nothing was ever as serious as Madeleine made it out to be.

She pulled on her boots and winter coat. As she walked up the shovelled path to the manor house she dragged her feet, mostly just to annoy Madeleine in case she could see her from the window. The snow crunched under her boots. The sky was clear and starry; there was a full moon. The cold, crisp air carried the scent of smoke from the fireplaces in the living quarters. Other glorious smells came from the dining room: freshly baked bread, *glögg*, and roasting ham.

When she knocked at Oswald's office door, Madeleine came out with a fretful expression and put a finger to her lips. Sofia could see Oswald on the phone inside.

'What took you so long?' Madeleine hissed.

Sofia didn't have time to respond. Oswald had just hung up the phone and was waving her in.

No Christmas decorations in his office. Not even a single Advent light or paper star lantern. Everything was bare and white, and, in Sofia's opinion, just plain boring.

'Come in, Sofia, have a seat.'

She sat down in front of him. He looked at her and nodded as if she had said something. She had come to understand that this implied some sort of approval. Sofia had been one of Oswald's favourites since the fire. She could tell because he would come and talk to her now and again after assembly. There were some staff members he didn't pay any attention to at all. He would even turn his back on certain staff if they tried to approach him.

'So here's the deal — I have to go away for a few days and I would have loved to take a look at your plans for the library before I go, but I don't have much time,' he said. 'I'll be back on December twenty-second. I was thinking we could devote the twenty-third to your presentation, and perhaps even the morning of Christmas Eve day, if we need it. That would work out very well for me. I heard you've got plans to go home and wonder if you can shift things around a little.'

The gears in her mind began to turn at crazy speeds. Images of her parents alone at Christmas dinner. The days she'd promised to spend with Wilma. Working on Christmas Eve! She had the uneasy sense that he was controlling her life. That this wasn't a suggestion but an order.

Before she could open her mouth, he went on.

'We're going to have a very special guest here this spring, a journalist named Magnus Strid. With any luck he'll write good things about us, so I'd very much like to have the library ready so he can make use of it.'

'But — this spring! Isn't that pretty far off?' It just slipped out of her.

'I'm a perfectionist, Sofia. I want to give myself plenty of time.'

A small wrinkle had appeared on his forehead. He was annoyed.

There went her Christmas plans. She hurried to respond, to make him understand that she could withstand a little pressure.

'Okay then. The twenty-third.'

'Great, Sofia. I look forward to your presentation.'

★

She worked just about around the clock until the morning before Christmas Eve day. He'd said he was a perfectionist, so she would live up to his demands. Everything would be better than he could possibly imagine. She was ready with a PowerPoint presentation full of images and summaries, finances laid out in clear numbers, a list with the price of each book, a demonstration of the computer system, and even samples of the fabric for the furniture. She spent the entire night before working, testing everything, practising her speech over and over.

After three cups of coffee in the morning, and with adrenaline pumping through her veins, she opened the door for him.

He had dragged along half the staff. Madeleine, of course, but also Bosse, Sten and Benny, some random people from the various units, and even Benjamin, who looked a little self-conscious as he stepped in. She wondered why everyone was there, and nervousness began to radiate from her stomach throughout her body until sweat broke out on her palms and forehead. She hoped no one would notice as she wiped her forehead with her sleeve.

There weren't enough chairs for everyone, but Oswald sat down in the visitor's chair and everyone else gathered behind him. They just stood there staring at her. It was so quiet she could hear the wind blowing outside.

She tested the screen again, cleared her throat, and wondered if she was about to start stuttering or become tongue-tied. But when she began to speak, her voice carried after all.

Oswald didn't say a word during her presentation, didn't ask a single question or make even a tiny sound. Now and then he gazed out the window, away from the screen, at nothing. The more she explained, the more disinterested he seemed. The room was still perfectly quiet.

When she was finished, everyone held their breath. They were waiting for the final judgment. It seemed to her that it couldn't possibly be good news, because when she tried to make eye contact he looked away. She had no idea what she was expected to do. She added that there was also a list of all the books, but Oswald put up his hand to stop her.

'I'll deal with the list later, Sofia.'

She looked at him in surprise.

'I knew right away that I would approve your plan. That was a professional presentation. Well thought-out. Good job, Sofia. I'd love to take the list with me so I can read it tomorrow.' He turned to Madeleine. 'See to it that she gets everything she needs — money, transportation, the whole lot.'

Sofia looked around. Benjamin looked relieved, but the others . . . perhaps it was her imagination, but she thought they looked a little disappointed.

After a while, Benjamin returned and stuck his head through the door.

'Great job!' he said. 'You sure know how to butter up Franz.'

'No way. I just put a lot of work in, that's all.'

He stepped in, his boots still on. She barely had time to stop him from messing up her freshly-polished floor.

'There's an organic Christmas smorgasbord in the dining room,' he said. 'I came to get you.'

'I'm coming.'

As he helped her put on her coat, he brushed her hair aside and blew on the back of her neck.

'You'll be the great heroine here for a while,' he said. 'But there will definitely be some folks who are jealous, remember that.'

'Who do you mean?'

'Oh, it doesn't matter.'

'Tell me!'

'Just the girls. No one in particular.'

As they came out to the yard she looked up at the attic again. It was midday, and yet a light was on up in the window.

'Look!' she said to Benjamin. 'There's someone up in the attic!'

He squinted at the building and shook his head.

'It's just the sun reflecting off the pane.'

'Then why isn't it reflecting off the other windows?'

'Oh, come on,' he said. 'Let's go celebrate Christmas.'

★

By the time Oswald approved her book selection, Christmas and New Year's had gone by. January began with a raging snowstorm that hit the island and effectively buried the manor. Sofia sat in the library, shivering. Her radiator couldn't warm the whole building when the temperature was under twenty below day after day. She sat there in her layers of clothing, wrapped in a big blanket. Long icicles hung from the gutters, glinting like amber in the late afternoon sun.

There was a knock at the door, and she recognized Madeleine's faint but impatient raps right away. Sofia opened up and her heart jumped as she realized that Madeleine had the list of books in her hand.

'April seventh!' she said firmly.

'April seventh?'

'That's when the library must be finished. So Franz has enough time to go through everything before Magnus Strid arrives.' She turned on her heel and trudged back through the snow.

Sofia sat down and paged eagerly through the long list. On the first page, Oswald had written 'OK, but with some changes.' He had crossed out two books but hadn't commented on anything else.

Then she saw his note on the last page.

Any book with religious or philosophical contents must contain a note that clearly states they are only here as reference materials, since we follow our own, clearly set path at ViaTerra.

That made ViaTerra sound like a cult. This was the first time it had seemed so clear from Oswald's words. She'd always thought of a cult as a group of fools walking around in sandals, rambling on about God and reciting random passages from the Bible. Pale failures of individuals. But ViaTerra wasn't like that at all.

She put down the list. Sure, he could have his idiotic notes. It didn't matter — she was too happy. Five months of hard work and now all she had to do was start putting her library together.

Today, though, she wouldn't do a thing but relax. *I've earned it*, she thought. She put on the coffeepot, kicked off her uniform shoes, curled up in a chair and went online. She decided to Google her own name. It was a good day, so surely she could handle any new blog entries and whatever other awful things she found.

But although she varied her wording, the spelling, and even her name she couldn't find any blog entries about herself. There was nothing there. There wasn't even a trace of Ellis.

She leaned back in her chair and closed her eyes. It seemed as if that hell was finally over.

I almost run right into him.

He's on his way to the barn. Why, I don't know. To sneak up on us, maybe.

Home. I know I have to run home before someone sees me.

But now he's there, and my brain short-circuits.

My first thought is to knock him out and stash him in the barn with Lily. But I get distracted by the horrified look he's giving me, and I realize I'm standing there in nothing but my underwear.

'Fredrik, what are you doing?'

I take off, running across the property as fast as my legs will carry me.

He follows. I hear his thudding steps behind me; I hear his panting breaths and cracking twigs and his stupid voice repeating my name.

But I'm faster and I fly across the yard and into the woods, across the paths. I know where I'm heading now, but I don't know why. The cliff is calling my name; I feel an incredible power pulling and sucking at me.

His panting fades away with distance.

By the time I reach the heath, I can't hear him any longer.

The full moon, the black sea, and the cliff are ahead of me, and he is somewhere behind me.

I run out onto the rock and hesitate for a moment. I turn around and watch him appear on the heath.

'Fredrik!' he shouts. He's so loud that he startles an owl, which flaps up against the dark sky.

Then I see the flickering of the fire I've left behind. The barn is burning.

I get ready, then dive. My body cuts through the water like a knife. And then I'm gone.

13

Spring came early. All the snow was washed away by rain in late March. A powerful area of high pressure settled just off the island and within a few days, the average temperature had risen from below freezing to thirteen Celsius. Everything came to life at once: birds, insects, and plants.

She was almost done with the library. Benjamin had outdone himself and brought all the books to her, thanks to innumerable ferry crossings, and now they were all arranged on the shelves, smelling terrific. The computer system had been installed and the furniture had arrived. It was five-thirty in the morning, and she was there for one final check. Everything had to be perfect before Oswald saw it.

A creak of the floor behind her, and when she turned around, there he was. She hadn't heard him open the door. He was wearing a leather jacket and blue jeans; his eyes were red and he had a day's stubble.

'I came here to get some positive energy,' he said with a yawn. 'At least there's someone around here who doesn't lie around snoozing while I work.'

He looked around, approached the shelves, and took out a few books; he tested out the sofas and played with the computer system. When she showed him how you could download and order books, he nodded in satisfaction. But what made him happiest was seeing the screensaver, which was a picture of the manor house with him in the foreground. At the top she had put his motto: 'We walk the way of the earth.'

He looked at the picture for a long time, then whistled in appreciation and smacked his palm on the desk. 'Looking pretty damn good!' was his final assessment. He made another round and suddenly she found him standing behind her. He placed his hands on her shoulders and began to massage her shoulder blades with his thumbs. They slid up and found a tender point on her neck, which he kneaded slowly.

'You've outdone yourself,' he said. 'Such a little pearl I picked up at that lecture. Look at this place! You have class, Sofia.'

All the air went out of her. She stood perfectly still, not even daring to breathe, because if she did the fire inside her would flow into his fingers and he would feel how excited she was. He bent down and put his head right up next to her own until his stubble scraped against her cheek. He whispered in her ear.

'Take the day off today. You've earned it.'

He let one hand slide down her spine and rest at her waist for a split second. She could barely tell when his hands moved away; her skin was still burning with his touch. She could only hear his steps as he left the library.

She didn't move; she couldn't seem to make her body do anything.

Why does he touch me like that? she wondered. *Is he teasing me, or is it perfectly normal? A friendly massage for a tired back? Am I just oversensitive? He's probably just happy that I do good work. Thankful that someone here actually does their job.*

Then she remembered that he'd given her the rest of the day off.

The others were still sleeping when she tiptoed into the dormitory, took out her backpack, and stuffed it with supplies for the day. She decided to ignore the ban and get her phone from the staff unit. The whole office was dormant, the blinds down. She opened her compartment in the cabinet where phones and other forbidden items were locked up, and stuck her phone and the charger in her pocket.

The sun was coming up as she walked into the yard. No breeze. Not a cloud in the sky. It was going to be a beautiful day.

She returned to the library building and made a cup of coffee while she charged her phone. Benjamin had given her the coffee-maker for Christmas so she didn't have to keep running to the little commissary where the staff could buy things like soap and shampoo.

She drank from her largest mug, nestled in the most comfortable easy chair, as her phone charged. She thought about Ellis — she didn't know why, but suddenly her memories of him kept popping up. She thought maybe he had found someone else by now. Some other poor woman who didn't know what awaited her.

She picked up her phone and texted Wilma.

Day off today, what's up there?

She decided to borrow Elvira's bike; she was sure the girl wouldn't mind. A quick ride down to the fishing shacks on the western shore, and she took a few pictures from the dock and sent them to Wilma with another message.

Are you awake, sleepyhead?

The response came almost immediately.

Nice pics! W.

It wasn't at all like Wilma to be so concise; something was wrong.

What is it?

No answer. She waited for a moment, taking off her shoes and socks and dipping her toes in the freezing cold water. At last she dialled Wilma's number.

'I knew you would call!'

'What's going on?'

'Don't freak out, but your tormentor is back to haunt us again.'

'What? What do you mean?'

'I ran into Ellis in town. He was being such an ass. He said he knew you'd joined that fucking cult and he was determined to get you back out again. He threatened to burn the place down and all kinds of awful stuff.'

Sofia's mouth suddenly felt dry. That familiar Ellis-related nausea rose in her stomach.

'Oh my god! But what can he do?'

'Nothing. I just didn't want to worry you.'

They talked for a while, until Sofia began to relax.

But she still felt distracted after their phone call; the day no longer seemed as lovely. She felt homesick for her parents, her friends, and Lund, the way everything had been before Ellis.

She called her mom and they talked for a long time, and then she headed to the village and had a sandwich for lunch. She strolled around for a while, amazed at how empty it was in the off season. Then she decided to bike to the lookout point to sun her face and read a book she'd brought from the library. When she got to the heath, though, she felt the cottage beckoning. She wanted to check in on it and see how it had weathered the storm and the winter.

Something felt different as she opened the gate and stepped onto the lot. At first, everything looked normal; the old wheelbarrow was full of leaves and flowerpots were strewn on the lawn. But then she caught movement out of the corner of her eye and realized the hammock was swinging back and forth. In it sat a woman, all dressed in black.

'Well, hello there, Sofia!' she said, her voice clear and ringing.

The woman had long, dark hair that was parted in the middle. She appeared to be around fifty. Her face was deeply wrinkled at her eyes and mouth, and her skin was tan and thick as leather. She was wearing a long, black skirt and a black blouse with wide sleeves.

'I'm sorry, I didn't mean to intrude —'

'Sure you did!' the woman said firmly. 'You've been here before.'

She stood up, and Sofia noticed that she was very tall. Tall and stout, but not fat. Her eyes were large and almond-shaped. She came up to Sofia and shook her hand.

'Karin Johansson. I own this cottage.'

'How did you know who I am?'

'I saw you last fall, you and your boyfriend. You had just left the cottage. I was here on a short visit to get everything ready for winter, and I must have forgotten to lock the front door. I saw you coming out. At first I thought you were burglars but you had left the cottage untouched. Then I asked around in the shops, and they know you. "Sofia and Benjamin from the cult up at the manor," they said. And now here you are!'

Sofia's cheeks flushed. She sincerely hoped that the woman hadn't seen them through the window.

'I'm not angry. In fact, it's nice to have someone looking in on the cottage once in a while. Would you like some coffee?'

'I'd love some.'

The cottage felt different with someone living there. The cabin smell had been replaced by the scent of food and freshly-brewed coffee. Sofia sat down at the little kitchen table while Karin put out the cups.

'I've always wondered about this location,' Sofia said. 'There's no road here, not even a path.'

'It's an old cottage. It's been in my family for a hundred and fifty years. They were fishermen. Back in the olden days, there was a gravel road down to the village, but when the Count built the manor my family started working there as servants. So they built servant quarters, and they moved up there instead. We kept the cottage, but when you don't use a gravel road regularly, it disappears. The grass takes over.'

She poured the coffee, placed a plate of cookies on the table, and sat down across from Sofia. Her eyes were such a dark blue they looked black. Her mouth was creased with laughter lines, and her nose was long and slightly bent.

'Are you just here for the summer?' Sofia asked.

'Now I am. But I used to work at the manor all year round. While it was empty I lived in town, but then a doctor bought the place and I got a job there again. I was a single mother then and I wanted my boy to experience life here on the island for a while.'

'Tell me more about what it was like here before,' Sofia said.

Karin didn't say anything; she looked hesitant. Then she stood up and went over to a bureau, where she opened a drawer and took out a thick bundle of documents.

'Move your coffee cup over,' she said, setting the papers down in front of Sofia. 'I used to be obsessed with the history of the manor. I thought it was exciting to listen to all the tales about it when I was a little girl, and as I got older I wanted to know more.'

She took a large sheet of paper from the pile and unfolded it. It was a family tree with sprawling branches and names covering almost the entire surface.

'I started digging through this in the summers. I made a family tree for the Count's line, and one for my own. Look at this! You can see who was married to who, and which ones worked at the manor house. The more I learned, the better I could see how our families grew together into one.'

Karin's tone was eager, and it rubbed off on Sofia.

'This is incredible! Why is all of this in the cottage? I bet lots of people in the village would be interested. The summer visitors, too.'

Karin shook her head.

'You have no idea what the kind of misery that family went through. It seemed like it would never end. Eventually I'd had enough. It really depressed me, so I put this all away here in the cottage. And then you come by asking about it!'

Sofia studied the genealogy for a long time. It was really made up of two trees: one began with the first Count, Artur von Bärensten, and the parallel trunk was for Karin Johansson's family. Little lines ran here and there between the two. Sofia used her finger to trace down to the last von Bärenstens. *Henrik and Emilie von Bärensten,* it read. They were the end of the line.

'What happened to them?' she asked.

'They moved to France. The manor house was empty for several years, before the doctor showed up and bought it.'

'Did you meet them before they moved?'

'Yes, I worked for them for a while.'

'So why did they move away?'

Karin shrugged. 'I suppose they got sick of the big house. Couldn't keep up with it. That whole family was from France originally. You know, like the Bernadottes.'

'I hope you don't mind my asking,' Sofia said. 'It's just so exciting.'

'No, not at all. That's why I'm showing you all this. But you have to understand, I have positive and negative memories of this island, and there are some things I'd rather not talk about.'

Sofia decided to take a leap forward in time.

'Were you here when that boy jumped off the cliff and died?'

Karin's eyes darkened as her pupils widened, almost swallowing her irises. She leaned back, her chair protesting with a creak, took a breath, and closed her eyes for a moment.

'He was my son,' she said at last.

'Oh my god! I'm sorry!'

'It's okay. You didn't know. Listen, I'm happy to talk about the manor house. On one condition.'

'What's that?'

'I want to hear a little more about what's going on there nowadays.'

*

It was dark by the time Sofia left the cottage. The fog had slipped in from the sea, and she had to use the flashlight app on her phone to find her bike on the heath. It had grown chilly, but the air was humid and gentle. She hadn't wanted to ask more about

Karin Johansson's son. Instead she had kept up the chatter, asking questions about the families and the island, and letting Karin drill her about ViaTerra.

'What is he like, that Oswald?' Karin had asked. 'I've heard he's a bit of a fanatic, not very nice to the staff.'

'Not really. He runs a tight ship, I guess, but it's probably necessary.'

'There are rumours about him. We hardly ever see him, here on the island. He never comes to the village, and when he takes the ferry he stays in his car. It's almost like he's a phantom.'

'No, he exists. He just has people to help him with purchasing and that kind of stuff.'

An idea began to take shape in Sofia's mind as she biked home. She could write a book about all this — the manor, the family history. A real thriller.

*

When she got back to ViaTerra, it was already eleven o'clock and her dormitory was dark. She fumbled her way to her bed and was just about to take off her jeans when she felt her phone in her pocket. *Shit!* She had to get it back to the cubby right away. She tiptoed back out of the dorm and up to the staff offices. No one was there, so she turned on the lights and was just about to stash the phone when she found that someone had left the drawer of a filing cabinet open. Curious, she flicked through the folders hanging in it. Each had the name of a staff member; they were in alphabetical order. She found her own and opened it. There was the questionnaire she'd filled out after Oswald's lecture, and the notes from her first interview with Olof Hurtig.

That's fine, she thought, reading on, but the following pages took her breath away. Someone had printed out Ellis's blog entries: the first one, with the Photoshopped images of Sofia naked and the one with the picture of Oswald with horns drawn on.

Last of all there was a note written in Bosse's scrawling hand.

Sofia Bauman, potential security risk. Full investigation required.

Her first impulse was to go straight to Bosse's room and wake him up. She was so angry that her belly felt like a ball of fire as she walked upstairs to the dormitories. An incessant voice in her head played out the dialogue she would have with Bosse; that voice, with its sharp arguments and keen wit would put him in his place. She tried to turn the voice off and think sensibly, but she couldn't get rid of it.

Tiny warning bells began to sound somewhere behind her enraged thoughts.

Calm down, get a grip.

She sat down on the stairs and breathed deeply, letting her mind follow her inhalations. She sat like that for a long time, until her rage ebbed away. For once she wouldn't act on impulse. After all, she had been snooping around and using her phone without permission. And it was partly true that Ellis posed some sort of threat, somewhere off in the distance.

She entered her dormitory and sat down on her bed in the darkness, still upset but determined to sleep on it.

But she didn't get much sleep. That night was the start of an inferno that would last for a few days. After that, the slim file would have vanished from her mind completely. Much bigger, darker clouds would have formed on the horizon.

I'm sinking.

The water is dark and cold and when I open my eyes I see the surface shining a deep green above my head.

For an instant, everything is still.

I don't know what to do.

Drown?

Swim up to the surface?

Help him put out the fire? But I know what's in the barn. How it will look.

Then a strange thought comes to me. A memory of a film. Prisoners escaping from Alcatraz. Bodies that were never found.

And all at once, I know what I have to do.

I swim as far as I can underwater, then slowly rise to the surface.

I bend my head way back, find the air with my mouth, and greedily suck it in, filling my lungs.

With any luck he can't see me; maybe he ran back when he saw the fire.

I keep swimming under the water, as fast as I can, as long as my lungs can bear.

Three, four, five times, up to the surface and down again.

One time, just before I come up for air, I roll onto my back under the water. I can see the stars above me, the surface like an infinite glass dome. Me and the universe, united.

A sense of calm returns to my body; it feels strong and lithe as it glides on.

I can see the jagged rocks under the water; I grasp a boulder and wiggle forward until the water is so shallow that I break through the surface. I crawl up on a rock.

It was a long swim — several hundred metres. For the first time, I look back at Devil's Rock. There's no one there.

The sky is red where the fire rages on at the manor.

14

The voices in her dream mixed with a different, louder voice that ripped her from her sleep. One of the blinds was drawn up a bit, so she could make out a silhouette in front of the window. Elvira's slim figure. There, the voice again, and running steps on the stairs and the sound of a motorcycle starting.

'What's going on, Elvira?'

'Someone is shouting outside the wall.'

'What?'

She got out of bed and went to the window. The lights were on in the yard and she could see Benny, or possibly Sten, heading for the sentry box on his motorcycle. She opened the window and stuck her head out to see what was going on, and then she heard the familiar voice — the one that had shouted outside a different window, in a different place.

'Sofia! I know you're in there. Sofia, come out, for fuck's sake!'

It was Ellis. That really was his voice. He was outside the manor wall. It was surreal, and for a moment she thought she was dreaming. He couldn't be there, and yet she could hear his voice so clearly, though it was clouded with jealousy and slurred like an angry drunk's.

Madeleine was awake now too; she sat up in bed.

'What's going on?'

'This is unbelievable,' Sofia said. 'I have to go down there.'

She pulled on her jeans, shoes, and jacket and ran out the door. A sleepy Bosse was standing in the yard. The shouting had stopped, replaced by angry voices outside the gate. It might be the night guard, talking to Ellis.

Bosse shot her an angry glare. Up at the manor, lights came on in several windows and curious faces popped up here and there. She wanted to disappear, to sink into the ground. She backed into the doorway where no one could see her.

'Stay here!' Bosse ordered. 'I'm going to find out what's happening.'

Sofia stayed put as Bosse walked to the sentry box. She had no trouble hearing the voices — the night was clear and still, and Ellis was still yelling. Benny, who'd been standing guard, was shouting by now as well.

'I know she's here, and I'm not leaving before I see her! You lot fucking kidnapped and brainwashed her.'

'We have no one by that name here. Now get out of here. We've already called the police.'

'I want to see that bastard Oswald too. You can't stop me from coming in.'

'Yes, we can. She isn't here. Leave.'

Bosse returned and whispered angrily to Sofia: 'Go hide! What's wrong with you? He can't see you here.'

It seemed idiotic. Ellis was on the other side of a solid wall, with no way to see in, but Sofia obeyed and slipped through the door of the main building. She wanted to go up to the gate and scream at him to leave her alone. But then she heard sirens and caught a glimpse of blue lights flashing beyond the wall, so she knew the police had arrived. Bosse came running over.

'So that's your boyfriend,' he said, shaking his head.

'My ex,' Sofia mumbled. 'I don't understand why he's here. It's unbelievable.'

'Yeah, you can say that again. Come on, let's go back in.'

'Where did he go?' Sofia asked as they walked up the stairs.

'The police took him; they're going to put him on the morning ferry. But I'm sure he'll come back if we don't do something.'

They sat down in Bosse's office and she spilled everything. How her last semester in Lund had ended in a nightmare when she broke up with Ellis, how he had hung her out to dry online. She avoided mentioning that she'd seen the most recent blog posts, saying instead that she'd heard about them from Wilma. When she was done speaking, Bosse looked at her gravely.

'You have to fix this,' he said.

'And how is she supposed to do that, Bosse?' a voice came from behind them.

It was Oswald. He was leaning against the wall and observing them. She didn't know how long he'd been standing there or how much he'd heard, but he was seething with rage.

'Explain yourself, Bosse. How is she supposed to just "fix" this?'

Bosse looked frightened. He cleared his throat, but Oswald jumped back in before he could respond.

'For Christ's sake, I thought it was your job to take care of the staff. Why is it that no one has told me about this? Magnus Strid will be here in just three days, so obviously I have plenty of time to handle it all on my own.'

'No, you don't need to do that,' Bosse said.

'Yes, I do. Fix it myself, just like everything else around here. Or do you want that idiot to show up and scream at us while Strid is here?'

'No, I swear —' Bosse tried. But Oswald walked up to him, grabbed him by the collar, and pulled his face close. There was a cruel gleam in his eyes. Bosse was white as a sheet.

'You are a bunch of incompetent idiots, you and your little biker gang,' Oswald hissed, his voice taking on a hard tone Sofia had never heard before. He let go of Bosse's collar and Bosse fell back into his chair. Oswald turned to Sofia. His voice had returned to normal.

'You can go back to bed, Sofia. This isn't your fault. You should have told us all about it when you came, but I'm sure you didn't know that idiot was still after you. You haven't been online.'

He must have read the blog.

Seen the pictures.

Fucking hell!

'Go to bed,' he said again. 'I'll deal with this.'

Sofia didn't dare protest. There was nothing to say.

She rose and left the room as Oswald continued to scold Bosse.

Madeleine was still awake when she got back to the dormitory, but Elvira was under the covers and snoring faintly.

'What's going on, Sofia?'

'It's a long story. I'll tell you tomorrow.'

'Please, tell me now. Is Franz upset?'

'I'm the one who messed up. It has nothing to do with you.'

She was sure she wouldn't be able to sleep after what had happened, but she was completely drained and slipped into deep sleep the moment her head hit the pillow. She didn't wake up until Madeleine gave her a gentle shake and told her it was time to get up again.

★

She was one of the last to arrive at morning assembly. The staff were restless as they stood in their lines.

'We're waiting for Franz,' whispered Elvira. 'He's going to lead assembly today.'

Oswald almost never came to morning assembly, so it could only mean one thing. He was angry with them, and it had to be about Ellis. The knot in her belly tightened. She felt nauseous, exhausted, and terribly unhappy.

When Oswald strode into the courtyard, he looked exhilarated. He had that look in his eyes that meant he held a trump card, which usually resulted in someone getting in trouble before assembly was over. He was carrying a thick folder under one arm. He stood still for a moment, observing them. It was so quiet you could hear a pin drop; everyone was staring straight ahead. Like soldiers at attention.

'Well, I came to ask you how things are going with the projects you were given yesterday. The preparations for Magnus Strid's visit.'

Nothing but surprised faces.

'Why the blank looks? Weren't you assigned projects yester-day?'

He turned to Madeleine, who turned bright red and stared at the ground.

'Surely Madeleine didn't go to bed before handing them out to you?'

He knew they hadn't received their projects, but he wanted to drag it out and make Madeleine feel horrible. And she did.

'That's too bad. And here I stayed up late writing them. Magnus Strid is an important part of our plan, as you know. He's a highly regarded journalist. He'll write positive things about us. That is, if we take advantage of this opportunity.'

Oswald waved Bosse over and gave him the folder.

'You hand them out. Make sure everyone reads them right away and gets started.'

Then he turned around and went back into the manor house. Madeleine was still staring down at the ground in shame.

Everyone remained silent until Oswald had vanished through the front door. Ellis had been forgotten for the moment.

Thank God.

The knot in her stomach loosened and she could breathe freely again.

Bosse handed out lists of varying lengths — all she got was a note with a short message from Oswald.

'The library looks good. Here are some of Strid's favourite authors. Make sure you have some books by them, and place an order if you don't.'

Only one of the authors wasn't yet represented in the library, and she ordered the books online. She had no intention of helping someone else with their project; she was still feeling drained after the night's incidents. Instead she sat down at the window with a cup of coffee and watched the staff running this way and that across the yard like industrious ants. She thought about what had happened in the night, how Oswald had transformed, threatening Bosse, shaking him by the collar, shouting at him. And how frightened Bosse had been.

On her way to dinner that evening, she spotted Madeleine on her knees, weeding a flowerbed outside the guest quarters. Katarina, the gardener, sat beside her. Madeleine was wearing jeans and a hoodie. There weren't many weeds yet, so she was yanking at whatever was there. She sneaked a look up at Sofia but quickly looked down again and continued to paw at the bare dirt.

Oswald didn't come to evening assembly, where Bosse preached about how important their projects were. When it was time to go, he called out to Sofia. She approached him, immediately noticing the peculiar expression on his face: a mixture of worry and triumph. He didn't say anything for a moment, waiting for the rest of the staff to leave the yard.

'You're being assigned a new job, Sofia,' he said at last.

I don't know how long I've been sitting here.

It must have been hours, because I'm so cold I'm shaking and my teeth are chattering.

Yet my mind is still crystal clear.

Devil's Rock is swarming with people now. Police, boats, divers.

And of course the usual group of idiots who start drooling the minute they get wind of a disaster. They're standing there like vultures, staring out at the sea.

The red glow in the sky is gone, replaced by faint blue flashing lights. So the police are on the property. It occurs to me that perhaps I should have cleaned up after myself a little better, but it's too late now.

I look at the crowd on Devil's Rock again. All this, for me.

It's exciting, almost exhilarating, especially the fact that they can't see me.

But then I spot her. She's standing at the edge of the cliff with her hands on her hips. It's impossible to mistake her posture, even at such a distance.

She's just standing there, gazing out at the water.

Any other mother would go to pieces. Cry and scream.

But not her. She just stands there staring.

Now that I've seen her, I have to go.

It's now or never.

I steal into the forest and find the familiar path to the cottage.

I have transformed into a phantom who wanders in darkness.

15

At first she had no idea what he meant.

'A new job? Do you need me to help out with something before Strid arrives?'

'No, I mean, you're changing jobs. Haven't you noticed what happened to Madeleine? Franz wants you to be his secretary.'

Oh my god! Not on your life!

'I can't. What would happen to the library?'

'Mona Asplund will take over as librarian.'

Mona Asplund was Elvira's mother. Sofia had never spoken to her. She worked on the farm; she was quiet and shy and mostly kept to herself.

'How will she manage that? This doesn't sound like a good idea at all.'

'Sofia, calm down. Why can't we ever just talk without you getting all worked up? Think of the priorities. Around here, nothing is more important than supporting Franz. Don't you get that?'

'We have to find someone else to be librarian.'

Her voice had risen into a falsetto. She was about to lose control.

'Franz wants you to spend evenings in the library as long as Strid is here. You can take Mona with you and show her how everything works.' He was unyielding, and it was too much. The disaster with Ellis and now this. The library was like her rock, and it was about to collapse.

She turned and ran across the yard, angry tears welling in her eyes. Bosse called after her but it only made her run faster. Through the door and up the stairs to her dormitory, where she slammed the door and locked it behind her. She threw herself onto her bed. Working with Oswald every day? It would be hell. All the closeness and energy and that tingle in her belly — and what if he blew up at her like he had at Bosse?

Her rage slowly retreated and was replaced by despair. What would she do? Could a person approach Oswald and say they didn't want to work for him? She thought about the Ellis situation. Oswald had seemed so sure he could handle it. Would he still help her if she refused to work for him? She considered all her options, but it seemed like she would come out the loser no matter what she did. Her despair gave way to a mute indifference, but the knot in her stomach was gone.

There was a knock at the door. She knew who it was.

'Come in!'

'It's locked, Sofia.'

She rose to turn the key, then sat back down on her bed.

Bosse was in the doorway. He didn't look angry, only nervous.

'Sofia, can't we talk about this?'

'I'll do it.'

'What do you mean?'

'I'll take the job. I don't really have a choice, do I?'

'Of course you do, but it's important for us to help Franz right now. You understand that, don't you?'

'Do you think he'll help me get rid of Ellis?'

'Yes, I know he will. He's already started working on it.'

'And you promise I can work with Mona until everything is in working order in the library?'

'Of course.'

'Okay then.'

The tense lines on Bosse's face smoothed back out.

'I knew I could depend on you. Now go to the office and see if Franz needs your help tonight.'

She went to the bathroom to spruce herself up, brush her hair and put on some lip gloss.

She tried to convince herself that this would all work out in the end.

★

Oswald's door was ajar and the office was empty, so she stepped in and looked around. Madeleine had a small desk in one corner, hardly large enough for a computer.

There were several neat stacks of paper on Oswald's desk. She sneaked a look at the top one and tried to make out what it said.

She heard his voice behind her.

'If you ever snoop through my papers, my computer, or anything else that belongs to me, you will be in big trouble, Sofia.'

She turned around and saw an amused smile on his lips.

'I'm glad you're here. Go down to the guards and sign all the confidentiality agreements they have. Then we'll get moving.'

As she was on her way out the door, she heard his voice again.

'This is going to be great. Really great.'

On the way down to the sentry box she made a decision. It came from deep inside her, a comforting thought that took root

148

and began to grow. She would move in with Benjamin. That way she could handle this new job, because she would have someone to talk to. And have sex with, of course. That tension with Oswald would disappear. And if things got too tough, Benjamin would be there when her long workdays were over.

*

The job wasn't anything like she'd expected. It seemed like nothing in her life ever turned out as expected, but maybe it was for the best. It wasn't hard to work for Oswald at first. Magnus Strid had arrived at the manor and Oswald accompanied him everywhere: to the guests' dining room, the garage (where Oswald showed off his cars and motorcycles), and the classrooms while Strid went through the program. Oswald hardly left his side.

When he wasn't with Strid he was on the mainland, giving lectures. Since new guests kept arriving on the island, Oswald remained in a good mood.

Sofia began to rearrange the office. She cleaned out Madeleine's mess and created her own computer system. She spent the first few days of her job anxiously trying to make herself indispensable to Oswald when he was there, running around the office and helping him with every minor task — like immediately fetching and stapling any papers he printed out — and refilling his water glass over and over. She even pulled out his chair for him when he was ready to sit down. But one day he waved her off.

'Calm down, Sofia. Relax. Don't get yourself in a tizzy over the goddamn water in my glass *again*.'

After that she let herself fall into a comfortable routine. When

Oswald was home, she made sure he had everything he needed. Breakfast and the morning papers had to be on the desk when he came in. His cars had to be washed by the household staff. She wrote congratulatory cards from him to the guests who completed the program and she typed out his lectures, which he always dictated. And she was expected to make sure that a few private things were on hand — like his cologne, which was specially made in Italy, and the muscle-building protein powder he mixed into drinks. But all she had to do was follow a checklist.

When Oswald was in the office, he always sent her off in the evening, saying, 'Go find out what's been accomplished today.' She reported any updates back to him, and that was the end of their workday.

The job was like child's play. At first.

She spent the rest of her evenings in the library with Mona, just in case Strid should come by.

There was something about Mona that Sofia couldn't quite put her finger on. She was the plainest person Sofia had met at the manor, pale and sullen with an evasive gaze. Mona was a nervous woman too. She bit her nails and her lower lip, and her anxious behaviour reminded Sofia of her own mother. Mona and her husband Anders were the only middle-aged people on staff; everyone else was young and presumably hand-picked by Oswald.

One night, Magnus Strid did come to the library. For once he wasn't in the company of Oswald. Sofia liked him immediately; he was short, hefty, and a little unkempt, with several days' worth of stubble and a large coffee stain on his shirt. But he had a warm, open smile and kind eyes.

'Do you have *Cleves* by Marie Darrieussecq?' he asked.

Sofia felt her cheeks flush. *Cleves* was one of the books Oswald definitely wouldn't have allowed her to purchase if he'd read it. The cover was innocent and lovely: a painting of a girl on a beach. But the contents were extremely erotic.

She helped the journalist find and check out the book. He began to ask her about the computer system, and soon she had shown him every detail of the library.

They started talking about books and must have been going on for hours, because by the time Sofia looked at the clock it was almost eleven. Mona had long since slipped out, and the staff had all gone to bed.

'I hope I can come by again before I go home,' Strid said before he returned to the annexe for the night.

'Anytime.'

When she stepped into the courtyard, the lights were still on in the office window, so she went up to turn them off and lock up for the night. To her surprise, Oswald was still there. African bongo music was streaming from the speakers on the walls, which meant he was in a good mood. He was reading a newspaper. He looked pleased when he looked up.

'So what did Strid think of the library?'

'He loved it. We talked for a few hours.'

'I saw you from the window.'

He looked like he had a secret.

'I have a little surprise for you, Sofia. You'll learn more tomorrow. I'll be on the mainland most of the day, but I'm sure Bosse will tell you.'

She was immensely curious, but she knew he wouldn't give her more right then.

Suddenly it just slipped out of her.

'I want to move in with Benjamin.'

Oswald knitted his brow thoughtfully. He studied her for a moment and gave her a cool smile.

'I know you two hang out, but is it really that serious? Or do you just want to have sex?'

She turned red and hated herself for it; she couldn't look him in the eye.

'I mean, we really like each other,' she mumbled.

'Well, I guess you can move in together in that case,' Oswald said and went back to reading the paper.

★

That night she did something she'd never done before. She went to Benjamin's dormitory and woke him up. She could do that now that she was Oswald's secretary. She knocked at the door and called in an authoritative voice: 'Benjamin Frisk. I have a message from Franz.'

Benjamin opened the door, his hair mussed, his eyes sleepy, wearing only boxers. She took his hands and pulled him into the hallway, placing him under the light so she could see his face better.

'We're moving in together!'

'What? Are you serious?'

'I just got the okay from Franz.'

He hugged her so hard she couldn't breathe.

★

The next day, she was in a terrific mood. Oswald was away, so she hung out in the office sorting papers, cleaning, and using

Oswald's stereo system for the first time although she wasn't sure he would approve.

When she saw Bosse in the yard she slipped down to the staff office to get her phone. She wanted to write to Wilma and tell her about Benjamin. While she charged the phone she discovered that she'd received a text from Wilma sent that same morning.

Did you read about Ellis? Awesome! was all it said.

At first she was confused. Then she got a hunch and rummaged through the newspapers on Oswald's desk for the local paper from Lund — Oswald had gone to the university there and still subscribed to the paper. The article wasn't long, but it was impossible to miss.

Internet Stalker Arrested

Under the headline was a picture of Wilgot Östling, the police chief, who stated that the police had traced a sexually offensive blog to a man in Lund. He had written his posts in various libraries and cafes, and when they performed a raid on his apartment drugs were found as well. The man was currently in custody. The article concluded with a statement from Östling saying that this was a breakthrough when it came to cracking down on the many sexual harassment cases online.

She read the article again. Word for word. She put down the paper and paced around the office, then read the article once more. She followed the text with her finger as if to reassure herself it was real. It had to be about Ellis. She paced the room again and looked out the window, where she could see the lookout point and the sea. Relief struck her like a warm wave as she stood there. That jerk was only getting what he deserved. All at once she felt tremendous admiration for Oswald. He had made this happen in only a few days. But how on earth had he done it? Would it turn into a trial? Would she have to testify if it did? Did she really hate Ellis so much she wanted him locked up?

Then another thought popped up. A thought she would rather push aside.

Because something wasn't right.

She knew Ellis had never done drugs.

The light is on in the cottage but I know she's not there.

The door is unlocked.

The heat strikes me as I step in.

She left the fire burning in the open hearth.

I feel the urge to set the whole cottage on fire, but I have more important things to take care of.

Now that I'm in the light, I discover how filthy I am.

I wipe my feet on the doormat; I can't leave any traces.

I take off my wet underwear and find a plastic bag in the kitchen to put them in. I have to remember to take them with me.

I walk into my room and close the door.

Look in the wardrobe for something ordinary; she must not notice anything missing.

I put on underwear, socks, a sweater, and pants. I find a jacket I never wear and the backpack is under the bed.

The clothes don't help; my teeth are still chattering and for an instant I wish I could crawl in bed to warm up. But I smother the impulse.

I sling the backpack over my shoulder on the way out.

Just then, I hear the front door opening.

16

She wanted to know more about Ellis, but Oswald was on the mainland and Bosse was in an interview with a colleague and didn't want to be disturbed. She paced the office, restless, until she found herself biting her nails and her pen and decided to take a walk on the island to calm down.

On the way out, she looked in on the staff quarters because she knew Benjamin was there. He had taken that morning off to move furniture into their new room.

She found him carrying a bureau through the door. He was shirtless, shiny with sweat, and didn't notice her until she was almost on top of him. When he did see her, he was startled and almost dropped the bureau. She helped him place it in the room, then looked around, pleased. Their room was plain, like all the rooms at the manor, but it was still their own. More space for clothes and belongings. Their own bathroom.

They sat down on the bed and Sofia told him about the article in the paper.

'But that's awesome!' Benjamin said. 'Why do you look so worried?'

'It's been so quiet. No one told me about it, and I'm worried that something's not right. It seems too good to be true.'

'But who would tell you? Bosse's busy. Maybe Franz wanted to tell you himself when he comes home.'

'And then there's the drugs. I know Ellis never used drugs. He drank, but I never saw him high.'

'Sofia, how can you be so sure of that? He must have hidden his drug abuse from you. You said yourself that he seemed so great but later he turned into a monster.'

'Just like you!' she said, bopping him on the nose.

They wrestled around on the bed for a while, but he was so sweaty she couldn't get a grip on him. So she lay still, her lips against his throat, inhaling his scent of sweat and saltwater. Though it was still early in the season, he had already started taking a dip in the sea each morning while everyone else was still asleep.

She left him with detailed instructions for how to arrange everything in the room.

★

The early summer morning was windy but warm. Clouds sailed across the sky, hiding the sun now and again. She told the guard in the sentry box that she had some errands to run in the village. Instead she took the path through the woods to the cottage. She hadn't been there since the day she met Karin Johansson.

The yard surrounding the cottage had come to life. The grass was tall and the dandelions and cowslips were racing each other along the walls. The key was under the doormat, just as Karin had promised. When she got inside, she took the family tree papers from the bureau drawer and placed them on the kitchen table. She made a cup of coffee and sat with her nose buried in the documents for a long time.

The family tree was clear but also impenetrable. The names of the Count's and Karin's own families were neatly lined up alongside each other. Some names had narrow, faint lines drawn between them. Some lines were red and others were green. She didn't understand what the different colours meant. Karin Johansson's name had both a red and green line to Henrik von Bärensten, the last Count in the family line.

There was also another name under Karin's: *Fredrik Johansson*. A small cross had been added next to it. Her son, the boy who jumped from Devil's Rock.

Something was missing. A man. A father for the son. She decided to ask Karin about the lines the next time they met.

Sofia began to flip through the newspaper clippings and pictures. At the top of the pile was an old photograph, a photostat copy — it must have come from an archive. In it, a large man in a suit and wide-brimmed hat stood with a shovel in hand. What appeared to be his family sat on a bench beside him. The woman, likely the Countess, had a new-born baby in her arms and a small boy next to her. The picture had faded, almost erasing the woman's features, but you could still tell how beautiful she was. Her face was open and sweet, with high cheekbones and large eyes. Her hair had been put up in a bun, but little wisps fell around her face. Without meaning to, the photographer had captured her worry — although her mouth was smiling, her eyes were anxious.

Breaking ground on the future manor! read the caption in elegant penmanship.

The next photo was of the Countess on a large white horse. She was wearing a black cape with the hood up. The picture had been taking facing the sea and everything was swept in fog. She looked serious here as well, but in a decisive way rather than a concerned one. It was a lovely picture, like a fairy-tale illustration.

Then came a small, yellowed newspaper clipping with a few lines about the fire at the manor. There was nothing about the Count's insanity or the Countess's jump from the cliff, but it said both had 'departed' under tragic circumstances. Next was a long article about the shipwreck, written in old-fashioned Swedish that was hard to understand.

So it all really happened, she thought. *It's not just ghost stories Björk made up. How can so much misfortune strike one place? There must be a reason.* A thought was niggling at her: maybe it would be their turn next. That it was only a matter of time before the curse hit ViaTerra. But then she decided her imagination was getting the best of her.

She sifted on through the pile and found several items from the church archives. Marriages, baptisms, and burials of various von Bärenstens; a few engagement announcements, a couple of wedding pictures. She toyed with the thought of looking up all the names in the family tree, but she had started to worry that Oswald might be home already, and wondering where she was.

At the bottom of the pile was an obituary:

My beloved
FREDRIK JOHANSSON
my son, my everything
has left me in irreparable sorrow and loneliness.
Rest in peace in the endless depths of the sea.
KARIN

He had just turned fourteen. She wondered what it would feel like to be dragged out to sea by the icy current and shuddered. A book about all of this would have to end with Fredrik Johansson's sudden death, she realized. And what a horrible ending that would be. She wondered what had happened to the von Bärenstens who moved to France. Maybe there was a better ending to be found in their fates.

Her pager buzzed, interrupting her thoughts. She'd received it when she began working for Oswald; she'd never seen such a gadget before then, but had heard they were popular in the nineties, before mobile phones became widely available. Text scrolled across the screen:

Return to the manor immediately. Party tonight. Bosse.

A party? She couldn't imagine what they would be celebrating. But at least it meant that Oswald was in a good mood, and that was positive news for everyone. Bosse would ask where she'd been; she decided to take the coast road home so she could pretend to have been in the village looking for office supplies. She arranged the documents into a neat stack and put them back in the drawer, then locked the cottage and jogged home.

★

When she reached the gate, sweaty and out of breath, she heard excited voices from within the wall. The lawn was full of staff setting up tables, chairs, and parasols, and music streamed from a pair of giant speakers that had been dragged out of the quarters. Bosse was waiting for her at the sentry box. He didn't even ask where she'd been.

'You have to go change clothes. Magnus Strid has completed the program and Franz wants to have a big barbecue for him.

All the staff and guests are coming. Franz wants you to oversee set-up, food, and all of that.'

She went to her room and changed into a short-sleeved black dress and sandals. Then she ran back to the yard and made sure everything was done properly: that tables were set up and decorated tastefully; that the food was prepared in the kitchen.

In the midst of it all, she noticed that the wind had died down and the clouds had broken up — it was going to be excellent weather for a barbecue.

When Oswald appeared, he was unusually chipper. He was wearing jeans and a pale jacket over a white shirt, and had a day's stubble just like Strid. His energetic force-field quickly enveloped the partygoers. He shook hands, laughed, and chatted with staff and guests.

'Perfect!' he praised Sofia in passing. 'And now that idiot who was after you is under lock and key. Contacts, Sofia, contacts are everything. It's good to have friends in high places.'

'But if there's a trial, will I have to testify?' she asked.

Oswald waved off her concern.

'No, I'll take care of it.'

She was just about to thank him, but he vanished before she could form words.

Almost a hundred people sat around the tables, eating and drinking, laughing and chatting. Benjamin was a little late coming from the staff quarters; he sat down next to her and whispered that everything was ready. They had their own room. She shivered with pleasure.

'Sofia!' Oswald's voice came from behind her, and when she turned around he was standing there with Magnus Strid. She rose and walked over to them.

'Sofia is my right-hand woman,' Oswald said, putting his arm around her shoulders.

She was probably the only one who noticed that he was stroking his fingers up and down her arm, but she still found all eyes on her. Anna, who was in charge of the annexes, glared from a nearby table, and Madeleine, who was sitting at the fringes of the group with Katarina, shot a hateful look her way. *Go ahead and glare*, she thought. *I've earned this.* She glanced at Benjamin, but he was absorbed in his meal and didn't even seem to have noticed that she'd left the table.

'Sofia and I have met,' said Strid. 'It's too bad she can't clone herself, because she was fantastic as a librarian.'

Oswald just laughed and moved on to another table with Strid. By the time Sofia was finished eating, Benjamin had helped himself to seconds, so she went down to sit by the pond for a while. The pair of swans that had lived there last summer hadn't returned, but a couple of mallards had nested there and were swimming around with a host of downy ducklings.

'Well, it's time for me to say goodbye, Sofia.'

It was Magnus Strid. He crouched beside her on the lawn.

'Oh, it was nice to meet you and chat about books a little.'

'I enjoyed it more than you might think,' he said. As it met her own, his gaze seemed inscrutable, even a bit concerned. 'May I ask what brought you here, to ViaTerra?'

She thought for a moment.

'I guess it was mostly the library. And the theses, of course. I felt amazing after the program.'

He nodded but his eyes didn't waver.

'Are you sure you're happy here? Is this right for you? With your education, you could have a completely different career.'

'Of course I want to be here,' she responded, but she wasn't without doubt. She hadn't thought about it that way. Everything had happened so fast, from one incident to the next — and now she considered what he had said. That she could do something different. That she didn't actually have to work at the manor.

'I only have a little over a year left,' she said. 'Then my contract runs out.'

'Sometimes it can be hard to get out.' His comment made her uneasy, and Strid noticed. At last he looked away.

'No worries. I just wanted to make sure. Of course you're happy here. It's a fantastic place.'

He took a card from his jacket pocket and handed it to her.

'If you ever want to get your foot in the door at a newspaper, you're welcome to contact me.' Quickly, gently, he patted her on the shoulder and stood up. 'Good luck with everything!'

'Same to you.'

She watched him head back to the tables like a lumbering bear.

The early summer evening was filled with laughter and elated voices. A blackbird sang ardently from the weeping willow by the pond. The pennant hung limp against the flagpole. It appeared to be the perfect night. Yet it felt like life was about to change in some vague, undefinable way. As if they had reached some limit and would soon hurtle downward with frightening speed. She wasn't sure why she felt that way, but the sensation was all too real.

I crawl under the bed and pull my backpack in with me. It's so cramped that I can feel the broken springs of the mattress against my back.

She's here.

I hear steps in the kitchen, a clatter.

I have no idea what that bitch is doing home. She's supposed to be out by Devil's Rock looking for me. Have they given up already? What's going on?

The door to the bedroom opens slowly, with a creak, and I see her feet on the doorsill.

She stands perfectly still for a moment and I don't dare breathe.

Then she sighs and turns around.

For a long time everything is perfectly silent.

Then there's a sound. At first I don't know what it is. Some kind of whining, sighing, sobbing.

She's sitting there. Fucking crying.

I've never seen her cry before. I thought she was tougher than that. I am disgusted.

I don't want to be there. I never want to see her again.

I just want to get far away from this horrible cottage.

Then the phone rings.

'Yes, I'm on my way.'

Joy rises within me when I hear the door open and close.

Never again, *I think.*

Never again will I have to see you.

17

Her stomach was a ball of anxiety when she woke in the morning. She extricated herself from Benjamin, who was wound around her like a creeping vine. She suspected she might have had a nightmare, but the feeling only got worse as she rose from the bed. The anxiety was making her almost nauseated. She cursed her mother — she must have inherited some sort of worry gene. There was no reason for this sudden anguish.

Two weeks had passed since the party for Strid. Oswald had remained in an unusually good mood since, joking and sharing little anecdotes with the staff during evening assembly. He'd almost completely stopped touching her that way. He brushed against her sometimes, or placed a hand on her shoulder while he spoke to her. But it felt friendly, and she sensed that maybe it always had been. Midsummer was just around the corner, the weather was lovely, and they had more guests than ever.

There was absolutely no reason to worry.

After a long, hot shower she felt a little better. Magnus Strid had woken something within her during their talk by the pond. She had started thinking about the future and what she would do when her contract with ViaTerra ran out. Maybe she could work at a paper. Or write that book. But she kept it all to herself, because she was sure Oswald wouldn't approve.

She sat on the edge of the bed to shake Benjamin awake before she left the room, and reminded him he had morning assembly in fifteen minutes. She didn't attend anymore. Instead she prepared the office for Oswald's arrival, and put everything in place: breakfast, the morning papers, and a list of his daily engagements.

Although it was summer, there was a thick fog covering the property that morning. When she stepped into the office, her nervousness returned. She opened the blinds to let in some natural light, but the office still looked dim and grey so she turned on some lamps. She picked up the morning papers, which appeared each day through a slot in the door.

She didn't usually read the papers, but that morning she browsed through them. She would never quite know what prompted her to do so. Maybe because she thought her bad mood was a result of something that had happened in the world. She did experience that sort of premonition from time to time.

She flipped through the papers, reading the headlines, but didn't find anything noteworthy at first. Fresh opinion polls for all the political parties, weather forecasts for Midsummer, and an elder-care scandal. Then she got to *Dagens Nyheter*.

The headline was impossible to miss.

New cult dawning on West Fog Island. Is ViaTerra the path to freedom or the path to terror?

It was the daily editorial. Her first thought was that it must have been written by someone else. Some imbecile of a journalist who didn't know the first thing about them. She quickly found the rest of the piece and there it was — a little picture of him. Magnus Strid, his hands over his round belly, that delightful smile on his face.

She buried her face in her hands and tried to get control of her breathing — she was suddenly panting. She stared at the darkness of her palms for a moment before looking back at the paper. The headline was still there.

It was eight o'clock. No word from Oswald. She had plenty of time to read. And read she must, before he arrived at the office.

She searched the text, trying to find something positive. This wasn't right. Strid was supposed to write nice things about them. He had praised the program; he'd always seemed happy, hanging out with Oswald. It was like this article had been written by someone else. A horrid, scandal–hungry journalist.

On a tiny, foggy island off the coast of Bohuslän, a peculiar New Age movement has taken root. They promise a better civilization and fresh hope for humanity. The name of the cult is ViaTerra, and their slogan is 'We walk the way of the earth.' Their leader, twenty-eight-year-old University of Lund dropout Franz Oswald, claims that their goal is to save humanity from toxins, stress, and other evils. Their doctrine — eat health foods, sleep, and exercise — is written down in philosophical terms, yet it seems to be just good common sense, nothing you can't do in your own living room or at the gym. A growing band of adherents pays hundreds of thousands of kronor to take part in this program and a few courses in self-discipline and relaxation methods.

Yet the most disturbing aspect is that ViaTerra seems to be a magnet for powerful players in influential circles, including the entertainment branch.

This cult — because it must be said that the operation fits into every definition of the word — claims that there is nothing strange about what they're doing, and yet their messages and methods bear frightening similarities to other groups who exploit their staff and members. The young, devoted workers live in a collective, sleep in dormitories, earn a few hundred kronor a week, and obey Oswald's every whim. And the same seems to go for our country's upper classes and celebrities, who always seem ready to hop on the next train to find meaning and satisfaction in their superficial lives.

This was a disaster. Worse than a disaster. A death-blow. Oswald would turn this place into a raging inferno.

The article went on in the same tone, revealing what they worked on and which guests took part in the program. And the ending wasn't any better.

It remains to be seen where this group, ViaTerra, is headed. The American author P.T. Barnum once wrote that there's a sucker born every minute. After speaking with Oswald and many of his underlings, one can only confirm that Barnum's words are as true today as they were in the 19th century.

She read the article again. A number of feelings spread through her as she did. Contempt, hatred, doubt, and fear blended into one. The doubt was mostly because there might be some truth to what Strid had written, because she couldn't spot any lies. Just a fresh point of view. A critical one that didn't *want* to see any positives. Then she thought of the book he'd borrowed from the library and wondered if he was a bit of a pervert. Or maybe she was the problem, if she couldn't see the path ViaTerra was on. But mostly she was afraid of what Oswald would do when he arrived at the office.

She toyed with the thought of hiding the paper, but that seemed absurd. Maybe she could go back to her room and pretend to have a fever. Oswald was a hypochondriac and didn't want sick people anywhere near him. This seemed like a good idea until she realized that someone would likely make her take her temperature. And wouldn't it just be putting off the inevitable? All hell would break loose when he read the article. It would be a mess, and she wouldn't get away unscathed.

Her pager buzzed with the usual message. He was on his way. She called the kitchen to order his breakfast. Time seemed to crawl by until he finally opened the door. He took one look at her shamed face and posture and knew something was wrong.

'What is it?'

'The article by Magnus Strid. It came out today.' She tentatively held out the paper to him .

'And of course you had to read it before I got the chance.'

'I thought I should —'

He snatched the paper from her hand, sat down, and began to read. She sat down at her desk and watched him in silence. Even when her bum began to hurt, she didn't dare change positions.

His face was impassive as he read; his features blank. Yet she could tell something was happening inside him because his jaw seemed to tense slightly and his skin slowly paled. Most of all, she sensed a horrible, dismal mood radiating off him and poisoning the air in the room. She suddenly became aware that he was looking at her. He hadn't moved a muscle, but his eyes were no longer on the paper — they were riveted on her own. For an instant she thought he would fly out of his chair and strike her. But he stood up slowly and put the newspaper on his desk, then left the office without closing the door behind him. His determined steps echoed down the corridor.

That was the last she saw of him for three days.

*

If it hadn't been for the kitchen staff, she would have worried something had happened to Oswald. But on the first day, he called to order food delivered straight to his room. Lina from the kitchen popped into the office to tell Sofia that 'Mr Oswald ate a good lunch.' Sofia relaxed. At the same time, the rumours about the article spread like wildfire among the staff and guests. A heavy, angsty mood fell over the manor. Grumpy faces and sad eyes everywhere. Bosse tried to pep up the staff at assembly, saying that Oswald would certainly help them out of their funk.

But no one knew what he was up to in his room.

Sofia walked around the office restlessly, with no idea what she should do. When she came in the next morning she found that the light on Oswald's answering machine had gone nuts: he had twenty-five missed calls. She played the first message, which was from a journalist with *Aftonbladet* who wanted a comment on Strid's article. The next message was from someone at *Expressen*. She unplugged the phone from its jack, sure that Oswald wouldn't want to give any comments.

She began to clean and sort papers and finally, when the office was spic and span, she began to read a novel on her computer. After each chapter, she took a turn around the office and looked down at the yard.

Around ten o'clock, she noticed a gathering outside the wall. All journalists and photographers with still and video cameras. They must have come on the morning ferry.

She checked the newspapers online and found that her fears were confirmed. Other newspapers had climbed on board with Strid's article, several with terrible speculations about what went on at the island. Her first thought was that her parents would faint when they saw this. But just as she was about to head for the staff office to get her phone and text them, there was a knock on the door. It was Lina from the kitchen.

'Mr Oswald says you're supposed to be there to meet the security firm when they come tomorrow morning.'

'The security firm?'

'Yes, he said they're going to install a barbed-wire fence on the wall so none of the idiots can get over. Those were his exact words.'

Sofia thanked Lina, hurried to get hold of Bosse, and told him about Oswald's strange message.

'It's not all that strange,' he said. 'There are tons of journalists out there. They would have no trouble climbing over the wall if they really wanted to get at us.'

★

Sure enough, the security firm showed up the next morning. Five men worked all day, before the eyes of curious journalists outside the wall and dumbfounded staff members inside. Slowly but surely, the fence took shape on top of the wall.

Sofia stood in the yard with Bosse, watching the wire wind its way around the property like a giant, razor-sharp snake. She'd always liked standing in the courtyard — such a nice mix of open space and nature. But now she thought it looked like a prison yard.

When it was all finished, the men approached her and Bosse.

'It's all done, just like your boss wanted,' one of them said. 'Now I'll show you how to turn on the current.'

'The current?'

'Yes, the wire is electrified, just as he ordered.' When the man saw the alarm on Sofia's face, he merely laughed. 'Don't worry. It's not that many volts. No one's going to get electrocuted. But it will deliver a decent shock.'

Bosse followed the men to the sentry box where the switch had been installed. She stayed behind, staring at the fence. It was like a dream, a dream so clear and sharp that it felt more real than real life.

*

That evening Oswald came to the office. He looked well-rested and energetic and not nearly as downtrodden as she'd expected. His eyes glittered with fervour; he almost looked a little crazy. Even that arrogant little tilt of his head was back.

'I want a meeting with the entire staff after dinner tonight,' he said. 'And I mean everyone. Every single person must be there.'

There's a tiny closet on the ferry. It's at the stern, where the cars are parked for their journey over. A tiny cleaning closet, not even high enough to stand up straight. But it's never in use while the ferry is traveling across the sound.

I was in there with Lily once. I locked her in to scare her, but that's another story, not important right now.

It's five o'clock and I can already see the coming light of dawn. The darkness has transformed into a thick, grey haze.

Three hours in a cubbyhole, then one more on the way over. But it can't be helped. This is the best hiding spot.

The odour of the fire has followed me here.

It's still draped over the island like a blanket.

But the sound of cars, sirens, boats, and voices is gone. So they gave up. I no longer exist.

I crawl into the closet and prepare for hours of darkness inside. I know all about darkness.

The darkness of the cellar in the manor house.

His horrible stench of sweat.

You can't see the blows coming.

I close the door behind me and sit down on a bucket. The words come to me, a mantra that will follow me on my journey.

'Eradicated, risen again, returned.' Like the bird rising out of the ashes.

Time stands still.

All at once, I find myself outside. I can see the whole island from above.

The first rays of sun brushing the landscape. The trees, the houses, the sea.

I realize I have left my body.

That I have greater powers than I ever expected. And that life has phenomenal plans for me.

18

It was perfectly quiet in the large dining room. The tables had been shoved alongside the walls and the chairs lined up so that fifty people could sit close together, their eyes on the podium that had been erected for Oswald. Typically, the dining room was full of chatter and noise. But now they weren't even talking to each other. It wasn't an awkward silence; rather, it was forced and anxious. They had been waiting for half an hour now.

Sofia was sitting in the front row with Bosse's gang and those in charge of the various units. In the very last row sat those who had landed in disfavour even before the newspaper article: Madeleine, and Helge, a guy from the household staff who had almost totalled one of Oswald's cars when he was supposed to bring it in to be serviced. In the middle rows sat the rest, grouped by team. This had all been done according to Oswald's instructions.

Now they could hear the familiar determined footsteps, but no one dared to turn around. Sofia was the only one who stood up to see if Oswald needed anything, but he shook his head and gestured at her to sit back down. He went to stand behind the podium and placed a sheet of paper on it. He looked up at them with an expression of mild concern.

'We're going to have a little chat,' he began. 'And figure out what's been going on in recent days.'

His tone was friendly. The tense mood in the room relaxed a bit.

'It's very simple,' he went on. 'We had a chance to spread ViaTerra to innumerable people. Most of us worked our asses off to help out. But someone here spread lies to Strid behind our backs, and now we must find who is betraying us all with wicked lies.'

His gaze had hardened, and he fixed his eyes on random individuals. It was still perfectly silent. Sofia could even hear Bosse's nervous breathing beside her. Oswald stared at Olof Hurtig.

'Olof, you were Magnus Strid's personal guide. You didn't spill any secrets, did you?'

Everyone turned around to look at Olof. This was the first time Sofia had seen him without a smile pasted on his lips. The corners of his mouth usually pulled up a little even when he was being serious. But now he was stiff and pale.

'No, Franz, absolutely not! We only talked about his program.'

'You can call me "Sir". That goes for all of you from now on. Like they do in the US. And you can be sure they have better control over their employees there than we do in socialist Sweden!' Oswald said. 'I hope you're not lying, Olof. Don't you see that Magnus deceived you?'

'Yes . . . sir. I do.'

Now Oswald turned to her.

Surely he doesn't think . . . ?

'What about you, Sofia? You had a long conversation with Magnus in the library.'

Her voice sounded rough and strange when she answered.

'We only talked about books, never about anything personal.'

He held her gaze for a moment. An icy chill ran through her, and images along with it. Strid down by the pond. His concerned eyes and questions about her future. But that had nothing to do with the article.

She stared back at Oswald and tried to look unconcerned.

'I believe you,' he said at last. 'Well, if no one will confess right now then you'll have to figure it out among yourselves. I have more important things to deal with. But before I go we need to talk about the rules.'

He began to read from the paper on the podium.

'One: I want reinforcements in staff administration. There must always be a guard in the sentry box by the gate and one patrolling the property. And Bosse needs someone to help him with staff ethics. Staff administration works under me. Directly. Understood?

'Two: Within staff administration there should be a program to handle those who have messed up. They will perform hard labour on the estate and will not be permitted to speak with the rest of the staff. They are absolutely forbidden from speaking to guests. They must wear a red cap so everyone knows who they are. You can call this program "Penance" or something like that.'

He turned to Bosse, who nodded eagerly.

'Yes, sir. I'll take care of it.'

'Three: All access to computer, cell phones, and any other electronic gadgets is banned effective immediately. Even during free time, which I doubt you'll have much of anytime soon anyway. The computer here in the dining room will be shut down. Bosse, you can gather up everything people are hiding in their rooms. We'll just have to confiscate it.'

An image of the laptop in her dresser drawer flew through Sofia's mind. She had to find a better hiding spot.

'Four: Tonight, before you leave the dining room, you will write a short but friendly email to your families and say you have a lot going on, that you'll be unreachable for a while, and that they shouldn't worry. You can write your messages by hand, and Bosse, your unit can send them from the dining room computer before it's shut down.' He chuckled suddenly. 'Don't look so upset! We'll get through this. Just a few weeks, and everything will go back to normal and you can tweet and text to your hearts' content.'

A few of the staff tittered nervously.

Oswald looked down at his notes again.

'And finally, five: No one here leaves the property without my written permission. Benjamin can make purchases as usual, but the guard will note the times he leaves and returns to the manor. I have more important things to deal with now. Sofia, you can stay here until all of you are done. But tomorrow I need you on hand in the office.'

'Yes, sir.'

Had she really said something so forced and ridiculous?

He gathered his papers and stepped down from the podium, then walked briskly down the aisle and closed the door behind him.

A screech came from the back of the room.

'Dammit, Madeleine! Why didn't you say anything? I saw you talking to Strid!'

It was Mona, and she had transformed. Her face was bright red and spit flew from her mouth as she shook her finger at Madeleine, who had flown up in response to the accusation.

'I didn't say anything! He just asked me how things were going and I said I liked working out in the sunshine. That was all.'

'You're lying! You talked for a long time.'

Katarina had stood up too. She was usually cool as a cucumber, but now her voice was shrill and strangely hoarse as she shouted at Mona.

'What about you? You had Strid alone in the library more than once. What did you talk about, huh?'

Sofia wondered why Katarina was defending Madeleine, but she supposed they had become friends as they weeded the flowerbeds together. Mona paid no attention to Katarina, she just moved down the lines to get to Madeleine. She planted herself in front of the other woman and gave her a shove.

'I know you're lying!' she shrieked in that new, strange voice. Then she shoved Madeleine again, harder this time. Suddenly everything happened at once: Madeleine was straddling Mona, whom she had dragged down to the floor. She pinned her arms to the parquet and screamed in her face.

'Shut up! Shut up, you nasty old bitch!'

Then, the unimaginable: Mona lifted her head from the floor and spat right in Madeleine's face. The glob of spittle landed in her eye and Madeleine howled in rage. Bosse came running and separated the two of them.

Sofia just stood there staring in amazement; she'd never seen anything like this at the manor — or anywhere else, for that matter.

Then she caught sight of Benjamin, who had a tiny smile on his face.

'Do you think this is funny, Benjamin?' she asked loudly.

'Yeah, it's pretty funny actually.'

Now everyone was looking at him. Even Madeleine and Mona were distracted.

'What's so funny about it?'

'This whole mess.'

'So it has nothing to do with you?'

'Nah. I never talked to Strid and I don't think screaming is going to get us anywhere.'

'Okay, okay!' Bosse had walked over to her. 'Benjamin is being an ass right now, but he's not wrong. We'll have to tackle this another way. You can come up one by one and account for what you did with Strid.'

Sofia eyed him with mistrust. 'All fifty of us?'

'Can you think of a better way? Franz said he wants to know who the rat is.'

She shrugged and looked at Benjamin, who was making a face. She suppressed the urge to walk up and smack him.

Bosse called the staff up one by one to interrogate them. Others joined in too, if they had questions. It took almost three hours and in the end it all went off the rails, because no one wanted to admit they had spoken negatively about ViaTerra. Sofia was so restless that her skin was crawling; she checked her watch again and again, thinking of the emails they were supposed to write to their families.

Bosse was looking increasingly desperate; they hadn't uncovered a thing. Everyone who was called up just stood there, stiff as a board, denying every accusation. At last Bosse turned to Sofia and whispered in her ear.

'What do we do now?'

'Write the emails we have to send.'

'Yes, but what do we say to Franz?'

'We say we're going to question them all one-on-one until we find the leak. It might not be so easy for the guilty party to confess in front of fifty other people.'

Bosse's face lit up.

'You're right! Let's do that.' He turned to the staff, full of energy again. 'We'll finish this later. Now you need to write to your families. Put your messages down on paper and include your email address and password.'

'I'm not giving out my password.' Benjamin again.

'Oh, come on! You can just change it next time you log in.'

Benjamin responded with a displeased grunt.

When Sofia sat down to compose her own email to her parents, her brain seemed to get stuck. Her throat was thick with repressed tears and her eyes were burning. But she wrote an awkward message to say she was very busy and wouldn't have time to call or write for a while. The tone wasn't at all like her, but she was exhausted and just wanted to go to bed. But they kept at it until early morning. Staff had to be assigned to Bosse's office. None of the unit heads wanted to give up any of their people, so a bitter fight ensued until the household unit and the farm unit each gave in and offered a few staff members.

Then, at last, they were done. The dining room felt sour and stuffy, and she went out to the yard for some fresh air. It was almost five in the morning; it was already light out and a pink summer sky with fluffy clouds suggested that it would be a beautiful day. She wandered around the lawn for a while, letting the dew drench her shoes and nylons. She looked up at the sharp, barbed-wire fence, trying to recall the sense of well-being she had felt when she was doing the theses, and had floated over the island like a swallow, but the feeling wouldn't return.

Benjamin had gone straight back to their room and was already asleep when she came in. His clothes were strewn all over the floor and he was snoring heavily under the blanket. She opened the dresser drawer and saw her laptop, still wrapped in a sheet, but she couldn't think of a better hiding place. It just looked like extra bedding, so she left it there. Slowly she undressed and hung up yesterday's uniform, then nudged Benjamin until he shifted over. The clock told her that she had to be up again in two hours; she turned off the light and floated into a deep slumber.

I'm going to pause the story now.

Just for a moment, so I can explain something. You may have wondered about Lily. Why it happened, or why I didn't drag her out of the barn that night.

So it's important for you to understand the way I think. The way I steer my life.

I see life as a game, and there are many ways a person can play — you just have to pick one.

But there must be clear rules, and Lily and I had our own. She was my slave at night. It was a game we played, and she liked it.

So much that she begged me, nagged me, to play. To take greater risks. To do more dangerous things.

Then, that night, she broke the rules.

She made quite a mess of things, with her screaming and the fire, of course, and put me in considerable danger. And at times like that, you must think of yourself first.

I think Lily had lived out her life, somehow. She never belonged here; she was too weak and gullible.

It's not as if I don't think about her sometimes. She was special.

But she was only a part of the game, a chess piece that had been knocked out, no longer playable.

So now I'm going to give you some advice. See life as a game; don't take it so seriously.

Other people are just game pieces. They can have different roles and can even cause trouble.

But you are in the main role and you always have a choice: use them or put them aside.

And don't be such a damn bleeding-heart, because they'll do the same to you, given the chance.

That's how it was with Lily, and now it's time to move on.

19

She was free. At least, for a few hours. She felt strangely proud of cheating her way into time off. And she knew exactly what she would do with it.

It was the kind of day when everything works out. Oswald had been in the office when she came in. For once he didn't treat her like she wasn't there. He didn't even complain that she was five minutes late.

'We're having a visitor today, Sofia. Her name is Carmen Gardell and she's one of the top PR experts in the country. She's going to help us regain control over all the lies that have been written about us in the media.'

Sofia knew nothing about what had been written because there had been a total ban on newspapers ever since Strid's article. She hadn't even sneaked looks at Oswald's papers, but she could tell from his tone that the media was gobbling up the ViaTerra story right now. And someone named Carmen, with a deep, gravelly voice, had called a few times asking for Oswald. Sofia had even wondered whether Oswald might have a girlfriend.

The day passed quickly. Oswald worked with great energy. He dictated various directives which she typed up and passed along to the staff. They mostly had to do with how to improve things on the property: a broken fence around the farm to fix, a withered flowerbed to replant. And something should be done about the fact that the new guards were running around in farmer clothes. Oswald hummed to himself between recordings. Now and then he looked up at her and smiled. It felt truly pleasant to work with him that day.

Around five, he stood up and turned off his computer.

'You and I are going to take a little stroll around the property and make sure everything looks good. I want us to take excellent care of Carmen. Bring your notebook.'

A fresh breeze met them in the yard. The sun was shining on the wilting Midsummer pole that was still up on the lawn. It had been erected solely for the benefit of the guests; the staff had no time to celebrate any holidays for the time being. Oswald's new rules had taken effect and were followed to the letter. It was understood that everyone had to work beyond the normal hours; it was proof of their devotion. A silent understanding had also arisen: as long as Oswald was still working it was wrong for staff to sleep. So it wasn't unusual to find people staring up at his window until the light went out before they dared go to bed at night.

The working days were long and a whole night of sleep was a luxury. No one would dare to point out that Oswald came to the office late in the mornings while the staff gathered at the crack of dawn. Furthermore, Oswald's personal staff had been increased to support him while he dealt with all the messes that no one else could handle. He now had a personal chef and someone in the household unit took care of his room, clothes, and other personal things. This was a positive development in Sofia's view; it lessened her workload.

But now Oswald pointed at the Midsummer pole in annoyance.

'That must be taken down immediately. Who the hell left it there? Get Bosse so he can take care of it.'

She was just about to say that Bosse actually wasn't in charge of Midsummer poles — the household unit was — but she had to bite her tongue because just then Bosse came out of one of the annexes and trotted over to them.

Oswald had gotten himself all worked up by now.

'Find out whose idea it was to leave that disgusting pole in the yard. It must be taken down immediately. It looks horrible. Clearly there's still no one here who cares.'

Sofia mumbled something and Bosse assured him he would deal with the pole.

'Let's go to Carmen's room,' Oswald said to Sofia. 'I talked to Anna yesterday about how it should look.'

Anna was responsible for everything to do with the guests: lodging, service, and food. She was already waiting for them by the annexes. With her hourglass figure and picture-perfect face, Anna was ViaTerra's own beauty queen. But in Oswald's presence she transformed into a total bimbo. She was so obvious about it that Sofia was mortified on her behalf. Anna would gaze at Oswald with glassy eyes and speak in a girlish voice trembling with zeal. They just plain clashed, with Anna's pining and Oswald's cool arrogance. He always found something to be annoyed about, and it usually ended with a teary-eyed Anna and a furious Oswald.

When Oswald wasn't around, Anna was happy to share little anecdotes about how Oswald had said this or that to her, as if they were best friends, and it got on the nerves of just about everyone else. Sofia sneaked a sideways glance at Anna and wondered what it felt like to go through life with that unrequited love.

Today's inspection started off well. The room had been aired out and made up with great care. Someone had placed a piece of chocolate on the pillow and set a bottle of sparkling wine on the nightstand. The bathroom was so clean it sparkled. A thick white bathrobe was hanging next to the tub. Oswald looked around several times and nodded in satisfaction.

But then a tiny wrinkle appeared on his brow.

'The flowers!'

'The flowers?'

Sofia looked at the vases, which were filled with white roses. 'I said peonies.'

Anna looked at Oswald, her face full of shame.

'Why did you fill the vases with roses?'

'Sir, we thought roses might be nice.'

Oswald's jaw was clenched. 'Are you that stupid? Do you think roses and peonies are the same thing? They don't even look alike. Don't we have any peonies on the property?'

'No, I'm sorry, but I'll take care of it, sir.'

'I don't trust you. Sofia, you'll have to fix this. I want peonies. I don't know when the florist closes; it might be too late. In that case you'll have to pick wildflowers, and I don't want just anything. Really lovely bouquets. Typical Swedish archipelago flowers. You have one hour until Carmen arrives. I trust you will manage.'

Sofia nodded. The florist closed at five, but it didn't matter — she knew exactly where to find beautiful wildflowers. She had seen them last year, growing along the stream outside Karin Johansson's cottage.

She dashed up to her room and changed into sneakers. They looked silly with her blazer and skirt, so ridiculous that she burst out laughing when she saw herself in the mirror.

Even the guard shot her a strange look before he let her out.

Once outside the gate, she stood still for a moment, inhaling the fresh air and feeling free and alive. Like a calf that has just been let out into a green pasture. She took the quickest route to the cottage, jogging the whole way. It was early July, and a weekend besides. There was a good chance Karin would be there.

★

She was sweaty and out of breath, and her hair had become tangled in the breeze. Her heart skipped a beat when she saw Karin in the hammock. Her hair was done in two thick braids and her pale blue dress set off her tan. Karin noticed Sofia right away; she glanced down at her sneakers and up at her uniform and the corners of her lips twitched.

'Hi! Is something up?'

'Quite a bit, but I don't have time to explain. It might sound odd, but I have to pick wildflowers down by the stream and then I can chat. Do you have time?'

'All the time in the world.' Karin looked at Sofia again and laughed. 'You might want to spruce yourself up a bit too, before you go back home. Do you need help with that cult over there?'

'No, it's not that. But I read the family tree and looked at the pictures and I have a few questions.'

'Then I'll get some vases for your flowers and make coffee while you're picking them.'

Sure enough, the grass around the stream was full of flowers. A breeze had come up, and heavy grey clouds were moving in from the west. The wind whistled through the treetops until the branches creaked. But down on the ground, the air was almost still. She wanted to stay longer and take a walk on the island again. To sit at the lookout point and gaze out at the sea. The days and weeks of free time had seemed self-evident before ViaTerra, but these days, free time was a privilege reserved only for the productive. And right now, the only person in that category was Oswald himself.

When she returned to the cottage, Karin had poured water into a few vases and lined them up along the wall. Freshly brewed coffee was waiting on a rickety little table in front of the hammock. The small yard was well protected from the wind, so it was warm, although clouds hid the sun from time to time.

'So, the lines on the family tree,' Sofia began. 'I was wondering what they mean. The red and green ones?'

Karin grinned.

'The green ones are for work and money, and the red ones are for love, of course.'

Sofia considered this for a moment, recalling the top of the tree.

'Okay, so there was love between you and the last Count?'

'No, not exactly, but there was a child.'

'Fredrik was his son?'

'Yes, but out of wedlock. Fredrik was never recognized, or anything. But he was certainly Henrik's son.'

'Did Fredrik know?'

'Oh yes, he knew. We lived at the manor until he was three; we moved out for reasons I don't want to get into. Later, when Fredrik realized he was Henrik's, he wanted Henrik to recognize him. But I wasn't interested. It only would have been about the money anyway, and we were fine without that.'

Sofia didn't say anything for a moment. She didn't want to stir up Karin's emotions.

'I looked at all the photographs and read the old newspaper clippings. It didn't say anything about the first Countess's suicide, or that the count set fire to the manor.'

'No, but that doesn't mean it's not true. There was a book; it was sort of a family history. The Count's daughter, Sigrid von Bärensten, wrote it. She was the little baby in the Countess's arms, you might have seen her in the first picture. She put it all down in that book.'

'Do you have it?'

'No, I wish I did, but it disappeared. Fredrik spent a lot of time with the daughter of the doctor who moved in later on. One day they found the book in the attic and it was like Fredrik transformed completely. He'd always been so angry at Henrik for leaving the island, but he read something in that book that made him furious. It was right before he jumped from Devil's Rock. Since then, the book has been missing. No one has found it.'

'Is the doctor's daughter dead too?'

She had a vague memory of Björk, the ferryman, mentioning something about her.

Karin nodded.

'How did she die?'

'There was a fire in one of the barns at the manor. But I don't feel like getting into details.'

'That's okay. You've already told me so much. I want to write a book about all this — the family's history.'

'I'm sure you could. But how will you manage, if you're stuck in that cult up there?'

'For one thing, it's not a cult. And my contract is up in a year.'

'Well, imagine that! I'll help you, then.'

'Great! I want to find that book. Do you think it could be at the manor?'

'Maybe.'

'There's just one thing I don't understand. That Count must have been filthy rich, right? Why did he build the manor way out here, far away from anything?'

'That's the kind of thing you'd only do if you're up to something shady, right?'

'But what was he up to?'

'It's in the book. I hope you can find it.'

'Won't you please tell me?'

'Maybe later, once we've gotten to know each other better.'

Sofia let it go; she realized there was no point in nagging Karin.

'But what happened to the ones who moved to France? Henrik von Bärensten and his family?'

Karin looked surprised. 'You don't know?'

Sofia shook her head.

'Then you haven't understood just how ill-fated the von Bärenstens were. Henrik and his wife died in a fire. This was several years ago. They lived in southern France, on the Riviera somewhere. The whole family was killed.'

'That's horrible! Is it really true?'

'Yes. It was actually Björk who told me about it. It was in the local gossip sheet, which I don't read anymore.'

'So there's no one left out of that whole family?'

'Not a soul. The woman who wrote the family history lived to be an old woman, but Henrik was her only child and she died in a nursing home a few years ago. When Fredrik died, that was the end of the family line.'

'And here I thought maybe there was a happy ending to my book.'

'I suppose there is, in one way. Not that I like your cult, but at least you've taken care of the place. The gate was open when I drove by last spring, and I couldn't help taking a peek inside. It's like the manor has gotten a new lease of life, isn't it?'

Sofia thought about it for a moment: the barbed wire on the wall and the gloomy mood of recent days. She hoped this wasn't the curse afflicting them too.

She glanced at her watch and realized she would be missed very soon, so she thanked Karin and promised to visit again as soon as she could. She dashed off with the flowers in her arms.

★

It had started to drizzle, and by the time she got to the gate her uniform was damp. The flowers had left flecks on her skirt, and out of the corner of her eye she could see her hair sticking out in all directions.

Bosse met her at the gate. He appeared to be calm, but she felt his seething rage right away.

'Where have you been?'

'First I went to the florist and then I was in the meadows picking flowers, see?'

She triumphantly held up her bouquet.

'Don't lie!'

'What do you mean?'

'I mean, don't lie. I was trying to reach you. Carmen Gardell is already here. But the florist said you were never there. They don't close at five anymore; they're open until six in the summer.'

Her heart jumped into her throat. Her hand searched her jacket pocket, but it was empty and she realized she had left her pager in the office. At first she thought she was screwed; she pictured herself in a red cap, weeding the flowerbeds.

'Did you say anything to Franz?'

'No, not yet, but I'm off to see him right now.'

'Please, don't say anything. I just thought wildflowers would be nicer than peonies. I had to search all over the island for them. And look what I found!'

Bosse grunted.

'Fine then. They do look very nice. But next time —'

'There won't be a next time.'

She marched straight to Gardell's room and knocked softly at the door. No one answered; the room was empty. Someone, probably Anna, had already removed the roses from the vases.

She made the prettiest arrangements she could.

When she came back into the yard, Oswald was walking toward the annexe with a woman by his side. Sofia was hoping to sneak to her room unseen and deal with her frightful appearance, but Oswald was heading straight for her.

'Sofia, come say hello!'

Carmen Gardell's high heels made her almost as tall as Oswald. Her face was so heavily powdered it looked like a mask. Her big eyes made her look constantly surprised, and her eyelashes were so long they reached her eyebrows. Her lips were full and pouty, like a duck's bill. Her hair was curled and feathered and arranged in a chaos that somehow still seemed perfectly designed. The suit she was wearing clung to her narrow waist and her large bust.

To Sofia she seemed to reek of perfume, even out in the fresh air.

'Carmen, this is my secretary, Sofia.'

Sofia quickly shook hands and tried to hide her dirty skirt with her other hand.

'Pardon me. I was taking care of something out in the grounds. I don't usually look like this; I'll go change.'

'Oh, it doesn't matter,' Gardell said in a deep, hoarse voice that Sofia recognized immediately. She was clearly amused by the sight of Sofia.

'Of course you can go change,' Oswald said. 'I just wanted you to meet Carmen. She's going to get us some good press, you see. Take some nice pictures. You'll get to help.'

'Sure, that sounds fun.'

'I'm going to have dinner with Carmen now, but perhaps you can make sure all the staff come to the morning assembly so I can tell you all a little about her project and what will be expected.'

'I'll do that.' She wasn't sure if she should add a 'sir,' but decided against it. She wasn't sure it would sound right in front of Gardell.

Sofia hurried across the yard to her room, where she showered and changed her clothes. She knew Oswald would be with Carmen for the rest of the evening, which meant free time she could use to explore the attic and maybe even find the family history.

After she'd straightened up in the office and sorted the mail, she took the stairs up to the attic. First she glanced at the staff office, which seemed empty. The stairs wound up around a wide pillar and ended at an old wooden door. She pushed the handle down, but the door wouldn't open.

Then she noticed the hardware alongside it. Two big, brand new brass padlocks.

Now let's get back to the closet on the ferry.

It's pitch black inside, aside from a tiny streak of light at the bottom of the door.

It smells damp, like seaweed and Ajax. The first minutes are the longest — they're nearly unbearable.

Then I am outside my body for a while, and when I return it's all warm in the closet and time no longer exists.

I am weightless.

Then come the familiar sounds. Cars parking, passengers boarding, the chatter and the laughter — it all reaches me as I sit on my bucket in the dark.

The ferry is far from full; it's the low season. These are the usual commuters and villagers heading for the mainland to shop. And here I sit, surrounded by darkness and sour smells, feeling perfectly clear in the head.

Like a polished diamond, a crystal chandelier in evening light. I feel no fear, no anxiety; I'm not even the least bit tense.

The darkness has become my companion.

I follow the journey by the sounds, which help me see. The ferry's engine's steady rumbling in the bay, its hacks and coughs as we reach land.

The cars starting up, driving off the ferry. The dragging feet of the passengers; their dull voices.

I can even hear the murmurs of the harbour before we arrive. And when the last few steps have echoed from the gangway I open the door.

I sneak off the boat like a shadow and bend my head so no one sees — yes, I almost pray, before I vanish into the crowd of people on the quay. I move faster, jogging, cheering to myself.

I have been eradicated and have risen again, all in the same day.

20

'May I have access to the attic?'

'The attic? Why do you want to go up there?' Oswald looked like he couldn't believe his ears.

'I thought I could put some of Madde's things there so I have more space here.' She gestured at the shelf behind her, which was full of books and notepads.

'The attic is unusable, didn't you know that? No one has access to it.'

A question about the padlock was on the tip of her tongue: why had someone bothered to use a new lock there? But she swallowed it; she didn't want to disrupt his good mood. Morning assembly was in an hour and Oswald would be speaking to the staff. The two of them had just finished going through his mail, and she had printed out his schedule for the day.

'Just toss all that crap. Why should we keep Madde's stuff? If you find anything valuable you can put it in the basement.'

The basement. Perhaps that would have been a good hiding spot for the family history. Sofia decided to search there too. She was obsessed with the idea of finding it, sure it would be the key to her own book.

There was a knock at the door and Carmen Gardell stepped in without waiting for a response. Her skirt was so short it was a miracle her crotch remained covered as she sat down before Oswald. She rested her elbows on the desk and cradled her face in her hands. The scent of her perfume wafted through the office.

'We should get started today, Franz, don't you think?' Gardell flashed a coquettish smile at Oswald.

'Of course, I just have to prepare the staff. You're welcome to go to the annexes and have a coffee in the meantime. I'll meet you there.'

Gardell ran her hands through her mane of hair and licked her lips to moisten them.

Didn't Oswald realize she was hitting on him? It was so ridiculous that Sofia had to clamp her lower lip between her teeth to keep from laughing out loud. But it seemed to have no effect on Oswald, who remained polite but cool.

She's not his type. He is turned on by something completely different. What, I don't know.

'Has the staff gathered, Sofia?'

'Yes, sir.'

Sure enough, everyone was waiting in their lines down on the lawn. Three red caps were conspicuous in the back. Stefan from the household unit, the one who hadn't taken down the Midsummer pole, had joined Madeleine and Helge in Penance.

Sofia stood beside Oswald at assembly these days, always with a notepad and pen in hand. It felt strange to stand in front of the staff; it gave her a certain amount of authority. She could see their faces and reactions. Today they looked a little nervous, as they always did when something new was going on. Change could have an immediate effect on anyone — it might mean an 'all hands on deck' situation, where people were expected to leave their usual jobs and help out with something else, sometimes around the clock. Or Oswald might make known that someone had messed up, and if anyone tried to hide something the assembly might take a turn for the worse.

'We have one of Sweden's top PR experts here,' Oswald began. 'You are not to blow this opportunity the way you did with Magnus Strid. Carmen's going to take pictures of you as you work, and she'll interview you and put together a story and a brochure we can send out to the media.'

A wave of relief washed over the group. She was surprised how easily she could see and feel it. In an instant, the lines of worry on their faces smoothed out.

'You must look respectable. Please talk with her about all the positive aspects of ViaTerra. But avoid trying to explain the philosophical concepts. I'll do that myself. And I think those of you in Penance should remove your caps for a few days. Bosse, you can turn the dining room computer on again. Just for the time being.'

No one said a word, but she could see tiny smiles pop up here and there.

'Sofia will go around inspecting your work areas so everything looks nice. I'll be spending most of my time with Carmen and our guests. It's important for you all to get enough sleep, by the way. No sleepwalking, please.'

A threefold relief: sleep, computer access, and a little free time. At least for Sofia.

'And no swearing. Don't leave any junk in the courtyard. Be polite to our guests and try to avoid tripping over me and Carmen when we visit your areas. Just a few days, okay? I want you to do your very best. Questions?'

A single hand went up. It was Mona's.

'Does . . . *sir*, does this mean that the rules you read last week no longer apply?'

Oswald stiffened.

'Are you serious? Are you really that stupid?'

'No, sir, I just wondered . . .'

Oswald turned to Bosse.

'Bosse, did I say anything about the rules ending?'

Bosse shook his head; he looked like an eager schoolboy who knew the answer to a tricky question.

'Absolutely not, sir. Not at all.'

'Did I say *anything* about last week's rules?'

'No, sir. You did not.'

'Good. For a moment there I thought I was being forgetful.'

Someone tittered but quickly checked themselves.

'All I said was that you're expected to behave yourselves in the coming days, right?'

'Yes, sir!'

'You might want to test Mona's IQ and make sure she's actually qualified to work here.' He turned to Bosse, who nodded and glared at Mona. 'Then that's that. I'm sure I don't have to list the consequences you'll face if one of you screws up again.'

He left them and headed for the annexes. Sofia lingered behind.

A small group of colleagues had gathered around Mona while the rest remained in their lines, curious about what would happen next. Katarina and Anna were the first to attack Mona. Anna strode up and grabbed her arm, while Katarina stood before Mona, who stared down at the gravel.

'Are you really that slow?'

'Do you want to ruin things for all of us, you bitch?' Katarina asked, giving Mona a little shove in the chest.

Mona didn't even try to defend herself; she just kept staring at the ground. Sofia felt a jolt of pity. She was also worried about losing Mona to Penance — that would mean an unstaffed library.

'Let her be!' she roared. 'Bosse's going to test her IQ. Didn't you hear Franz?'

Anna and Katarina were startled out of their attack. Katarina was about to open her mouth again, but Sofia interrupted her.

'That's all. You can all get back to work now.'

A pleasant mixture of warmth and strength spread throughout her. *This is what it feels like to have power,* she thought. *I work for Oswald and no one can say a damn thing, because he's not here and I'm in charge.*

The staff scattered and soon only she and Bosse were left in the yard.

'Do you *have* any IQ tests?' she asked.

'I don't know. If we don't, we'll find some online. We'll manage.'

She spent the hours before lunch walking around the property finding out how the projects Oswald wanted done were progressing. She took notes and spoke to the staff. Back in the office she turned her notes into a checklist on the computer. Her feet were sore, but her realization was still intoxicating. Being Oswald's stand-in meant sharing in some of his power.

★

'That was quite a performance at assembly,' Benjamin said when she came home that night.

'A performance? They were going after her; it was nuts!'

'Right. You restored order.'

202

She couldn't keep herself from telling him about the cottage and Karin Johansson. She just had to talk to someone, because she was so excited about all of it — the family history, the history of the manor, and the thought of writing a book — she thought she might burst.

But the more she shared with Benjamin, the more upset he looked.

'What's wrong?' she asked at last.

'I don't want you going to the cottage anymore, Sofia. You have to stop snooping.'

'But why? What's wrong with you?'

'That has nothing to do with ViaTerra. You'll only get distracted. Don't you realize how important your job is?'

She was immediately annoyed. Like he was the boss of her. As if his role in the ethics unit meant he had the power to keep her under control. She said the first hurtful thing that came to mind.

'Do you think I'm going to work here forever? That this is some sort of lifelong assignment?'

'It is, Sofia. And you're breaking all the rules right now.'

'I'm so damn tired of your negative attitude. God forbid you do something that's against Franz's stupid rules for once.'

They fought long into the night. Even after they finally made up the air seemed to tremble with spitefulness, and she couldn't fall asleep. She didn't understand him. How could he have turned from the best guy in the world into a whiny, nagging idiot?

He dozed off before she did. She laid her head on his chest and found that his heart was still beating fast and hard. He was upset even in sleep. *In a way, he's right*, she thought. *I can't dig through all of this and do my job at the same time, yet I can't just let it go.*

The fight had left a bitter taste in her mouth, and it was still there when she woke up in the morning. But it vanished quickly after that, because everyone seemed so happy out on the property. Anna had cleaned the annexes so that every surface gleamed. Katarina waved from the flowerbeds, where she was watering new plants. Even Simon in the greenhouse looked freshly shaven and alert, and the new security guards had received their uniforms.

Everything she'd requested had been done. And when Carmen Gardell walked by and flashed her that perfect, snow-white smile and said, 'Thanks for your help,' she felt truly valuable.

Who am I, really? It's become a constant question during my journey. I think about it as I gaze out of dirty train windows, wander unfamiliar streets, and rest at night with only the sky above me.

Fredrik Johansson is dead and probably already buried. So who has risen again; who is leading this search for truth?

There's something magical about having no name or identity, like finding yourself in the thin mist between dream and reality.

The feelings from my dream linger, but real life slowly becomes sharp and clear.

I know where I'm going and who I'm looking for. But I don't know who I will become.

Right before I leave Sweden, I happen across the article.

I'm standing in a dusty little convenience store, flicking through the daily papers — it's become something of a morning routine. And suddenly, as I turn a page, the little story turns up.

'Tragedy on West Fog Island,' it says.

I read it, feeling strangely pleased; the article is short and insignificant. It says I hit my head on the underwater boulders at Devil's Rock and was pulled out to sea. They are incompetent idiots. Those rocks are way too deep down; you can't hit your head below that cliff.

It's almost too good to be true.

Fredrik Johansson isn't just gone, he has been completely erased.

21

The pager vibrated stubbornly in the dark.

At first she thought it was just Benjamin snoring, but then she turned on the light and saw the little gadget dancing all over the nightstand. They'd only been sleeping for a few hours. Her whole body was heavy and limp; it didn't want to give in to the unpleasant racket. Benjamin groaned and pulled the covers over his head. She grabbed the pager and read the illuminated message.

To the office immediately, bring Benjamin.

All at once she was wide awake; something wasn't right.

Why both of them, and why in the middle of the night? It must have something to do with their relationship.

Her stomach knotted. She sat up and poked at Benjamin.

'Oswald wants to see us. Right away.'

'What? You mean you, right? Not me.'

'No, both of us.'

Benjamin sat up in bed, also fully awake.

'Shit! What could it be?'

'No idea, but we'd better hurry.'

They didn't bother with their uniforms and pulled on jeans and T-shirts instead. She racked her brains on the way up but couldn't think of anything she and Benjamin had done that was against the rules.

They dashed up the stairs and were out of breath when they reached Oswald's door. Sofia gestured at Benjamin — *wait a minute*. Oswald didn't like when people came into his office still panting.

There was a glow at the bottom of the door. It was past three a.m. and this didn't feel right at all.

★

Oswald had changed after Strid's article, had become tougher. Sofia realized he was putting on a pleasant face for Gardell, but that he was furious about the article; he took some of that fury out on her. He was always looking for a reason to carp at her, and his whole nature had grown harder and more stubborn.

He had started touching her again, but there was no gentleness left in it. There had once been a tenderness to it, like when you can't help touching a beautiful flower. These days it only felt vulgar. But it didn't matter; her body still responded compulsively, as if he were striking a match.

One day when he was more annoyed than usual, he had crossed a line. Yet she hadn't said a word. She realized that she had become afraid of him. He had spent that day insisting on her attention, asking her to perform tiny, silly tasks in the office. The sorts of things he certainly could have done on his own. He had also spoken so softly and quickly that she kept having to ask him to repeat himself, which annoyed him even more.

For a short time, she was absorbed in a text that needed editing and hadn't noticed his eyes on her. He stood up, walked over to her, sat down, and folded his long legs under her little desk. She didn't dare look at him.

Suddenly she found her thighs clamped between his own. He squeezed them so hard she let out a small groan. For an instant, it was dead silent.

She looked up and he slowly released her legs.

'Do I have your complete attention now?'

She nodded. The air had rushed out of her lungs.

'Good. You must become more intuitive, Sofia. Sense when I need something, so I don't have to nag.'

'Of course.'

Then he went back to normal, like nothing had happened. And that was the worst part — those abrupt endings. As if he was getting worked up about something else, something she didn't quite understand.

★

Now they were standing outside his door at three in the morning, and Sofia did not have a good feeling about it.

She knocked cautiously, then opened the door. They stood in the doorway for a moment, waiting. Oswald was bent over a document on his desk. When he looked up, he looked tired and rather worn out.

'Come in and have a seat.'

They gingerly sat down in front of the desk.

Oswald stared at Benjamin first, until Benjamin looked away.

'I want you to find a hiding spot for the theses,' Oswald said at last.

Benjamin raised his eyebrows as he always did when he was mildly confused.

'There's been talk of a police raid. But we have friends high

208

up in law enforcement, so I'm sure nothing will come of it. At the same time, you can never be too safe.'

Sofia tried to think of a reason why the police would raid the manor in the first place. And how Oswald could know about that sort of police business.

'No one must get their hands on the theses,' he went on. 'We will delete them from the computers and print them out on paper instead. Bosse will have to set up a system so guests hand them back once they've read them. There will not be any copies. I hope the guests were never allowed to keep them . . .' He was talking to himself. 'But we still have to find a hiding spot. Somewhere on the island. Not on the property. We need to write them down on paper that can handle being stored outdoors. What do you think, Benjamin?'

She wondered why Benjamin was there instead of Bosse, and assumed it must be because he knew the island so well.

'Maybe the cave?' Benjamin said, then gasped as if to pull his words back in.

Oswald raised his eyebrows.

'What cave?'

Benjamin squirmed anxiously in his chair.

'None in particular. I thought maybe we could find some cave here on the island; I heard there are some around.'

'That's a horrible idea. Think of all the storms and moisture and everything.'

Sofia was about to point out that the theses would be safe in *that* cave, but Benjamin gave her a look of warning and she closed her mouth again.

'Oh well, that will be your project, Benjamin. Find the perfect hiding spot. And not a word to anyone else. Understood?'

'Yes, sir. I'll take care of it.'

'Good, you can go. But Sofia, you stay here.'

Benjamin left the room. Oswald bent forward. He held her gaze for a long time, but she didn't look away.

'You haven't found the leak yet, have you?'

'No. Bosse has interviewed the whole staff. He really grilled them, but no one confessed. We've even promised to be lenient if they do confess.'

'I thought as much. I think we have an infiltrator, Sofia.'

'A spy?'

'Right. Someone who was sent here by the press to report on us. Someone who wants to make my life hell. We have to rethink everything when it comes to security around here.'

'Of course, what can I do?'

'First I want Tom to taste my food before he serves it to me. You must be there to watch. Just go down to the kitchen. And make sure he always uses fresh goods and doesn't take shortcuts when he's preparing my meals.'

Tom was Oswald's personal chef; he made meals and snacks just for Oswald.

'Sir, surely you don't think he's trying to poison you?'

'Don't be so naïve, Sofia. He arrived on the island just about when our problems began. I just want to be sure. The kitchen is full of idiots I don't trust.'

'Okay. I mean, I'll take care of it.'

She was beginning to feel uneasy. There was something creepy about all of this. The theses and the food. The idea that someone had it in for him.

'Then I want you to get lids and straws for my glasses. You can order them from the mainland, those little paper lids that protect your beverage from germs, dirt, flies, and things like that.'

And poison, she thought, but she just nodded.

He thought for a moment, gazing out the window at the darkness. She didn't want to disturb him, so she waited until he turned toward her again.

'Was there anything else?'

'Yes, one more thing. Talk to Bosse tomorrow and make sure all the rules I wrote down a few weeks ago are still in force. People on Penance need to wear their caps and the computer should be turned off. Everything we discussed.'

'Yes, sir.'

Why this, all of a sudden? Carmen Gardell had left the island a few weeks ago, noticeably disappointed that she hadn't got Oswald into bed. But she had worked hard, interviewing and photographing the staff, all dressed up and wearing makeup, and she promised to put together a lovely brochure for them.

But Oswald was nervous. Really nervous.

'You can go now. See you tomorrow.'

As she left the room, he was staring out the window again, deep in thought.

★

Benjamin was sitting on the bed and waiting for her. He looked concerned and a little pale underneath his tan.

'Sofia, you must never say a word about the cave.'

'Wait a second. You're the one who mentioned the cave, not me.'

'It just slipped out. It was stupid of me. Please, never talk to Franz or anyone else about that cave, promise me.'

'Why are you acting so weird? What is so secret about that cave?'

'It's my hiding spot. I want to keep it for myself.'

'Are you nuts? It's just a cave!' Her voice had risen half an octave, and this would turn into a fight again if she didn't check herself. They'd been arguing a lot in recent days, but she wasn't sure why. There really wasn't anything to disagree about. All they did was eat, sleep, and work, yet they were always on each other's nerves.

Her whole body ached with exhaustion. She couldn't remember the last time she'd gotten a full night's sleep. Her head was heavy and her eyes burned.

Maybe that's why we fight so much, she thought. *We're so tired and irritated that we just snap at each other.*

She didn't even have the energy to hang up her clothes, so she tossed them on the floor and crawled under the blankets. Benjamin's back was to her; he was already breathing heavily.

The cool pillow felt nice against her cheek. She knew it would only take a few seconds for her to fall asleep. But just as she was dozing off, her pager vibrated again.

To the office. Just you.

'I have to go back to the office,' she said, but Benjamin was already asleep. She turned on the bedside lamp, pulled on her clothes, and looked in the mirror, which showed her a pale face with sunken eyes.

★

Oswald was in the same position as when she'd left him.

'One more thing, Sofia. You'd better sit down.'

She slowly sank into the chair in front of him, afraid of what was coming.

'I want cameras installed in every room and office. Surveillance cameras. The kind no one can see. I think that's the only way to catch the infiltrator. I've contacted a security company, and they'll be here the day after tomorrow. I want you to help me when they get here.'

'All the rooms?'

'Right. The panel of screens will be here in the office. No one must know, not even Bosse and his idiots. I think we'll send the whole staff out to pick blueberries in the forest while we do it. Are blueberries ripe right now?'

She nodded even though she had no idea. She still wasn't sure she'd heard correctly.

'So you want cameras in every room, even the bedrooms?'

'Yes, what did you think I meant?' he snapped. 'Do you think this bastard sends in his reports in front of the whole staff?'

She wanted to ask if cameras were truly necessary. Or even legal. She didn't think they were, but what would be the point in asking? He would only find someone else to help him, and send her to Penance.

'A gang of technicians will come by to set it up. I'll take care of the main building and you can be in charge of the annexes and the classrooms. Maybe the basement too. Can just anyone go down there?'

'Yes, I think so.'

'Good. Then that's settled. And we don't need cameras in the guests' rooms, just the dining room, the staff work areas, and the classroom. That way we can keep an eye on them while they're doing the theses. That's all we're interested in.'

'What do we say if the guests ask what we're doing?'

Oswald grinned, looking satisfied.

'I've already thought of that. An obligatory study day in the dining room for all the guests: they'll be reading a new, ground-breaking briefing I wrote. Hurtig will be there and Anna will prepare sandwiches before she leaves the grounds. But they don't know about any of this. Only you and I know about the cameras. Understood?'

Sofia nodded.

He stood up and opened the cabinet on the wall, where all the keys to the estate hung. He took down a fat key ring and handed it to her.

'These are the keys to all the buildings outside the manor house. It's best I give them to you now so I don't forget. I'll talk to Bosse about the blueberry picking. Go to bed now, it's late.'

Just as she was about to open the door, he said, 'If you tell anyone about this, and that means Benjamin too, you'll spend the rest of your life mucking-out cow shit in the barn.'

She nodded without even turning back around.

Slowly she went back down the stairs.

Her room was pitch black, and Benjamin was snoring loudly. It seemed to her that this all had to be a mistake. That Oswald would realize he had overreacted and would change his mind.

But then a faint ray of light appeared in her tired mind.

The key cabinet. She knew the keys to the attic had to be there. She just knew it.

The villa sits in a little hollow, a valley among the sloping rocks that face the sea.

It's enclosed by a substantial wall, but from the top of the slope I can see everything. The perfect lawn. The neat flowerbeds. The pool. The shaggy little dog who always pees on their lounge chairs.

The housemaid and the gardener and the little kid who runs around in a swimsuit, shrieking.

This is the second day I've spent sitting here, and I am restless and impatient.

But I can't go down yet. I have to be sure he's home first.

And it won't hurt for me to have slept outside a few days, because it can only be a good thing if I look ragged. My appearance in their life should be dramatic.

A silver Mercedes glides up the winding roads to the house.

Right away I know it's him.

The iron gate opens, and the brat stops playing and runs up to the car.

Hatred for the man burns inside me even before he has stepped out of the vehicle.

Here he is, living in the lap of luxury as though nothing ever happened.

But soon, everything will change.

For some, punishment is immediate. For others, fate strikes back when they least expect it.

As the red sun takes its last trembling breath on the horizon, I rise and walk down the incline.

It is time.

22

A burst of stale, stuffy air greeted her when she opened the door to the basement. She turned on the light, which barely illuminated the steep staircase. The walls were covered in dirt and spiders' webs, and it didn't improve much as she reached the basement itself. She had expected a large room full of junk, but someone must have cleaned it out when the group moved in. All that was left now was the staff's belongings, everything that didn't fit in their rooms. All their things — clothing and various items of furniture — had simply been deposited willy-nilly on the floor. A sheet of paper with the name of the owner lay before each pile. It looked a mess. What was more, it all smelled mouldy.

There was no family history down here; she was sure of it. But she had to keep Oswald from discovering this mess. He would be furious, and it would surely lead to another renovation project with the whole staff working day and night. She had to talk to Bosse and arrange for boxes and storage, then get everyone to clean up their own property. Until then, it was probably best to keep the basement locked.

On her way back up the stairs, she thought about what she would tell Oswald. She couldn't let this turn into one of those days when he ended up in a rage and they had to work all night.

Today was the eighth of August — her birthday. Birthdays

weren't celebrated at ViaTerra. The kitchen staff would bake a little cake you could have at dinner, with a candle in it. That was the extent of it. And you certainly didn't get a cake if you were in Penance.

She supposed her parents would try to call to wish her a happy birthday. They would try her cell phone first, and when she didn't answer that they would call the phone at the sentry box. She wondered what the guard would say. Probably that she was unavailable. Maybe Oswald would let her ring them up for a quick chat. As long as he was in a good mood. A very good mood.

She turned out the basement light as she left, and just as she was about to take the stairs up to the office she heard sounds from one of the other rooms. Muffled sobs. She followed the sounds and found herself at an open door at the end of the corridor. Mona was lying on one of the bottom bunks in the dormitory, crying piteously.

'Mona, what's wrong? What are you doing here?'

'You can send me to Penance. I don't care.'

Sofia sat on the edge of the bed.

'Tell me what's going on.'

'I'm so tired. I can't even think anymore. I can't handle these working hours and I'm worried about Elvira.'

Sofia hadn't talked to Elvira recently. The last time they saw each other, the girl had been working in the kitchen, looking happy, healthy, and lovely as always.

'Is something wrong with Elvira?'

'No, it's just that she's fourteen and she's supposed to be in school.'

Sofia took Mona's limp hand.

'Listen, we can fix this. It will get better. Sometimes when you haven't been sleeping, everything seems hopeless. Just stay in bed until you feel rested. I'll tell Bosse you have a fever.'

'You're so nice.'

'Hardly, but I want you to stay in the library.'

Mona laughed and snuffled. Her eyes were lined with red and sunken into deep, dark shadows. Sofia thought no one who worked at ViaTerra should look like that.

She mulled things over on the way to the office. There was no longer any work schedule for the staff. Everything Oswald wanted done had to be done 'tonight,' 'before the end of the day,' or 'before you go to bed,' so everyone just kept working until the task was finished. If there wasn't enough manpower in your own unit, you just borrowed from another. Mona was constantly being loaned out. After all, guests never visited the library at night. And now the whole staff was suffering from exhaustion.

Sofia decided to bring it up with Oswald. Maybe he didn't know how little sleep they got — he himself never showed up before late morning.

He looked up as she stepped through the office door.

'So how did the basement look?'

'Oh, it needs some cleaning, but we don't need any cameras down there. It's just the staff's extra belongings. We can put a padlock on the door.'

'Great. I have some good news.'

Thank god. He's changed his mind. No surveillance cameras.

'The security company will arrive after lunch. And the whole crew is already gathering in the yard for blueberry picking. I even got Bosse to arrange for caps so they look like a real team. See how funny they look?'

She went to the window and looked down at the yard. The

entire staff was lined up, wearing blue caps and carrying blueberry rakes and buckets. She noticed Benjamin, who was standing very straight like a soldier heading to battle. The whole scene really did look comical. She held back a giggle, but she felt a pang in her heart — they all looked so clueless.

She put on her most sincere face and turned to Oswald.

'Sir, there's something I want to talk about.'

'Out with it.'

'I found Mona in her room. She's sick with a fever. I understand she's been working almost without sleep for several weeks. I thought it might be a good idea to come up with a work schedule for the staff.'

Oswald considered this for a moment. Those little wrinkles appeared on his forehead.

'Lack of sleep doesn't make people sick, Sofia. Viruses do. When you're running a business, you can never put your staff first. If you do, it will all go to hell. Someone has to think first and foremost of the operation. That's especially true at ViaTerra. Do you have any other solution to all the misery in the world?' He was annoyed.

'No, of course not.'

'But you're right about one thing. I don't want a bunch of epidemics around here. We have to find a spot to isolate the sick. What do you think about the basement? Could we fit a few beds down there?'

'Maybe. But it's dark and kind of damp in there.'

She avoided mentioning the mouldy smell. If he heard about that he would hit the roof, and go take a look, and then her chances of calling home would be zero.

'Oh, a little moisture won't kill anyone. Being sick isn't meant to be comfortable. Talk to Bosse. The two of you have to work it out before the fall bugs start going around.'

'Okay, we will.'

'What about Mona?'

'Mona?'

'Yes, you told her she had to go berry-picking too, right?'

'No, I thought . . . with her fever and everything . . .'

'What is wrong with you? Is she supposed to stay in her room while the security company installs the cameras?'

'No, I forgot . . . I mean, I wasn't thinking . . .'

'That much is clear. Unless she has a fever of like 40 degrees, she's going with everyone else.'

'I'll fix it.'

It felt like she was betraying Mona, but that didn't stop her from sending a message to Bosse's pager asking him to fetch Mona for their outing.

'Bosse will deal with it.'

'Good. And please, don't touch anything in here until you've washed your hands. I don't want to get whatever it is Mona has.'

She obediently headed for the bathroom to wash her hands.

'If you're worried about the schedule, bring it up with Bosse. Of course the staff can sleep. As long as they finish what I ask of them first,' he said to her back.

She sat on the toilet lid for a moment, steaming. What a fucking birthday. And it probably wasn't going to get much better.

★

A little while later she watched as the staff marched out of the yard in the direction of the woods. They were still in neat lines. Their caps slowly shrank into tiny blue dots in the distance.

The security company showed up soon after. Five young, talkative guys installed the cameras.

'This is the best system there is,' one of them assured them. 'The cameras are so small they fit in the air vents. It's almost impossible to see them. You can turn them on and off with a remote control within a radius of three hundred metres. Incredible, isn't it?'

Oswald nodded. He had grown increasingly exhilarated as the installation progressed. By the time everything was finished and the technicians showed him the control panel full of screens, he was so worked up he couldn't stand still. He paced back and forth, rubbing his hands.

He had sent Sofia out to oversee the installation in the classrooms, the personal advising rooms, and the work areas out on the property. He had stayed behind in the manor house.

She'd stopped to peek in the dining room, where the guests were reading Oswald's briefing. They were deeply absorbed in the material, perfectly unaware of what was going on throughout the estate. Olof Hurtig had nodded at her as if to signal that everything was under control.

When she returned, Oswald was testing out the system. He laughed and joked with the technicians.

'Hi there, I have a little birthday present for you,' he said when he spotted her.

Her heart skipped a beat. He knew it was her birthday. Maybe he would let her call her parents after all.

'There won't be a camera in your bedroom,' he said. 'You're the only one to be spared. So you and Benjamin can do whatever you want at night.'

He gave a loud guffaw. The technicians joined him in his roar of laughter.

★

Oswald's enthusiasm about the new system lasted all day. When the staff came back, their buckets full of blueberries, he didn't even hear their eager voices from the yard. He was entranced by the screens and buttons.

'Listen, I think we should include Bosse in all this. You're hardly going to have time to use the system, are you?'

She nodded in relief; the last thing she wanted to do was sit around spying on the staff.

'Tell him to come up here after dinner.'

Bosse shared Oswald's enthusiasm for the system from the start. They were like little boys on Christmas Eve, all shining eyes and rosy cheeks. They stared at the screens long into the night while she worked at her own little desk. It was getting too late to call home.

She was frustrated and ready to cry.

'Look at this, Bosse!' Oswald cried.

She sneaked a peek. The screen showed Eskil, who took care of the animals. He was in bed, and there could be no doubt that he was jerking off under the covers. The volume was up so high that Eskil's groans echoed off the walls. Oswald began to giggle. She'd never heard him giggle before. Bosse was bent almost double in laughter. Sofia shook her head and gave Bosse a pointed look. Just then, Oswald got hold of himself and turned off the screen.

'Seriously, though, Bosse. I want you to be in charge of surveillance. The idea is to keep all areas under watch. Regularly.

Eventually we will find that damned mole. He'll have hidden a phone or laptop. And he'll be texting or emailing from places where he thinks no one can see. Got it?'

Bosse nodded eagerly and gazed admiringly at Oswald, who turned off the surveillance system, stood up, and yawned loudly.

'I think I'll head to bed. What a day! Sofia, clean up here and then you can go to bed too.'

He left the office so quickly she didn't get a chance to ask about the phone call. Now she was sure it was the worst birthday she'd ever had.

Then she thought of the laptop in her bedroom. She decided to at least send an email to her parents. She couldn't use the desktop computer; all the outgoing email was censored by Bosse. She didn't even dare to think about using Oswald's computer, which was the only exception.

Benjamin wasn't in their room when she arrived. She took the laptop from the drawer as it was, wrapped in the sheet, and dashed up the stairs with the bundle in her arms. If anyone asked she could say that they were installing new electronics in the office, which certainly wouldn't be a lie. Curious eyes stared at her here and there, but no one said anything.

She plugged the charger into the wall outlet behind the desk, so nervous that her fingers trembled as she logged in; she was thinking of what Oswald had said about the traitor, how he would have a computer or phone hidden. She thought about locking the office but worried that Oswald might come back.

The login took forever; she hadn't used the laptop for so long that the screen was full of irritating pop-up notices.

When she finally accessed her email, she found a new message from her parents. They had called, but the guard who answered had told them she was busy.

She wrote and wrote: she was fine but missed them. Yes, her birthday had been nice. She had been celebrated and received presents and everything.

Her fingers flew over the keyboard. Her anxiety grew and grew, driving her on. Just as she clicked 'send', she heard a noise: the familiar creak as the door opened. She inwardly let out a long string of curse words, but there was nothing she could do. No chance of hiding the laptop.

And there he stood in the doorway. Not Oswald but Benjamin. Darling, wonderful Benjamin. She had never been so happy to see him, yet the tears came pouring forth. The dam holding back all the day's frustrations burst, and she sat there crying until her tears splashed onto the keyboard.

Benjamin looked at her in horror.

'Sofia, what's wrong? What happened?'

Now she noticed that he was holding a bouquet of flowers, drooping willowherb he must have picked on the blueberry outing. But still.

He came over to embrace her.

'I just came to get you. Happy birthday!'

Only then did he notice the laptop.

'Did you get an extra computer?'

She shook her head and told him about the secret in her dresser drawer.

'It's been like one last connection with the world, you know, so Mom and Dad don't start to worry.'

Benjamin looked at her for a moment and laughed.

'You're too damn funny.'

'So what do we do? About the laptop, I mean.'

'We'll keep it in the dresser,' he said. 'It might come in handy.'

They went to the yard to unwind for a bit before they went to bed. There was still a bit of light in the sky, and the dew had begun to gather. The air was cool and a little raw. It would soon be autumn. She didn't even want to think about it. The storms, the wind, the thunder, and that thick fog. Autumn on the island didn't feel even the slightest bit exciting anymore.

'It will get better,' Benjamin said, pulling her closer.

'Are you reading my mind?'

'No, but I think everyone is feeling the same right now. It started with that bloody newspaper article. We've been making no progress since then. But we have to remember why we're here. That ViaTerra is the way out.'

'Benjamin, I don't think I can handle another autumn and winter out here. Not if things keep on the way they have been.'

'It will get better,' he said firmly. 'At least it can't get any worse, right?'

The guard in the sentry box at the gate looks at me like I'm an alien. They've even made him wear some sort of uniform, a black blazer and tie.

The iron gate is massive and the wall is higher than it looked from above. This place isn't easy to get into. I wonder what the old man is so scared of, why he has to hide away like this.

But he's filthy rich, of course, and probably wants to feel secure here among all the snobs of the Riviera.

'What do you want?' the guard asks. In French, naturally.

But I understand. I've already begun to pick up the language.

'I want you to tell Henrik I'm here,' I respond in English.

'And who are you?' he asks, still in French.

He looks like he can't believe his eyes. A dirty, long-haired teenager wants to talk to the Count? His tiny brain simply can't put it together.

'Fredrik from Fog Island.' I hate that I have to use my old name, but it can't be helped. 'You can tell him that Fredrik from Fog Island is here and wants to see him,' I say.

He nods, then picks up the phone and pushes a button.

There is a lengthy silence. At first I think he's going to hang up and pretend the Count isn't home, but then he starts babbling in French. He sounds servile and apologetic.

Then he doesn't say anything for a long time and glances up at me, uneasy. He slowly puts down the receiver.

'He's on his way,' he says at last.

23

'Sofia, come look at this!'

She was at her desk, waiting to go to bed, exhausted as usual. But Oswald was watching the surveillance screens again.

'Just look at what the staff gets up to while I'm working my ass off.' He pointed at one screen: Katarina was lying in bed and reading a book.

'She's lying there reading some trashy novel like she's on vacation.'

He switched the picture to show a couple of girls sitting on the floor and chatting in a dormitory room. Oswald zoomed in on Corinne from the household unit; she was eating a sandwich.

'Look at this fucking feast! She stole that from the kitchen, of course.'

Sofia couldn't quite grasp the gravity of all this, and Oswald noticed her hesitation.

'Don't you get it? I work like a dog day and night. Trying to handle the media. Repairing our image. And the staff just laze around. As if everything's just fine.'

'Of course, sir. It's totally wrong.'

But he was wound up and didn't feel validated at all by her comment.

'No, it's not *wrong*. It's all gone to shit. This is treason. Are you that slow today? Do you think this fatty understands how important it is for us to spread ViaTerra's message? No, she's just sitting there enjoying her sandwich.'

Sofia knew nothing she said would make any difference, so she just nodded and tried to look concerned. Sometimes when he got really angry his eyes grew cloudy and his rage transformed into tiny arrows that flew through the air to strike her. There was no defending herself. She just had to sit there and take it.

'Go get Bosse and his crew of idiots. Benny, Sten, and the new guards. All of them. Make it quick!'

She ran down the stairs and found Bosse and his henchmen straight off, in the staff office. They were sitting around a table covered with cell phones.

'What are you doing?'

Bosse looked up at her, preoccupied.

'Going through the staff's phones to look for suspicious texts. That's how we'll find the mole.'

Shit. She thought of all the forbidden texts she'd sent out.

'Franz wants to see all of you. Now!'

She put a little extra authority and strength in her voice. Bosse was startled and stood up.

'Of course. We'll get back to this later, guys.'

They didn't even notice when Sofia hung back in the room. When the last man was out of sight, she searched the pile and found her own iPhone. It had a little post-it note with her name on it. She sent up a silent prayer that it still had some battery and breathed a sigh of relief when the screen lit up. Then she deleted every text on it, put it back in the pile, and ran as fast as she could to the office. The men were lined up before Oswald's desk.

'Where have you been?' he asked, irritated.

'Someone had left some personnel folders out. I took care of it. Sorry to make you wait.'

'Good thing you handled it,' Oswald said, content with the explanation.

Bosse shot her a look of alarm, but she just raised her eyebrows.

'Men, we need to get a handle on all the laziness and indolence in this group,' Oswald said. 'Right now, I am the only one getting anything done — and maybe Sofia too. Everyone else is walking around like zombies when they're not sitting around daydreaming. Understand?'

'Yes, sir.'

'I want you to bring me suggestions of punishments to be used when someone messes up. We don't have to call them punishments . . . consequences, maybe. After all, there should be consequences when people don't perform their jobs properly, shouldn't there?'

'Are you thinking of someone in particular who's messed up?' Bosse asked, curious.

Oswald shook his head angrily.

'You don't get it. Half the staff is walking around in a daze. Not a single one of those bastards has any motivation. We have the solutions to all the world's problems, but why should they care? You should just see what they get up to at night.'

Bosse swallowed and nodded.

'I want your suggestions before you go to bed.'

He turned to Sofia.

'I want you to find out what book Katarina was reading.'

'Now?'

'Yes, now!'

She went to the second floor and knocked at Katarina's door. A moment went by before the door opened, but Katarina didn't look at all tired. *She probably couldn't tear herself away from her book*, Sofia thought in irritation.

'Katarina, I have to make sure all the windows are closed and secured. Franz asked me to.'

'The windows? Why?'

'No idea. Is Bengt asleep?'

Bengt was Katarina's husband, and indeed he was asleep, splayed out on his back with his mouth open, snoring gently. The book was on Katarina's side of the bed, but it was too dark in the room to make out the title.

Sofia approached the window and pretended to check it.

'What are you reading?'

Katarina immediately looked ashamed. Before she could respond, Sofia went to the bed and picked up the book. It was a Harlequin romance, *The Elasticity of Love* by Myra Loft. The cover showed a woman gazing out at the sea, her long hair waving in the breeze.

'There are better love stories in the library,' Sofia said. 'If you're interested, I mean.'

Katarina flushed. 'Okay, I'll check it out sometime. I just grabbed this one in the village when I was buying plants.'

*

Oswald looked at her expectantly when she returned.

'You were right. It was a Harlequin romance.'

'Like I said! She didn't get it from the library, did she?'

'Definitely not. We don't have that sort of book there. She said she bought it in the village while she was shopping.'

'Well, there you go! I thought Benjamin was going to take

care of all the shopping, and I haven't given her permission to leave the property. This just gets worse and worse. It's insane, it's like we're running a nursery! No wonder we're treading water around here.' Just then, Bosse and his gang returned, looking eager and a little self-important. Bosse proudly handed a piece of paper to Oswald.

'Here are the Consequences.'

Oswald gazed at the document for a long time. That wrinkle of annoyance appeared on his forehead. Then he looked out the window for a moment, shaking his head.

'Fantastic. Really terrific, Bosse. You've outdone yourself.'

Then he read aloud, imitating Bosse's southern–Swedish accent.

"One: Reprimand. If a staff member is found to be uneffective or makes repeated mistakes, he or she will be given a warning. Two: After three warnings, the staff member in question will forfeit a week's pay."

Oswald laughed.

'Uneffective? That's not even a word. Help, I'm shaking in my boots! I can only mess up three times or I'll be out five hundred kronor! Ohhh, it burns!'

He ripped the paper into little strips and turned on his Dictaphone. He spoke into it clearly and with no hesitation. He paused between each point to stare at Bosse, who by now looked like a scolded puppy.

'One. Laziness and lack of productivity: the guilty party shall complete a compensatory project that requires at least ten hours of extra work, beyond the usual working hours.

'Two. Repeated failure: rice and beans for two weeks, with no access to the kiosk; meal breaks shortened to fifteen minutes.

'Three. Treachery, disloyalty, betrayal, and lying: the guilty party shall jump from Devil's Rock in front of the entire staff, in the hope that he or she will realize the consequences of his or her behaviour. If this has no impact on behaviour, he or she will be dismissed and sent back to the mainland.

'Four. In special cases, when the person in question shows remorse and regret, he or she may be allowed to undergo Penance.'

He thought for a moment. It was dead silent in the room; the only sound was his fingertips drumming against the desk. Then he spoke again.

'Jumping from Devil's Rock will occur in full uniform, and the head of ethics will recite the following to the guilty party before he or she jumps: "May you leave your betrayal in the depths and rise to the surface pure and full of devotion."'

He turned off the Dictaphone and nodded in satisfaction.

Benny was the first to speak. He typically remained silent during meetings and assemblies, but something was weighing so heavily on him now that he dared to open his mouth.

'Sir, I thought people could die jumping from Devil's Rock.'

Oswald burst out laughing.

'Have you been listening to the old gossips in the village? I can't believe my ears. No, it really isn't dangerous. As long as you can swim.'

Then came another peal of laughter. *He almost seems a little crazy*, Sofia thought. The thought was unwelcome; she knew he was doing all of this for the good of the group. That glow in his eyes had to be devotion, not madness.

Maybe I need to do some soul-searching, she thought. *Come up with things I've done that go against the group.* She thought of her laptop and cell phone, and it was as if the mouldy smell from the

233

basement floated by as she stood there. But then Oswald's voice brought her back to the office.

'I believe I've found our first candidate for Devil's Rock. Katarina. She's lying around reading trashy books this minute, while we work. And as if that isn't enough, she buys them in the village during working hours. No wonder the yard looks like shit.'

Bosse gasped and Sten let out a horrified moan.

'She will jump tomorrow morning, after assembly. The whole staff must be there, except for those who serve breakfast for the guests. I'll be there, believe me. I don't want to miss this.'

★

They walked across the heath in two straight lines. Katarina and Bosse were in the lead; Oswald was off to the side a little way. The fog was thick and the ground was so dewy that shoes and trouser legs were soaked through. They walked slowly, as if on a death march. Everyone was looking toward the sea, serious and solemn.

The whole coast was wrapped up in fog. There was no horizon, only the blanket of fog and the black water.

Katarina's face was tight and grim. She was scared; Sofia could see and feel her fright.

When they arrived at the grassy slope that abutted Devil's Rock, Bosse and Katarina took off their shoes before climbing down to the rock cliff. They stood at the edge and waited for a signal from Oswald.

Katarina's head was drooping like a wilted flower. Sofia could tell she was crying; her back was trembling. Bosse grabbed her shoulders and straightened her up.

Oswald nodded at Bosse, and everyone listened breathlessly

as Bosse read from the notes he had taken from his pocket: 'May you leave your betrayal in the depths and rise to the surface pure and full of devotion.'

Katarina nodded. She hesitated, gazing down at the dark water that was as still as a black mirror below the cliff. Then she jumped, her back straight and her hands at her sides. The splash when her body hit the surface was muted by the fog and died out so quickly that it hardly reached their ears.

All eyes were drawn to the rings on the water where she had gone under. Then she popped up, sucked in air, and gasped for breath with wide eyes.

She swam to the rocks and pulled herself up. Her wet uniform hung heavy on her body. Little rivulets dripped from her clothing and onto the rocks.

Slowly she made her way back up to the grassy area with everyone else.

Bosse was holding a large towel and was just about to hand it to Katarina when something happened. She turned away from him, her hands grasping her belly. A gurgling, bestial sound came from her throat and she threw up on the grass.

No one spoke. All they could hear was the screeching of a few gulls and the sound of a motorboat way out in the bay. They looked at each other in shock, and then at Oswald.

'Well, damn,' he said at last, shaking his head. 'Guess she swallowed some water.'

Katarina looked up and her eyes met Sofia's. They were black with hatred.

★

There it was again, that bitter gaze coming from the far side of the dining room. It had been going on for a week now. Katarina seemed to seek out Sofia wherever she was so she could nail her with hostile glares, whispering and tittering with other staff members.

Sofia didn't dislike Katarina. She wasn't even sure if she thought the punishment had been just, but it didn't matter — right now, all she wanted to do was walk up and smack her. What had she expected? That Sofia would lie to Oswald? Tell him that Katarina had been reading *War and Peace*?

This just could not go on. Dealing with Oswald's moodiness and outbursts of rage was one thing, but doing so while the rest of the staff actively worked against her was completely different. Katarina had to disappear for a while — perhaps even for her own good.

She rose from the table, scraped her barely-touched food into the compost bucket, and placed her plate and cutlery into the dish tub. She looked at her watch: fifteen minutes before she had to be back at work, and fifteen minutes would be enough.

Bosse was bent over a big stack of papers in his office, just as she'd hoped. Oswald had instituted a system in which the staff were encouraged to write a report whenever they saw something unethical. She herself had handed out piles of report forms to the staff. 'Declaration,' read the top of the sheet, which was otherwise empty. Once you had finished writing, you sent the report to the ethics unit, which was expected to deal with whatever you had written. Oswald had called it 'peer pressure', but Sofia had read a few of the reports and thought they mostly consisted of whining.

'Have you gotten any reports about Katarina?' she asked Bosse.

'What?'

Bosse seemed completely overwhelmed by the large pile.

'I asked if you've gotten any reports on Katarina.'

'Oh, does Franz want to know?'

'What does that matter? Could you answer me now?'

'I don't actually know,' he said, staring down at his papers.

'Let's find out,' she said, dividing the stack in two and starting to read through the reports. It wasn't difficult — the names of the people being tattled on were written in capital letters at the top of the sheet.

In the end they found three reports on Katarina. One said that she had complained about the food, another that she had borrowed someone's soap without permission, and a third claimed she had whined about jumping from Devil's Rock.

The last report had been written by Elvira. Sofia thanked her silently as she read.

'I knew it! Katarina hasn't changed a bit since she jumped. Now she's complaining about Franz. Look at this — she belongs in Penance.'

Bosse read it and shook his head.

'Dammit, you're right. I'll bring it up with Franz.'

Sofia wasn't there when Bosse spoke to Oswald, but the conversation must have happened because two days later she saw Katarina in the barn with Madeleine, sporting a red cap. They were feeding the pigs, the most recent newcomers to the property. It wasn't easy for Sofia to contain her laughter.

Great, now you can glare at the sows instead of at me, she thought, feeling a little ashamed at her schadenfreude.

She realized that Katarina had noticed her, but she shrank from Sofia's gaze, turning her eyes to the ground.

An eternity passes before he arrives.

But then I see a shadow moving across the yard. Quickly, jerkily. I can feel his irritation even from here.

He thinks it's a mistake, a bad joke, a mix-up, anything but the truth. I have disturbed him and he just wants to get it over and done with. Confirm what he already knows. That it's not me. He wants to go back to whatever he was doing that was so important.

But he did come out here.

All at once, I know he received my letter.

He knows who I am. But he doesn't know what I have in my backpack.

The light from the sentry box illuminates his face. He looks older now than when I last saw him. His face is furrowed and his eyes are heavy, like an alcoholic's. He's tanned, but tired and worn out.

At that moment, I feel nothing.

Neither hate nor love.

Neither contempt nor admiration.

He stops and looks at me for a moment, from a distance. The iron gate still separates us.

Then he comes closer and grips the iron bar.

Stares at me as though I'm a ghost.

'But you're dead!' he says.

His first words to me.

My father.

24

There was still something magical about life there, about the way everything could turn on a dime. It was like they were riding on waves in the sea. Each time they came to the crest of a huge swell, about to be flung against the rocks, something happened. The wind calmed. The sea smoothed. Again. And it certainly had been rough seas at the manor in the past few weeks. Oswald's rules quickly became law. Punishments were dealt out in a steady stream. The pile of reports on Bosse's desk grew higher as Oswald's fuse grew shorter than ever.

The workdays were long and sleep was a luxury. Although Sofia was tired almost constantly, she often lay awake brooding at night. She wasn't sure she wanted to stay on the island. Her thoughts made her feel guilty and put her in a constant state of anguish as she worried that Oswald might notice something wasn't right with her. At the same time, a voice in the back of her head told her that everything would go back to normal eventually. Back to the way it had been in the beginning. Because there were nice moments too. When Oswald said that he and she were the only ones who got anything done. Or massaged her tired shoulders. Or called her a gem. And then there was Benjamin — she didn't want to be separated from him, but he would never betray Oswald and leave the island with her. It was complicated.

It's this damn lack of sleep, she thought. *Everything will be better once we can sleep at night.* But sleep didn't seem to be on the horizon for those on Oswald's agenda.

He had become terribly irritable and the more trivial the thing he was annoyed by, the more vulgar he was in expressing himself.

'Can you tell that fucking cook to stop putting parsley on my fish?'

Or, 'Kick Bosse in the ass next time he comes around here smelling like B.O.'

After that he would drone on for what seemed like an eternity about how the person in question was useless and incompetent. Now and then he would take a short break from his tirade, and she was expected to validate him. But sometimes she just didn't have the energy. This, too, got him extremely worked up.

'Don't stand there gaping at me like a fish.'

At the same time, he would simply shrug off bigger problems, like a flooded barn. She just didn't understand him anymore. One thing was for sure — something needed to happen to put him in a better mood.

★

And then, one afternoon, the phone rang.

She recognized the deep, hoarse voice right away.

'Is Franz there, Sofia?'

'Hi, Carmen. No, he's not in the office. Can I take a message?'

'No, it's best if you go get him. Is he there on the property?'

'Yes, I think so.'

'Please tell him to call. I have some good news.'

Sofia seldom sent messages to Oswald's pager, but this sounded important. And good news couldn't hurt.

Oswald appeared almost immediately. He had begun to use the

speaker and a microphone when on the phone in the office. He said you could get brain cancer from the radiation in a cell phone or a headset. Sofia was thus able to listen to every conversation he had. She always pretended to be working, but her ears remained on high alert.

Gardell almost chirped when Oswald got hold of her.

'I've found our spokesman, Franz. You'll never guess who it is. Someone we never could have dreamed of.'

'Who?'

'Alvin Johde.'

'You're kidding.'

'I'm not! And that's not all — he wants to come out and do the program right away. Before it gets too cold and nasty out there.'

Oswald and Sofia stared at each other in disbelief. Alvin Johde was a singer who mostly went by just plain 'Alvin.' It was like saying Zlatan — everyone knew who he was. He had become a world-famous artist and had even toured in the U.S. This had all happened before Sofia came to the island; these days she wasn't up-to-date on all his success, but Gardell made it sound like he was still a bright star in the constellation of Swedish celebrities.

'Hello, are you still there?' Gardell laughed. 'He's promised to do TV interviews and ads for us if he likes ViaTerra. But he doesn't know anything, of course, so he needs to be — how should I put it — indoctrinated, while he's there.'

'Of course, I'll take care of that.'

'Good. Then I'll try to get him out there next week. Can you receive him then?'

'Absolutely!'

'Make sure he gets the best personal advisor you've got.'

'I have a girl who's very good. He does like chicks, right?'

'Sure does. Maybe a little too much.'

When Oswald ended the call, she noticed that the wrinkles on his forehead, which she'd thought had become permanent, were gone.

Then he did something extremely unexpected. He bounced out of his chair and pumped his fist in the air.

'Do you know what this means? If we get Alvin Johde, basically the whole of Europe will be at our feet, not just Sweden. We'll have to start thinking about getting multilingual staff and everything.'

'Incredible,' she said, hoping she sounded enthusiastic.

'Do you like his music, Sofia?'

She didn't think Oswald was a Johde fan; most of what he played in the office was gloomy, like Wagner or Mahler, with a little African or Indian music thrown in if he was in a good mood. But never pop.

'No, I can't say I do.'

'Right? It's pure crap. But that's the point. Almost every teenager likes him. That's what matters.'

Sofia nodded. She thought about Alvin Johde and ViaTerra's message about tranquillity and getting back to nature. The two didn't really mesh, but she supposed Oswald knew what he was doing.

'The whole staff has to gather right away so I can share this. *Everyone.* Even the kitchen staff. They'll just have to take a break from cooking. This is big.'

A buzz of astonishment spread through the lines when Oswald told them who would be coming to the manor. Most of them knew of Alvin Johde, and those who didn't jumped on the happy bandwagon anyway. Oswald went on about everything that had to be done before the arrival of their celebrity. Sofia's pen flew over her notepad.

'The garden must be perfect. I don't care if it's autumn. Katarina, you take care of it. You can take a break from Penance. We'll put the caps away for the time being. And for god's sake, no digging any ditches while he's here. No, I think it's best we get rid of Penance for now.'

Oswald's cars and motorcycles had to be washed and polished. Johde's room had to be readied, with all the amenities. He went on until Sofia had filled several pages and didn't stop until his phone jangled in his pocket. Then he moved to the side to take the call, and returned with a smile on his lips.

'Three days, gang! You have three days, and then he'll be here.'

He sent the staff away but asked Sofia to remain.

'I have to take the five o'clock ferry to the mainland to get a haircut and consult with Carmen. I'll be back on the morning ferry. Make sure everything gets underway. Did you write down everything I said?'

'Yes, sir.'

'Good, Sofia. I'm depending on you.'

She hurried to the office and typed up her notes on the computer, then copied the list and ran around handing it out to the staff. By the time she was finished there was an hour left until bedtime, but her feet hurt and she decided to stay in the office. She wondered how she would get everything done and still get any sleep the coming nights.

That's when she caught sight of the keys. They were on the edge of Oswald's desk, and they were the ones that opened his little wall cabinet, which held key rings to every building on the property. And, with any luck, the padlocks on the attic door. He must have forgotten them in his mad, happy rush.

She opened the cabinet. A whole row of keys were hanging there, but only one of them held small keys of the sort that open padlocks. She stuffed them in her pocket and locked the cabinet again.

The wooden steps up to the attic creaked under her feet. She glanced nervously back at the office area, but she didn't see anyone there. One by one, she tested the keys in the locks. The first lock opened right away, with a click. The very last key opened the second lock. She prepared herself for a terrible mess. Stale air. Maybe even mould. But the air was cool and fresh when she stepped through the door.

It was pitch black. A faint hum was coming from some sort of ventilation system. She fumbled for a moment and found the light switch. At first, everything was so bright that she was blinded. But then the room took shape: the walls and ceiling were white and looked freshly painted. An enormous canopy bed held court in the centre of the room. She saw a nightstand, a large wardrobe, a couple of chairs, and a table; they all looked new and expensive. The floor had recently been polished. At one end of the room was a fancy bathroom with a jacuzzi, a shower, and a toilet. As she stepped in, she caught a faint whiff of lemon.

The buzzing had stopped, and now it was so quiet she could hear the rush of the sea through the attic window. Who lived here? It all looked so new. There wasn't a speck in the sink or a single strand of hair in the shower. The room seemed unused, waiting — but for what? *This is something he's created for himself,* she thought. *But why?* Should she ask him? The thought made her feel vaguely ill, and a warning seemed to hum from deep in her marrow.

This is his secret.

The raids. Naturally. This would be his hiding place if the police come. Of course he wants to keep it a secret. That has to be it. There was no other logical explanation.

★

Three days of preparation, almost without a wink of sleep for anyone on staff. But despite the crazy schedule, it was like all discord in the group had been blown away. There was no time to write reports or bicker, Alvin Johde was coming!

When Oswald's car pulled onto the property on the third day, she was standing at the window in the office and spying from behind the blinds. Oswald stepped out and tossed the keys to a guard. Then Alvin appeared. He looked short and scrawny next to Oswald. He had bright purple tips in his hair and the rips in his jeans were visible even from Sofia's position. There could be no doubt that it was Alvin. *Think how lucky I am, that I get to meet him*, she thought. It never would have happened at a different job.

And meet him she would. She would make darn sure of it.

★

Everything changed. They spoke almost exclusively about Alvin.

'I saw him.'

'He said hi to me.'

'God, he's so cute!'

The rules were forgotten for the moment. The staff were allowed to sleep and take long dinner breaks, and Penance dissolved and those in it became members of the group again. Oswald was in a brilliant mood, always at Alvin's side. They rode around on Oswald's motorcycles, listened to music in his private room, and even played volleyball with some of the other guys on staff.

For a while, everything felt like it had in the beginning, back when she had first come to the island. Back when there was time to gaze out at the sea, breathe the fresh air, and feel like you were part of something much bigger and more important than the boring old regular life on the mainland.

Everything will be fine, she thought. *Now that Alvin's here, nothing can go wrong.*

We're sitting in one of the three guesthouses on the estate.

He rushed me over here, away from the astonished looks of the guards and curious eyes in the illuminated windows of the villa.

I decide I like this place — the grand house, the enormous lawns, the guard and the gate.

It has style; there's no denying that.

He's looking at me so gravely now, trying to look strict, but the worry shines through his affected expression.

He is terrified.

Is this what I'll look like when I'm older? *I wonder, studying his worn face with disgust.*

I decide that I look more like Mom after all. Thank god.

'Fredrik, I'm sure you understand that I have to contact the Swedish authorities,' he begins. 'Everyone thinks you're dead.'

'It's better than that,' I say. 'They've even buried me.'

'This really isn't funny,' he says. 'You're in a dreadful situation.'

'So are you,' I snap. 'I don't think you should contact anyone. If you do, you'll find yourself in a bit of trouble.'

'Oh? Why is that?'

'Because it will come out that you're my father. And if that happens, the pictures you all took up in the attic will be released on the Internet.'

He squirms.

I think about telling him that I remember everything.

The darkness in the basement. The threats, the blows.

But he suddenly looks depressingly pitiful. I had expected much more resistance. It must be his guilty conscience; maybe he's been expecting this moment. Expecting fate to catch up with him.

'So you came here to threaten me, is that it? What is it you want? Money?'

I shake my head and don't say anything for a moment to let it all sink in.

The consequences.

'You are my father, after all,' I say at last. 'And all I want is a new life.'

25

Oswald was standing in the doorway of the office with one foot in the corridor, on his way back out again.

She had been waiting for him, knowing he would come.

'Mona has to jump from Devil's Rock,' he said. 'You know why.'

Since Alvin's arrival on the island, Oswald had been practically glued to his side. In fact, it seemed unimaginable that he should leave the celebrity just to see to the punishment of a staff member as insignificant and meaningless as he considered Mona to be. But Sofia knew why Mona had suddenly become so important. And why Oswald was there.

She gazed out the window at the cold, windy fall day. Leaves and twigs swirled around the yard. The sky was thick with clouds, and there was a gale at sea.

'Sir, is there anything else we can do to punish her? It's so windy, and it will already be dark by the time dinner is over.'

Oswald stepped in and approached her desk. For a brief moment she thought he was going to throw himself at her. She knew it was just her imagination, but his posture suggested a predator ready to attack.

'The water's cold. Okay. Is it frozen over, or something?'

'No, no, it's not frozen.'

'So there *is* water for her to jump into?'

'Yes, sure, of course.'

'And we haven't lost all our flashlights?'

'No, I don't believe so.'

'Then that bitch will jump for what she did. Do you hear me?'

He was shouting by now. The strength of his voice made her recoil; she hit her back against the bookcase behind her desk. She clasped her hands in front of her and stared at the floor, trying to look submissive. *Don't defy him. Don't provoke him.* She pressed herself against the bookcase, and he took another step. He was dangerously close now. He banged his fist against the table and her pen holder fell over; pens flew every which way. Her water glass shook but made it through. She hardly dared to breathe; she kept staring at the floor.

'I'm sick of all your objections. Do you hear me?'

'I understand; I won't —'

'That's right. You will not disagree with me again, dammit!'

This would never turn into a dialogue. All it would take would be a facial expression he found annoying, or a poorly chosen word, and he would be in her face again. She had to get out of the office, and fast, because she was running out of oxygen.

'I'll take care of it. I'll go see Bosse right now.'

'Get a move on.'

She felt like she was floundering; it was overwhelming — it was unlike her to be at such a loss. She hadn't even tried to stand up for herself. But she slinked past him and out the door, her tail between her legs, hating herself for it.

She ran down the stairs to Bosse's office and told him what had happened with Mona in the library. Why she had to jump. Bosse didn't look concerned in the least; instead he was exhilarated.

He seemed to get a kick out of disasters — the more serious, the better.

'Heck, it's only water. She can handle it. I'll take care of it.'

It seemed to Sofia that Bosse had started to talk like Oswald, to use the same intonation and gestures. What was more, he'd let his hair grow out, and it was just long enough to put in a ponytail at the back of his neck. He even wore tight T-shirts under his uniform, exactly like Oswald. But Bosse was scrawny, so it just looked silly.

Sofia didn't want to go back to the office in case Oswald had lingered there, so she went to the staff bathroom and locked herself in. She sat on the lid of the toilet with her head in her hands. Dammit, now that she had time to think about the fateful incident earlier that day, the tears came.

★

Oswald had wanted to show Alvin the library and Sofia was to be there when he did. She and Mona had been awaiting their arrival for an hour. They had already cleaned, dusted, and made sure that every book was standing up straight on the shelves. They must have tested the computer program at least a hundred times. Now they were just sitting around waiting and having coffee. Mona was anxious; she bit her nails, as always, and kept glancing at the door.

'It'll be fine,' Sofia assured her just as Oswald and Alvin came in. This was the first time Sofia had seen Alvin up close. Her first impression was that he looked like a doll. His gelled hair stood on end in hundreds of black and purple spikes. His face was powdered white and he was wearing eyeliner. But even stranger were his jerky movements. He seemed incapable of standing still; he twisted his body and squirmed, pacing as he spoke, cracking his knuckles, gnawing at his lower lip. If she hadn't known better she would have thought he was high, but she'd heard he just had an excess of energy, inexhaustible reserves of vigour and vitality.

She showed him the whole library. He didn't seem particularly interested in the books, but when she showed him the computer and its screensaver with Oswald's picture and motto, he whistled.

'Shit, this is awesome, Franz! You've really put your stamp on this place.'

He liked the fact that you could order books and download them to your phone or laptop. She asked if he wanted to try it out, so he eagerly took a seat and ordered a book for himself. When he stood up again, he placed his hand over Sofia's and winked at her. She didn't know what to think — other than that he was a little pleasantly nuts.

When the tour was over, Oswald gave Sofia a pleased nod. Mona had remained standing behind the librarian's desk throughout. She looked lost but relieved now that it was all over.

Then she reached across the desk to shake hands with Alvin in a farewell gesture. And that's when it happened. She knocked over her coffee cup with a thud, and the coffee splashed onto Alvin's trousers, leaving big brown stains on his white jeans. Everyone was shocked into silence, and then a flood of apologies poured from Mona's mouth.

'Oh, it's no big deal,' Alvin said. But it was clear from his expression that those jeans hadn't exactly come from a second-hand store.

Mona said she would wash the trousers for him, but he shook his head.

'Sofia will take care of it later,' Oswald assured him.

As they left, Oswald turned around and shot Sofia a malevolent look, and she knew it was going to be a terrible day.

★

She rose from the toilet lid and wiped her tears. Once she'd washed away the mascara that had clumped around her eyes, she ran her fingers through her hair and made a face at her reflection. *He will not break me*, she thought. *Never.* But then she thought back to what had happened. Mona's imbecilic clumsiness. That oafish idiot. Perhaps she had even spilled that coffee on purpose. Seriously, how much could Oswald be expected to put up with?

She thought about Mona, then Oswald. His field of energy. How he could charm anyone and fit in anywhere. Even Alvin looked up to him. Oswald might be unpredictable and temperamental, but he was never boring. Then her thoughts returned to Mona. Her sullen presence. She adjusted her skirt and jacket and opened the door.

Duty called.

★

The procession struggled on, into the wind. The roving beams of their flashlights sought out the narrow path. A light drizzle wet their faces. Sofia walked beside Bosse, who was holding Mona by the arm. Oswald was at the gym with Alvin, so he'd directed Sofia to take his place. She just wanted to get it over with and be back inside, out of the cold. But something was horribly wrong. She could hardly see Mona's features in the dim light, yet she could feel the other woman's fear. She wasn't crying; she wasn't making a sound. But terror seemed to radiate from her body. She was like an animal walking to slaughter.

Sofia felt vaguely ill and tried to convince herself that Mona was just a coward and this might even do her good. But there was something overwhelming about Mona's fear.

By now they could see the terrain around the cliffs. Everything was dark grey: the sea, the sky, the rocks. Only the foam on the water glowed white.

Mona kept herself together until she was standing on the very edge of Devil's Rock. But then a long, frantic howl rose from her throat and stunned the whole staff.

And then: 'I can't swim, I can't swim, I can't swim . . .' She repeated the phrase like a mantra. It began softly but increased in volume until she was howling again.

'Why didn't you say so before?' Bosse roared, shaking her arm.

'I was afraid to. I'm so scared.'

Benny separated himself from the pack and approached them. 'You're lying! You're just trying to get out of it.'

Sten stepped forward as well, always ready to have Benny's back.

'She's definitely lying. Look how fake she looks. She has to jump; Franz said so. If she can't handle it, we can always pull her out. Right?'

He turned to the group for their approval. It started as a buzz but soon rose into a steady, persistent chant:

'Jump! Jump! Jump! Jump!'

So she jumped. She yanked her arm from Bosse's grasp and slipped over the edge of the cliff. There was a loud splash as she hit the water.

When she came up, it was all wrong. She was flapping her arms, spitting and hissing. Gasping for breath. She vanished beneath the surface. Bobbed up again, screamed, but swallowed water and went under. After that, she didn't come up again. All they could see was the dark water and the foaming waves. The whole group stood there helplessly, staring down at the water. Sofia knew she should jump in and rescue Mona, but it was as if her feet were rooted to the ground.

A grey arrow darted by at the edge of her vision. Someone had pulled away from the group to fly into the water. They might have been staring for a few seconds or a whole minute, until the bodies appeared on the surface. Benjamin, his arms around Mona's chest. He dragged her to the rocks and helped her up. He held her as she coughed up water, gagging and crying all at once.

One by one, they woke from their trance. Bosse had the towel; Katarina brought her down jacket. Soon the staff had flocked around Mona.

That was when Sofia heard it.

Far out in the sea, it called and echoed. The intermittent tones came in on the wind.

The foghorn.

At first she thought it must be her imagination.

But she wasn't the only one who heard it that night.

*

No one let on to Oswald what had happened, not even a hint. No one wanted to be the bearer of bad news. But Sofia knew he would fly into a rage if he found out Mona had nearly drowned. He wouldn't be mad at them — just Mona. He would probably dismiss her and send her back to the mainland. And then the library would be empty. The images from that night haunted her thoughts, as did the thought of what might have happened if it weren't for Benjamin.

★

Alvin completed the program and left the island satisfied and happy.

Oswald had accompanied him to the mainland and returned late that night. Sofia was still up, working on a computer system that would keep track of everything Oswald wanted done. He glanced over her shoulder as she typed at the computer, realized at once what she was doing, and mumbled in approval.

'That's looking good. Put a time limit on everything. If you don't receive a report within a certain period you can use the Consequences. First, three warnings. Then — boom!'

He laughed and Sofia immediately understood what he was getting at. A sort of obedience tool. He sat down before her and stared at her. She'd learned not to look away even if she did feel nervous butterflies in her stomach.

'Things with Alvin went well,' he said. 'He's going to talk about us on TV soon.'

'Fantastic!'

'And now that he's gone, I'm going to stay here for a while. Deal with the staff.'

He kept staring at her as if he was trying to read her mind.

She held her gaze steady, but her mouth went bone-dry. At last she had to say something to put an end to the silence.

'Sir, may I ask you something?'

'Of course.'

'When Mona jumped from Devil's Rock, some of us heard the foghorn. But it doesn't work anymore, does it?'

The corners of Oswald's mouth turned up.

'Oh, didn't that Björk character tell you? When the wind blows a certain direction, it causes the horn itself to make a howling noise. That's all you heard.'

'I see, okay.'

There was a glimmer in his eyes.

'Although the villagers say there's more to it, of course.'

'What's that?'

'That it means someone's going to die.'

'This is Fredrik,' he says to the little girl, whom I dislike immediately.

Her eyes bulge out too far, and she has pigtails, a pointy nose, a nearly invisible chin, and one of those superior 'my daddy is rich' smiles that reveals a terrifying mouthful of braces.

Just you wait, I think, but I smile back. My very best smile.

He convinced me to shower and put on new trousers, socks, and a sweater he's pulled out of nowhere.

'Fredrik is going to stay with us for a while, in the guest house,' he says.

We'll see, I think.

I look around the large room we're sitting in.

Marble floors. Everything is beige, white, and blue. It's sparsely furnished but all the fabrics are expensive.

Huge windows with heavy drapes. The painting on the wall looks like an actual Picasso.

Mediterranean deluxe, I think.

I've never seen anything like it.

It smells pleasantly clean, not of soap or floor cleaner but of furniture polish and aired-out rooms.

Then my eyes fall upon her. Emilie, the Countess.

The daughter must take after her, because she is not beautiful.

Her nose is a little too long and slightly crooked. Her chin is small and her eyes are almost colourless. But she has a thick, blonde mane of hair *that tumbles over her thin shoulders, and her body is slim and narrow, like a girl's.*

She looks at me with surprise and curiosity.

Her eyes wander over my face and body and stop, just for an instant, at my crotch.

It only lasts a fraction of a second, but I notice it. And she knows I noticed.

Don't get any idea, bitch, I think. You're way too old. But then I think of how useful she could be.

She might even be the key to everything.

I look back at her, letting my eyes roam her body.

Like a lighthouse beam sweeping the sea on a raw, cold night.

26

They had gathered in the dining room in front of Oswald's TV, which was already on, the sound muted. Now they just had to wait for the program to start. Alvin was the featured guest and would talk about ViaTerra. They'd even been permitted to dress in civilian clothes and everyone had dressed up a little in honour of the evening.

Sofia was sitting in the first row, next to Anna, who smelled like sweet perfume and was wearing large, dangly earrings. It was comical somehow, these moments of vanity in front of a television. As if Alvin would be able to see and smell them through the screen.

'If you all had a little of Alvin's ambition, we would get more done,' Oswald said. 'So take a lesson from this program.'

Just then, the segment began and Oswald signalled to Bosse to turn up the volume. It started off well. Alvin seemed to have an answer to every question. He used words like *presence* and *tranquillity*, which sounded a little odd coming from his mouth. But that was probably the whole point — that this boisterous guy had found peace on the island.

Sofia sneaked a look at Oswald. He was standing close to the TV, his arms crossed over his chest. He nodded approvingly now and then.

But then the magic spell was broken; something unexpected happened. The TV host took out a blank sheet of paper and held it up to Alvin.

'So this is ViaTerra's secret, what people pay hundreds of thousands of kronor for?'

Alvin didn't know what to say. Then he started to giggle. He tried to speak, but he couldn't stop laughing.

'But it's actually pretty cool,' he said once he had collected himself. 'It has to do with dreams. That you can achieve anything in life.'

Sofia squirmed anxiously and glanced at Oswald, whose face had clouded over. She sent up a silent prayer that the host would let this topic go, which, thank god, he did.

But then came the final question.

'So what was the most memorable part of your time on Fog Island?'

Alvin considered this. He looked away from the cameras for a moment. Once again he had lost the thread, and when he opened his mouth all that came out were little mumbling sounds.

Come on! Sofia thought. *It's a simple question! Just answer and give us our happy ending.*

At long last, a huge smile spread across his face.

'I guess it was the chicks. They have a whole ton of hot girls who work there.'

The studio audience burst out laughing and Alvin joined in. The camera zoomed in on a couple of guys in the front row who were bent double and had tears in their eyes. The contrast between what was happening on screen and the suddenly subdued atmosphere in the dining room was so stark that Sofia felt a sinking feeling in her stomach. *It's probably not that bad*, she told herself. *Alvin is what he is.*

But Oswald's expression was dark. He walked over and turned off the TV. The show wasn't even over.

An unbearable silence ensued.

Everyone was waiting for Oswald to say something, but he just moved to stand in front of the staff at one end of the front row, then slowly walked along the chairs until he had taken in every face. He passed Sofia and stopped in front of Anna.

'You!' he roared. 'Stand up!'

Anna flew out of her seat so quickly that her chair overturned and was caught by Eskil, who was sitting behind her. She stood there with her dangly earrings, terrified, waiting for whatever Oswald was about to say, but he just moved on. He went past the guys in Bosse's gang, past Mona, at whom he aimed a scornful look, and came to the next row, where he stopped in front of Mira, who had been Alvin's personal advisor.

'Definitely you!' he said.

Mira just stared up at her from her chair.

'Stand up!' he shouted so loudly that someone in the back row squeaked in fear.

Mira flew up, suddenly so close to tears that her lip trembled.

Oswald moved on and Sofia realized what he was doing. He was picking out the most beautiful women, the 'hot girls.' Madeleine, of course, and Katarina. He stopped in front of Elvira, but then he shook his head.

'You're too young.'

Once he'd made his selection, twelve women were standing.

'There they are,' he said. 'Might as well get started. I want to know everything they did with Alvin. Every last detail. Does everyone understand? Surely you're not so stupid that you think he made this up? Seriously. None of you will go to bed until

262

you've squeezed the truth out of them. This is so disgusting that I think I have to go vomit.'

He was just about to leave when he noticed Sofia. It was like she had been invisible to him before. He slowly approached her. At first she felt the impulse to stand, but she pressed her quivering legs into her chair.

He crouched down beside her and stared into her eyes. She stared right back. His face was right in front of hers. The whole room blurred out, leaving only his eyes, black as a coal mine in the dim light. The image was so sharp that she could see tiny red lines where blood vessels had burst in the whites around his irises. She wondered if that happened when a person was extremely angry. Sweat popped out on her palms. She didn't understand why she was so nervous when she hadn't done anything wrong.

'I'll deal with you later,' he said at last.

Then Oswald stood up and walked down the aisle to the exit.

Bosse stood up and all eyes were drawn to him. He turned to Sofia for support, so she stood as well.

'Benny, run and get pens and paper,' he said. 'So they can write down everything they did with Alvin.'

A laugh came from the far corner of the dining room; there stood Oswald, who hadn't left after all.

'What's wrong with you? Write down what they did? I'll show you how this is going to work.'

He came back and pulled out one of the tables that was lined up along the wall. He yanked and tugged, but waved Bosse off when he attempted to help. Then he placed one chair on either side of the table.

'Sit down!' he directed Bosse, pointing at one of the chairs.

Bosse hurried to take a seat.

'Sofia, give me your notepad and pen.'

She handed them over and he placed them on the table in front of Bosse.

'You take notes, Bosse. All the shit they've done must be put down on paper. Then they can sign their confessions. Mira, we'll start with you. Come sit in the other chair.'

Mira trotted over to them and sat down. She was wearing a ruffled white blouse and her hair was piled on the top of her head. *Like a Barbie doll under interrogation*, Sofia thought.

Oswald waved at Sofia, and Bosse's henchmen.

'You stand here behind Bosse. If she dodges the question, just have at her.'

Oswald opened the interrogation.

'What did you do with Alvin?'

Mira cleared her throat. 'I, hmm, I didn't do anything in particular. We joked around a little. But we never touched each other, I swear.'

Oswald banged his fist on the table.

'Don't lie!' he shouted. 'Out with it!'

Mira searched her memory. Sofia could see her thoughts now and then, as they flickered across her face like shadows. There was something she touched on but didn't want to think about.

'That!' Oswald cried. 'What were you thinking right then?'

Oswald chased the thought, which kept returning, faster now, and with such power that sweat began to bead on Mira's forehead.

'There! There!'

But she didn't want to reveal her secret.

'For Christ's sake, answer me!' Oswald said, banging the table again.

'Well, um, there was this one time when we were talking

about his program. His feet brushed mine under the table. They only brushed. But I think it was on purpose.' Her cheeks turned red and her gaze flitted here and there.

'Bullshit! I don't want to know what *he* did, Mira. I want to know what *you* did.'

'Well, I guess I rubbed a little too. We sort of rubbed our feet together. It was only for a minute.'

Oswald looked at them in triumph.

'There you go! See what a pathological liar she is? I'm sure she had sex with him too. Go ahead, you can all ask questions as well. And don't be kind to her. You'll have to get tough, because people like her only respond to threats.'

Soon Mira was being bombarded with questions. As soon as she hesitated or seemed evasive, Bosse struck the table with his fist. Just as Oswald had done.

Bit by bit, the confession came out, and so did the tears. Yes, there had been hugs, yes, and touches. His hands under her shirt. And they had kissed the day before he left the island. No sex, she assured them, but Oswald seemed satisfied. He told her to stand up and turned to Benny.

'Send her to Penance, but keep her under watch around the clock. Otherwise she might decide to run away.'

Benny nodded and swallowed, overwhelmed by Oswald's presence.

'Now that I think about it, I think you'll have to create a special Penance for her,' Oswald added. 'Otherwise she might poison those already in it. Now do the same with all the others. I have more important things to take care of. But every confession must be signed before you can go to bed.'

It was six in the morning by the time they were finished. Things had progressed slowly at first, but later it seemed like some sort of virus trickled into the room and spread among the twelve accused. Maybe they were just tired of the shouting and threats, but they started confessing at a dizzying pace. 'I flirted with him,' 'brushed by him,' 'winked at him.' If someone hadn't done anything at all, she could always confess to thinking about Alvin while masturbating and talk about it in great detail. Sofia was soon tired of hearing where and how they'd touched themselves, and she wondered if they were too stupid to realize what the consequences would be.

When they were finished, a whole pile of confessions lay before Bosse on the table.

Sofia looked at the women, who were lined up against the wall. She suddenly felt sorry for them. *I must have a screw loose*, she thought, because what they had done was completely scandalous. Yet something ached inside her. Maybe it was their nice clothes and their tears — it felt like they had just crushed these girls' few minutes of joy about their brush with celebrity. A stolen glance or a gentle touch they could recall and use to warm themselves when life felt cold and lonely behind the barbed wire.

I'm turning into a bleeding heart, she thought. *And that's not a good thing at all.*

'What do we do now?' Bosse asked, looking at Sofia and then at the line of twelve women.

'You can go to bed,' she told the staff; they were still sitting as if nailed to their chairs. A faint murmur spread through the group. She wasn't sure if they were relieved to be done or disappointed that the show was over, but they strolled out of the dining room.

Bosse looked euphoric. A second wind had brought him out of exhaustion; his adrenaline had taken over.

'This will be a new program,' he said. 'Penance squared, sort of. You'll have to be really tough on them, Benny. Can you handle it?'

'Definitely!'

She left Bosse and Benny in the dining room and glanced at the women one last time, sincerely grateful that she wasn't standing against the wall with them.

*

When she arrived at the office, Oswald was already there. He was freshly shaven and looked well-rested. She placed the pile of confessions in front of him in the centre of his desk.

'Most of them flirted with him. A few did worse things.'

'I knew that already,' he said, shaking his head. 'Almost a million TV viewers saw that crap, Sofia. Do you understand what a terrible betrayal this is?'

'Yes, I do.'

'What about you, then? I saw Alvin checking you out in the library.'

'I didn't do anything with him.'

She stubbornly met his gaze and it felt really good. She was not about to confess to something she hadn't done. He could shout and bluster all he wanted. It wouldn't make a difference — she was too tired and numb to feel anything.

There was something else too, a defiance that had grown out of something she'd heard while Alvin was on the island. The quiet conversation she'd eavesdropped on made the night's incidents seem unfair.

It had been late at night. Oswald had been in his room,

hanging out with Alvin, and asked her to bring down some bottles of water. When she saw that the door was open, she stopped just outside. Maybe it was because she sensed that a private conversation was taking place, or maybe she was just curious.

'But there's nothing wrong with a little bondage, is there?' she heard Alvin say.

'Oh, that's so passé after *Fifty Shades* and everything. Like Hans Scheike, whipping little girls with twigs. Instead imagine that you have a chick in front of you, hot as fuck, with a belt around her neck. You pull on it and the life goes out of her eyes, but then you give her life back again, all within a few seconds, while you — well, you know what I'm saying.'

No one said anything and she heard a faint, appreciative whistle. From Alvin, definitely.

Her mind raced as she stood there outside the door. Those were just fantasies, not something he actually did, he had the right to his sexual preferences, maybe he was just joking. Yet at that moment, she found her admiration for him had cooled.

She cleared her throat loudly before stepping into the room, but she couldn't bring herself to make eye contact with the men. She hurried to put down the bottles and leave.

But now that she was standing right in front of him, she thought that what the girls had done was trivial compared to his fantasies.

'Well, I suppose I have to trust you,' he said.

She didn't move, just kept looking him in the eye. It was a quiet battle she didn't realize had begun. She couldn't look away. His own gaze seemed odd, and suddenly her whole body went cold.

'What are you staring at?'

'Nothing, sir, I'm just tired.'

And that was no exaggeration. It felt like her legs were about to give way beneath her. She had a vision of resting her head on a soft pillow, and she couldn't hold back a yawn.

Oswald looked at her in irritation.

'Surely you don't think you're going to go to bed right now? The day has just begun.'

In that very moment, the realization struck her for the first time. It shot up from her belly like an electric jolt and flourished in her brain.

This was just the beginning.

Everything that had happened so far had been child's play.

And life did not, in fact, have any rock bottom.

For the most part, people are weak and gullible.

There is one thing hardly anyone can resist: a little flattery.

And Emilie is no exception.

She is alone and restless in that big house.

Flattery is like a drug to her.

Though you have to be careful with it, because in large doses it becomes sickly sweet and hackneyed.

But I was born with the ability to make others feel important.

I slowly make progress with her. Offering help.

Laughing at her jokes. Listening when she talks. Listening when she complains. Listening when she rambles.

Looking enchanted, as if everything she says is incredibly meaningful.

Giving her little compliments.

Letting my self, my aura, surround her until she feels all warm.

Filling her cold emptiness with my energy. And it works.

'I like having you here,' she says one day. 'Thanks for always being so helpful.'

'I'm the one who should be thanking you,' I say. 'It feels like I've finally found my home.'

She begins to confide in me.

I'm allowed to move into the house, into my own room upstairs.

And one night, it happens — what I've been waiting for.

I'm sitting on the stairs, listening to them talk in the living room. It's become a habit.

I keep an eye on them.

They can't see me, but I can hear them.

'I like Fredrik so much,' she says. 'I want him to stay with us.'

'That won't be easy,' he says. 'You know, the paperwork and everything.'

'You can take care of it,' she says. 'You have contacts.'

I've heard enough. I'm satisfied. Everything is going as planned.

Just as I'm about to get up and go back to my room, I see her.

Bugeye.

She's on the top step, staring at me. Her little fig-shaped ears are pricked.

I decide it's time to deal with her. Fast.

27

'Listen to this! "Sleep deprivation can be used as a method of torture and has also been used to bring about visions in certain religious circumstances".'

Sofia was curled up on her bed, her laptop balanced on her legs, Googling 'sleep deprivation'. She recalled students at the university who could hardly go one night without sleep; it would wreck them for the rest of the week. At ViaTerra, functioning without sleep was a daily reality.

It was hard to remember what it felt like to be well-rested. Her body was always wrapped in a fuzzy, uncomfortable buzzing that made each motion seem to take forever to complete. It was hard to focus her gaze and there was a metallic taste in her mouth from all the toxins her body couldn't manage to get rid of.

Benjamin groaned loudly from under the blanket.

'Sofia, please, can't we go to sleep now? You're only torturing yourself with this stuff. And by the way, didn't we agree you would only use the laptop in emergencies?'

But she didn't stop reading.

'"In the long term, severe sleep deprivation can result in psychotic reactions or epileptic seizures. Acute effects of sleep deprivation include drowsiness and problems concentrating and learning".'

He sat up in bed and gently removed her hands from the keyboard. He looked at her with those lovely eyes, eyes that had once been so alert, had seemed to see through all the hypocrisy and lies, but now just seemed tired and sad. She wondered if he truly saw with them anymore.

'Sofia, I understand how you feel,' he said. 'But shouldn't we turn out the light now so we can get some sleep for once? It seems like everything is going to get better.'

Better? Maybe. But she wasn't so sure. She had felt uneasy in recent days, full of an unpleasant, anxious feeling she couldn't shake. Perhaps it was due to the lack of sleep, but deep down she was sure it was something else. That Oswald was up to something.

It had started with the number of guests dwindling as Oswald stopped giving lectures on the mainland. One evening when she peeked into the dining room she noticed that only three guests were at dinner. Something wasn't right. She didn't dare to ask Oswald; she was afraid it had something to do with their bad reputation in the media. That it had become more difficult to tempt people to visit the island.

A second worry was Penance, which just kept growing. Twenty people were running around in red caps by now — almost half the staff. All the women who had flirted with Alvin were in 'Penance Squared.' They wore red caps and black scarves and weren't allowed to talk to anyone, not even those in regular Penance. Now that half the workforce was missing, it was hard to get everything done.

And then there was the escape attempt, which happened one afternoon right after lunch. Sofia had been in the office with Oswald, who was working on something on his computer. Whatever it was, it must have been secret, because he had shifted the screen so she couldn't see it.

It was raining outside, a heavy, persistent rain that washed the windows clean.

Suddenly, an alarm blared — something had touched the fence. At first she thought the rain had set it off, or that a squirrel had tried to jump over and got zapped to death. But then she heard a furious scream from the courtyard.

Angry voices. Motorcycles. The sounds reminded her of the time Ellis had shown up. She went to the window but couldn't see anything through the sheets of rain. The alarm was still sounding.

Oswald stood up.

'Can you see what's going on down there?'

'No, but there are people. And motorcycles.'

The rain was beating against the window now; they had to raise their voices.

'You'd better go down and see what's up,' he shouted.

She ran down the stairs, stopped by her room to grab her raincoat, and hurried out to the courtyard. At first, all she could see was a few figures by the wall. The rain was falling hard enough to kick up pieces of gravel. As she approached, she saw that Benny and Sten were holding onto Mira, who was screaming, kicking, and trying to yank her arms loose. Bosse stood before them, trying to reason with her. He looked up and noticed Sofia.

'She was trying to run away! But we stopped her!' he called triumphantly.

Oswald had come out as well. He was standing behind Sofia in a big, black rain poncho and staring at Mira. The very sight of him made her recoil and stop kicking. She was shivering and shaking, soaking wet. Her jeans were ripped and blood was flowing from one bared knee.

'So you were on your way to Alvin,' Oswald said. 'What a little idiot you are. He's not interested in you; don't you know that?'

'She tried to go over the fence,' Bosse said. 'But she got caught on the barbed wire. I suppose we'll have to fix up that cut.'

Oswald didn't seem to care about her wound, but he switched to a milder tone.

'You know why you wanted to escape, don't you, Mira?'

She shook her head in confusion.

'It's your conscience nagging you. If we let you leave, we would truly be doing you a disservice. You haven't confessed everything, you see. Once you do, you'll feel better. Do you understand?'

He didn't wait for her response; instead he turned to Bosse.

'Keep her under supervision around the clock. Use someone we can trust. Hard labour. And work on her at night. Find out everything she's done.'

Mira was led off toward the barns. Sofia wondered why she hadn't just gone to the gate and said she wanted to leave. What would have happened? But she suspected she already knew the answer to that question.

Later that night, the staff gathered for a conversation with Oswald. They met in the staff office for a change; Oswald wanted to be in more relaxed surroundings for his little chat with them. There was even coffee. The people on Penance were there too, but they had to sit in a row at the very back of the room.

As Oswald began to speak, his voice was strangely weak.

'I can't do all this work myself,' he nearly whispered. 'Get all the guests here, handle the media, and do the dishes at the same time.'

That last bit was probably meant to be a joke, but the group's laughter was tentative.

'But let's be serious now. My life has become unbearable recently. I've been responsible for getting every last bastard into the program and made sure they received services. I've squeezed in as many lectures as I could and handled inquiries from TV and newspapers. All without any real help from you lot.'

Shame settled over the room.

A couple of girls tried to impress Oswald by taking notes, but they soon thought the better of it.

'If you don't put down those pens, I will throw them, and you, out the window.'

Then he continued with a grave monologue about all the hard work he had to do and how worthless the staff were.

An idea began to grow somewhere beyond Sofia's consciousness, like a little hum, but it soon pulled her along into a stream of questions. Oswald's voice became a dull rumble in the back of her mind. What did he even do all day long? She knew he had a couple of computer guys who sat around writing nice things about him online all day. He spoke to a private investigator who was shadowing Magnus Strid, whatever that was supposed to lead to. He contacted a law firm now and then. But what else? Aside from the steady stream of instructions and directives he captured on his Dictaphone, she truly had no idea what this back-breaking was made up of. What did he actually do besides spew out words, words, and more words, occasionally sprinkled with curses?

'Sofia!'

His voice yanked her from her thoughts. For an instant her mind was perfectly empty.

'Sofia, did you hear what I said?'

Luckily she had left her mental recording device on — it registered everything she heard even if her mind wandered.

'Yes, sir. You said we absolutely must return to the founding principles of ViaTerra. Bring fresh life back into our goals.'

'Right! Well done, Sofia.'

He stood up and paced back and forth.

'How many here have completed the ViaTerra program?'

Seven hands reached for the sky and waved eagerly. The personal advisors, of course, plus Sofia, Benjamin and Madeleine.

Oswald shook his head.

'This can't be true! No wonder you're a bunch of blockheads. You don't even understand why you're here!'

Sofia thought it was strange that he didn't realize no one on staff was studying — they didn't have time thanks to their insane schedule. He was anything but dumb.

'We're going to fix this,' he said. 'As you may have noticed, we have almost no guests left. The last two are heading home tomorrow morning. We'll close guest services for the autumn and winter, and all of you can go through the program. We're going to create a real team.'

Everyone exchanged mumbles, nods, and looks of agreement. He had ignited a spark of hope.

'But we have to have peace and quiet while we do it,' he went on. 'So write to your parents and friends tonight and say that you'll be busy for the next few months. That way they won't have to worry.'

The meeting lasted until one in the morning, and then there were lots of emails to write, and suddenly it was three a.m. Luckily Oswald stuck his head in at two to tell them they could sleep in the next morning.

★

And now she was sitting there like an idiot, Googling 'sleep deprivation' when they were finally allowed time to sleep. Benjamin had given up and pulled the covers over his head; he was already breathing heavily. She closed the laptop and stuck it back in the drawer, then crawled under the blankets and pressed herself to Benjamin's back. She rested her cheek against his neck and inhaled his scent. He murmured softly and contently, and they fell asleep like that, heavy and warm.

★

She woke up early the next morning, then lay gazing up at the ceiling for a while. She tried to go back to sleep, but she felt something drawing her to the courtyard.

She pulled her robe on and stuck her bare feet in her shoes, then went downstairs and opened the front door. At first, all she could see was the fog. It was so thick she could hardly make out the annexes.

But then her eyes adjusted and she saw a pair of guests talking to Sten over by the sentry box. They were carrying suitcases and seemed to be saying goodbye. Then they passed through the gate, which closed behind them with a creak.

The last two guests.

The fog grew denser; it seemed alive, floating across the yard and alternately enclosing and releasing the trees and buildings.

All that was still was the sharp points of the barbed-wire fence.

It struck her that they could simply vanish now. The whole staff could go up in smoke, and no one would miss them for a very, very long time.

The island God forgot.

*

She had begun to think of them as 'seances,' Oswald's drawn out conversations with the staff each evening. They often lasted late into the night. At first she thought he talked about so many things, and so fast, that she would never remember it all. But then she realized he always came to the same conclusions. That ViaTerra was the solution to all the world's problems, that he was the only one who ever got anything done, and that the staff were all incompetent. She was astounded at his ability to use so many words and yet say so little and wondered if she was the only one having such horrible thoughts.

On this particular night they'd had to wait for Oswald for a while. She stared out the window — the wind was ripping at the trees. They'd lost almost all their leaves, but this was the first time she'd noticed.

Oswald began speaking as soon as he came through the door. Today was about the theses, and he was all fire and brimstone.

About half an hour into his lecture, she noticed that Simon, who worked in the greenhouse, looked unusually tired. He was a large guy, and a bit clumsy. He was difficult to talk to, but he was a genius when it came to gardening and thanks to him they had fresh vegetables year round. Sometimes Sofia stopped by the greenhouse just to watch him work, to see how he tied up the branches of the impressive tomato plants, whistling as he watered and touched the plants so gently with his huge hands. The greenhouse was peaceful in a way that didn't exist anywhere else at ViaTerra.

Now, Sofia noticed that Simon was nodding off here and there. She caught his eye and shook her head in warning. If there was anything Oswald hated, it was when people fell asleep during his lectures. But Simon couldn't keep his eyes open. His eyelids fluttered and his head lowered. She knew how it felt when exhaustion tugged at your body while your brain went numb, so she tried to help him, signalling to him to get hold of himself. But then Oswald caught sight of him as his eyes were closed and his chin was resting on his chest.

'Oh, Simon, do you find this boring?'

Simon started and looked around in shame.

'No, not really. Just a little sleepy.'

Oswald leaned across the table and fixed his gaze on Simon, who was wide awake by now.

'*Not really*? Did you hear this fucking dumbass? *Not really*! Here I work like an animal, trying to drum a little sense into your brains and this fat pig just sits here snoring.'

Simon's face had turned bright red. He glared at Oswald, fighting an internal battle to keep a lid on himself, but something wanted out and was about to overflow.

'You can continue your snoring in Penance,' Oswald said. 'Who needs your goddamn plants?'

The whole staff stared at Simon: this was the moment when one usually showed remorse and begged forgiveness. But nothing was usual about Simon that evening.

He jumped to his feet.

'I quit,' he said.

'What?'

'I'm done with this. None of the shit you say makes a lick of sense.'

Everything happened so fast that Sofia's eyes could hardly keep up. Suddenly Oswald was standing in front of Simon, grabbing him by the collar with both hands. First he shook him, and then his palm flew up and struck Simon's cheek with a loud crack that echoed in the silent room. Oswald brought his hand down on Simon's head several more times, hard. The veins on Oswald's forehead were standing out and his eyes were wild.

'You fat, disgusting pig!' he shouted in Simon's face.

Simon tried to shove him away, but both men lost their balance and were suddenly on the floor in a tangle of arms, legs, and wrinkled clothing.

Oswald had a stranglehold on Simon's neck, but Simon grabbed Oswald's hands with his huge paws and pulled them away to get free.

The guys only hesitated for a moment, and then they were in a ring around the two men. Bosse's whole gang. They grabbed Simon's arms and legs, holding him fast as Oswald extricated himself and stood up. He adjusted his clothes, his face crimson. Spit flew from his mouth as he screamed at them.

'Do you see that? This is the kind of shithead who ruins things for the rest of us!'

He marched out of the room, stumbled over the doorstep, and vanished into the darkness of the hallway.

Simon was still on the floor, in the grasp of Bosse's crew.

'He hit me. That son of a bitch hit me,' he whimpered.

Bosse stood with his arms crossed, staring down at him.

'Get up, you bastard!'

Benny and Sten still had hold of his arms. By now the rest of the staff had recovered from their shock and jeers rained down.

'Traitor!'

'Rat!'

'What's wrong with you?'

Even those in Penance Squared chimed in.

Sofia watched it all from above, as if she had flown to the ceiling when the first blow landed. She didn't want to be there. She didn't really want to see what was going on, on the floor. So she fled upward, but the ceiling stopped her and she couldn't get away from the horrors going on below.

It wasn't just that Simon was standing there, thoroughly degraded. It was also something she had suspected: you couldn't just walk away. The gate was, and would remain, closed. The barbed wire on the fence was all too real.

Bosse looked to her for support. Oswald wasn't there, after all. But she just stared at him and shrugged. Simon was led away, and she got a lump in her throat when she saw his hulking body and ruffled hair vanish through the door.

The rest of the staff were starting to leave the room. The show was over.

She knew she should go to the office to ask if Oswald needed anything, but instead she went straight to her room.

Benjamin was sitting on the edge of the bed, getting undressed.

'I don't even want to talk about it,' she said firmly.

'Talk about what?'

'For Christ's sake, he's started to hit the staff. This is nuts.'

'It's not great. But we're the ones who drive him to it, aren't we? He works like a dog. And that idiot stands up and says he wants to quit. Plus he fell asleep during the lecture.'

'So it's okay to hit him?'

Benjamin sighed. 'Listen, let's go to bed. Bring it up with Franz if you don't like it. You work with him around the clock, after all.'

His last remark made her furious. Mostly because it was true. She didn't dare talk to Oswald about it.

Benjamin lay down with his back to her and pulled the covers over his head.

She sat on the edge of the bed for a long time, staring into the darkness, knowing she would never fall asleep. The scene between Oswald and Simon played on repeat in her mind, complete with sound and crystal-clear images.

Then she remembered the diary. The little black journal Wilma had given her.

She turned the light back on. Benjamin grunted under the blankets. The diary was in the top drawer, under her shirts. She opened it and stared at the first, blank page for a while. Then she took a pen from the nightstand and began to write: first the date, then 'O violent toward Simon.' She went back in time, writing down everything to the best of her recollection. The first abusive words, the first bans. The first jump from Devil's Rock. The more she wrote, the better she felt.

Once she'd depleted her memory, she felt almost rested despite not having slept a wink.

It was as if someone had pressed a reset button in her mind.

We're almost to the top of the hill now, struggling up the last little bit of the slope.

She follows me like a faithful dog.

She insisted on dragging her little cart behind her, with a Barbie doll in it; she has a hard time pulling it, but still she keeps up with me. At the top, we stop to catch our breath.

It's dusk; the sun is bathing in the sea like a blood orange.

I take the items from my backpack. Bone-dry kindling, gasoline, and matches. She looks at me expectantly, hugging her doll.

'Are you sure you want to use that doll?' I ask. 'I thought it was your best one.'

'No, I dropped her in the toilet when I was going to wash her hair in the sink. She smells all weird now.'

'Okay, it's up to you.'

We build a little pyre at the very top of the slope and place the doll on top.

'Now she can see all of Antibes,' I say, 'and everyone can watch as she is punished.'

She nods gravely.

I take out the plastic bottle of gasoline and show her how to pour it all over the wood and the doll.

'Can I light it?' she asks.

'Yes, if you're careful.'

Her hands are shaking, and she lets go of the match so quickly it goes out before it reaches the pyre. She lights a new one and this time it catches. The doll burns; soon its hair is charred and its face becomes a black mask. The flames lick at the evening sky.

'Now she has been punished,' she says. 'That dumb doll.'

'That's right!' I say, sitting down in front of her and taking her hands. 'Sara, you understand, don't you, that if you tell Mom and Dad about this we can't play this game anymore.'

The flames are reflected in her eyes. They're really glowing.

She's so excited that her chin is trembling.

'I'll never say a word,' she says, pressing her lips into a thin line. 'Never, ever.'

28

'Now we're going to play charades!' Oswald exclaimed once they had taken their seats.

Little waves of uneasiness spread through the room. Sofia tried to figure out if this was a joke they were expected to laugh at, and turned up the corners of her mouth, but then she realized Oswald was serious. His eyes were amused and sharp all at once.

He'd asked her to call all the unit heads to the office. Bosse's whole gang. Mona for the library; Olof for personal advising; Anna for the annexes and Katarina for the garden. Yes, Anna and Katarina were to come too, whether or not they were in Penance. Plus Benjamin for the transport team and Ulf, who was responsible for the farm.

'I hope you don't find this degrading. After all, you didn't protest when I was wrestling with that disgusting fatty the other day. So I thought maybe you were in the mood for a game.'

No one said anything. Being in his presence had started to feel like walking a tightrope. You had to react properly, avoid missteps, or else you would tumble into a pit of uncomfortable surprises.

'I'm sure you know the rules. I've even made the cards myself.'

There was a pile of index cards in front of him, and he held up the top one. Bosse's name was written on the back in marker.

A shrill laugh broke the silence. It was Ulf from the farm; he had misread the situation and thought Oswald was joking. Or maybe it just slipped out. Oswald stood up and clenched his fists until his knuckles went white. Ulf had already swallowed his laughter, but Oswald was heading for him.

Now he's in for it, she thought. Yet she noticed that the urge to intervene was weaker than it had been last time. It was too dangerous, even idiotic, because it wouldn't help. Instead she summoned that voice of reason from the back of her mind.

I'll deal with this later. There's nothing I can do right now.

But Oswald stopped before he reached Ulf.

'I can assure you, Ulf, that this is no joke.'

'No, sir, I understand. Forgive me.'

'Good, because it's very simple. You will each receive a card with your name on it. On the back is one word. You have to get the rest of the group to guess the word. Without speaking, of course. You may only use gestures and sounds, just like in charades. And I'll time you!' He held up a stopwatch. 'When you're done, you will fasten the card to your uniform with a safety pin so the whole staff can see it. The safety pins are over there on the table.'

He pointed at the table in the corner where she usually put his mail. He really had planned this carefully, arranged it behind her back. That needled her. Not so much the ridiculous game, but the fact that he'd excluded her from his plans. That she was one of those to be humiliated.

'And there's a prize, of course,' he went on. 'Whoever is fastest doesn't have to wear their card. So hurry it up, we don't have all day.'

He picked up the pile of cards and walked around placing them on each person's lap, name up.

'Bosse, you may begin.'

Bosse stepped up in front of the others and stood so the group was in front of him and Oswald, who was sitting at his desk, was behind him. He looked down at his card, embarrassed and clearly off balance.

'The clock is ticking,' Oswald said.

Bosse squatted down, shuffled forward, and flapped his arms.

'Bird!' someone shouted.

'Rooster!'

'Duck!'

Bosse shook his head frantically and clucked loudly.

Suddenly it came to her. The word Oswald often used to describe Bosse.

'Chickenshit,' she called.

Bosse nodded and shot her a grateful look as he stood up.

'Come here and give me the card, Bosse.'

Bosse hurried over to obey.

'Turn around.'

Oswald fastened the card on Bosse's back so everyone could see the big, sprawling letters. CHICKENSHIT.

'You may not take it off until I give you permission. Once you've shown some initiative. Maybe even a little leadership. Your turn, Ulf.'

Ulf was one of the hardest workers on the property. He always pitched in when help was needed; he was almost imposingly cheerful, laughed nervously at his own jokes, and always tried to please everyone. But now he looked terribly unhappy as he stood there gazing down at his card and scratching his head. He pointed at his leg.

'Leg!'

'Knee!'

'Kick!'

He shook his head. Again he gestured down along his leg, then pointed to his teeth and his head.

'Bone!' Benjamin called.

Ulf nodded, patting his hands on his head again.

'Idiot!'

'Head!'

'Skeleton!'

Ulf shook his head, at a loss. No one said anything for a moment; their ideas had run out. Ulf got down on his knees and banged his head against a chair.

'Bonehead!' Anna shrieked.

Ulf exhaled and picked up his card.

Most of them had gotten caught up in the game. The mood was jolly — after all, it was only a game and Oswald looked so cheerful as he watched them.

Now it was Anna's turn. She giggled when she read her card. Oswald shot her a warning look, so she stiffened and thought for a moment. She tugged at her shirt, flapping its hem. She shook out her whole body. Went back to the shirt. She alternated between the two several times. It took ages for someone to catch on; in the meantime people called out everything from 'hot' to 'seizures.'

'Loose.'

Madeleine had finally figured it out.

'Ooh, damn!' Oswald said. 'That took almost two minutes. That's what happens when you have an excess of hormones and a shortage of brain cells.'

Anna's cheeks flushed as she went to fetch a safety pin. She began to fasten the card at the bottom edge of her blazer.

'Not there,' said Oswald. 'Right over your chest where everyone can read it. Either there, or I'll put it on your back.'

She quickly moved the card up and Oswald nodded at Benjamin.

His eyes were locked on Sofia's for a moment as he stood before them. Then he looked down at the card and smiled. He began to dart his head this way and that as if avoiding flying objects. Dodger, of course. Oswald's great complaint about Benjamin was that he always shirked his duties. The answer was on the tip of Sofia's tongue, but she waited for someone else to guess. She didn't want to attack Benjamin. She was still having trouble getting to grips with this peculiar game.

But Oswald was on top form. He could hardly contain himself each time a new person fastened their card to their clothes.

Mona, who was next to last, stiffened when she read her card. Her eyes moved between the card and the group again and again. She couldn't seem to start; her legs were shaking and all the colour had drained from her face.

'We don't have all day,' Oswald said, drumming his fingers on the desk.

Mona couldn't get a grip on herself. She stood perfectly still, her mouth open as if her jaw was locked. Her eyelids fluttered as if she might faint.

Oswald came over to her.

'You stop this nonsense, or there will be consequences. We don't have all day here.'

Mona turned away and stared down at the floor.

'Come here, Anna!' Oswald called. Anna quickly minced up to him.

'Look at her,' he said, pointing at Mona. 'This is how she looks after three days on the ViaTerra program. She can't even play a child's game. How do you feel when you look at her?'

'Angry,' Anna responded. 'Really angry, in fact.'

'Go closer,' Oswald said. 'Look at that sour face. Do you know what it says on her card?'

'Nope,' said Anna.

'It says "sourpuss", of course. And she doesn't want to admit it, that she walks around here poisoning ViaTerra with her negative energy.'

'Ugh, nasty,' said Anna.

'That's right. What do you want to do with her now?'

Anna tried to make eye contact, but Mona wouldn't look at her. Anna grabbed her head and pulled it up. Mona's gaze was still distant, like a little kid who doesn't want to give in.

'I actually feel like I want to smack her,' Anna said.

'Then do it!' Oswald replied. 'Why do you all make me do your dirty work? There's no peer pressure here. Do whatever you want to her, Anna.'

Anna didn't hesitate. Her hand flew up and cracked against Mona's cheek. And again, even harder. Mona didn't speak or move, but an angry red patch flared where Anna's palm had struck her. A single tear trickled down her cheek.

'Stop being such a pussy,' said Anna.

'That's right,' said Oswald. 'You can both sit down again.'

Sofia watched them: Anna's haughty expression and Mona's awkward presence. She wondered why Oswald had chosen Anna in particular. She supposed he knew she would do anything for him.

'Your turn, Sofia. I saved the best for last.'

When she looked at her own card, she burned with rage,

because the word there was so unfair and unwarranted. Then again, it wouldn't be hard. She stuck her hands out and pretended to straddle something. The group was well warmed up by now.

'Witch!'

'Five seconds. No label for you, Sofia. Congratulations, you won!'

Benjamin's eyes found hers; she saw a gleam of amusement in them.

You stupid little Oswald clone, she thought. *I'll deal with you later.*

They were allowed to take a break after the game.

'Get back to work so you can get something done before dinner. We'll discuss this later tonight,' said Oswald.

*

The mood at dinner was subdued. No one on staff wanted to ask about the labels. But they certainly stared and whispered. Sofia found that she felt some schadenfreude over being spared a label. She tried to ignore the general mood and was spearing a few beans on her fork when her pager buzzed in her blazer pocket.

Same gang to my office again after dinner.

She knew he meant everyone with the labels. She quickly wrote all their names down on her notepad and walked around the dining room to let them know. Everyone was there but Mona, so she sent a message to her pager.

The chairs were as they'd left them in the office. She sneaked a look at the desk: no papers or cards. Just Oswald, who was reading something at his computer. He must have showered, because his hair was damp and the office smelled like soap and aftershave. He was wearing one of those white shirts that never seemed to wrinkle.

'Are the idiots coming?'

'I told them to.'

'Then you can sit beside me. After all, you won the contest.' He pointed at a little stool in front of his chair. She sat down and felt immediately ridiculous, like a schoolgirl who had gotten the best grade on a test.

The others came up the stairs, panting. They collected themselves, then slipped in and sat down.

'Is everyone here?'

Bosse looked around and nodded.

'I just want to know what you learned from our little game today,' said Oswald. No one dared to answer at first, but then Ulf raised his hand.

'Well, if we don't deal with situations around here then you have to do it. And that makes us more like training wheels instead of the engines in our own machinery. Sort of.'

Oswald considered this and nodded slowly.

'Yes, maybe. But you're not even training wheels. You've become completely destructive. You're not even cogs or spokes — you're a wrench in the works.'

The room filled with a dull murmur of agreement.

'I hope you've learned something,' he said. 'Because next time we'll play musical chairs and the losers will jump from Devil's Rock — all except for the one who gets the last chair, of course. And after that we can play duck duck goose.'

He was dead serious. Sofia let her eyes rest on Benjamin's face for a moment. He looked grim and tense.

That was when she noticed the empty chair behind him.

Mona's chair.

'Mona's missing!' she cried.

She stood up so quickly that her stool tipped backwards and thudded onto Oswald's foot. But by the time he yelped she was already halfway out the door. There was only one thing on her mind. She had to find Mona, and fast.

'We need to have a little talk about your future,' he says solemnly.

I don't get why he always has to be so bombastic. As if everything he does is a great sacrifice.

I don't believe he actually likes me, but it's become convenient to have me here. Less bitching from his wife.

And he had to think about the future — with Bugeye as his sole heir, it wasn't looking so hot.

I know all of that.

And yet I force myself to give him a grateful look.

'You have to have an identity,' he says. 'You know, a name and so on. Fredrik Johansson no longer exists. And he's not going to rise again.'

You have no idea, I think.

He can tell that my thoughts have wandered for a moment, but his reading of me is all wrong. As usual.

'Don't worry, we can still call you Fredrik if you like. As a nickname.'

'Can't you just adopt me, so I can be a von Bärensten? That's what I am, after all.'

'It's not that simple, Fredrik. You can't adopt someone who doesn't exist, as I'm sure you understand. You need a name, a birth certificate, all of that.'

'I still really want to be named von Bärensten,' I say.

'I'm sure we can work that out.'

'I have to thank you,' I say. 'For everything you've done for me.'
Jesus, it sounds so smarmy.

But he swallows it hook, line, and sinker.

'You're welcome, Fredrik. You've really come to be part of our little family.'

That's the least a person could say. I'm Emilie's confidant and Bugeye has been following me around like a shadow ever since we started our games.

'A man is coming tomorrow to help with the paperwork,' he says. 'You'll be there, but I'll handle the talking.'

'Does he know who I am?'

'No, he doesn't. And he's not going to ask.'

29

She dashed down the stairs like a maniac, almost stumbling at the landing, but she caught the railing and flew into the corridor where Mona's room was. Loudly, impatiently, she banged at the door and yanked it open when no one answered.

Inside, Mona was hanging.

Her feet were still touching the chair; it looked like the tips of her toes were glued there, while her body had fallen forward, supported by the noose. Her head was turned toward the door so Sofia could see her wide-open eyes bulging from their sockets. Her tongue was protruding between her lips and something gooey and thick hung from the corner of her mouth. But she was moving. One leg was twitching as if it were trying to shake itself loose from the chair.

There was a deafening scream, and suddenly she realized it was coming from her own mouth. She took a few steps toward the chair but was shoved aside by strong hands and she fell to her knees.

'Dammit, don't touch the chair!'

It was Benjamin's angry voice. All of a sudden he was up on the chair, lifting Mona's head out of the noose. He held her in his arms, balancing her body for a moment and then stepping to the floor. Sofia's mind was working furiously but her thoughts were completely illogical: she thought it looked not like a noose but some sort of cord. How peculiar that Benjamin had saved Mona a second time. And she thought she had read somewhere that hanging with a short rope took more time than with a long one.

Mona was limp on the floor and Benjamin was blowing into her mouth. Sofia sat down and took her hand. She didn't know what else to do. She looked down at Mona's pale face and was flooded with relief, because she could see life in it: a faint blush in her cheeks. Tiny beads of sweat popping out on her forehead. Her eyes seemed to have sunk back into their sockets. Benjamin blew and blew countless times, and Mona began to cough and gurgle. She turned her head to the side and threw up. A pool of stir-fried beans from dinner formed on the floor. Sofia found that this was the first time she had ever been happy to see someone vomit.

Curious colleagues crowded into the doorway, but no one dared to come in. Oswald had arrived by now and shouted, 'Get out of here! Everyone leave. Right now!'

The others scattered and fled like cockroaches. Oswald stepped into the room, stood behind them, and stared down at Mona. Sofia didn't want to look up at him. She clutched Mona's hand and fixed her gaze on the other woman's roving eyes.

Benjamin turned to Oswald.

'We have to call an ambulance. She needs medical attention.'

Oswald crouched down beside them.

'Let me look at her.'

Sofia reluctantly let go of Mona's hand and moved aside.

Mona shied away from Oswald, but he took her wrist, felt her pulse; lifted her eyelids and looked at the whites of her eyes. Then he placed his hands around her neck and she whimpered.

'Does it hurt?'

'Just a little.' Her first words. So she could talk.

'We don't need an ambulance. She'll recover,' Oswald said firmly.

'But she tried to kill herself. Don't we have to report that sort of thing? And shouldn't she see a doctor?' Benjamin was clearly exasperated.

'Have you forgotten I studied medicine? I'm telling you she'll be fine.'

Benjamin swallowed and mumbled something incomprehensible. 'The noose was a little crooked around her neck,' he said at last.

'Yes, that's probably why she's still alive,' Oswald said. 'She couldn't even do that right.'

'No doctor,' Mona whispered from the floor. 'Don't need one.'

'You heard her,' said Oswald. 'Who here takes care of the sick?'

'That's Elin. She's a personal advisor, but she does double duty, sort of.'

'Does she have any education?'

'A little, she's a nursing assistant.'

'Then she can take care of Mona around the clock until she's better. You know we can't bring in the police or doctors. She's looking better already.'

Mona tried to sit up but sank back to the floor. She looked awful. Her face was sweaty, her hair was stringy, and her skin was a pale greenish tone. You could see the angry red marks around her neck where the noose had cut in. Mona had hanged herself with an extension cord. She'd wound the knot carelessly around the hook the ceiling light was suspended from, and had placed the noose around her neck at an angle. She'd done it all in a rush, so her habitual clumsiness had saved her life.

'Listen to me,' Oswald said to Mona. 'Try not to stand up yet. Benjamin and I will lift you into bed. Sofia, make sure someone cleans this up.' He eyed the vomit on the floor in distaste.

'Benjamin, I want you to talk to Mona's husband — what's his name again?'

'Anders.'

'Right, Anders. You'll have to explain what happened. He'll have to move to a dormitory so Elin can stay with Mona for the time being.'

He was talking about Mona as if she wasn't even there. But then he nailed her with his gaze.

'Are you out of your mind, Mona? Surely you're not trying to prove me wrong as I try to sort out this mess around here?'

'Not at all . . . sir,' Mona whispered.

Oswald looked up at the ceiling, where the cord was still dangling from the hook.

'Take that down, Benjamin. And stay here until Sofia has fetched Elin.'

As Sofia went down the stairs her hands began to shake, and no matter how hard she tried it was impossible to make them be still. Then she felt her legs begin to quake, so she sat down on the steps for a minute to collect herself.

The whole staircase seemed to be swaying, and she felt so sick that she had to close her eyes. But the darkness behind her eyelids didn't make the swaying go away, and when she peeked again it was as if the staircase had been erased. She thought she might feel better if she went to throw up, so she forced herself to stand and staggered down the stairs.

Fresh, cold air met her in the yard. It was dark; someone had forgotten to turn on the outdoor lights. She stood still for a moment, breathing slowly through her nose and letting the air out through her mouth. She felt the chilly air settling on her trembling body like a cold blanket. After a while, everything became still. She thought about defying Oswald and calling the emergency number or the police, but it seemed pointless. After all, Mona had said she didn't want that.

Elin was cleaning in the annexe. Sofia could tell by the expression on her face that the rumours about Mona had spread like wildfire.

'Well, there aren't any guests anyway,' Elin said. 'I'll come right away.'

'Bring a nightgown, toothbrush, and stuff from your room, because you'll have to sleep there,' Sofia said. 'See you upstairs.'

She resisted the urge to spill the whole story to Elin, to blurt out how horrible it had been. On the way upstairs she took a mop and bucket from a cleaning closet. She would clean up the vomit herself. She still felt dizzy as she walked up the stairs — they started swaying again. It became hard to breathe and her chest ached. Just as she was about to sit down and catch her breath, she caught sight of Oswald on his way down.

'Well,' he said. 'Now I have to tell the staff. Why do I always end up getting stuck with the really fun jobs around here?'

Then he noticed the state she was in.

'What is it? You look awful.'

She mumbled something about how she felt a little strange.

'You're just in shock,' Oswald informed her, looking at the mop and bucket. 'Go on and clean up. Then you can let Elin take over and you can come up to the office. I'll help you. Understand?'

She nodded and stood still as he passed her on the stairs. She dragged her feet the last few steps to Mona's room. Benjamin was still there, and they exchanged meaningful looks.

'Later,' he said.

Mona was in bed, looking pitiful and pale with her stringy hair spread over the pillow. Sofia cleaned the floor first, then sat on the edge of the bed and took Mona's hand.

'You don't have to say anything if you don't want to. It's probably best to save your voice. Elin will be here soon to take care of you. Get some sleep now.'

Mona gave a rattling cough.

'Anders and Elvira?'

'They'll come visit once you've gotten some rest.'

'What have I done? It was all so dark. I'm sorry.'

'You don't have to say anything.'

'It was mostly for Elvira. I thought if I was gone Anders would get to take her back to the mainland. This place isn't very good for her.'

'Why not?'

'I just know it,' Mona said, pressing her lips together. 'I can feel it.'

There's something she isn't telling me, Sofia thought. *There's something fishy about all this.*

'But can't you just leave the island when your contracts run out?'

'Oh, you know how it is. The contracts are just symbolic. You can't just leave ViaTerra. It's a lifelong mission. A calling.'

Just then, Elin stepped through the door, her cheeks flushed with zeal.

'I'll take over now,' she said firmly.

Benjamin had left the room without anyone noticing. Sofia spoke to Elin for a minute and promised to check in again later.

Just as she left the room, she recalled what Oswald had said on

302

the stairs: he would help her. She hoped he wasn't going to chew her out, because she was totally exhausted. It was hard enough to get her body to move, and her brain seemed to be lagging even farther behind.

★

'Have a seat, Sofia,' he said as she walked into his office. He had placed her desk chair in front of his own desk. 'That's just so you won't fall asleep in the easy chair,' he said.

So he had been waiting for her.

It felt strange to sit down in front of him. Like she was a visitor.

'Everything okay with Mona?'

'Yes, Elin's there now.'

'You've had a shock. It's no wonder, but I'm going to help you.'

She nodded, wondering what on earth he was going to do.

'Do you remember thesis number two, the one about infinite strength? When you recall moments you were strong and draw energy from them?'

'Of course. That one and number four were my favourites.'

'Good. But now we're going to flip it around. Instead of drawing energy from the events, you're going to release energy. Get rid of your negative energy. Do you understand?'

'Yes, but can you do that? Change the theses?'

'What do you think?' he snapped. 'Who do you think wrote them?'

'Okay. I understand.'

'Good. Now close your eyes. Take a deep breath and let it out through your mouth. Relax. You should close your eyes as we do this.'

She stared at the darkness of her eyelids, noting that the sensation of swaying had almost stopped, but she felt strangely weak.

'Recall a time you felt helpless.'

'Now?'

'In the past, of course. Tell me about the first memory that pops up.'

His voice had grown deep, almost hypnotic, and it pulled her into a muddle of images swirling by. Her brain became numb and her body felt heavy.

She told him about everything that popped up. Memories of feeling weak and helpless. It was strange to find that they were so neatly lined up, in chronological order. All she had to do was select each one. And every time an incident came up, he told her to go through it and let go of the negative energy.

'Release the energy!' he said. 'Let it float up to the ceiling. To the sky.'

His voice had grown hazy and thin, and yet it reached into the deepest parts of her.

And then came *that* incident. Perhaps it was the very first one. It had been during the winter, when she was five or six, and it was snowing — tiny, pretty flakes whirling in the wind. She had run up to the highway even though she wasn't allowed. At the edge of the road lay a little dog, whimpering softly. It was on its side and it must have been run over, because it was lying there so limp and still. A gust of wind blew a bit of snow off the road, and a light dusting fell over her and the dog. She could recall the exact way it had looked at her, with sad black eyes. Its nose had been cold and wet when she touched it. And somehow she knew, just knew, that it was going to die.

The memory was painful. Her chest ached and she felt a thick lump in her throat; she couldn't get any words out, didn't want to say more.

'Go through the incident again,' Oswald said. 'Release all the harmful energy. You can handle this, Sofia!'

She started to cry.

What is this?

Why does it feel like this?

Oswald made her tell him about the dog several times, until her tears stopped and she felt completely drained.

'Now you can open your eyes,' he said.

The first thing she saw was his hand on the pen, and the notepad. He had written down what she'd said. When she met his gaze, he looked pleased.

'There's the answer, Sofia! That's why you're such a bleeding heart sometimes. You've gotten everything all mixed up, you see. Mona's no puppy. She's a grown woman who is responsible for her own actions. Do you feel better now?'

'Yes, I do,' she lied. Because she didn't want him to keep digging through her memories on any account.

'You see, Mona did all this on purpose,' he went on. 'To gain sympathy and to get out of working so hard. She's weak and has no willpower, and she doesn't belong here. We will send her to the mainland. After she's signed every goddamn confidentiality agreement we have, of course.'

'What about Elvira?'

She couldn't help but ask.

'Elvira can make her own decision about where to go. She's not a child. And if you ask me, she's made of much stronger stuff than Mona.' He suddenly stood. 'Listen, I'm going to retire early tonight. You can clean up here and go to bed once you're done.'

He walked around the desk and stood behind her, grasping her hair and pulling her head back until she was looking up at him. He took one hand from her hair and placed it around her chin to bend her neck even farther, until the muscles of her jaw hurt.

'You have to learn to relax. Stop taking everything so seriously.'

Something hard pressed against her back.

Ohmygod that's his erection!

He let go of her chin and let one hand fall to her breast, where it rested for an instant. His hand was limp, but he began to rub his palm over the exact location of her nipple as he pressed his hardness against her shoulder blade.

'You're so stiff. Relax, for Christ's sake.'

His hands went limp again and moved off her body.

She was sitting with her back to the door and couldn't see as he left the room; she only heard his steps and the door closing.

Once again she was shaking. She didn't move for a moment, just sat exactly as he had left her. She noticed that she didn't feel anything. No excitement. No arousal. *Well, that's the first time*, she thought.

She wondered what he wanted with her. What would happen if she spoke up. She tried to think of someone she could talk to. The thought of going to Bosse was so absurd she laughed out loud. The thought of talking to Benjamin made her feel sick. She knew exactly what he would say: it was her imagination. She was just shaken up by what had happened to Mona. She could even hear his voice saying, *How do you know? Did you see it? Maybe he just had something hard in his pocket.*

It would be unthinkable to talk to one of the other women.

They would only be jealous and hate her more than they did already.

She was always alone with him when he touched her. It would be her word against his, so in fact there was only one way out. *Let him do it*, she thought. *If he really tries to come after me I can always knee him in the crotch, and who would he turn to then?*

She tried to shake him off, but it was too quiet in the room. She could still feel him against her back. The breast he'd touched felt warm; the air in the office was heavy and stifling.

She went to a window and opened it wide. Something was glowing down in a little grove by the annexes. She tried to make out what it was and discovered Anders sneaking a cigarette. Probably worried sick about Mona. She left the window open and paced the room for a while. It would be impossible to sleep now, and she would make Benjamin's night hell if she went back to their room.

Then she sat back down and sneaked a look at Oswald's surveillance screens, mostly because she was curious about how the staff had reacted to what had happened to Mona. Most of them were still awake, sitting and chatting on their beds. They looked a little shaken. *So they do care*, she thought.

When she got to number seven, the button that showed her old dormitory, she found another, blank button after it.

This was the first time she'd noticed it. She pushed number seven first, and saw a wide-angle view of the dormitory. Madeleine was sitting on the bed and Anna was already under the covers. Anna had moved in when Sofia moved out, so the residents of the room these days were Anna, Madeleine, and Elvira.

Madeleine was speaking loudly and eagerly. Sofia didn't dare turn up the volume but she could make out phrases like, 'What the fuck got into her?' and 'When will all this misery end?'

Then she pressed the blank button.

A new image flickered, then grew clear on the screen. Apparently there was an extra camera in her old room.

On the screen was Elvira, and she was in the shower.

The party is in full swing.

I'm standing off to the side, bored as hell.

I've been given everything I desired in these past few years, but still, nothing.

My good name.

The best schools.

Thousand-euro trousers.

But it's the people, these fucking people, who bore me to the point of insanity.

I look around the great room and can't see anyone, not a single person, I like.

Dad with his bloodshot piggy eyes. He's become a closet alcoholic.

Emilie, tugging at her trashy short skirt. Her anxiety, those constant worry vibes radiating from her. So timid and sympathetic it makes me want to puke.

The chicks in the corner. Their giggles, glances, and smiles.

But I don't smile back. Not tonight.

I've had enough. I'm tired of these people.

Then I spot Bugeye.

She's all by herself in another corner. Her dress is too big and hangs off her like a sack. It's like putting a Chanel on a walking stick.

Picking at the tip of her nose and looking around uncertainly.

She doesn't fit in.

She never will. She turns her face toward me.

That face I've been forced to look at for almost six years now. And it sure hasn't gotten any prettier with age.

Her eyes stick out of her skull like little balls. That mouth, thin as a line, and her pointy nose.

She's got pimples now too.

I can't bear to look at that face a single day more.

Not even an hour, a minute, a second.

And then, at that depressing moment, the idea strikes me.

That one could break a person down, erase who they are, and build them up again in a new way.

Like the phoenix rising from the ashes.

But on a whole different level.

More like casting iron with a hammer and tongs.

And all at once I know who will be first.

She's scraping her foot against the marble floor. Sending pleading looks my way.

'Save me, Fredrik, save me from all this!'

Doesn't fit in.

Never will.

And that's the whole point.

30

She would bring it up with him. Stand firm. She would not be a coward.

Three days had passed since the Mona incident. On the first day, Sofia had visited Mona's room again and again. She hadn't dared to let her out of sight. But Mona had recovered quickly and now she looked perfectly normal again, aside from the marks on her throat. Sofia had started to hope that Oswald would make good on his threat to send Mona away from the island. She'd read somewhere that people who attempt suicide and fail usually try again.

And then there was Elvira. Who really shouldn't have been there.

At night, Sofia puzzled over the camera in the shower, and on the third night everything became crystal clear. Elvira worked in the kitchen. The kitchen staff worked until nine and showered afterwards, before going to bed. And it was always nine o'clock, or a little before, when Oswald sent Sofia out. 'Go down and see what got done today,' he would say.

That must be it.

I know I'm not wrong.

That must, must, must be it.

Then she remembered something else: how Oswald usually

looked at Elvira. Up and down and up again, the way you might look at a woman. Not a child.

So now she was standing before his desk and gathering her courage. Her stomach was full of butterflies and her palms started to sweat.

The camera in the shower had to come down. She didn't even care about what he'd seen — all that mattered was that the goddamn camera had to go.

Say it now! Out with it!

'Sir . . . I noticed there's an extra button for the surveillance cameras, one more button after number seven.'

His expression didn't change; he just kept reading the paper. He didn't even look up.

'Oh, so you've started using the system to spy on the staff. Did you see anything exciting?'

'No, not at all. I wasn't spying. I was just dusting and I noticed the button.'

'Those idiots put the camera in the wrong spot. It was supposed to be aimed at Madeleine's bed. I wanted to keep an extra eye on her; she was acting so strange.'

He's lying, what a hell of a lie.

She wondered if there was any polite way to say it, to tell him that he was a liar and she was no idiot. *Oops, we put the camera in the shower instead of the bedroom.* Did he really believe she was that stupid?

He looked up from the paper, stared at her, and shook his head.

'Let it go, Sofia! Why are you so hung up on a bloody button? Don't you know we have more important things to deal with?'

A hardy mosquito had sneaked through the window and was sucking blood from his temple, but she didn't say anything. She thought about how funny the bite would look the next day. Her mood went sour; the conversation was over. At least for the moment. But she wasn't about to give up. She was determined to confront him again.

And maybe she would have, if the epidemic hadn't broken out that very day.

★

A fresh sort of calm lingered on the property when she went to lunch. The sun was peeking out after several weeks of fog, rain, sleet, and wind. It was the third week in December. Although the sky was clear, the air smelled like snow. Heavy grey clouds gathered on the horizon, apparently on their way to the island, but frost still glinted off the trees and bushes in the sunlight.

There would be a meeting after lunch. As soon as it was over she would talk to Oswald again. She was not about to give up.

The meeting was unusually relaxed. They pulled up chairs and sat in a circle around Oswald. He hadn't brought any papers and was wearing jeans and a wool sweater. He almost seemed relaxed. For a while he spoke about what had happened in the past few months — the staff was doing better now that they understood the theses. He explained that he would be going to the mainland in the next week to reconnect with his contacts there. He was thinking about opening the annexes to guests again in the spring. He was acting so friendly that Sofia found herself thinking that the camera in the shower really might have been a mistake made by the technicians. She struggled with the thought for a moment, but her conviction that he was lying to her returned.

All of a sudden, someone sneezed. One, two, three times — it was Ulf, who was sitting in the front row. He was quick to bury his nose in his elbow, but the first sneeze had reached Oswald unhindered. The room grew deadly silent. Oswald threw his hands into the air in a gesture of hopelessness.

'This is just ridiculous. Am I supposed to work with children who don't even have the manners to cover their mouths when they sneeze?'

He stood up and looked at them with distaste — not just at Ulf, who was holding both hands to his face and trying to hold back another sneeze. Oswald was already on his way out, but suddenly he turned on his heel.

'Check that idiot's temperature. He looks fucking sick.'

Sure enough, Ulf had a fever. And so it began. When Sofia told Oswald about Ulf he was beside himself.

'I told you in the fall! You and Bosse were supposed to fix up the basement so we could isolate sick people down there. You have to handle this. Get the basement in order. Take everyone's temperature. Anyone with a fever must be isolated for at least twenty-four hours.'

He was shouting. Tiny, invisible droplets of spittle hit her cheek.

'I'll take care of it.'

'And no more chats with the staff until everyone is healthy again.'

She wanted to point out that, in fact, only one person was sick so far. But she knew he was terrified of anything to do with viruses or bacteria.

Besides, while using her computer in secret, she had read that the flu was sweeping the mainland. And she knew who would shoulder the blame — only Benjamin had been outside the manor walls in the past few months.

She dragged Bosse down to the basement with her. It still smelled like mould down there, and it was cold and damp after the very rainy autumn.

'Maybe we can bring down some electric heaters,' Bosse suggested. 'And tealights and stuff, to make it a little cosier.'

Sofia looked around the gloomy, ice-cold room sceptically, sincerely happy she wasn't sick.

'What will we do with the staff's belongings, then?' She looked at the piles on the floor in concern.

'Oh, we'll just shove them in the corner over here. There will still be room for at least ten beds. And hey, we can use bunk beds so there will be twenty. There are a bunch of extra beds in one of the barns; I've seen them before. Those on Penance can fix it all up tonight.'

Sofia knew at once that this would be one of the most loathsome projects she'd ever taken part in. But she couldn't come up with any other solution, so she decided to let Bosse handle most of it. She would keep her distance as best she could.

'Okay, you get the room ready and I'll make sure everyone takes their temperature.'

She went up to Mona's room to order Elin to make the rounds with a thermometer — she wasn't about to do that herself. The thought of being close to all those disease vectors and passing the virus on to Oswald was unbearable.

Before she went upstairs, she peered out the glass pane in the door that led to the yard. It had started to snow. Big, thick flakes swirled around and caught in the tops of the trees. The lawn was already white. The sky was leaden and grey.

She found Elin at Mona's bedside. Sofia suggested that one of the guards stay with Mona while Elin went around taking temperatures.

As soon as she reached the stairs up to the staff office, she heard scattered sneezes and coughs. *It's just psychosomatic,* she thought.

But it soon became clear that Benny, who was dozing in the sentry box, also had a fever. And Lina in the kitchen had glassy eyes and was coughing and sneezing almost continuously. They really did have an epidemic on their hands. When she looked out the window, she spotted the group on Penance trudging through the snow with the beds. It was already getting dark.

Once the beds were arranged in the basement, it looked even worse. They were so close together that you had to worm your way through the narrow spaces to get in or out. They were also so tall that they blocked the faint light from the ceiling fixtures.

The mattresses were old and worn and smelled stale. Elin had gathered some herbs and teas for the sick, but when Sofia asked if she had anything for the fever, like paracetamol, Elin gave her a look of horror.

'That stuff is absolutely against the rules here, Sofia. Franz would never allow it.'

As they stood and looked at the horrid room, Oswald came in. He was wearing a face mask over his nose and mouth, the sort of mask they had used while renovating the living spaces. Sofia held back a giggle; he looked rather comical. At the same time her chest constricted, because she was sure he would fly into a rage when he saw the wretched state of the sick bay.

'This isn't so bad,' he said instead. 'At least they'll want to get better fast.'

★

It only took a few days before half the staff was sick. Luckily Elin had managed to avoid getting a fever, although she was coughing and sneezing. Mona was helping them care for the sick now.

Sofia went back and forth between Oswald's office and the basement, but tried to hold her breath as much as she could down there, and avoided touching anything. Every time she came back to the office, Oswald told her to wash her hands and to avoid coming anywhere near him. She washed her hands so often that they became red and chapped. Every surface had to be wiped down with alcohol several times a day.

In the midst of all this, Oswald called the unit heads to a meeting in the dining room. At first Sofia thought she had misheard.

'Sir, more than half the staff are sick with fevers right now.'

'Then they'll have to put on masks, because I want to talk to them.'

With Bosse's help, she collected masks for everyone and gathered the coughing, sneezing, glassy-eyed group in the dining room. They looked like mummies in their masks. *This sort of thing doesn't happen in real life*, she thought when she looked at them. *This is a bad dream and I'm going to wake up soon. God help me, let it be a dream.*

Oswald was over half an hour late and several of the staff had already nodded off.

'Look at that, you all seem hale and hearty!' he said when he came through the door.

He stared straight at her and raised one eyebrow. She smiled dutifully, but her insides flooded with something as cold as ice.

'I'm going to the mainland the day after tomorrow to reconnect with people, so we can get the ViaTerra program up and running again. I'll be gone for a week. I have a list here with things that must be done while I'm gone. Sofia, you can make

317

copies for everyone tonight.' He handed her the list, which appeared to have at least fifty points. She wondered how in the world they would get it all done with half the staff incapacitated. It was December 22, but there wasn't a trace of Christmas around the property. She found herself wishing that the bays would freeze so the ferry wouldn't be able to return. That he would be stuck on the mainland for a long time. For once she wasn't ashamed of her thoughts.

She looked down at the list again. Their Christmas present.

'You can't infect me if I'm not here, so you can work even if you aren't feeling so well,' he said.

Not a sound from the staff. Not even the usual murmur of agreement.

But then Benjamin stood up.

No, Benjamin, be quiet, don't say anything stupid!

'Sir, don't you think everyone needs to rest at least until their temperatures have gone down? Surely we can't have people running around working with fevers?'

She knew what was coming before it happened. Knuckles whitening as Oswald clenched his fists. Jaw muscles tightening. Eyes narrowing into thin lines. She tried to make time go backwards. Erase Benjamin's comment. But Oswald took a few big steps and was right in front of Benjamin. He grabbed him by the collar and shook him. He smacked his open hand down over Benjamin's head.

Benjamin didn't put up a fight, but his eyes were burning.

'I'm tired of your nonsense, Benjamin!' Oswald roared. 'Who do you think brought this fucking flu here? If you disagree with me again, I'm sending your ass back to the mainland. Permanently. Sofia will stay here.'

Oswald shoved him back into his chair.

Benjamin still didn't say anything, but he was trembling with pent-up rage.

Oswald looked at the rest of the group.

'Anyone else who wants to challenge me?'

No one responded. The dining room was perfectly silent. Even the coughing and sneezing had stopped.

★

The next day she had a splitting headache, a sore throat, and aching joints. She could hardly drag herself out of bed. Not even the hot water of the shower could revive her; instead she found herself cold and shivering. She knew she had a fever but decided to power on and trudge through the day, because Oswald was scheduled to leave the island the next day. Once he was gone she would sleep off her illness in her own room.

After lunch she felt weak and so dizzy she was afraid she might faint. She sat at her little desk and tried to look diligent, but she felt Oswald glancing at her over and over.

Soon after, the chills set in and her eyes and nose began to run. She bent her head toward her keyboard, hoping he wouldn't notice.

'Shouldn't you be out on the property making sure everything is getting done?'

She opened her mouth to respond but no words came out. Instead her throat released a croak — no matter how hard she tried, she couldn't speak.

He caught on right away.

'Are you nuts? Have you been sick this whole time? Are you

trying to infect me before I go? Get down to the basement. Pronto. But before you go, wipe down every single object and surface you've touched with alcohol. And don't come back out of the basement until you're well. Got it?'

She had neither the desire nor the strength to protest. Instead she was relieved, because her legs nearly collapsed underneath her when she stood up. She managed to drag herself around and sanitize everything she'd touched as he glared at her furiously.

The stale, damp basement felt like the overcrowded hospital once she'd dragged her body down the stairs. Almost every bed was occupied. There was coughing and groaning here and there, and the air smelled sharp with herbs and sweat. But she managed to find an empty bed and lay down on top of the blanket, still dressed, and fell asleep as soon as her head hit the pillow.

When she woke up eighteen hours later, her clothing and blankets were soaked with sweat. The fever seemed to have broken, but she was utterly wrung-out. Her mouth tasted bitter and metallic. Elin wasn't there and everyone else seemed to be asleep. According to her watch, it was six o'clock.

She lay still and gazed up at the dirty mattress of the bed above her for a while. A tiny spider was crawling through the dust and she watched it go. She heard snores, and someone was coughing in the bed next door.

It's Christmas Eve, she thought. *It's Christmas Eve and I'm lying here in this filth. I haven't bought a single present for Mom or Dad. I haven't even sent them a Christmas card. And the worst part is, I never even considered it.*

Images of the first part of her stay on the island flickered through her mind. Walks in the woods. Quiet moments at the lookout point. Visiting the cottage with Benjamin. The day when the library was ready. The parties early on, when they'd celebrated successes.

Then came images of the way things were now.

The wall and the barbed wire. The thick, constant fog. Punishments and abuse, both verbal and physical. Mona's face as she hung from the ceiling.

All at once, she knew it would never get better. Every time she'd felt hopeful, a new catastrophe turned out to be waiting just around the corner.

For a brief moment, she felt perfectly free as she lay in the stale room.

She had made up her mind.

I look down at my watch.

Four hours have passed.

Four hours, and she hasn't made a peep. She's tougher than I thought.

I put my ear to the wardrobe door to listen, but I don't hear a sound.

It strikes me that she might have died of fear in there. A skeleton in the closet, literally.

But then I hear a tiny sigh and a breath.

'Fredrik!' It's Emilie's anxious voice, from downstairs.

'Yes, Mom!'

'Do you know where Sara is?'

'No idea. Should I look for her?'

'No, we can wait a while. I'm sure she's just with a friend.'

Idiot. As if she has any friends.

Four hours, we agreed. Four hours in the dark. But I'm waiting, letting her stay in there a little bit longer.

You always have to show them that they can handle more than they think.

And of course, this is nothing compared with what will come later.

Four and a half hours, and I open the door. She blinks like an owl when the light hits her.

It takes a while to drag her out — she was squeezed in among suitcases and shoeboxes.

Then I unroll the sheet I've wound around her. She is cocooned like a caterpillar. Totally helpless.

'You did it! Four and a half hours.'

'But I thought —'

'Just a little bit extra. It's part of your test.'

She lights up; her eyes sparkle. 'What's the next part?'

'The water test,' I say, letting her relish the words for a moment.

31

Benjamin simply stared at her; he seemed to think he had mis-heard.

'You heard me. We have to get out of here. Leave. Escape!'

'Are you crazy?'

'Don't be such a hypocrite. I know you want out too. It's never going to get better around here.'

'But can't we just wait and see?'

'Wait and see if he kills someone? Benjamin, there's no debate here. I've had enough, and I'm leaving whether you do or not.'

It had taken a few weeks for her to gather enough courage to talk to him. But she had made up her mind, and it would not be swayed. She thought about it almost constantly — what it would feel like to be free. Go wherever she liked. See whoever she wanted to. Little things that had been trivial before she came to the island had suddenly become desirable. She wanted to watch TV, take a bus anywhere she wanted, eat a hamburger. She even found herself fantasizing about working at some crappy job and coming home after work and having time off, being totally free. She closed her eyes and tried to sense the buzz of people on the mainland living their regular old lives. She was so jealous of them it made her chest ache.

A nearly overwhelming restlessness was about to conquer her.

She wished she could teleport herself to the other side of the wall; she just wanted to get it over with. Because even though she had made up her mind, the fear of being caught gnawed at the back of her mind. What if she was stopped and detained? Forced back down off the wall, like Mira? Sent to Penance for an indeterminate amount of time, under guard around the clock?

And what about Oswald? She shuddered every time her mind touched upon what he would do if he knew. He had just returned from the mainland, and he had sensed a change in her right away. He was suddenly like a bloodhound on the trail of a fresh scent. His eyes followed her everywhere, suspicious. He squinted searchingly every time he spoke to her.

'You seem a little distracted, Sofia. Not quite all here,' he said one day.

'No sir, not at all. I'm just so glad everything went well on the mainland. That we'll have guests again in the spring.'

She no longer had any scruples about lying. She knew she could always butter him up with a little flattery.

'Yes, but it's going to take a lot of work to get everything ready on time. I'd really prefer not to be dragged into the zombie gang before then.' He sighed, his attention diverted for the time being.

*

She could see now, in Benjamin's eyes, that he wanted to leave too. It was like nudging two marbles over the crest of a hill. They were rolling. Almost on their way.

A little fuel to the flames wouldn't hurt.

'Haven't you had enough of being humiliated? Do you want

him to beat you into the dirt? It's not going to get any better, don't you see that?'

In some ways, he was her ticket out, because he knew every nook and cranny of the island and the ferry. And she wasn't one hundred percent sure he wouldn't tattle if he stayed behind.

'If I leave, Benjamin, he'll kill you. Or put you in Penance for the rest of your life.'

Doubt was raging inside him; she could see it in his eyes. But then it disappeared and his usual, energetic expression returned.

'Okay,' he said. 'Let's do it.'

That was suspicious — she had expected much more resistance. 'Seriously?'

'Yup. We'll get out of here. I've had enough too.'

She threw herself on top of him and he fell backwards onto the bed. She straddled his stomach and peppered his face with kisses.

'Oh my god, I'm so happy! We have to start making a plan. It has to be watertight. Because if he figures out —'

'I know how we can get out,' he interrupted her. 'I'll put a ladder up against the wall, somewhere in the back where no one can see it. We'll sneak out in the middle of the night; we can jump over without touching the wire. We'll run like crazy for the cottage and hide there overnight. In the morning we can walk the path over the cliffs, to the ferry. It will take some time, but no one will see us there.'

'But isn't it cold and slippery? How will we manage that?'

'I know how. Trust me.'

'But if they discover we've run away they'll be waiting for us at the ferry.'

'Yes, but they probably won't miss us until morning. At the morning assembly, at the latest. We have to be on the ferry before then. I know where we can hide — there's a tarp in the stern, where all the cars are parked.'

'We have to lie under a tarp in the cold for hours?'

'We'll wear warm clothes and keep each other from getting too cold.'

He's already got it all worked out, she thought. *Running away. We hadn't even talked about it. And I didn't even guess.*

'I'm still worried about the fence,' she said. 'All it would take is one brush against the barbs and the alarm will sound.'

'I can jump over without touching it. And I'll help you over. If the alarm does go off, we'll just have to make a run for the cottage. We'll have a head start.'

'But what if it's one of those nights when everyone's up working?'

'Then we'll have to do it the next night, or the night after that.'

'What if the water freezes and the ferry can't cross?'

'Then we'll be in trouble! Sofia, stop being such a worrywart. I'm sure we can check the weather online. You've got your laptop, after all.'

She took out her laptop and looked up the forecast. The next few days were supposed to be above freezing, with no snowstorms on the horizon.

'What do we do when we get to the mainland?'

'We'll head to my sister in Gothenburg and lie low there for a while.'

'Should we email her and let her know we're coming?'

'No, too risky. I'll call her tomorrow when I'm on the mainland. I'm supposed to take the eight o'clock ferry to make some purchases and I'll be back at five.'

'And then we'll go to the police and report that bastard.'

'The police? Are you crazy? Why do you want to go to them? Won't getting out of here be enough?'

'Oswald has to be held accountable for attacking staff members.'

'We'll never get to him, Sofia. It would be our word against everyone else's. They'll say he's the kindest leader in the world. They're terrified of him. If they want out, they'll have to escape on their own.'

Sofia thought of the people who would never be able to escape. Mona and Elvira. Simon, who was still in Penance. Devoted, thoroughly brainwashed Bosse, who didn't even understand that anything was wrong. Suddenly it felt like she was betraying them. She wondered if Oswald would punish the whole staff after she and Benjamin escaped. More cameras, rules, and prohibitions.

'There is another way,' she said. 'We can blog about it once we're out.'

Benjamin shook his head slowly, but he didn't say anything.

'Should we pack everything up tonight?' she asked.

'No, that's too risky as well. We'll do it tomorrow evening.'

'I won't be able to fall asleep.'

'But you have to. You'll need to be able to run fast tomorrow night. Count sheep, breathe deeply, do whatever it takes. But you have to sleep.'

In just a few minutes, he was snoozing beside her. *His brain must be missing the part that makes you worry*, she thought. She lay there ruminating for a long time, trying to repress all her scattered thoughts. When she finally dozed off, her sleep was restless and full of dreams.

She woke in the middle of the night to Benjamin sitting up in bed and looking at his pager. When she asked what was up, he only mumbled, put down his pager, and fell back to sleep.

The next time she woke up, he was already gone. *He could have escaped by himself*, she thought, feeling warm inside. *Could have just taken off while he was on the mainland. But he's going to stick around and help me over the fence.*

By the time she got up, her stomach was full of butterflies and her skin was crawling with anticipation. She wondered how she would make it through the day without Oswald noticing. She decided to spend it running around the property. She could tell him she had to make sure everyone was working on his projects in preparation for spring.

She was so nervous that she was starting to have doubts — she just wanted to be rid of the suffering and restlessness. Maybe they should hold off for a while, give themselves time to get used to the thought of escaping. There might be other ways to get out. Her mind flashed on an image of herself jumping from a second-storey window; they would have to take her to the hospital and then she could escape from there. It seemed like a plausible scenario — but no, she pushed it out of her mind and decided that Benjamin's plan would be fine. She gritted her teeth and concentrated on her morning tasks, and showered, dressed, and tried to think positive thoughts.

It will be fine.

We can do it.

One more day, just one more, and it will be over.

*

The feeling that something wasn't right came to her as she was climbing the stairs to the office. There was nothing concrete, just an unpleasant premonition. Then she felt an impulse to simply turn around and walk back down the stairs. But she decided it must just be because of Oswald, because she was afraid of looking him in the eye while she was keeping this huge secret. *He can't read my mind*, she thought. *Only my body language. Just look cheerful and unconcerned. Or maybe a little grumpy. He'll never suspect a thing.*

When she opened the door to the office, Oswald was already at his desk.

Bosse and his henchmen were standing to his right.

On his left was Benjamin, a sheepish smile on his face.

The lake extends maybe half a kilometre from the little beach.

We drove for a long time to get here.

I hope she isn't going to disappoint me.

She's standing on the dock in her ugly swimsuit. Shivering already — it's only spring.

We're alone out here. Not a soul in sight.

For some reason, I no longer find her annoying. She's my pupil now.

There's a tiny islet about a hundred metres off the dock. It's a little hill with a lone, wind-whipped cypress tree.

'Do you see that little island?' I ask, pointing. 'You have to swim to it, under the water. If you come up for air, I'll see you and you'll have to start over again.'

'I can't!'

The words fly from her mouth. I can tell she regrets them immediately.

'Okay, then I guess you'll just die out here today. Under the water.'

'What?'

'I'm just joking. You can do it. Now jump in!'

I sit down on the dock and dip my fingers in the water. It's freezing. But she jumps in with a splash and vanishes below the surface.

This will do her good.

I already know she'll never manage it.

That's part of the test.

Her little head pops up above the water. Again and again.

She never reaches the islet.

I start to laugh — she looks like a little duck bobbing out there in the water.

'Come here!'

Obediently, she swims back to the edge of the dock. Her face is so white, and her lips are starting to turn blue.

I pull off my trousers and take off my watch, piling both on the dock.

Then I step down into the cold water, which comes up to the edge of my underwear.

I grab her hair out of the blue, causing her to lose her balance, and pull her under the surface so she's on her back.

Her face shows shock and terror.

The water is clear, so I can see her eyes.

I put one hand over her body and keep my grip on her hair with the other as she splashes and kicks.

Bubbles pour from her mouth to the surface.

Then she figures out the rules. She relaxes and goes still.

Her wide eyes make her look dead.

And I hold her down and wait. For a long time.

I wait until I see the panic in her eyes and pull her up just before she can take that fatal breath.

She gasps and spits, coughing and sputtering.

Her already wet eyes fill with tears. I just stand there watching her until she collects herself.

'I understand now,' *she says at last.* 'You have to take it to the very limit.'

'Exactly!'

I pat her wet head and she looks at me like a submissive little puppy.

32

'I changed my mind. It's for your own good, Sofia.'

Benjamin was almost whispering, and his gaze was focused somewhere over her head so he wouldn't have to make eye contact. She stiffened, then realized he had betrayed her — a realization that hurt so much she wanted to bend over double and collapse to the floor. For an instant her body stopped working. Her chest constricted, her muscles locked up, her heart stood still, and she was flooded with the feeling that her whole life had come crumbling down. Benjamin still wouldn't look at her; he turned his head and stared at the wall. Oswald and his henchmen had turned into shadows. All she could see was Benjamin.

Her body began to allow for new feelings: disappointment and despair and at last a seething hate so strong it bubbled in her ears. There was something about Benjamin's posture, a nonchalant indifference that he had to be putting on. That sanctimonious little coward with his crooked smile, as if he were playing a practical joke on her.

All she could think as Benny and Sten came over and took her by the arms was that she needed those arms free so she could claw out Benjamin's eyes.

'Don't send her to Penance,' said Oswald. 'She's not getting off that easy. Pair her up with Simon instead.'

He turned to Benny, who was still holding Sofia tightly by the arm.

'They will do the shittiest, most horrible job there is. In black caps so no one can mistake them for Penance.'

He stared at her, but she averted her eyes.

'Benjamin says she hid a laptop in their room,' he said to Bosse. 'Go through every email and find out what she's been up to. Who knows, maybe we've found our mole at last. Check her phone too.' He waved his hand dismissively. 'Now take her away. I don't want to see her deceitful mug any more.'

He speared her with his gaze one last time.

'You will never get out of here. Just so you know,' he said.

*

She felt empty and mute as they led her out. *Maybe this is what it feels like to be catatonic*, she thought. *Or maybe the worst part comes later.*

But it wasn't until after dinner, when she was running by with Simon, both in their ridiculous black caps, and she saw the double bed she'd shared with Benjamin being carried out of the manor house, that her heart hurt and tears burned behind her eyelids. It was freezing out and the icy north wind made its way under her clothing; she could feel it in her bones. The warm light of the manor house windows gazed down at them.

She and Simon were relegated to a corner of the stable. They would spend the night in sleeping bags on the straw floor. A small electric heater had been brought in, but it would hardly make a difference — the wind could find all the holes and cracks in the stable walls.

They would have to shower in the barely lukewarm water in the basement shower, which was so full of dirt, mould, and spider webs that she'd had to hold her nose with one hand and wash with the other during those times she'd had to use it when sick.

Their work would consist of shovelling snow, mucking out stalls, and taking care of the pigs. Benny had a few other enormous, unfeasible tasks planned for them, such as cleaning all the toilets with nothing but a toothbrush and polishing every hardwood floor in every building by hand, but only at times when the staff and guests wouldn't spot them. They were also under orders to run whenever they moved around. No talking or making eye contact with the rest of the staff. If they messed up, they had to run around the estate three times. Their schedule gave them eighteen hours of work and six hours of sleep.

She stopped for a moment and gasped for breath. The air was so cold it burned her lungs. The courtyard was cold and deserted in the frosty darkness. It occurred to her that she could refuse orders. Just say *no, I won't do it, I won't run another step, I won't sleep in the stall, and I won't do your shitty jobs*. But they still wouldn't let her out. If she even knew whether *out* was all she wanted. There was something else she was after. Revenge. She hated Benjamin so much it hurt deep down in her chest, and the thought that he would get away with this, continuing to live his meaningless life as if nothing had happened, was unbearable.

Another thought was niggling at her without quite becoming fully formed, but it had something to do with patience. *Oswald will miss me when the next secretary starts screwing up*, she thought. *It takes a certain amount of freedom to escape from here. And the only scrap of freedom there is, is at the top. Have to grit my teeth and just deal with the humiliation. Be smarter than to trust anyone next time.*

When she got into her sleeping bag that night, she lay shivering for a long time, staring up at the dark roof of the barn. Simon was sleeping deeply; he didn't move a muscle there in the straw.

This is hell, she thought. *Being so completely stuck.*

Her whole life had been stolen from her before she had even begun to live it. She had ended up in hell and she wasn't even dead.

How can a person become so powerless?

She imagined the infinite vault of stars over the roof and imagined herself floating in outer space. She felt her pulse slow and at last she fell into a bizarrely deep sleep.

★

One morning as they were mucking out stalls, Simon started talking to her. He spoke in a way no one else at ViaTerra had ever done. Benny was in the bathroom and had left them alone for a short time.

'Do you think Oswald is just plain mad?'

She stiffened. This was forbidden territory. It was one thing to think a thought, and something else entirely to let it come out of your mouth. In speaking, things became too concrete; it was hard to erase them later. Words like 'blasphemy' and 'treason' flickered through her mind. But she was curious. And after all, Benny wasn't there.

'What do you mean?'

'Well, logically he's like our boss. He's responsible for everything. So if it all goes to hell, how can it be everyone else's fault but his?'

'Sure, but he has to handle the media and all of that himself.'

'Okay, but think of all the crap that's been written about us. It's not like he's doing a super job.'

He scraped away some cow manure with his shovel — he didn't seem at all troubled by what he'd just said. His voice was clear, matter-of-fact, and steady, without a hint of shame.

'But . . . then how could he have created all this? The whole program, the place?'

'Oh, I'm sure he's not stupid. But that doesn't mean he hasn't lost his mind.'

She was still on guard. What if Benny had instructed Simon to test her? To see whether she really was a traitor? She glanced at Simon. His expression was peaceful and serene. This slave labour didn't seem to bother him. It seemed no one could make that strong back and rough hands crack. He just kept working, rhythmically and cheerfully. Yet he was hiding these dark, forbidden thoughts.

'Are you saying you want to leave, too?'

'Nah, I'll wait until it all comes crashing down. It will eventually.'

She was about to contradict him, but realized he truly meant it. There was no stress or hurry about Simon. He did what he'd always done: work.

'What about the greenhouse?'

'Well, I'm sure it's completely ruined by now. I'll probably end up there again once they run out of vegetables.'

She wanted to laugh out loud — they were so different and yet so alike. But she held back her laughter, because the barn door creaked and Benny was on his way back.

'You might be right about Oswald,' she whispered quickly, before Benny was within earshot.

★

That's how it began. When Benny was around, they talked about permitted topics. Gardening and farming, stuff Simon knew about. They could even talk about books, because he'd read quite a bit. In the brief moments when Benny wasn't looming over them, they talked about forbidden things. About Oswald and what was happening with ViaTerra.

Laughing and giggling were absolutely forbidden, so if their conversation sounded too chipper, Benny immediately got after them.

'Stop laughing, for Christ's sake. You have nothing to laugh about. Franz is working his ass off while you're just loafing around here. That's three laps around the manor.'

So they plodded around the manor in their heavy winter boots and grinned at each other when they were out of Benny's sight. Sofia had thought about the Benny situation — could they turn him? Get him on their side? But there was no spark in Benny's eyes; his gaze was so listless that it never quite lit on any particular spot. It was as if the individual himself had checked out, leaving only an obedient shell behind.

She scratched a line into a wall of the barn for each passing day. She felt grief when she accumulated a week's worth of lines, but her eagerness to get away was fading and she fell into a routine. The hard work took its toll on her body. Her hands were soon calloused, red, and chapped, and her knuckles were so dry they split and bled. Her back and joints ached from all the toiling and the relentless cold. She'd always been thin, but she didn't even dare to guess what she weighed now. Her ribs stuck out so much she could feel them through her thick winter coat. At last Benny took mercy on her and made her drink milk, straight from the cow. It tasted horrid but her body began to recover.

The days were still short and it seemed like they were surrounded with endless darkness. She thought of her parents every night when she went to bed, closing her eyes and recalling their faces. Sometimes she could barely remember what they looked like, and the details got fuzzier the harder she tried. Sofia and Simon were not allowed to send emails or make phone calls under any circumstances, but they were allowed to send handwritten letters. It was hard to come up with anything to write. It was mostly all 'I'm fine. I miss you. I love you.' But she still wrote. And didn't receive a single letter in response. When she asked Benny about it, he just shrugged.

What if Oswald makes me stay here for years? She thought sometimes. *What if he forgets I even exist?* The very thought seemed like it might tip her over into insanity, so she let it go and focused on her work. She tried to concentrate on the positives: they could spend time outside and breathe the fresh air. They would get to experience spring when it came to the island. And the pigs were happy and healthy now that she and Simon were taking care of them.

★

The landscape around the manor was barren and colourless that winter. The winter before, the whole courtyard had shimmered with lights and lanterns. Now it was naked and cold in its winter garb. The fog was thick almost every morning, which meant it was impossible to see past the walls. The yard had transformed into a field of black and white thanks to the dark, bare tree trunks and the endless snow that covered the ground, the roofs, and the treetops. The pond was frozen and empty. The manor house itself, which gleamed white in the summertime, looked greyish against the snow, and the warm lights glowing from its windows at night just made it seem even sadder. But she wasn't looking forward to the summer. It was easier to be ostracized, frozen out, when everyone else was suffering in the cold as well.

Oswald had expelled her from the manor house on January fifteenth. Forty-two days later, she saw the first snowdrop. Rays of sunshine had just freed it from a snowbank, and the tiny flower bowed its head, dangling in the light breeze. She touched it so very gently, deciding that it must be a sign.

'I guess spring is coming after all,' said Simon.

It was the day Sofia saw Benjamin again for the first time.

He must have been intentionally avoiding her, because he was the only person she hadn't seen pass by now and then. Benny was gone for a while that morning, and suddenly Benjamin was there.

All the pent-up feelings welled up afresh as she looked at him. He was just standing in front of her, a small, wrinkled note in hand. She thought she could see his legs trembling slightly.

'It's not like you think, Sofia,' he said.

'I never want to speak to you again.'

He held up the note.

'Take this,' he said. 'In case you ever need it. In case you manage to get out of here.'

She took the note from his hand. A series of numbers was written on it. She let go of it so it floated to the ground, then turned her back on him. When she turned around again, he was gone. Simon gave her a pointed look.

'He's a pig,' she said.

'Maybe, but that note might be good to have one day.'

She bent down and picked it up. The moisture had almost erased some of the digits, but she could still read it. A phone number. And a name. 'Vanja Frisk.' She sighed and stuffed it in her pocket.

★

That was the day their little crew grew. Sofia knew Madeleine was Oswald's secretary again. She'd seen her walking by, at first with a superior smile on her face, but more recently she had looked browbeaten, running around the property with a hounded expression Sofia knew well. She was immediately filled with delight at Madeleine's pain.

Madeleine was so easy to bully. She was much weaker than Sofia, who thought smugly that Madeleine's days were numbered. That it was only a matter of time. And later on, Sofia would make sure she was visible from the manor house windows now and then.

Benny was gone for a long time that evening. His pager had gone off, and he looked upset when he read the message. He shot out of the barn like an arrow, leaving Sofia and Simon to their task of spreading straw in the stalls. He was gone for several hours, and Sofia had almost started to think they might have a chance of escaping over the fence. But one glance out of the window and she changed her mind. Snow was whirling through the air. Just when it seemed that spring was on the way.

She and Simon worked slowly and chatted as they absentmindedly covered the stall floors with straw. All to remain in the warmth of the barn for as long as they could.

When Benny returned, he was not alone. He was leading a teary-eyed, pale Madeleine by the arm.

'Here's a new team-mate for you,' he said.

A tiny, evil spirit turned somersaults in Sofia's heart.

They can't see me, but I can see and hear them from my spot behind the tree.

I know exactly who he is. She has described him to me.

And what an attitude. A conceited, fat idiot; I can smell the creep on him from way over here.

She doesn't spend breaks alone anymore. There's a little gang she hangs around with now. They're all like her — awkward, ugly, ungainly — but even so, they're a group.

He comes up behind her, grabs her by the back of the neck, and squeezes. He knees her in the back.

The others scatter, but she stays put. She says something to him, then points in my direction.

He follows her up to the wooded area where I'm waiting.

'Do you want a beating, you little witch?' he says, shoving her until she nearly falls.

But I come from behind before he notices me.

I lock his arms and breathe down the back of his neck.

He screams when he looks back and sees me in my mask.

And that's when she strikes. She pounds her fists into his stomach and groin, hammering until all the air goes out of him.

'Hold on,' I say. 'What do you want to do with him? What do you really want to do?'

'Kill the pig,' she says with no hesitation. She's excited. Almost beautiful. Her eyes burn.

'Then do it! Come on!'

She pulls the switchblade from her pocket and holds it up for him to see. The tip is aimed at one eye, and he roars like a madman.

But break is over. No one can hear him now.

Then she stabs him. First in the arms — tiny punctures that drip blood. She kicks him in the crotch with all her might.

He hollers and collapses, but he can't get out of my grip.

She's not done; now she's aiming for his chest, but I pull his heavy body out of range.

Instead she falls to her knees and drives the blade into his leg, all the way up to the hilt.

She's just about to withdraw it and attack again, but I stop her with a yell.

'Stop. Have you forgotten the rules?'

'To the very limit,' she pants.

'Right. Let's get out of here,' I say.

I let go of him and he falls to the ground with a thud.

We run into the woods.

She's giggling.

All the while, we can hear him groaning and whimpering.

33

Madeleine cried almost constantly, whenever she wasn't complaining. She whined about the cold, blisters on her feet, and various other pains, but mostly she just leaked quiet tears wherever they went. Sofia suspected Madeleine was experiencing some sort of mental breakdown and brought it up with Benny in the stable one day. She suggested they let the other woman rest up in an empty stable, but Benny wouldn't hear of it.

'She's been going on like this for a week, Benny. It's not normal.'

'Well, she's just going to have to pull herself together, damn it. Go show her how to muck out stalls and get her moving.'

'Maybe it would be good for her to get outside for some fresh air. I saw some weeds in the flowerbeds.'

That was as far as she got, because Benny's eyes, which typically roved every which way, were suddenly nailed to something over her head. When she turned around, she saw Oswald coming briskly down the centre aisle. He stopped right next to her. Her skin still seemed to tingle when he stood so close. But he hadn't come to see her.

'Where's Simon?'

Simon peered out from one of the stalls, shovel in hand.

'I'm here, sir.'

'My cook says there are no vegetables in the greenhouse anymore.' He was clearly furious; his voice was rough and hoarse, but he was keeping himself in check.

'I don't know, sir. I haven't been there in months.'

'So you think I should eat frozen peas from the store?'

'No, of course not.'

'Then you're going back to the greenhouse, effective immediately. You have one week to get things growing in there again.'

Simon put down his shovel, shot Sofia an apologetic look, and walked down the aisle and out of the stable. Oswald, too, turned to leave. Sofia noticed he had manure stuck to his shoe and muffled a giggle.

'Is something funny, Sofia?'

'No, I'm sorry, I thought I was going to sneeze.'

'I thought maybe there was something you wanted to say to me.'

'No, I mean, yes, I'm sorry for my betrayal and all that.'

He observed her for a long time.

'I'll think about that.'

A jolt of loss flowed through her when she realized that Simon wouldn't be returning. One thing was certain: life would remain miserable if Madeleine didn't stop crying. She thought maybe there was something Madeleine didn't dare to say while Benny was around, so she decided to talk to her once they'd crawled into their sleeping bags for the night. Benny slept in a stall near the door in case they tried to escape. But he was out of earshot if they spoke in whispers.

'Hey, we've been working together for almost two years and I don't know a thing about you,' Sofia began.

'Oh, there's nothing to know.'

'But what did you do before you came here?'

'I was a secretary, like I am now, or was before everything went to shit . . .' Madeleine began to blubber again but soon got herself back under control. 'I mean, I worked for one of the directors of a pretty big IT company in Stockholm.'

'But why did you come here?'

'I went to a lecture Oswald gave. He came up to me afterwards and said he'd been looking for someone like me for a long time. He took me out for dinner. That was before we had the manor.'

Her voice had taken on a dreamlike tone.

'It seemed like he already knew all about me. He understood me like no one ever had. I knew right away that I was meant for ViaTerra.'

He hand-picked us, Sofia thought, *and he knows just how to do it.* This insight was followed by a quick series of thoughts, almost flickering by, and yet they were fully formed. All the staff members were white and looked 'typically Nordic.' Aside from Abayomi in the kitchen, of course, who Oswald called 'the blackhead' and 'big lips' and complained it would take a year to learn to pronounce his name. Oswald said all this in such a mild and joking tone that no one challenged him. He had even said once that Abayomi just 'sneaked in' under his nose.

Then Sofia's thoughts turned to the guy on the farm who turned out to be gay — Oswald had sent him back to the mainland before anyone had time to react. One day he was just gone, never to be heard from again. Out of these thoughts was born a suspicion: Oswald was trying to create the ideal worker. Their Nordic appearances were the template and the slavery and humiliation the tools.

Madeleine hadn't realized that Sofia's thoughts were wandering, so she blathered on. She seemed to come to life when she spoke about Oswald.

'It's like he's above everything. His vision, that is. It's greater than we can understand.'

She's fucking in love with him, head over heels.

'But then what happened? You seem totally wrecked!'

It was like turning on a faucet. Sofia wondered how it was even possible to cry so much. How could there be so many tears in a such a tiny body?'

'Come on, tell me. I'm listening.'

'Shit, Sofia. I don't know what to say. I hate myself. This is the second time I betrayed him. I feel awful. And everyone else just keeps messing up. It's like the whole staff is working against him. The punishments don't make any difference. Where will it all end?'

Now Sofia was all ears. 'What punishments?'

'Well, Tom, you know, his personal chef, served him frozen peas from the grocery store. Can you believe that? What a jerk. It goes against absolutely everything we stand for. But he paid for what he did. Franz made him eat an entire package of frozen peas. But then Tom still couldn't fix things so Franz could be given truly local food.'

'A whole package of peas? Seriously?'

'Yeah, what did you think? Franz sat him down in the middle of the staff office where everyone could see him and it took such a long time. And that horrible sound when he chewed.'

'What else has been going on?'

'Well, Anna hadn't emptied the trash cans in the dining room for probably a whole week, and it smelled like rotten fruit in there. She had to stand in a trash can with a sign that said *pig* around her neck. Bosse and his crew poured water on her now and then so she wouldn't doze off. How hard it is to empty a few trash cans? To clean up after yourself? What is Franz supposed to do? Empty them himself?'

'How long did Anna have to stand there?'

'Oh, it was like three or four hours. In the end Franz asked what she'd learned and she said something, I don't remember what, but he let her go.'

Sofia tried to make out Madeleine's face in the darkness to see if she even understood how insane this all sounded, but it was too dark. But she deduced from Madeleine's monotonous voice that she had no clue.

'And then there was Bosse himself. He didn't get a damn thing done so he had to clean out a blocked drain with his bare hands.'

'Oh, damn.'

'Right.'

'No, I mean damn, that's disgusting! It's revolting!'

'You don't understand, Sofia. Franz tries to put his foot down, but it doesn't help, and it's so darn frustrating.'

'What about you? How did you end up here?'

'I screwed up too. I spilled coffee on his desk while he was reading the paper. I don't understand why we're all so clumsy, why we can't get anything done. We're working more and sleeping less, and still nothing gets done.'

So it had gotten worse. And just when Sofia had thought it had reached rock bottom. She was disgusted to picture Anna in a trash can and Bosse cleaning out drains, but the peas were what made her see red. As if his goddamn peas were the most important thing on earth. She didn't know which was worse: everything Madeleine had just told her, or Madeleine's attitude toward what was going on. She wondered how many of the staff had become as brainless as Madeleine and who still had a few brain cells left. Maybe she and Simon were the only ones.

★

Their workday began at six in the morning, an hour before everyone else got up. They usually started with a lap around the manor to warm up, and then they mucked stalls and fed the animals. That gave Eskil, the animal caretaker, a break in his otherwise long day.

The morning after her conversation with Madeleine, the sun peeked out. The sky was pale pink and yellow. The snow had melted and it smelled like spring.

Sofia noticed a light glowing over in the greenhouse. So Simon was up too. She missed him. His calm breathing as they worked. Their friendly conversations.

The manor house was still dark, aside from a light in the attic window. She imagined Oswald must be up there and wondered why. It wasn't like him to get up so early in the morning. The night's conversation with Madeleine returned to her.

At least I've learned something new, she thought. *It can always get worse.*

A figure approached briskly from the gate. It was Sten, the guard who had the morning shift.

'Did you turn off your pager?' he asked Benny, irritated. 'I tried to reach you like a hundred times.'

Sten went on before Benny could answer.

'Message from Bosse for Sofia and Madeleine. You have to remain in the courtyard after eight. I think Franz wants to talk to one of you.'

It could be about any number of things. Oswald might have spotted them walking instead of running. Maybe he wanted Madeleine back, or maybe he was angry about the manure on his shoe. But deep down, she knew what was going on. She had understood back in the stable when he looked at her like she was an object he'd forgotten and suddenly rediscovered. She didn't even know if she wanted to go back, but it didn't matter — her body still buzzed with anticipation. After all, it would be a victory of sorts. And the world outside would be closer. She thought about what she would say to him when he spoke to them at the courtyard later, practising different sentences in her mind. She ran through the conversation several times, until she found she was mumbling out loud.

★

He came at eleven. They were pulling weeds in the sunshine. Or, rather, they were pottering around because there weren't all that many weeds yet. He came up on his motorcycle and braked hard in front of her. She hurried to stand up and brush the dirt from her coat. As usual, he looked well-rested. His hair was still damp from his morning shower. The scent of his aftershave floated on the air. She fixed her eyes on his hands, which were resting on the handlebars, because she didn't want to look him in the eye until he had addressed her.

'Have you come to any realizations, Sofia?'

'Yes, sir. I was only trying to run away from myself. My transgressions made me feel like a burden to the group. That's why I wanted to leave.'

'That's true, but you were a burden to *me*. You understand that, don't you?'

'Yes, sir.'

'Good. You can go to Bosse. He'll make sure you're brought up to date on everything that's happened while you were gone.'

Madeleine cleared her throat and was about to open her mouth.

'It's best for you to keep your trap shut,' he said to her. 'Not a single word out of your lying mouth.'

He turned to Benny.

'Madeleine shouldn't be weeding flowerbeds. She should be doing the worst of the hard labour. Back-breaking, dirty work. That's the only thing that can get through to her type.' Oswald turned back to Sofia.

'What are you waiting for? Run and find Bosse now, before I change my mind!'

★

Bosse wasn't in the staff office, so she had to run around looking for him.

Her body was singing. She felt almost free, and she couldn't keep from stopping by the greenhouse.

Simon was crouching down to plant things, and he gave her such a warm smile when he noticed her.

'It was all destroyed,' he said. 'I had to start over from scratch.'

'He's putting me back in the office!'

'Oh? How do you feel about that?'

'Like it's probably the only way out.'

'I suppose you're right.'

He didn't stop digging through the dirt.

'Please, Simon, come with me if I find a way to escape.'

He responded without hesitation.

'No, I'll stay here until the walls fall. But good luck. I'm sure you'll make it out. Come by and visit again sometime.'

She finally found Bosse in one of the annexes, where he was talking to Mona. Both looked embarrassed when they spotted her, as if she were barging in on a delicate conversation. Mona quickly stood up and looked at her tentatively, unsure whether Sofia was still in disgrace.

'I'll be going now,' she whispered.

Bosse gestured at Sofia to take a seat. He looked at her dirty hands and stained winter coat.

'You can't get rid of me that easily, Bosse.'

'So I see. Franz said you were coming back. Some things have happened while you were away. Pretty major things, actually.'

'All right.'

'I don't know where to start. Oh, the lodging situation. There was too much trouble with couples living together, so Franz got fed up. Everyone lives in the dormitories now. Guys with guys, girls with girls, of course.'

'Even married couples?'

'Yes, everyone. I mean, a couple of girls got knocked up. Katarina and Corinne. It's been taken care of now, but that was the end of that.'

'"Taken care of?"'

'Yes, obviously we can't have kids running around here. But I didn't think you'd care, after what happened with Benjamin.'

'No, I don't care, but it sounds like they didn't have a choice.'

'What do you think? *Is* there a choice between ViaTerra and a screaming baby? Of course they had abortions. We didn't even discuss it with them.'

She swallowed the remark on her tongue. It simply wasn't the right time or place to have a talk with Bosse.

353

'But you'll be back in number seven. Your belongings are already there,' he said.

'Okay, anything else?'

'You won't be getting your laptop and phone back, but I'm sure you knew that.'

'Of course, but how is everything going, Bosse? Will guests be coming this spring?'

'Nothing has changed, Sofia. Franz still has to do all the work. He's totally worn out.'

She was about to say that he'd looked to be in fine form that morning, but instead she just nodded.

'Staff rules are extremely tough. No email or phone calls. We run everywhere. Lunch and dinner have been shortened to fifteen minutes. But we mostly only get rice and beans. The greenhouse went to hell after Simon —'

'I heard.'

'Well, there you have it. Not much has changed.'

'And there will be guests this spring?'

'Yes, dammit. That's what everyone's working on. Trying to get everything ready. The annexes have to be in tip-top shape, the menus, planting, we've been full up. We have a project that Franz has written up. There are several copies on your desk. And Franz is working on something else too. New theses. But I'm sure he'll want to tell you about that himself, so I won't say too much.'

She was just about to stand up and leave.

'Shit, I almost forgot. Until the greenhouse is up and running, Franz's food is being flown in from some place in Italy. It arrives at the airport on the mainland. Organic food. The very best. Benjamin picks it up every day. You have to warm up the food and serve it, because Tom screwed up and is in Penance.'

354

Bosse looked exhausted. His hair was greasy and uncombed, his eyes were red, and his tie was loose under his dirty collar. He seemed glad to have her back, as if she would bring a ray of hope into his misery.

'Anything else?'

'No, that's all. Your uniform is probably in your room, but I don't know if Benjamin had time for the dry cleaning.'

'It's fine, Bosse. I'll manage.'

The door to her old room, number seven, was ajar. Bosse must have sent someone over, because it was so neat and tidy it almost looked unnatural. She peeked into the wardrobe and drawers. All her clothes and belongings were there, even the diary. She sincerely hoped no one had read it. Her uniform was hanging in the wardrobe.

She took off her dirty clothes and put them in the hamper, then went to the bathroom. She suddenly recalled that there was a camera in the shower and started to look for it. She found it almost immediately, mounted over the stall. A tiny eye staring down at her naked body. She left the room and found a black marker in the dresser, then got back in the shower and blacked out the eye until it would no longer be able to see anything.

When she was finished in the shower, she sat on her old bed and looked around. That was when she noticed that there were no sheets on Elvira's bed. She opened the girl's wardrobe.

It was empty.

'Fredrik, I want to speak with you.'

For once, there is authority in her voice. I know exactly what this is about; I've been looking forward to it.

We walk into her office and she sits down, biting at her lower lip.

'This is serious, Fredrik. The rector at Sara's school just called. He said Sara stabbed a classmate. Our Sara. I don't know what to do.' She starts to cry.

I put on an expression of surprise.

'Are you serious? Surely you don't believe it.'

'No, I mean, Sara isn't an aggressive person, is she?'

'She would never harm a fly,' I say firmly.

'But this is serious. And he said she was helped by a masked man.'

I laugh.

'That sounds ridiculous. What a story!'

'Yes, it sounds preposterous, but what am I supposed to say?'

'You should say that it's the dumbest thing you ever heard. That the guy was obviously in a knife fight and is looking for a scapegoat.'

She stops her sniffling and collects herself.

'Of course, that must be it.'

'Definitely. And then say if they don't convince this guy to withdraw his accusations you'll pull Sara out of the school and that will be the end of all the charity work you do for them.'

Her face lights up. She chuckles.
'*Fredrik, darling. I don't know what I would do without you.*'
Yes, one really does wonder, *I think.*

He slammed a thick pile of papers down in front of her so hard that the legs of the small desk trembled.

'These are the new theses, or rather, propositions. They will complement the original theses.'

She looked at the stack and hoped he would explain what she was expected to do with it.

'They're the lectures I gave for the staff during autumn and winter. Madeleine transcribed them all, but there are some problems with them and that's where you come in.'

He pointed at the top sheet. A sentence was underlined in red pen. 'Read this!'

She read silently to herself: ' . . . *but I suppose this is beyond your ability to draw conclusions.*'

'That has nothing to do with the proposition, does it?' said Oswald. 'It's just a comment on the group's collective level of intelligence, understand?'

She nodded.

'There's a little of that sort of thing here and there. The lectures simply need to be cleaned up. They'll be issued as supplements to read after thesis number four. Our new guests will be totally pumped when they read it.'

He wants me to get rid of his curses and derogatory comments about the staff, plain and simple, she thought. *Seems like there will be a lot of them.*

'Each lecture will become one proposition,' he went on. 'It's as simple as that. But you have to be able to tell when I'm theorizing and when I'm just chatting with someone.'

He turned to another page, where he'd marked red lines in the margin alongside a paragraph of the text. In this section, he was picking on someone because their uniform was dirty.

'This isn't part of the reasoning, as I'm sure you understand.'

She nodded.

'So your job is simply to bring out the true propositions from all this.'

'And how does this relate to the fifth thesis, the one that hasn't been released yet?'

'This *is* the fifth thesis, you moron! I've just expanded on it. Turned it into a number of propositions. Like you can do with a piece of music. Do you understand?'

Sofia nodded and accepted the instructions with a deep, inward sigh, but then she had an idea. She could save what she removed from the texts and create a folder of all the degrading things he'd said about the staff in his lectures. It was risky, but she could always say she'd done it to be on the safe side, in case he wanted to keep any of what she'd edited out.

'Did you hear what I said, Sofia?'

'Of course, sir, every word.'

'Then you understand what you're supposed to do?'

'Definitely.'

'Show me when you're done with the first proposition, and then we'll go from there.'

She fiddled with the first text until lunchtime. Oswald had said he would be in his room and was gone for the rest of the morning. As she worked, she glanced out at the sea now and then. There was a streak of glittering sunshine way off at the horizon, but otherwise the water was grey and still. She felt antsy; she wanted to stretch out her legs and go for a walk on the island. She couldn't seem to focus her attention on the words in the document and her eyes began to wander aimlessly; time and again she had to force them back to the task in front of her.

Oswald returned just before lunch and nodded, pleased, when she showed him what she'd accomplished. 'Right, so you understand how I want it to be. It sounds really good, doesn't it?'

'Very good, sir.'

He was startled. A sudden flash of suspicion passed over his eyes.

'You've been so pleasant ever since you came back. Almost excessively obliging. I hope everything is as it should be with you.'

'I feel fine, sir.'

*

It was strange to eat in the dining room again. For the past few months, Benny had brought food for them to eat in the stable. Most of the time, it was already cold. She took the seat beside Mona, who was looking lonely. They chatted about the library for a bit.

'I'm trying to keep it in order,' Mona said. 'But no one visits anymore. We don't have any guests and the staff are so busy. So mostly I've been working on other projects.'

'But doesn't the library have to be perfect if guests will be here soon?'

Mona sighed.

'Yes, but I guess some things are more important.'

Sofia decided to change the subject. She didn't want to know how much the library had suffered; it would only ruin her pleasant day.

'Did Elvira move to a different room?'

Mona looked surprised. 'So you don't know?'

'No, I hardly know anything about what's been going on while I was gone.'

'She's on the mainland, finishing school. Franz sent her. She had to go sometime, of course, so now it's finally happening.'

'That's great. But why aren't you there with her? Is Anders there?'

'No, she's living with my sister in Lund.'

Sofia would have expected Mona to look relieved, but instead she seemed troubled.

She's lying. There's something she isn't telling me.

They ate the rest of their rice and beans without a word. A sudden, painful silence hung in the air in the wake of Mona's lie.

*

Oswald was still away after lunch. She continued to clean up the documents. The lectures he'd given while she was gone rang with a completely new tone. Now he was talking about reincarnation and how the body was a home for the soul, but it was also constantly wandering. She thought it sounded forced and pious, not at all like his original, down-to-earth lectures. The folder in which she saved his curses, abuse, and nagging began to grow. She took a break and walked around the office. She was feeling restless again and wanted to be out on the property. Her pager buzzed in her pocket.

Taking the five o'clock ferry. Back tomorrow.

She knew Oswald hadn't left ViaTerra for a long time. He'd said he would stay until everything was ready for the guests. And yet here he was, leaving. On her first day back on the job. That had to mean something. A sign for her to take advantage of this opportunity.

At four o'clock she stood by the window and watched until she saw his car drive through the gate. She'd already turned off the computer and straightened her desk. She forced herself to linger for a moment and then headed downstairs and out to the yard. She didn't even know where she was going; she just wanted to stretch her legs and get some fresh air.

Then she decided to stop by the mailroom and see if she had received a letter from her parents. She could always pretend that she was picking up Oswald's mail.

The small room was behind the annexes; it was really just a storeroom where mail was sorted into plastic boxes and handed out to staff and guests. After careful inspection by the ethics unit, of course. The door wasn't locked. It was dark, draughty, and cold inside. The radiators weren't even on.

After some fumbling, she found the light switch. The fluorescent tubes flickered and bathed the room in an unpleasant, greenish light. The whole room was full of boxes stuffed with mail. She crouched down and began to sort through a random box. It contained outgoing mail from the staff. Hundreds of items. The letters hadn't been sealed, so the ethics staff could read them before they were sent out.

She sifted through them, checking the dates. They went back

as far as January — right after her escape attempt. She searched on and at last she found them: her letters to her parents. She couldn't even remember how many she'd written, but all at once she knew they were all there in the box. Rage overtook her so quickly that she couldn't help herself. She stood up and kicked the box until she stubbed her toe and cried out in pain.

As she began to root around in the other boxes, she found that they were labelled. 'Outgoing staff mail,' 'incoming staff mail,' 'outgoing staff packages,' 'incoming staff packages.' And then the final box, the only one that was empty: 'Franz Oswald.'

She sat down on the cold concrete floor and searched once more through incoming staff letters. There was only one addressed to her, from Karin Johansson. She stuffed it in her pocket. Among the packages was one large box from her mother.

She took her pager from her pocket and sent a message to Bosse.

Mailroom, stat.

He was there within minutes.

'What on earth is all of this, Bosse?'

'Mail.'

She walked up until she was right next to him, so close she could smell his breath. It was sour, as if he hadn't slept or brushed his teeth in a long time.

'I'm already furious, and if you make it any worse I'll tell Franz about this.'

A look of alarm passed over Bosse's face.

'It started in January when Franz sent you to Penance and we went through your computer. We found the emails you sent your parents and friends. He flew off the handle and said not even letters were allowed anymore. If we thought a particular letter was necessary, we could run it by him. But obviously we didn't want to send staff letters up to his office, not with everything he had going on. So they . . . well, they've just been lying here.'

'What were you planning to tell the staff?'

'I hadn't gotten that far.'

'Jesus, Bosse. This is awful.'

'Not as awful as all the shit we make Franz deal with.'

'No, it's worse. This is insane. And it's illegal. I don't think Franz knows all this mail is here. I'll check with him.'

'No, don't,' Bosse whined. 'What are we going to do?'

'You'll have to send them. That's better than keeping them here. People might complain when they notice the dates, but that can't be helped. If you want to read them before you send them out, you'll have to do it now. Franz is coming home tomorrow, so you'd better get them on the morning ferry.'

Bosse nodded, but a shadow fell over his face. He certainly didn't look like he was happy about another night with too little sleep.

'Hand out the packages today. So it doesn't look like belated Christmas when Franz gets home tomorrow. And I'm taking this,' she said, holding up her package.

'Wait! You know I have to check the contents.'

'So open it. But hurry.'

Bosse gently removed the brown wrapper. Inside was a package wrapped in Christmas paper. Something wasn't right — she had already received a Christmas present from her mother. In October. That's the sort of person her mom was. She had all her presents ready to go in November. But Sofia didn't let on as Bosse removed the paper. Inside was a white box. He opened the lid and the two of them gazed down at cute black boots. How odd.

Her mother never bought clothes for her, much less a sexy pair of boots. But there they were.

'Are you satisfied?' she asked.

Bosse nodded and handed her the box. She closed it, put it under her arm, and marched out of the room, still angry, but triumphant.

She remembered the letter in her pocket as she hung her jacket on her office chair. It was a thick envelope addressed in an ornate hand and bearing a ton of stamps. She opened it and removed the contents. The letter itself was brief: 'Here's some material for your book. Hope to see you this summer. Karin.' There was also a small, yellowed booklet.

The Tragic Fate of the von Bärenstens: Fact and Fiction, it read over a blurry, black–and–white picture of the manor house. She pored through the booklet and found herself so captivated that she completely lost track of time. The man who had written the booklet was a professor of history and had a summer cottage on the island. He'd become fascinated by the history of the manor. His words about the family's life were laboured but exciting. Love affairs, children born out of wedlock, accidents, illnesses, and other miserable events — they were all there. Her desire to write a book about them returned.

She wrote a short response to Karin by hand, then stamped and sealed the envelope.

There was a knock at the door. She rushed to shove the letter and booklet in the top drawer of her desk.

'Come in!'

Benjamin's face, full of shame, peered in.

'Go away!' she snapped.

'Listen . . .'

He looked so unhappy that she took pity on him.

'I'll only speak to you if it's absolutely necessary.'

'It *is* necessary. I have to deliver food.'

'How the hell *could* you?'

He took a hesitant step into the room and tried to gather himself. He had grown thinner and his face more hollow. The carefree charm that had once radiated from him had vanished. She suddenly longed to see him the way he had once been. Her heart ached.

'It's not what you think, Sofia, not at all.'

'You can leave the food here each day. And anything else you have to deliver. But don't expect any small talk from me.'

'That's fine. I just wanted you to know how sorry I am.' He hesitated, searching for words. 'I've missed you so much.'

'You could have thought of that before.'

'I know. See you.'

She had trouble concentrating once he'd left. But at last it was ten o'clock. She straightened up the office and turned off the computers. When she looked out the window she could see that the lights were on in the little mailroom. Bosse had taken her at her word.

She carried her package to her room and placed it on the bed. Then she returned to the mailroom. Bosse's whole gang was reading letters and hardly noticed her when she stepped in. There was a large plastic box next to the door; she crouched down and inspected its contents. It was full of sealed envelopes from the staff, ready to be sent out to friends and family. She felt warm inside and placed the letter to Karin in the pile; no one noticed.

'How's it going?' she asked Bosse.

'Good — we'll have all the letters on the morning ferry, and we've handed out the packages.'

'Did you find anything suspicious?'

'No, it's all fine. So far.'

It would be a long night for a bunch of guys who were already suffering from lack of sleep, but it couldn't be helped.

When she returned to her dormitory, she sat down on the bed and took the boots from their box. They had high heels and smelled good — of leather. What on earth had gotten into her mother? Never had she bought anything like this for Sofia. She mostly sent books, gift cards, and money these days. She pulled on the first boot, which slid smoothly over her leg, but as she put the second one on she felt something hard in the bottom.

She removed her foot and fished out a tiny package.

It was a cell phone.

With a charger and everything.

The dew has begun to settle on the ground, which is too bad because it will put a dampener on the fire.

We've come to the chicken coop. It's off to the side, a few hundred metres from the farmhouse. I've chosen this place with great care.

A dog starts barking over by the house.

I make Sara sit down. We crouch before the coop, perfectly silent for a moment.

The rooster struts up and peers at us with one eye. The other is covered by his drooping comb.

'Look at his eye!' I say. 'See how empty it is?'

She nods.

'There's no life in there. Most animals are like that. Like robots. It's the same with people. You can tell how much life they have by their eyes.'

She's entranced.

'Some people have those empty fish eyes. They have almost no life at all. Which means they're totally worthless.'

She nods eagerly.

'Like Dad — sometimes,' I hurry to add.

I can tell she's considering this as we prepare.

We drench the coop and the stupid, cackling hens in petrol, which we've brought in soda bottles.

The idiotic birds flap their wings and squall.

Then we dribble a line of petrol over to a tree. Mostly for effect's sake. The dog has stopped barking.

I hand her the matchbox.

'It's time!'

She hesitates for a moment; a veil falls over her eyes.

'They're stupid, soulless animals, Sara. There's no life in them.'

So she lights a match and drops it with a dramatic gesture.

The flames flare up right away and lick the sky with their greedy tongues. They spread to the coop, and suddenly the chickens are burning. Flapping and screeching, throwing themselves against the walls.

Sara laughs out loud.

The tree is in flames by now too.

The dog is barking again, restless and full of alarm. We can hear doors slamming in the farmhouse.

'Let's get out of here!'

We run as fast as our legs can carry us. Into the woods. She can't stop laughing.

35

Oswald was sitting in front of an open newspaper. He snorted, crumpled the paper into a ball, and threw it at her. It bounced off her head and fell to the desk.

'Read this shit, but get hold of Bosse first.'

She sent a quick message to Bosse, unfolded the crumpled paper, and had no trouble spotting what had caused Oswald's outburst.

Madeleine was gazing up from the page. It was a graduation photo, complete with the traditional white dress and cap. *Prisoner of the diabolical sect on Fog Island*, read the caption.

Oswald loomed over her as she read. He was breathing heavily, and his presence was so palpable that it was hard to focus. But the article was short. It said that Madeleine's parents, who lived in Stockholm, had been trying to get in touch with her since New Year's Eve. They had called, emailed, and sent letters, all in vain, and at last they took the ferry to the island but were turned away.

We couldn't even get through the gate. A rude young man told us she was busy and didn't have time to see us.

The article concluded by saying that the police would investigate Madeleine's disappearance and take all necessary measures to reunite her with her parents.

Bosse had appeared in the doorway. He must have come

running, because he was panting and sweat was dripping from his forehead.

'Come in and close the door,' said Oswald.

Bosse obeyed but leaned against the doorjamb, staying as far from Oswald as possible.

'Have you stopped sending out the staff mail?'

'No . . . yes, I mean . . . After what you said . . .'

That was all it took. Oswald's marble paperweight went flying and Bosse barely had time to duck. It struck the doorframe and left a mark in the woodwork before it fell onto Bosse's foot. He cried out. Sofia couldn't help picturing blood spurting from his forehead — it had been such a close call.

'So *I'm* the one who stopped the mail?' Oswald shouted.

'No, sir, no, not at all. I mean . . . the letters were there for a long time, but a few days ago Sofia found them. And we sent them out.'

Oswald looked at Sofia. 'What's this?'

'I found a bunch of letters from the staff in the mailroom. I knew you would never allow them to lie there for months, so I directed Bosse to mail them.'

Oswald didn't say anything for a moment.

'What does that matter now? This rag will take credit for the fact that we released the letters at last.'

'They can't,' Sofia said. 'The letters will have been postmarked two days ago. Before the article came out.'

'We can say we were having issues with the mail,' Bosse suggested.

'If you don't shut your mouth, I will superglue your lips together,' Oswald said.

But he looked calmer. He turned back to Sofia.

'I'm going to make a few calls. You go talk to Madeleine. She needs to call her parents right away and say that it was her choice not to contact them. And she can say she'll visit them this weekend. Sten will listen in on the conversation, as always — and make sure he records it too.'

He fixed his eyes on Bosse, who was still standing with the paperweight between his feet and his back pressed against the door.

'She can't go alone. Send a chaperone. Someone who can handle it if Madeleine gets any ideas. Katarina, maybe. Drill into Madeleine's feather-brain what she is and is not permitted to say. We can turn this whole mess around to our advantage.'

★

Sofia found Madeleine in the stable with Benny. They were fixing the door to the pigpen and didn't notice Sofia until she was almost on top of them.

She decided to get straight to the point.

'Madeleine, your parents went to the police.'

'The police?'

'They haven't heard from you since January.'

'But I wrote to them.'

'The letters were never sent. Your parents came to the island asking about you.'

'Oh no! Does Franz know?' She was nearly hysterical.

'What do you think? It was in the paper today.'

'The paper? Oh my god, I'm so ashamed.'

'Yes, but he's giving you a chance to fix it. You have to go see Sten and give them a call. Tell them it's all a big mistake.

That the mail got lost. And you're going to go visit them next weekend. With Katarina.'

'Katarina?'

'Yes, just say she's your best friend, and she's really been looking forward to meeting them.'

Madeleine nodded frantically. 'Sure, I'll do whatever it takes. Just so Franz doesn't fire me.'

'He won't. Do you know anyone who's left ViaTerra?'

'Just Elvira.'

'She'll be back, believe me.'

Every time Sofia spoke to Madeleine it felt like there was an infinite gap between them. As if everything she said just bounced back to her from the invisible walls of the void — even her barbed comments.

Once she had delivered Madeleine to Sten, she went back to the office. The door was ajar and she could hear Oswald's voice. He was on the phone and sounded livid. For once he wasn't using the speakerphone, so she couldn't hear the other end of the conversation.

She lingered outside the door to eavesdrop.

'Yes, you heard me. Some idiot misplaced the mail. She's calling her parents now and she'll be visiting them this weekend. Right, it's all a misunderstanding.'

Silence for a moment. She was just about to enter the office when he started talking again.

'That sounds good. As usual, thanks for your help, Wilgot. You have to visit us this summer. I've released the fifth thesis. Total dynamite.'

Wilgot. She could picture him at dinners in the annexe. The chief of police who had sat at her table with his wife, the accountant.

'Then that's settled. Yes, just call the parents later so they can confirm it. I'll handle the newspaper. They're damn well going to publish a public apology.'

She walked in, pretending nothing was wrong, and sat down at her desk to clean up one of his lectures.

He ended the call, then sat down to type something on his computer. For a while they worked in silence. But something was wearing on him and creating a cloud of irritation in the air between them.

'Did Bosse tell you I was the one who asked them to stop the mail?' he asked at last.

'Yes, I suppose he suggested as much.'

'And you still told him to send it?'

'Bosse always acts like a robot, you can't keep track of everything around here.'

'Right, right. It's just a little too . . . perfect. You aren't up to something, are you, Sofia?'

'No, of course not.'

'Good, then that's that.'

★

On that same day, she was struck with serious doubt. It wandered into her mind sometime after lunch. Everything had seemed so simple just a few days ago. She wanted out. The cell phone had arrived like a gift from heaven. All she had to do was call home and say, 'I'm stuck here. Help me.' Or call the police directly. But nothing seemed quite that easy anymore. Not at all.

She thought of what had just happened to Madeleine. Wilgot Östling was so tight with Oswald. And there were other things to consider, and now she didn't know which way was up.

If she just left, what would happen to all the others? Simon, his hands busy in the earth, waiting for the walls to fall. Benjamin, who she both loved and hated. How long could he hold out without transforming into a passive bag of bones?

But why did she even care? They were all there of their own free will. Although that wasn't entirely true. No one could know how another person truly felt inside, and there was so much they weren't allowed to talk about. She was torn, and it felt like her doubt might drive her to madness. She wished she could come to a decision and turn her thoughts to something more sensible.

I need ammunition, she thought. *Proof of everything that's going on around here. If I run now, he'll send the whole police force after me.*

She had hoped Oswald would take the five o'clock ferry for his meeting with the newspaper and leave her alone with all her troubling thoughts, but he decided to call the paper instead. The conversation didn't seem to go as he'd hoped. The calm, authoritative voice he started out with soon grew annoyed and angry, until at last he slammed down the phone. The barrage of curse words he aimed at the paper were ones she seldom even used in her mind.

It was going to be a gloomy evening. Even the weather was horrid. A storm had moved in during the afternoon, and the wind and rain pounded the windows. Thick black clouds hung over the estate and extended off over the sea. The trees were bending in the wind and leaves and flower petals flew across the yard like butterflies. Just as she was considering which excuse she could use to get out of the office for a while, the phone rang. It was Benjamin.

'Sofia, the five o'clock ferry is cancelled due to the weather. I can't bring Franz's food over today. I don't know what to do.'

'There's not much you *can* do, is there?'

'No, but try to explain to him, please. I spoke with Björk but he said the winds are too high. It's too dangerous.'

'I'll take care of it,' she said, hanging up.

Oswald glanced in her direction.

'Who was that?'

'It was Benjamin. They've cancelled the five o'clock ferry. Your food won't be coming, but I'll make sure the kitchen fixes you something.'

'No you will not. He can make sure the ferry goes instead. I want my food.'

He was thoroughly worked up after his conversation with the newspaper.

'Benjamin said he talked to Björk, but the wind is too strong. It's too dangerous.'

'It's nothing! Look out the window. Look, I said! This weather is child's play for anyone who knows the first thing about boats. But this whole damn village is full of cowards, and Benjamin is even worse. I never understood what you saw in that idiot.'

'I understand.'

'No you don't, not at all, because you don't know how many times I've had to eat crap when he's screwed up. Go ahead, go to the kitchen, but I bet it will be something nasty, as usual.'

She was on her way out of the office, but he had risen to block her way. He walked up to her, and with every step he took she backed up until she was standing with her back to the wall. He grabbed her wrists, pulled them up above her head, and held them in an iron grip.

'Benjamin this, Benjamin that,' he hissed.

Her body was stretched out before him, and when she tried

to pull her arms back he only squeezed her wrists harder. He moved even closer and pressed his body firmly against hers. His face was right up next to hers. She could feel him breathing into her ear, in little starts.

'Is there something misfiring in that head of yours, Sofia? Don't you get that what you need is a man with drive, not a whiny little brat?'

A voice inside her head was screaming at him to stop, but no words could pass through her compressed lips. He pressed against her even harder, and she felt his erection against her stomach.

Do something! Kick him!

Just then, he let go. He stepped back and shrugged his shoulders.

'Now go get that bloody food.'

*

The rain was pouring down outside. She opened her umbrella, but the wind caught it and blew it inside out. She bent it back and aimed it into the wind instead. By the time she'd battled her way to the annexes, her legs were soaked and the hem of her skirt was dripping.

She forced the images of what had just happened from her mind. *The way out is through his office*, she thought. *I have no choice. Unless I want to go to Penance again. And I don't. I'd rather die. I've got to get out of here, I've got to.*

Negotiations with the kitchen staff about what to make for Oswald took a long time. The pantry was low on stock and at last they decided to make spinach-and-cheese ravioli.

'We have a good French cheese to use in the filling,' said Inga, one of the cooks.

'Do you have fresh tomatoes?' Sofia wondered.

All at once, the cooks looked dejected.

'No, only tinned ones. But we do have some fresh lettuce from the greenhouse.'

Sofia considered this for a moment. It seemed like the best solution.

'Okay! But you'd better start right away.'

She didn't want to go back to the office, so she waited in the kitchen as they prepared the food. The tomato sauce smelled delicious as it simmered on the stove, and she got her hopes up that they might be able to appease Oswald despite his horrible mood.

The rain had let up by the time the meal was ready. She asked Inga to help her carry the food to the office, because she didn't want to be alone when she served Oswald.

They stood quietly in the doorway until he nodded at them to come in. Inga placed the tray on the desk in front of him. The kitchen staff had arranged the food with care and garnished it with basil Simon had already managed to grow in the greenhouse. When he first lifted the dome from the plate, Oswald looked pleased.

'What's this?'

'Ravioli with spinach and cheese, sir,' said Inga. 'The cheese comes from Brittany. And the lettuce in the salad was grown here, of course.'

'Hmm . . .'

He poked at the sauce with his fork.

'You didn't use canned tomatoes, did you?'

They deflated. Neither of them dared to answer. Inga's cheeks had gone bright red.

'Yes, sir,' said Sofia. 'We simply didn't have any —'

The tray came hurtling at them so fast it flipped end over end in the air. The plate shattered into hundreds of tiny shards and the ravioli bounced off the floor here and there. Their legs were splattered with tomato sauce and water from the glass, which had also smashed to pieces.

Suddenly everything was still, except for the plate dome, which was spinning on the floor with the unpleasant scraping of steel on marble.

'Get out!' he screamed. 'Get out of here and don't come back!'

At first she didn't know where to go. She sent Inga back to the kitchen and went to her room, where she sat on the bed and forced back the tears that were burning her eyes. *I won't go back there*, she thought. *I will not suck up to him for the sake of fucking canned tomatoes. He can clean it up himself.*

Her pager buzzed.

Come back to the office.

She went anyway. Her legs stood up on autopilot and trudged up the stairs.

But if he keeps complaining about the tomatoes, I'm leaving, she thought. *I'll just walk away without a word.*

He smiled at her as she came in, as if nothing had happened. As if the wreckage and the food on the floor didn't exist. She almost slipped on a piece of ravioli as she approached him but caught herself just in time.

'It's not your fault, Sofia,' he said. 'Frisk is the one who hasn't done his job. He's been messing with me for a long time now. I think he's trying to take over.'

'Take over?'

'Yes, take over my job. I'm sure that's why he got hung up

on you. Because I'm the one who brought you here. He wants anything that belongs to me, you see.'

'But he only ever has good things to say about you.'

'Exactly, he can be so ingratiating. You don't know him, Sofia. Get this into your skull. I know what I'm talking about. You saw what happened when you wanted to run away. Anyone with a speck of initiative would have just stopped you. But not Benjamin. He didn't dare. He came crying to me instead.'

She wanted to challenge him, but she reacted too awkwardly. She cleared her throat, but no words came out. He stood up and came over to her desk.

'I can read people. Believe me. Benjamin is a deceitful jerk, and you should be glad things ended the way they did between the two of you.'

'I'll make sure the ethics unit investigates.'

'Not necessary. Just make sure he comes by as soon as the ferry arrives in the morning. I'll deal with him myself.'

It's by sheer chance that I overhear their conversation.

Sara has gone to bed. I've been chatting with them in the living room, or the salon, or whatever the hell it is.

Once again I've suggested that I should move out. Get my own place.

It's not something I truly want to do, but it seems polite to suggest it.

Show them I don't want to be a burden. Once again, I allow them to convince me to stay.

'The house is so large'; 'Emilie feels safer with you here'; 'Sara would be crushed.'

The same old arguments. And I pretend to buy them. I head for the kitchen, planning to make a midnight snack.

But they think I've gone upstairs and I can hear their voices clearly through the cracked door.

'I have to take a look at the will,' he said. 'Fredrik is like one of our own, but it's still not proper for him to have the same right of inheritance as Sara.'

'What does it matter?' she says. 'I don't understand why you're bringing it up. We're not going to die.'

'You can never be too careful. We'll leave him enough money to manage, of course.'

She doesn't say anything.

I hate them. It takes effort to keep myself from walking in and slugging them one. Those ungrateful idiots. After everything I've done. All these years of toiling, fawning over them, and immaculate behaviour.

I stare out the giant window that faces the sea.

How much money is in question here? I'm sure it must be billions.

Enough money to live whatever life you like. Instead they live here, mincing around on their marble floors.

Throwing pathetic parties for boring people.

It's almost criminal to waste resources like that. My course has been so steady; my plan clearly staked out.

But now it's time for Plan B. And it has to happen fast.

36

There was a small hill behind the manor house that afforded a view of the sea. She decided to stop there on her way to work the next day. The clouds had all but blown away but the strong, icy wind had remained. She stood up on the hill for a while, letting the wind tear at her down jacket and whip her hair about. The waves were so strong that the foam was thrown all the way up to Devil's Rock.

She was just about to head back when she heard a sound. It came in bursts and blended with the howling of the wind, like a trumpet sending a song of lament over the bay. She thought of what Oswald had said, that it was just the wind blowing through the old foghorn. Yet she felt ill at ease as she walked to the office.

What's more, she was late. Oswald and Benjamin were already there when she opened the door.

They were staring at each other like a couple of angry bulls and didn't seem to notice her appearance. The air was trembling with rage. Her heart jumped into her throat, and not just because Oswald looked so furious — Benjamin was staring daggers right back. She had never seen anyone look at him that way.

'You should be licking the floor before my feet,' Oswald said.

'Never. It's not my fault that the ferry couldn't cross.'

'Get down on your knees!'

'I will not!'

Oswald moved toward Benjamin until there were only cen-
timetres between them. He shoved Benjamin in the chest with
both hands, but Benjamin wouldn't back down. His narrowed
eyes were fixed on Oswald and he didn't budge a millimetre.
Oswald exploded, screaming in Benjamin's face, attacking him
like a machine gun.

'You ungrateful little shit! You are nothing but a loser! Riding
back and forth on the ferry, refusing to lift a goddamn finger
for this place.'

Each time Benjamin opened his mouth, Oswald started in
again.

'Shut your mouth and listen up! I said, shut your mouth! What
have you done for this place? Not a thing. You are nobody. Do
you understand me? Can you get that into your thick skull?'

He shoved Benjamin again, harder this time, but Benjamin
stood his ground. He was seething with an incredible rage; it was
like a switch had been flipped. She had never seen Benjamin truly
angry and thought it was odd that Oswald hadn't yet attacked
him with his fists. Then again, Bosse and his gang weren't there
to back him up.

She sneaked past them and slid down into her desk chair.

'Down on the ground, or else you will jump from Devil's
Rock. Your choice.'

This challenge seemed to throw Benjamin for a loop. Sofia
cast a quick glance out the window. The waves were crashing
against the rocks and she could hear the endless thunder and
roar of the sea all the way up in the office. Suddenly, she felt an
impulse so strong that it sucked the air from her lungs: *Run up
and get between them. Put an end to this.*

Don't do it, Benjamin! Don't agree to it! He's only messing with you.

'I'll jump, but I won't lick the floor.'

Idiot, idiot, you goddamn idiot!

'Then that's settled!' Oswald said. 'Sofia, the whole staff must be there. It will be a good lesson for them. I'll come too. You can bet on that.'

He had regained control of his voice, but he was far from calm. His breathing was quick and his hand was trembling ever so slightly. But she could see it.

Then he nailed Benjamin with his gaze again.

'Don't think I don't get what's going on. I know exactly what you're after.'

Benjamin stormed out of the office, leaving the room in awkward silence. She pretended to be rummaging through her desk drawer, where she found a few pages of his theses she hadn't yet typed up and set to work. She felt his eyes on her for a long time and then heard the door open and shut.

He came back just before lunch.

'Benjamin will jump after assembly,' he said. 'Make sure the staff sticks around until I come down.'

But he came down before assembly was over and shooed off Bosse, who was harping on as usual.

'That can wait. Come on! The whole gang. We're going to Devil's Rock.'

★

The closer they got to the sea, the stronger the wind blew. The sun peeked out now and then from the clouds, which had gathered again. The sea was like a dark, foaming blanket that reached for the horizon, roaring as the wind whipped it up. Thick lines of waves rolled in toward the island and crashed against the rocks. Stones and gravel from the sea floor clattered against the rock faces, only to be pulled back out into the depths.

It's impossible to jump right now, she thought. *Not even Benjamin can manage.* She prayed to a higher power, any power at all that would listen, for Oswald to change his mind. For him to realize the incredible strength of the current. And how cold was the water? Seven or eight degrees, maybe. Could a person be paralyzed by the cold and swept out to sea?

They were standing near the edge of the cliff — Benjamin and Bosse, and, behind them, Sten and Benny. In case Benjamin tried to run.

Benjamin took another few steps toward the edge and looked down at the water. He took off his shoes. Oswald nodded at Bosse, who read the short proclamation.

'May you leave your betrayal in the depths and rise to the surface pure and full of devotion.'

And then everything went wrong. Usually, the guilty party jumped from Devil's Rock with their hands at their sides. But Benjamin took a running start and flew over the edge like an arrow. He dived like a professional — it was strange to see him spear the middle of a wave in his uniform. But the wave didn't toss him ahead of it; instead he vanished under the surface. At first she thought he would be fine, because his entry had looked so smooth. She scanned the water for a head popping up. But she saw nothing.

She thought perhaps he had taken a few strokes under the surface, that he wanted to mess with Oswald. So she looked a little farther out, but all she could see was more waves. She turned around and noticed the tense expressions and anxious eyes of the others. Whispers began to go through the ranks. 'Where did he go?' 'Do you see him?' They stood where they were for a moment, whispering to each other and staring down at the water. Their concern grew as hope began to fade, only to return each time a wave crested or a dark spot was seen amidst all the foam. But there was no Benjamin.

An empty space grew where he had so recently been standing on the cliff.

Then, Bosse's voice: 'We have to go after him! He's not coming up!'

And Oswald, roaring: 'No, it's too dangerous!'

He took command. 'Bosse, take the bike by the sentry box and ride to the harbour, fast. Make them take out the pilot boat. He might have been dragged out to sea. Benny, get all the guys and search along the rock edges down there. But watch out for the waves!'

The women drew closer together, awaiting instructions, something to do. But Oswald just shot an irritated glance their way.

'You can go home. I'll handle this.'

Sofia took a step forward.

'Not on your life! I'm staying until we find Benjamin.'

The others mumbled their agreement.

Oswald shook his head, shrugged, and allowed them to stay. He fished his phone from his pocket and made a call.

Tears welled in her eyes and began to force their way out as the uncertainty became too much to handle. But it was a certainty that broke the dam. The certainty that no one could manage down there in the sea for so long. Not on a day like this. Things were truly serious now, and if she stood still much longer she would lose her mind. Others had started crying as well.

'Let's go down to the rocks and search for him,' Sofia said to them. 'We can't just stand here.'

Oswald was busy talking on the phone and didn't attempt to stop them. The wind carried his angry voice down the slope as they went. He was talking to Bosse.

They took off their shoes and tossed them into what became a strange, grey pile in the grass, then continued down the rocks barefoot. As she neared the water, a wave swelled and drenched her legs.

It was even colder than she'd expected, and her feet went numb almost immediately.

Soon after, she was wet up to her waist. But the others kept following her, staring out at the sea and trying to spot something — a body, an article of clothing, any sign of Benjamin.

Anna was the one who found the blazer. It was on a rock sticking up from the water. She hollered and tried to reach it but was thrown back by a wave. At first Sofia thought she had lost her footing and fallen into the water. But she had been washed onto a boulder and was sitting on it and gasping for breath. Sofia climbed over to her and made Anna hold onto her as she reached out and retrieved the blazer. She held up the wet bundle for Oswald to see. He signalled at them to come back up, so they climbed to the grassy slope. Oswald ripped the garment from her hands.

'That idiot,' he said. 'That goddamn idiot.'

At first she thought she had misheard. But no, he was standing there cursing Benjamin, who was surely dead in the icy water. *It must be the shock*, she thought. *He must be completely beside himself.* She was wet up to her chest by now, and freezing — she was shivering, and her teeth were chattering. Anna was soaked head to toe.

'Go home and change immediately!' Oswald directed Anna. He looked at Sofia but she shook her head vehemently. Oswald walked to the precipice, gave a sharp whistle, and waved at the men, who climbed up the rocks like spiders.

'I've called the police,' he said once everyone had gathered. 'They're bringing divers. You can't keep climbing around on the rocks, it's too dangerous.'

He observed them for a moment.

'Those of you who got wet must go and change immediately. The police will want to talk to you. It's important for us to stick together now, so everyone knows what to say.'

The power in his voice was muted by the wind, and yet he managed to reach them.

'This is what happened. Benjamin made a bet with some-one — let's say it was you, Benny — that he could jump from Devil's Rock despite the wind. He made the whole staff come along as witnesses. I wasn't here, of course. Bosse called me later. Understood?'

No one protested. Some nodded or mumbled agreement. Some didn't say anything. Sofia had so many comments on the tip of her tongue: *You're lying! That's not what happened! You were the one who* — But not a sound came out. It all got stuck in her throat. Her word against theirs, that's what it would be. And she was so thoroughly exhausted and chilled to the bone. She tried to force her brain to work, to analyse the situation. The police. The police would be coming. She would tell them everything. They would take her with them. She would beg and plead until they did. Best to keep her mouth shut until they arrived.

They sat in the grass in small groups, waiting. Her feet and legs had gone numb; her hands were shaking. Tears overtook her again as strange memories of Benjamin popped into her mind. How he tossed his clothes on the floor, always left the wardrobe door open. Stupid details. But it was so incredibly painful to think about them. And that goddamn foghorn. She should have known.

But her body was far too cold and tired to handle all these thoughts, and the landscape began to blur around her.

The police vessel that finally showed up seemed to move in slow motion. It took a while for them to come ashore in the waves. Oswald and a few of the guys went down to help. She squinted at the sun and tried to make out the figure stepping off the boat, a man in a uniform who took a few staggering steps onto a big rock and steadied himself on Oswald's arm.

It was Wilgot Östling.

All sensation in her body had vanished. Something was flickering, sharp and full of static, at the edges of her vision. Everything went sparkling grey, then white, and at last her surroundings disappeared completely. She made one last attempt to brace herself and get up, but she fell back and drowned in the infinite darkness.

'You have to promise not to say a word about this.'

That's how I begin the conversation.

She's all ears, and on edge, because she can hear the gravity in my voice.

'Of course, what's wrong?'

'Well, I heard Mom and Dad talking. I didn't mean to, but . . . oh, maybe it's not that big a deal.'

'No, tell me. Tell me!'

'They said they were thinking of changing their will. Sara, you won't say anything about this, will you?'

'You know I won't. What did they say?'

'Well, Dad was saying that they were going to make me the main heir. You'll only get part of it. Shit, Sara, I don't even know why I'm telling you this. But it feels like you've become my best friend, you know that, right?'

She nods.

To think that she doesn't see. How stupid can you get?

I could have any friends I want. I can pick and choose.

Yet she believes me.

'It doesn't seem right, Sara,' I say. 'It seems like we should share everything. Forever, I mean.'

'I hate them,' she says.

'Me too,' I say, taking her hands. 'It would be better if it was just you and me, wouldn't it?'

She nods.

'You're so nice, Fredrik.'

'Aw, I'm only looking out for you.'

The seed has been sown. Now it just needs a little time to sprout.

37

A persistent buzzing noise roused her from sleep. She slowly opened her eyes to find a fly on the nightstand, cleaning its legs. She must have forgotten to close the blinds properly and the light filtering in under the edges was bright and white. For a moment she found herself suspended between her dream and the cold morning light, but then her eyes focused and she saw bodies in the other dormitory beds. She felt empty down to her marrow and her memory was full of holes. She battled the emptiness for a moment, and then the images returned.

The sea and the wind. Benjamin on the cliff. And how it all went black in the end.

She was overwhelmed by great sorrow. It must have even been with her as she slept, because her heart was heavy and aching and tears burned in her eyes.

But now it took on enormous proportions and nearly threatened to smother her. Benjamin's scent seemed to waft through the air, the scent of seaweed and salt that often came from his skin when he returned from his morning dip. She could almost feel his warmth under the blanket and regretted every mean thing she had ever said to him. As miserable and useless as she felt, she wished she could just go back to sleep and never wake up. But then she felt a faint flicker of hope. Maybe, against all odds, they had found him.

She moved her body, extending her fingers and stretching her legs. Everything seemed fine, except for her merciless headache.

One of the bodies in the other beds moved, sighing and turning toward her. It was Anna. She opened her eyes and met Sofia's gaze.

'Good morning. How are you feeling?'

'Like shit. Did they find him?'

Anna shook her head slowly.

Sofia gave a sob. She turned her back on Anna and buried her face in her hands as she curled into a ball. She sniffled and cried and pressed her pillow to her face until she was gasping for breath. Eventually her voice went hoarse and her lungs whistled as she drew in air — she must have been lying there for a long time. She felt the mattress shift under her and knew that Anna had come to perch on the edge.

'You've had a shock. Just rest until you're feeling better.'

Sofia turned over and wiped her tears. To keep from crying, she pressed her lips together.

'What happened?'

'The police and the divers said he must have hit his head on a rock, and his body was dragged out by the currents. The water was so rough that at first the divers couldn't even go in. When they could dive, they searched for hours but didn't find him.'

'Oh, Anna. He's dead!'

The last word caught in her throat and she started crying again. Anna took her hand.

'Everyone's so sad, but I know it's worst for you. Elin and I are going to move in here so you won't be so alone. Franz is on the mainland, talking to the police and Benjamin's family. He said you don't have to work until you feel better.'

'How did I get here?'

'The guys carried you. You fainted. Franz said it was the cold and the shock, and your wet clothes. It was just too much, he thought.'

'I faint pretty easily. I think it has to do with the blood flow to my brain.'

Tears continued to flow.

'Sofia, I'm so sorry.'

It seemed to Sofia that Anna didn't look particularly sorry. Her eyes were too steady and her face too stiff, aside from a fake sympathetic smile. She could only imagine what Oswald had said to the staff while she was passed out in the grass. Goddamn hypocrisy was what it was, and a wave of rage washed over her.

'What the hell is going on, Anna? Why do you look like everything's fine? Why does everything feel just like it always does around here? Is everyone totally nuts? Benjamin is dead, dammit!'

'Yes, and it's horrible. But he was the one who wanted to jump. He knew it was a risk. It was an accident . . .'

'You don't know one fucking thing about how it happened.'

'But Oswald said —'

'Of course he did. What did you tell the police?'

'What we agreed upon with Oswald, obviously.'

'Goddammit, you're all such liars!'

'You need to sleep, Sofia. You're not really yourself right now.'

'I'm done sleeping!'

'Oswald said Elin has to check your blood pressure before you're allowed to get out of bed.'

'Okay. Elin!' she called loudly.

Elin groaned from her bed.

'It's five-thirty in the morning,' Anna said. 'Let Elin sleep. We'll deal with everything later, I promise.'

'Sure, you two go right ahead and sleep. I'll just lie here thinking for a while.'

She turned to look at the window and listened to the others breathe as they fell back to sleep. She squinted at the pale light filtering in under the blinds. So many feelings were battling inside her. Grief was just waiting to swallow her up again. All she had to do was throw herself down into it, let a mute depression take over, and close herself off from the world outside. But then there was her rage at the hypocritical playacting that had taken place out there at Devil's Rock. A piece of theatre with blind marionettes who had followed Oswald's script to the letter. And most of all, she was disgusted with herself for playing her supporting role without speaking up, for just waiting obediently for the cops to arrive and take care of everything.

This isn't working anymore, she thought. *Cry when no one's looking. Silently, in the dark, at night. But now that pig is going to pay for what he does to the staff.*

The last thing she wanted to do was go work in that loathsome office. But Oswald wasn't home. There was a computer there, and she could lock the door and be left alone. She got another whiff of saltwater from under the blanket and realized that she was the smelly one. They had put her to bed fully dressed in her wet uniform.

When she got to her feet, the room began to sway. She grabbed hold of the bureau and stood still for a moment, but she couldn't free herself from the dizziness — it fell over her again as she walked across the room. She realized it was somehow linked to the unpleasant, seaweed smell emanating from her body.

The dizziness faded after some time in the shower. A tiny bit of seaweed that had been nestled in her armpit slid down her body and vanished down the drain. She rubbed and scraped at her dirty hands and scrubbed her knees, which were green from the grassy slope. There was no clean uniform in the wardrobe, so she put on jeans and a hoodie. She searched for her phone and its charger among her underwear, found them, and stuffed them into her pocket.

There's still a camera here, she thought. She looked for the vent and found it in a corner near the ceiling.

She cautiously pulled over the chair next to her bed, climbed onto it, and stared into the vent. There it was — a tiny eye, not much bigger than a marble, staring at her. She jumped down to get her pocketknife from the top drawer of her bureau, then climbed back up and stuck the blade through the grating. The glass shattered with a crunching sound and a few shards fell onto her head.

'What are you doing?'

It was Anna.

'It's so cold in here. I was just aiming the vent away from my bed.'

'Get back in bed, Sofia.'

She didn't know where it was coming from, this new courage. But it was comforting. She dug through her handbag for something to handle her headache — and there it was, in one of the inside pockets, a paracetamol left over from before she had come to the island.

The light seemed garish when she walked into the yard, despite the thick fog that blanketed the property. There was no wind, and the world was silent. She didn't want to go to the kitchen, but the greenhouse lights were on. Simon was watering tomato plants when she came in.

He noticed her right away, and put down the hose to walk over to her.

'Oh my god, Sofia. It's horrible.'

She nodded.

'We can talk about it later, when you feel up to it.'

She started crying again. He pulled her close and held her for a while, stroking her back with his dirt-covered garden glove.

'I actually came by to look for some food,' she said.

'Food?'

'I didn't want to show my face in the kitchen. You don't have anything I could eat in here, do you?'

'No, nothing has grown enough yet except for some herbs and lettuce, but I have this.'

He pulled a flattened sandwich from his back pocket.

'My breakfast. We can share it.'

He also had a thermos of coffee. They sat and ate the sandwich in complete silence. It tasted good, and it felt calming to sit quietly next to Simon.

'But didn't Benjamin *want* to jump?' he broke the silence at last.

'No, he didn't. He had to choose between jumping and licking the floor at Oswald's feet. Terrible, right?'

'That's so disgusting it's crazy.'

'It's weird, though. We weren't a couple anymore, but that almost makes it worse. I feel mean — there was something he wanted to tell me. "It's not like you think," he kept saying. But I wouldn't listen to his excuses. And now I'll never know what he meant.'

She started crying again; this time it was just quiet tears running down her cheeks.

'Someone really should put that bastard behind bars,' said Simon.

'Oswald?'

'Right. Lock him up.'

'How do we do that?'

He thought for a moment.

'By snooping. Find out what he's *really* up to.'

'What do you mean?'

'I mean, the way he acts, there's something he's hiding. If we could find out what it was . . .'

'How would you go about that?'

'Not me. I'm just a dumb farmer. But you could do it. You work in his office.'

She considered what he'd said.

'I think I'll head for the office now. Thanks for the sandwich,' she said as she stood up.

'Don't even mention it. Be careful, Sofia.'

★

The paracetamol had kicked in and her headache was gone by the time she reached the office. It was dark and cold inside, but her papers were still on the desk just as she'd left them. The chairs weren't pushed in; it seemed that Oswald hadn't been back.

She turned on the lights and the heat. The wave of energy she'd recovered suddenly vanished and she felt like she sinking to the marble floor. Images from the scene between Benjamin and Oswald moved through her mind unbidden. *Last time I stood in this room, Benjamin was alive*, she thought, as a suffocating sense of hopelessness filled her. Regret closed in on her again.

Why hadn't she convinced Benjamin to lick the stupid floor? She even could have gotten down on her knees to do it herself, just to shut Oswald up. Or she could have started screaming out on the cliff, made a scene, anything to put a stop to Benjamin's idiotic recklessness.

Tears sprang to her eyes again, but she forced them back down.

One step at a time, that's the only way to get through this.

She cleaned up a little as the phone charged, then locked the door from the inside. She sat down in front of Oswald's computer. She had never used it before — that was a line she hadn't dared to cross — but now she didn't care. How could things get any worse than they already were?

Oswald's big tub of muscle-building vitamin powder, the stuff he mixed into his drinks, was on the edge of the desk. Suddenly she found herself very irritated by it. Who on staff had time to think of building muscle? She picked up the tub, went to the bathroom, poured the entire contents into the toilet, and flushed. All at once her mood improved a bit. She laughed so loudly it echoed off the bathroom walls. Back at the desk, she set down the empty tub, logged into the computer, and checked her email and Facebook.

There were several emails from her parents and Wilma, and a few from friends she hadn't heard from in a long time. The level of anxiety in their messages rose the closer to the present day she got, and concluded with a deafening crescendo, a heart-rending plea from the mainland.

Where are you, Sofia? Answer, answer!

She answered every one. Wilma had written one email about Ellis. He had received a conditional sentence and had to pay a fine; he even owed Sofia some money. All this, and she hadn't even been present. She thought about Oswald's network of contacts and shuddered. Ellis suddenly seemed as insignificant as the buzzing little fly that had woken Sofia that morning. She even felt glad that Ellis hadn't ended up in jail. Her hatred for him had cooled.

She surfed the net for a while, trying to figure out what had been going on in the world. She Googled the name 'Vanja Frisk' and found the woman's address, cell phone number, and everything; she wrote it all down on a Post-it. Then she deleted the browser history before turning off the computer. The phone was fully charged, so she checked her texts and responded to them. Then she dialled her parents' number. Her mother picked up.

'Sofia, honey! We've been so worried. Where are you?' Right away, her mom started crying.

'I'm here on the island, Mom. Everything's fine. I'm so, so sorry that I haven't called. I miss you so much.'

Her throat was thick with grief; she tried to swallow and sound cheerful, but her voice still sounded choked.

'Sofia, are you crying?'

'No, no, I just have a cold.'

'Darling girl. Come home!'

'I'll be home soon, Mom, I promise. There's just something I have to finish up here. I'll be home before summer.'

'We can come visit you.'

'No! Don't do that! I mean, it would be too tricky. I promise I'll come home soon.'

They spoke for a while, but she never did get the lump out of her throat.

'Can I ask you a few favours?' Sofia asked before they ended the call.

'Anything.'

'I have a friend who lost someone. I mean, we have an acquaintance in common and he died. I wonder if you could send her a card and flowers from me. It's a little complicated from here on the island. But send them in a few days, if you don't mind, once she's had time to recover a little.'

And when Oswald isn't at her house to see them.

'Of course I will, darling.'

'Her name is Vanja Frisk.' She gave her mother the address. 'Just write "I'm sorry for your loss, Sofia" on the card, and include my mobile number.'

'I'll take care of it.'

'Thank, Mom, just one other thing.'

'Anything.'

'I need to borrow some money. I promise to pay you back once I get home.'

'How much?'

'Ten thousand kronor or so. It's for something I need to do. I promise I'll pay you back.'

'Don't they pay you there?'

'Sure, this is just for something extra.'

'Of course you can have the money. I'll deposit it in your account. Will that work?'

'Yes, thanks, Mom.'

'Can't you take the weekend off to come and visit?'

'Soon, I promise. But not yet.'

After their conversation, she sat down and gazed out the window for a while. Tiny leaves had sprouted on the birches, creating a green veil that swept over the landscape. It reminded her of that first spring with Benjamin. She wondered how she could shut out such painful memories, and remembered what Simon had said, that Oswald must be hiding something. She mentally wandered around the manor and found her mind settling on the attic. She rose and walked to the key cabinet on the wall. It was open, but the keys to the attic padlocks weren't there. He must have taken them with him, which only made her more curious.

Whatever it is he's got up there, it's something of value to him, she thought. So there had to be cameras up there. Another screen. A keypad he didn't want anyone to find. She thought of how eagerly he had sent her away while the system was installed; he'd wanted to take care of everything himself. Her thoughts were drawn to his room. She didn't visit it often, but she had fetched items from it now and then, or straightened it up when he complained that the household unit had slacked off.

It was only six-thirty; she had half an hour before the staff would start coming down to breakfast.

The door to his room was ajar. It was actually a suite of three rooms, like the guest suites in the annexes. A bedroom, a large living room, and a private gym. He had all the latest workout gadgets, and staff were forbidden entry, but the celebrities exercised there with him. There was even a tanning bed in the gym.

When she opened the door she heard faint voices and was afraid someone was there, but it was just the TV. The room looked neat; it had recently been cleaned. She spent a long time searching for a screen but didn't find one; it wasn't in one of the wardrobes or cabinets.

The TV, she thought. *The cameras could be linked up to it.* There were two remotes on the coffee table; she picked one up and turned the TV on and off with it, then selected the DVD input. The other remote had several numbered buttons and a few larger buttons in various colours. She pressed the red one and the TV screen turned blue. When she pressed the button labelled with the number one, a room appeared, viewed from the ceiling.

It was the room she had shared with Benjamin. Someone else lived there now, but she recognized the wall mirror — Benjamin had had quite a time dragging it over from the mainland for her. *So much for that goddamn birthday present*, she thought, because she remembered the day Oswald had told her that as a special birthday treat, there wouldn't be a camera in their room.

Then a thought sneaked up on her.

Maybe it really hadn't been like she thought, that night when they were planning their escape.

Maybe she had misjudged Benjamin.

She was sitting there on Oswald's couch and pondering this when she heard a quiet knock at the door.

I let her take the first step.

I wait. Certain it's coming.

It's night-time, and we're sitting up on the rise and gazing at the sea. The night is clear, full of glittering stars. I've brought her here intentionally, knowing that she likes to sit here with me.

At first she doesn't say a word, but then she breaks the ice.

'I've been thinking about what you said.'

'What?'

'About Mom and Dad. How it would be better without them.'

'Oh.'

I pretend to be surprised; I want it to seem like her own idea.

'So what do you think we should do?'

'Get rid of them. For real, I mean,' she says. Her voice quavers.

We're into dangerous territory here. She's afraid I'll protest. And I do, but only a little.

'But it's not that bad, is it? I mean, it's not like they beat you.'

'No, but what they do is even worse. They freeze me out. Stare at me like I'm a monster.'

Silence again, a lengthy one.

Then I turn to look at her. So sincere.

'I'll help you in any way you want,' I say. 'You know that.'

'But if they disappear,' she says hesitantly. 'If they disappear, it will just be you and me?'

'Just you and me,' I say with great emphasis.

38

She turned off the TV, put the remote back on the table, and went to the door. There was another knock, harder this time. Her pulse quickened. She thought about hiding in the wardrobe, but opened the door after all. Outside was Corinne from the household unit, holding a big tray and staring wide-eyed at Sofia.

'What are you doing here?' she asked.

'I was just about to ask you the same thing.'

'Oh, I'm sorry, Sofia. I thought you were in bed. Someone mentioned you were. I only came by to drop off food for Franz and to clean.'

'Food? He eats in the office.'

'Not that food. He's ordered extra food, because he works out after lunch and dinner. Didn't you know?'

Extra food? Two workouts a day? Sure, he had been out of the office an unusual amount lately, but she'd never asked where he was. *Simon's right*, she thought. *There's something fishy going on.*

She quickly recovered her wits.

'You can put the food in the fridge, but I've already done the cleaning. I came to get something and it was a real pigsty in here. You people need to shape up.'

Corinne looked around the neat room in surprise.

'Oh, right, I'm sorry. But I have been cleaning this room every day.'

'You can't tell to look at it. I've taken care of it now, so you can go.'

'Okay. You won't say anything to Franz, though, will you? I mean, that you didn't think it was nice in here.'

'No, I certainly won't. He has more important things to worry about.'

Corinne placed a sandwich and a big smoothie of some sort in the fridge and aimed another baffled look Sofia's way.

'As long as you're here,' Sofia said, 'I don't have any clean uniforms. I don't know who's in charge of that now, but I can't look like this when Franz gets home.'

'Of course not. I'll take care of it. We didn't think you would be back on your feet so soon.'

'But I am, as you can see.'

Corinne nodded and vanished.

Sofia waited for a while, then closed the door and locked it. She knew Oswald liked to record what he saw on the screens in the office. He liked showing Bosse short clips of the staff in humiliating situations. She'd learned to recognize the rough bursts of laughter that meant he had found something to save. Surely he did the same here in his room, and all she had to do was figure out how to use the remote.

She pressed different buttons until she found a registry that was just a column of letters. She selected the first one: B. The picture quality was incredibly sharp. It was Bosse, jerking off on a bed and moaning. Very loudly. She tried to turn down the volume but couldn't figure out how at first. At last she found the right button.

Either he's a perv, or he's saving this as some sort of blackmail material, she thought. How illegal was it? Could he be thrown in jail just for this? She scrolled down to the letter S and steeled herself for what she was about to see, because she knew who S was. She was almost certain it would be a sex video starring her and Benjamin. *But how often did we have the energy?* she wondered. She found herself hesitating — she didn't want to see Benjamin or hear his voice. But her curiosity got the best of her.

She left the volume low and selected the S.

She and Benjamin were under the covers, chatting. She didn't even have to raise the volume to know what they were saying. She knew exactly when Oswald had recorded this. That moment in bed was still clear in her memory; they'd been like calves eager to get out into green pastures.

Oh god, he caught us red-handed!

Scattered memories suddenly became a cohesive whole. Benjamin with his pager in the middle of the night, his sheepish smile, the repeated 'it's not like you think.'

You idiot! Why didn't you say anything?

Her fist flew to her mouth and she bit down to keep from crying as she pounded her other fist on the sofa. She threw herself back on the sofa, hitting her head against the wall with a thud. For a moment, she just stared at the ceiling as she tried to get her breathing back under control.

There was a crash in the corridor outside. She started, suddenly hyperaware that she was in Oswald's room, on his sofa, with his whole system up and running. And he would soon be on his way home across the sound. She listened but didn't hear anything else. She sat up on the sofa, selected the TV screen, and turned the volume back up to its original level. The remote went back on the coffee table, and she straightened the room until there were no traces of her left.

She looked out the window before leaving and found the yard bathed in golden sunshine. *The fog has lifted*, she thought. *I'll be damned, the fog has all but been wiped out.*

★

Oswald looked surprised when he saw her behind the desk.

'What are you doing here?'

'Working, sir.'

'But you've had a shock.'

'It passed.'

'So quickly?'

'It's just that I realized a few things. No one forced Benjamin to dive like that, you know, head first. He betrayed us, plain and simple. So now I don't want to talk about him anymore; I just want to work and finish the propositions.'

Oswald still looked surprised, but he nodded in satisfaction.

'You do understand. Imagine that. I have to admit, I underestimated you.'

'That's okay.'

Her face was impassive, but she noticed some twitching in her legs. It spread up through her body, and she hoped he wouldn't notice.

'So,' he said. 'The propositions. They have to be ready in two weeks.'

'I can manage it.'

'Good. I'm really just here to make sure you're okay,' he said. *Liar!*

'That's kind of you.'

'I'm going to the mainland over the weekend to give a lecture for some big-shots. To drum up some more guests for the spring program.'

She racked her brains. What day was it? Thursday, she thought, or maybe Friday.

'Maybe you can even finish your rough draft of the propositions before I get home?'

'Of course. I can do that.'

She went back to work typing up the documents but felt him glancing at her now and then. They worked like that, in silence, all day. She printed out proposition after proposition and lined them up neatly on his desk. The hours crawled by as she waited for him to leave for the mainland; she hoped he would take the five o'clock ferry. But he stayed put. Each time he looked at her, she felt like her body was one big, teeming anthill and she became overly conscious of every move she made, how much she was blinking, and the way she was breathing.

At nine in the evening he stood up and yawned loudly.

'I think I'll go to bed. I'm taking the morning ferry.'

'Okay, sir. I'll handle everything here.'

But instead of leaving the office he walked up to her desk and stared down at her for a moment. She gave a hesitant smile but when he didn't say anything she went back to editing documents on the screen. From the corner of her eye she saw him walk around the desk and position himself behind her. His hands slid under her blazer and blouse and grasped her bare shoulders. He let one finger trail across the back of her neck and down her spine, causing her to jump. His hands moved back up and he grabbed the chair, which creaked as he leaned over her.

411

'Look at me!'

He placed a finger under her chin and forced her face up. A tendril of hair had escaped his ponytail and was brushing her cheek. His eyes looked hard in the cold light. He smelled like soap and aftershave — how could such a pig smell so good? It was probably part of his game.

She allowed her body to sink back into the chair as she tried not to breathe the air around him, but that made her dizzy. She forced herself to look innocent and stared back at him until he turned away.

'I'm glad you've seen through Benjamin,' he said. 'You're smarter than the rest of the idiots here.'

His face disappeared and she saw his back heading for the door, but then he stopped.

'I hope for your own sake that you're playing an open hand. You know there will be consequences otherwise.'

'Of course I am.'

'I have big plans for you, Sofia.'

She was about to ask what they were, but he was already out the door. He didn't even close it behind him. For a long time she sat still, listening for his retreating steps. Her skin felt sticky and warm where he'd touched it. She wondered what was wrong with her — why did she let him touch her like that? A scene played out in her head: she screamed, kicked him, and clawed his face, but it only turned into a farce and didn't get her anywhere. Except to Penance. A few minutes, and Bosse and his henchmen would arrive. Another six months, at least, mucking cow shit out of stalls, feeding pigs, and freezing at night.

I have to get out of here, she thought. If that meant she had to put up with his groping, so be it. Because she *would* get out, and she would rather suck him off than stay. In which case she would just have to go throw up in the toilet and keep working. If she didn't escape soon she would lose her mind — this was her last chance.

She stopped working, because the very thought of editing any more of his drivel made her ill.

What would she say if she locked the door but he came back? Maybe that she wanted to work in peace and quiet. That she didn't want anyone else to see the propositions. He had said they were secret, after all.

She locked the door and sat down at his computer. He had turned it off, so she had to wait as it rumbled its way through start-up and the screen lit up again.

She'd learned the password by sneaking peeks over his shoulder. Once inside, she scanned through his folders and documents.

At first everything seemed perfectly ordinary. Questionnaires from lectures. Financial documents she didn't understand in the least. Emails he'd received from celebrities and saved. But then she found an unnamed folder — its icon told her it contained photos. She opened it and found a ton of pictures. After some searching, she found a way to display them as a slideshow.

When it started, she was astonished. Close-up images of a woman's body, blurry in a lovely way, like they were shrouded in mist. A breast, a hand, the inside of a thigh, the outside of a vulva. They were exceptionally erotic without being pornographic, it was like they were spun cotton. There were upwards of a hundred pictures in the folder, but no face. No identity.

Yet she suspected, almost knew, who it was. There was something familiar about the pale body. Those little freckles under the breast.

Elvira! But how —?

There had to be more pictures. She feverishly searched the hard drive and eventually found a whole series of image folders, all created within the last month. But when she clicked on them, she received a message that they were locked and inaccessible. She sighed in disappointment — they were password-protected, and if she knew him it would not be easy to guess. She tried the password to the computer, but it didn't work.

There's only one option, she thought. *Make a copy. Unless I can crack the password here and now.*

Her next idea was so stupid and rash that she pushed it out of her mind several times. But it kept coming back, and her stomach tingled to think of it. She logged out, turned off the computer, and walked around the office a few times as she tried to let go of this completely insane plan, but it was no use. It was as if she'd already made up her mind. She only knew one person who knew everything about computers and then some. It seemed incredibly unlikely that he would help her, but at the same time he never turned down an opportunity to show off how goddamn smart he was.

She took her phone from her pocket and turned it on. She still remembered his number, and her fingers trembled a little as she sent the text.

Want to call it even? I need your help cracking the password on some computer files.

'You have to imagine what will happen,' I say. 'You have to truly see the accident in your mind, like a hundred times. Until you're totally sure. Understand?'

'Not really,' she says. 'But I'll try.'

'Listen to me,' I say. 'Look at that big kerosene lantern in the corner. If it tips over, the kerosene will spill on the floor. It'll splash all over. Can you picture that?'

She nods.

'And what happens then, Sara? You'll have to use your imagination for this part.'

She doesn't speak as she looks inward. I go on.

'Dad likes to work on the cars. He enjoys doing it. What if he brings a rag covered in petrol or diesel into the living room? By mistake, I mean. He places it on the bannister, and the fire spreads upward.'

'But he wouldn't do that, would he?'

'You little idiot. It doesn't matter. All that matters is what could happen.'

Her eyes finally light up. We talk through the plan.

Over and over.

So many times that I almost lose my voice, but now we're on the same page.

She even comes up with ideas herself.

'The guard has a night off this week,' she says. 'Dad is too lazy and cheap to find a replacement. He's off Friday night, I think.'

'There you go! You can think for yourself.'

'And he drinks a whiskey sour each night before bed. If we put something in it he would get really tired . . .'

'Right! Great! Now we're cooking.'

It strikes me that she has never once expressed doubt or tried to back out. That scares me a little. I wonder if she's going to flip out at the last minute and panic.

Whether there's some sort of dam inside her that will burst when it's time.

'You're sure you want to go through with this, right, Sara? It was your idea, after all.'

'Of course I do. But you'll help me, right, Fredrik?'

'You know that already.'

'And then what?'

'Then it'll just be you and me.'

39

She waited for Oswald by the gate. She was shivering a little; the air was cold although it was a beautiful spring day. Morning assembly was in full swing in the yard and Bosse was lecturing the staff in an insistent tone. Everywhere she looked she saw new foliage and flowers: the tulips stood in tight bunches around the pond and the lilac bushes had just leafed. She glanced at the winding gravel road outside the gate. A gust of wind came over the wall, carrying the scent of saltwater and seaweed.

It smells like freedom out there, she thought.

Oswald's car came from the garage and slowed down once he caught sight of her. The gravel crunched under the tyres and flew up at her legs.

He rolled down the window and gave her a puzzled look.

'I just wanted to make sure you have everything you need,' she said.

'Okay. But shouldn't you be in the office working on the propositions? Time is getting short.'

'I'll handle it.'

'Good. The lecture is at ten so I should make the five o'clock ferry back.'

She felt a jab of disappointment — she'd hoped he would be gone overnight. But she still had time.

He waved at the guard, who saluted him and opened the gate. She stayed put and watched the car vanish down the gravel road. She just knew he was staring at her in the rear-view mirror.

★

Instead of going to the office she hurried for the library.

Morning assembly was over and Mona was strolling across the lawn. She looked old and clumsy in the faded winter coat she wore over her uniform. Her hair was uncombed, her face worn and tired. A flash of concern appeared in her eyes when she caught sight of Sofia.

'I want to talk to you, Mona. Can we go in?'

'Of course.' Mona fumbled as she inserted the key into the lock. She opened the door to the library, which felt cold and draughty and empty, as if it had been abandoned for a long time. Mona turned on the ceiling lights and sat down at her desk without taking off her coat. Sofia took a seat on the chair in front of her.

'Where is Elvira?' She wanted to get right to the point.

'I told you.'

'Don't lie to me.'

'What do you want, Sofia? You've become so unpleasant.'

'I want to know where Elvira is.'

'I told you, she went to the mainland.'

'And I want to know the truth.'

Mona's lower lip trembled and her eyes darted this way and that. She was at the breaking point — all it would take was a little nudge, one last shove.

'This is serious, really serious, and I want you tell me the truth.'

'Sofia, I can't. You know I can't. Franz —'

'Franz just left. He can't see us. He's on his way to the ferry.'

Suddenly she felt uncertain and looked up at the ceiling in search of cameras, but she realized that Oswald had stuck to the manor house during the installation. There were no cameras in the library.

Mona hadn't even noticed Sofia's wandering gaze. She was just staring at the desk, sullen and reticent.

'Tell me where she is!'

'But I promised, don't you get it? I swore not to tell!'

'For Christ's sake, she's only fourteen!'

'Age doesn't matter. Franz says she's the chosen one.'

'Chosen one? What does that mean?'

'She's his soulmate. He's known it since he first laid eyes on her. He just knew she was the right one. At first she was just here to work and so on, but then he decided she was ready.'

'Ready for what?'

'They have some sort of spiritual relationship. That's all I know.'

She felt the sudden urge to smack Mona and wondered if she was really as stupid as she seemed. Did she even care? Did she really think this was normal?

'Can't you hear yourself? Are you completely braindead?'

'No, I most certainly am not! Don't you know what this will mean for her future?'

'Mona, listen to me. He doesn't care about her. He just likes young girls. I've seen the pictures on his computer . . .'

Mona's face crumpled until she looked like a raisin. She jabbed a spindly finger at Sofia and started shouting at her.

'You're lying, you're lying! Stop lying!'

Sofia tried again, praying that no one could hear them outside the building.

'He's taken nude pictures of her. I saw them. You ought to be put away for this, just like him.'

Mona had begun to sob. Shit! It would be impossible to get her to talk in this state. Sofia switched to a gentler tone.

'She's up in the attic, isn't she?'

'Yes, but it's really nice up there.'

'Do you ever see her?'

'No, but . . .'

'But what?'

'It's not good for her while she's undergoing preparation. To see us, I mean. But he takes good care of her. He gives her food and stuff.'

Sofia didn't say a word for a while, figuring that she wouldn't get any farther with Mona; the woman was just another cog in a big wheel, not useful at all, only worn out and broken.

'I know you're doing this for her own good,' she said, and Mona relaxed a little. 'But if you tell Franz I asked about her, if you even mention it, I will tell him you were the one who came to me. That you were super worried and wanted my help to get Elvira out. And which one of us do you think he'll believe?'

Mona pursed her lips. Her eyes were narrowed lines.

'I'm not saying anything. But what are you planning to do?'

'I'm going to find out what he's doing to her.'

Mona buried her face in her hands. Her head trembled and her back shook. When she looked up again, her eyes were red.

'He's so nice to me, Sofia. He's taking care of me now, making sure no one picks on me. He's been so sweet, and he promised I can stay at the library. I'm sure he's being really nice to Elvira too. Please don't poke your nose into this . . .'

Sofia didn't respond; instead she placed her hand over Mona's and squeezed it, then stood up. She went back outside, into the spring sunshine. She wondered if Anders would be of any use, but quickly let go of the thought. Anders would never question Oswald's actions.

She had to talk to someone — her head felt like it was about to burst with all this. But she didn't know who she could trust. Maybe not even Simon. What if he had bought his way back into the greenhouse by spying for Oswald? She could see him right now; he was out in the vegetable garden putting up a fence. He waved at her with his huge glove.

'I think I'm going crazy,' she said as she walked up to him.

'Better tell me what's up.'

'You're not a spy, are you, Simon?'

'A spy? Are you nuts? How many times do I have to tell you I'm just a simple farmer?'

'I almost forgot.'

'I can keep working while you talk. That way it'll just look like you're chewing me out, as usual.'

He didn't say a word as she told him what she knew; he just kept placing the wire fence around the neat lines of plants. When she was done, he stopped and looked her right in the eyes.

'Jesus, this is nuts!'

'I know. What should I do?'

'What you're already doing, I think. Snoop around. Gather evidence.'

'I'm so, so scared he's going to catch me, Simon. I don't know what he would do with me if he did.'

'You're going to manage it. I just know it. To escape, I mean.'

'But what about Elvira? How do we get her out?'

421

'I don't think she wants to get out. She's probably, like, totally out of it. But he's a paedophile, and if you can prove it he'll end up behind bars.'

'So I have to find out what he's doing to her, don't I?'

'Maybe. But it's more important for you to get out. If he finds you out and sends you to Penance again, I'll help you run away.'

'Oh, I'm sure he would come up with something even worse. Like forcing me to jump from Devil's Rock when it's windy as hell. "Oops! Another fatal accident!"'

Her phone dinged. As she opened the text, her hand trembled.

Simon stood before her, breathing down her neck, as they read it. Ellis wrote that she should transfer the files to a thumb drive and mail it to him, along with some other information about the computer and the system they had come from.

And his irritating conclusion: *Problems with the cult out there? Thought as much. E.*

'I have to copy those files,' she said. 'And take them with me when I escape.'

'How can you be so sure Ellis isn't tricking you? He was evil to you before, and now he might be after revenge for the court case,' Simon pointed out.

'He has a hugely swollen ego; he wants to prove he knows everything. Plus, he was sort of right when he came here to yell about freeing me from the cult, wasn't he?'

*

She jogged up the stairs and hesitated for a moment but decided to stop by Oswald's private room before going to the office to copy the files. She wanted to confirm her suspicions: if she knew Oswald, he had cameras in the attic.

Once inside, she locked the door and turned on the TV. None of the buttons on the remote brought up an image of the attic, no matter how much she fumbled with them. *Think*, she commanded herself. *Some rooms are linked to the office, and some go here. Bosse and I have access to the system in the office and that can only mean one thing. The camera in the attic must be linked to this system, but how the hell do I bring up the image?*

She tested out various combinations of digits and almost gave up, but then she tried 666 out of sheer desperation — and there it was.

The white walls and furniture seemed to glow on the screen. Elvira was sitting on the bed, the covers drawn up to her waist, but her upper body was bare. She was reading a piece of paper on her lap. There was a tray of food on the nightstand.

Sofia studied Elvira's face to see how she was feeling, but she seemed totally focused on whatever she was reading and didn't seem concerned in the least. *Simon was right*, she thought. *She's in a dream world, like a Hollywood film where she's the chosen one. This is totally off the wall.*

There were two beds in the room now, one against each wall. At first she thought perhaps Oswald slept there sometimes, but then she recalled the words he'd said the day before.

I have big plans for you, Sofia.

What if he wants me in there too, she thought. *No, I'm just imagining all sorts of shit now.* But something inside her whispered to be careful, and she felt a sense of urgency, hot as his panting breath, as she headed for the office.

Yet she forgot to start transferring the files from his computer

— that pile of propositions on her desk distracted her. The certainty that they had to be finished before he got home.

It wasn't until lunchtime that she remembered the folders; she almost choked when she realized how little time she had.

As soon as she was back in the office, she set to work. She knew where Oswald kept his thumb drives, so she found the one with the greatest capacity and deleted everything on it.

She began to copy the folders and watched the little bar that showed the progress.

One percent. Two percent. Dammit, it seemed to be taking forever. She decided to finish up the propositions to distract herself. She worked quickly and methodically.

She went back and looked at the bar again. Seventy-five percent now. Nervous, she circled the computer and mentally urged it to hurry up.

Then the unthinkable happened. There was a buzz of static and a click, and suddenly all the electronics in the office seemed to take a deep breath and go silent, all at once. All the screens went black. *The power!* The fucking power had gone out. She opened the door and found the corridor bathed in light. She realized it must be a fuse and fumbled through the fuse box until she found the right one. She replaced it and everything returned to life.

She rushed to turn off everything but Oswald's computer and her own; she didn't want to take the chance that it might happen again.

All she could do was start the file copy over from scratch.

She finished editing the propositions and felt a sense of satisfaction even as her anxiety was about to do her in.

Eighty-two percent. Almost finished. Soon all his shit would be on the tiny drive.

She printed out the propositions and placed them in a neat pile on his desk, then decided to transfer them to his computer so they would be there when he got home. He would probably be happy. Even thrilled.

She used her own thumb drive for that transfer, then pulled out the drive and stuck it in her pocket. She stared impatiently at the first drive, which was still inserted, the progress bar crawling toward the goal. A glance at the clock told her it was quarter to three. She had plenty of time, and the bar was almost to the end. Ninety-eight percent.

But then she heard steps in the corridor, and they were so familiar that the hair stood up on the back of her neck. It was impossible, but she heard them. Her mind whirled. She could pull out the drive, but evidence of the transfer would still be on the screen. There was no time. There was simply no solution.

Jesus fucking Christ, what am I going to say?

The handle turned. Shock washed over her as she saw him in the doorway, his eyes wide.

'What the fuck are you doing with my computer?'

The yard is empty.

It's so quiet I can hear her inside the house. A few noises: rustling, the lamp falling to the marble floor.

Everything seems to be going according to plan.

I think I can hear the crackle of the match as she lights it. But it must be my imagination; that door is thick.

I'm sitting with my back against it, keeping guard. Just as I promised. I went up to look at them one last time, knocked out in their beds. Dad snoring heavily and Emilie curled up in a ball like she was in hibernation.

I know I won't miss them. Their lives are so completely meaningless. They've never done anything great, and they never will. There is no room for people like them on this earth.

She must be finished.

The flickering light from the fire reaches me. I imagine what it must look like inside. Flames leaping for the stairs, blocking the way out.

The big glass windows downstairs. Like walls. Impossible to open.

There is only one way out for her. And this is it. Right where I'm sitting.

Thirty seconds. That's all she has left.

Thirty seconds, max. Maybe twenty, if I'm lucky.

And now her hand is on the handle.

She tries to turn it. First calmly, but then more frantically.

Until at last she's yanking furiously at it.

But my hand is there. Firm and steady. And my back, pressing against the door.

The smoke must be thick by now.

She pounds and kicks at the door like a lunatic.

'Fredrik! The door is stuck! Help! Fredrik!'

And she starts coughing from the smoke.

I stay put, pressing my back to the door, listening to the rustling, the coughing, the pounding. The rasp of her nails against the wood as she falls. I picture the flames catching up to her.

The door has grown very hot and I have to move out into the yard. I think, the door was actually open the whole time. All she had to do was try. But she didn't.

Now it's burning. The whole fucking thing is burning.

I stand in the yard, admiring the magnificence.

I see a flash of something in an upstairs window. A shadow, the face of someone who has crawled their way over. A black dot popping up for an instant.

And falling back again, into the flames.

40

Later on, she decided she must have had a guardian angel. Someone must have spoken through her, because the answer had just fallen from her lips.

'Sir, it was supposed to be a surprise.'

He stepped through the door and approached the desk. A bolt of panic ran through her, but she stood perfectly still.

'A surprise?'

'Yes, I finished the propositions.'

The computer dinged.

Success — the files had finished copying. She pulled out the thumb drive and stuck it in her blazer pocket.

'I was just transferring them to your computer from my thumb drive, because I thought you would want them there. I printed them out too, of course.'

She pointed at the stacks of paper.

He didn't move as he considered what she had said. His eyes reflected his thoughts: first doubt, then relief, and then he was back to normal. Arrogant and superior.

'I thought you were coming back on the five o'clock ferry. I wanted everything to be ready when you got here.'

'A friend was sailing over in the nice weather,' he muttered. 'I caught a ride with him. As if it's any of your business.'

'Of course not.'

She moved away from his computer and sat back down at her own desk.

He was still standing in the centre of the room.

'I don't like you messing with my computer, Sofia.'

'But I didn't. I just thought you would want to have the propositions on it.'

He grunted and sat down at his desk, then opened the file with the propositions and glanced through it.

'Sure enough, it seems like we're done. You can be sure everyone at my lectures can't wait to read the propositions. Everyone who was there today will be coming here this summer.'

'Wonderful!'

'Yes, it is.'

He leafed through the piles of documents on the desk.

'Listen, we need to take good care of these. Tomorrow I want you to print them out on archival paper and place them in individual sheet protectors. Frisk had some of those in his little shed by the annexe. I'm sure there are more boxes left. Put them all in a binder. Can you manage that?'

'Of course. I'll start today.'

'You do that.'

It seemed like he had forgotten about the computer incident for the moment. He spent the time before dinner surfing the internet and making a few calls. Enar, who had taken over the transport unit after Benjamin, brought his dinner at five thirty, and Sofia warmed the food and served it with mineral water. Oswald put on some Indian sitar music and gazed at the sea for a while.

'Well, I'm going to go have dinner,' she said.

He didn't respond. She cursed herself for continuing to ask his permission to eat, and during dinner she worried about whether he would notice she had fiddled with his computer. She decided there was no way — he was pretty clueless when it came to technology; he was always asking for her help.

By the time she returned to the office, Oswald had read through all the propositions. He was nearly euphoric.

'Jesus, this is incredible! The whole staff must read them. They can study outside of working hours; there's going to be a lot to do before the guests arrive. I'll talk to them at noon assembly tomorrow. And you and I have to inspect the property and make sure everything is perfect.'

He muffled a sudden yawn, as if the burst of emotion had been too much.

'Listen, I think I'm going to head to bed.'

At seven o'clock?

She could only nod. His jacket was on the back of his chair, so she helped him into it and watched as he disappeared out the door. His steps echoed down the corridor.

She had an idea where he was going, but she waited for a long time, knowing that what she ought to do was go down to Benjamin's old shed and get the sheet protectors. But there could only be one thing Oswald might long for at seven in the evening when he was so excited. And it wasn't sleep.

After charging her phone for a moment and straightening the office, she turned off the computer but left the light on so it would look like she planned to return. She tiptoed past the staff room, but no one seemed to notice her. The lights were out in the stairwell but came on automatically when they sensed her presence.

She hurried to his room, wondering if he was there. Frantically, she attempted to think of some plausible lie as she opened the door, but the room was empty.

At first she locked the door from the inside but changed her mind and unlocked it again. *If he comes, I'll jump out the window,* she thought. *I'll hear him coming, and I can do it before he can open the door.*

She opened the window and left it ajar. A look down at the yard and she was sure it would work. All she would have to do was hide in the bushes alongside the house and blame the household unit. She could say they must have been airing out the room but forgot to close the window.

She turned on the TV and scrambled to press *666* on the remote. Just as she'd expected, Oswald was there. He was fully dressed and sitting on the edge of the bed. Elvira was just lying there and staring at him. Oswald sank both hands into her golden mess of curls.

'Have you been waiting for me?'

Elvira nodded. Her shoulders were bare, but the covers were drawn up. Oswald let go of her hair and pulled down the blanket. Her skinny body looked like a child's, with her small breasts and narrow hips.

'I feel cooped up,' Elvira said hesitantly. 'I think I need some fresh air.'

'Of course,' he said, standing up and cracking a window. 'Better?'

'Yes, thank you.'

'I'm going to show you something. It's part of your preparation.'

He fumbled with his trousers, yanking at something.

What the hell is he doing?

431

He had pulled his belt from its loops and held it up before Elvira.

'If you put this around your neck and tighten it, it decreases the oxygen in your brain and it feels fantastic,' he said. 'Like you're floating on a cloud.'

Elvira looked confused.

'And that will bring us closer, spiritually. It's an incredible experience.'

Have to record this, have to get it on film.

She turned on her phone camera and propped it against a vase on the coffee table so it could capture what was happening on the screen.

Elvira caught her breath and looked up at him beseechingly.

'You don't have to worry,' he said. 'We're only going to practise a little today. I'll show you.'

She nodded, but she still looked frightened.

Sofia wanted to shake Elvira, shout at her to wake up from her trance.

Why is she so goddamn stupid? I know her. We shared gum while we were doing renovations, and laughed at all the people who kept screeching at everyone to work faster. What happened to her?

Oswald bent forward to place the belt around Elvira's neck. He rested his hand on her forehead for a moment, as if to calm her. Then he took hold of the belt with both hands and pulled. It happened so quickly that Elvira cried out, gasped for breath, and stared at him in astonishment. He loosened the belt a bit and let her catch her breath. But then he tightened it again and Elvira almost lost it — she tried to scream. He silenced her by pulling harder, and her face went beet red.

He's going to kill her!

Suddenly, Oswald let go of the belt and let Elvira draw in air. He gave her an unctuous smile Sofia had never seen before.

'You'll come to like it,' he whispered. 'I'll go slowly. We'll only practise until you're used to it. It's going to be great. Really great.'

A sticky layer of sweat had settled on Sofia's body. She hadn't even noticed any perspiration, but now she realized she was shaking too. The room began to sway and her stomach turned inside out.

I can't throw up in here, I can't —

She ran to his bathroom, fell to her knees, and grabbed the toilet seat. The vomit gushed into the bowl. Then more. Bile, or whatever it was. She stayed there for a moment with tears in her eyes, but then she worried that he might be done and was on his way back. She wiped her mouth, stood up, adjusted her clothing, and flushed. It still smelled like vomit, so she took the bottle of expensive aftershave and poured some into the toilet. She hurried back to the room and looked at the screen. Now he was chatting with Elvira.

Sofia turned off her phone, put it in her pocket, and turned off the whole system.

As she closed the window, she noticed that her legs were still trembling. She made sure that her phone really was in her pocket and hurried into the corridor, where she remembered she had left the light on in the office. She ran up the stairs with her heart in her throat, turned off the light, and locked up. She thought she heard his footsteps upstairs as she ran toward her dormitory. At the last second, she changed her mind.

Have to talk to someone, got to find Simon.

When she reached the yard she felt a sharp chill on the back of her neck, like an icy cold draught. She turned around and

433

saw Oswald's face pressed against the windowpane upstairs, but thought it must be all in her head. She must be so shaken that she was seeing things. She ran for the farm, where Simon was bumping along with a wheelbarrow. She ran up to him and grabbed his arms.

'Listen to me! For God's sake, listen!'

'Sofia, I'm listening!'

The words came at a frightening speed and he had to stop her now and then to keep up.

'We have to call the police,' she said when she had finished her story.

Simon scratched his head and thought for a moment — for so long that Sofia began to stamp her feet anxiously.

'Don't do it,' he said at last.

'What? Are you crazy? Jesus, he's raping a minor!'

'Did you see him rape her? Did she resist?'

'No, but what does that matter? She's fourteen!'

'Think about it, Sofia. Think about what will happen if you make the call. The police will come, and the first stop is the gate. No cop gets through that gate without Oswald's permission, I can promise you that. He'll suck up to them and say he's got this girl who's a little nuts — that is, you. And if that doesn't help, he'll call Östling. And anyway, the attic is locked and he'll assure them that it's completely unusable. Then he'll chuckle and offer them coffee and by the time the cops leave they'll be best friends. I don't think I have to tell you what happens to you after that. You have to learn to think like him.'

This was the longest speech Sofia had ever heard from Simon.

'What about Elvira?'

'Did it seem like he was going to kill her?'

'No, not exactly. More like it was the start of a whole ton of perverted things he plans to do to her.'

'Right. That's why it's so urgent for you to escape.'

He had made her feel a shred more relaxed. Her thoughts cleared. Getting out was what mattered. There were no solutions inside the walls; there was no refuge, no justice. Get out or be ruined. Those were the options.

'I'm terrified,' she said at last.

'I'll help you,' he said, squeezing her wrist in his large gardening glove.

*

When she got to her dormitory, it was only a little past eight. The room was silent. She sank down on her bed, turned on her phone, and played the video from the attic. The image flickered a bit, but she could plainly see and hear what was going on.

She opened the wardrobe and took out her backpack to dump out its contents: a few napkins, silverware, a blanket, and a thermos. She filled the thermos with water from the bathroom tap and stuck it back in the backpack. The thumb drive from Oswald's computer went into a pocket.

For a moment she wondered if she should take the SIM card out of her phone and put it there too, but she decided she still needed the phone. A pair of jeans, underwear, and a few sweaters went in the backpack, which she stashed under the bed. Way back, where no one would see it. She sat back down on the back and realized that her blouse was damp with sweat.

It's time, she thought. *I have everything I need. All I have to do is plan my escape.* She thought of Elvira, and then of Benjamin, who God hadn't saved even though she'd prayed He would.

Please God, save Elvira at least. Don't let him kill her.

Her phone rang. It was so loud in the quiet room that she jumped. *Private number*, said the screen. She let it ring a few more times, but her curiosity got the best of her.

'Sofia? Is this Sofia Bauman?'

'Yes . . .' she said cautiously.

'This is Vanja. Vanja Frisk.'

I stand in the front drive for a long time.

The burning house is strangely beautiful. It's not like an inferno, more like sparking fireworks.

The whole second floor is in flames by now. It smells sharp and scorching, but also of cedar and pine, like their furniture.

Then I walk down to the sentry box and make sure that the cameras really are turned off. And the fire alarm, of course.

What an idiot, the guard who forgot all about those . . .

I sit down in his chair.

It's time for my transformation, a complete metamorphosis. I work myself up into a state of panic and desperation. I imagine how it must feel, plunging into the emotions — emotions I can create, but don't have.

I dial the number and bawl when they answer.

'You have to come! Jesus, shit, it's on fire! The whole house is on fire!'

Words, shouted and slurring. I give them the address.

I leave the sentry box and walk through the gate to the car I parked there.

The Mercedes. I'm glad I've saved it from the fire. Shit, I love this car.

Headlights appear down the gravel path. A neighbour has spotted the flames.

He dashes from his car to where I'm sobbing on the hood of the car.

'Where is everyone?' he shouts. 'Your family!'

I don't respond, just press myself to the car, sobbing and sniffling.
I point at the house.
'Inside. I couldn't . . . I got here too late. I'm sorry!'
He grabs my shoulders and tries to calm me.
Then come the sirens and the flashing lights.
I did a good job, *I think.*
The firemen unroll their hoses. Someone runs to me from an ambulance. I take a deep breath and make my heart beat faster.

41

Sofia's mother had sent the flowers right away, of course. She'd rushed to do it, just as she did everything else in life. And now Sofia had Benjamin's sister on the phone and didn't quite know what to say. She tried to explain that she and Benjamin had been together without getting into how they had come to break up. It sounded muddled, and she wondered if Vanja understood, because she didn't say anything for a long time.

'Well, Benjamin mentioned you. Said he'd met a girl out there on the island. You must be so sad. Just like me.'

'Yes. I can't wrap my head around it. But I'd like to meet you and tell you something. I mean, something about Benjamin.' She could feel the other woman's hesitation. 'A little later,' she hurried to add.

'Sure, of course we can meet,' said Vanja. 'But maybe not right now. With the funeral and everything.'

'A funeral? Already? But they haven't even found his body!'

'No, but they probably never will. It's better to get it over with. Franz Oswald was here, and he took care of all the costs. He was so kind. Maybe you'd like to come to the funeral?'

'I would like to, but I think it would be too difficult for me,' she said, which certainly wasn't a lie.

'I understand. Please feel free to call me again sometime.'

She felt ill at ease once they had hung up. Something was missing — there was no hint of sadness from Vanja's voice. But then again, she and Benjamin hardly ever saw each other. Maybe they hadn't been close. And how well did *she* know Benjamin, really. It was like she had never really gotten a grip on him. What had Oswald called him again? Dodger. He had slipped through her fingers and would remain an unsolved mystery forever more.

She felt sad and burdened at the thought that Benjamin would be given a funeral while his body was still far out at sea, being eaten by fish. And now she couldn't even picture his face — it was like he was being wiped out. There weren't even any ashes to bury.

She closed her eyes and tried to remember what it had felt like to touch his skin, but all she could recall was his scent.

When she finally went to bed, sleep eluded her. She was haunted by the images of Oswald and Elvira in the attic. And the harder she tried to fall asleep, the clearer the pictures became. She sat up in bed, turned on the light, and took out a notebook.

She began to outline an escape plan. She could always use the plan she and Benjamin had never set into motion, but spending a night in the cottage alone would drive her to madness. And how would she get over the fence without setting off the alarm? Surely Simon would help her. She had to talk to him, to run through everything and get her thoughts in order.

Her phone jangled again.

Mom.

She had to be more careful and silence her ringer when she wasn't using the phone. The thought of dealing with her mother's anxiety was so overwhelming that she rejected the call and turned off the phone. She decided to wake up at six, so she could talk to Simon before everyone else woke up.

'It's not going to work,' he said straight away.

'Why not?'

'The electric fence doesn't work that way. It's not just touching the barbed wire that sets off the alarm. If you jump over, the vibrations when you land will be strong enough to trip it.'

'How do you know that?'

'I've been snooping around a little, just like you. Farmers need hobbies too, right? Mine has always been electronics.'

'Then what can I do?'

'The best solution is probably a power outage. You can simply turn off the main switch. It takes ten minutes for the backup generator to kick in. But there's always the risk that someone will flip the main switch back again.'

'That sounds insane. Ten minutes? How far can I run in ten minutes? They'll come after me on their motorcycles.'

He thought for a moment.

'Not if you run through the woods. They can't drive there.'

'In the middle of the night? I don't know if I can do it. And what about when I get to the ferry?'

Simon chuckled.

'One thing at a time. What if I run to the main generator once you've turned it off and pretend something's wrong with it? After all, I do help with the electrical systems sometimes.'

She felt hope rising.

'Benjamin said you can hide under a tarp where the cars park on the ferry. I'll just have to lie there until the ferry leaves.'

He nodded and closed his eyes as if he were trying to picture it all before him.

'Couldn't you check the weather forecast on your phone? If

441

there's moonlight it will be easier to find your way through the forest.'

She turned on her phone and found the weather site.

'This good weather is supposed to last all week.'

'But there could still be fog in the morning. You have to leave at night before the fog comes in and when the moon is at its brightest.'

'If there is a moon,' she said, looking for the phases of the moon on the site. 'It's only a half-moon right now. Maybe I should wait a few days.'

'I think you can do it,' Simon said.

'At least it's the start of a plan.'

'We should probably both think about it for a while,' he said, and his hands were suddenly back in the earth.

★

She lugged the large box of plastic sheet protectors across the yard, wondering how long it would take to print out the propositions and insert each page into a sheet.

At least she could think about her escape plan while she was finishing Oswald's stupid project.

Suddenly she felt that surreal feeling again, in the middle of the yard — this all had to be a dream. It couldn't be real, everything that had happened in the past week. Those things just didn't happen in real life. She tripped over a rock and almost dropped the boxes. As she carried them up the stairs to the office, she broke out in a sweat and swore inwardly.

Oswald laughed when he saw her. He waved her in.

'Damn, are you going to encase every last piece of paper in this office?'

'No, just the propositions,' she muttered.

'Don't be such a grump, Sofia. It doesn't suit you. Now get this over with and don't forget about our little tour of the property — or that I want to talk to the staff tonight.'

She didn't respond, just lugged the box to her desk.

Her silence provoked him.

'You know you have two roles when you're working for me, don't you?' he said.

'No, I didn't know that.'

'But it's true. First there's your job as my secretary, and in that role you're extraordinary if I may say so.'

'Thanks, I'm glad to hear it.'

'Yes, but then there's your role as a woman.'

'Okay . . . what does that entail?'

'Nothing, of course. You're simply supposed to keep up with all the twists and turns. Be submissive, I suppose is the right word. I do like that word.'

He laughed, but she knew he wasn't joking. She fingered the pocketknife she always kept in her blazer pocket these days. A ridiculous defence weapon in case things should get out of control in the office.

'Oh, Sofia!' he said. 'Don't take everything so fucking seriously.'

She attempted a smile, but it turned out stiff and foolish. Under a cloud of increasing irritation, she tried to focus on her sheet protector task and finished just before evening assembly. She put the plastic pages into a binder, and as soon as she was done he took it from her hands.

'I'll take care of the binder. It has to be stored in a very special place. Do you understand why this is so important?'

'Not really,' she confessed.

'Well, if every computer in the whole world stops working, we'll still have this.' He held the binder up triumphantly.

★

Later that evening, when she was finally able to rest her legs after their long, boring tour of the property, her thoughts returned to what he'd said. Why hadn't he just put the binder in the safe? Then she remembered how he'd asked Benjamin to hide the theses somewhere on the island. She'd never asked Benjamin where he'd put them. That was just one more thing she'd forgotten because something else suddenly seemed so much more important.

A police raid, she thought. *That must be what he's afraid of. He's so paranoid he thinks the whole state and government are out to steal his nonsense.*

It was starting to get late. The sun was setting, painting the whole office red.

'I'm going to take a little stroll before bed,' Oswald suddenly said.

He had the binder of propositions under one arm. Never before had she heard him use the word 'stroll.' A ride on the motorcycle maybe, but he didn't seem to care about the nature of the island. And dusk was falling.

As soon as he'd left, she rose to look out the window. He walked across the yard, spoke to the guard, and vanished through the gate.

She was terribly curious and felt an irresistible urge to follow him. What could she say to convince the guard to let her out? He would just call Oswald. Then she caught sight of his phone on the desk. It was like it was waiting there just for her. She stuck it in her pocket and rushed down the stairs.

'Franz forgot his phone,' she told Benny, who was sitting in the sentry box. 'He's expecting an important call.'

Benny hesitated.

'I have to call him first.'

'You can't, I have his phone.' She held it up.

Benny muttered but opened the gate for her. She thought about taking advantage of the situation to escape, but it would all go wrong without her backpack, and with such haste. Furthermore, she was far too curious about where Oswald was heading. Darkness was falling and she figured he was already out of sight, but then she caught a glimpse of a figure across the meadow. He was heading for the cliffs.

She hurried to follow him but moved almost silently. She hoped he wouldn't turn around. But he did, when he reached the precipice, so she ducked behind a tree.

He was climbing down the rocks now, and his silhouette was stark against the sky, which burned orange and red like a crackling spring bonfire. The sun had almost dipped below the horizon. She recognized the spot he was climbing down to, from the time Benjamin had brought her there. Oswald was on his way to the cave. Benjamin's cave. What the hell was he doing there? How was it all connected? Had Benjamin hidden the theses there? It seemed he had lied to her about it all, and now she didn't know up from down.

An eternity seemed to pass before Oswald came up again. She thought about running over to surprise him on his way up, at the very spot where it made you dizzy to look down and you had to keep a firm grasp on the boulders. She could shove him so he fell and hit his head on the rocks and ended up in the sea with Benjamin. And then he would go straight to hell, where he belonged. But then his head popped up over the cliff and she could see his long figure striding toward her. She backed into the forest, caught sight of a large boulder, and lay down flat on the ground behind it.

Dew had already settled, and the moisture seeped through her skirt and the front of her blazer. He was close now. She could hear twigs and heather rustling under his feet. Her heart was pounding so hard and so fast that she felt out of breath.

She waited until everything was perfectly silent, then waited a little longer. She stood up and slipped up to the cliff. The sea was still and it was almost fully dark. Trying to remember each footstep Benjamin had taken, she began to climb down. Her eyes searched for and spotted the grassy patch where the cave entrance was. She shuffled down and found herself standing at the opening.

It was dark and damp inside the cave. The scent of Oswald's aftershave lingered in the cool air. There had to be a hiding spot, there just had to be. She walked around feeling the walls with her hands — a few times over — but she couldn't find anything. She was about to give up but then she reached higher, made one more turn, and found a large hole between the rocks.

She stuck one hand in and it was almost sucked into the void. At first all she felt were the spines of two binders: the propositions and the theses, of course. But when she reached farther, her hand hit something hard. A small box. She got a grip on it and pulled it out.

It was a tin. She opened it, and all she had to do was touch what was inside, because she held a similar instrument in her hands each day. A tape recorder. The type Oswald used for his dictation.

She thought he must have a good reason for hiding it there, because he certainly didn't climb around the cliffs on a daily basis.

She closed the tin and stuck it in her pocket but left the binders where they were. After all, she could probably rattle off the goddamn theses and propositions by heart.

On her way back up, her body began to tremble and she stumbled a few times but made it to the top unscathed. She knew she looked a mess. A run in her stockings, already considerable, was only getting bigger. Her blazer and skirt were damp and must have been stained by the moss.

Now that darkness had fallen, the moon was up, peeking through the thin clouds now and then. She ran home, sending up a silent prayer that Oswald hadn't asked after her.

Benny shot her a look of bewilderment when she reached the gate.

'I went looking, but I couldn't find him.'

'He's back.'

'Did he ask about me?'

Benny shook his head and opened the gate. His eyes betrayed his guilty conscience over letting her out.

Oswald's phone and the little tin rattled in her pocket as she ran across the yard. She knew she had to put the phone back quickly, before he had time to miss it, but not while she looked like she had been fighting a bear in the forest.

There was no clean blazer in her dormitory, only an extra skirt, so she dried her wet blazer with a towel and put on the fresh skirt and new nylons.

Anna came in just as Sofia was on her way out.

'You've certainly been going to bed early in recent days,' Sofia said as she rushed past her.

447

The office was empty, so she put the phone on his desk. Her hand brushed the tin box in her pocket. She opened his desk drawer and found the other recorder, the one he used each day. So this was a different one. Curiosity overwhelmed her — she wanted to listen to the recording, but it would have to wait. She would put it in the backpack under her bed with everything else she could collect before her escape.

It was almost eleven o'clock and she didn't think Oswald would return, so she turned off the computers and the lights and was just about to lock the doors when she heard footsteps in the corridor. He was heading for her at a terrific speed, obviously furious.

'Where have you been?'

'Sir, I've been looking everywhere for you. You forgot your phone, and I thought you would want it. I've been running around like crazy.'

'Why don't you have your pager on you?'

She patted her pocket.

'Oh no, I guess I forgot it . . .'

'Next time send a fucking message to my pager! Now *I've* been running around trying to find my goddamn phone. Don't you have a single brain cell left?'

'I'm sorry. I'll do that next time.'

'You're such a stupid bimbo sometimes,' he said, ripping the phone from her hand.

'I'm sorry . . .'

Her voice faded; he was already gone.

She wondered how much time she really had.

'So your name is Franz Oswald von Bärensten?'

I look down at the tape recorder and then up at his stern face.

'Yes, but my parents called me Fredrik.'

I squeeze out a few tears.

'Strange nickname for Franz,' he says.

'It sounds more Swedish. We're from Sweden.'

He looks at me in concern, then drops the bomb.

'We have received the results of the investigation. It seems that your sister set the fire. She tried to get out once it was burning, but apparently the door was jammed. She died of smoke inhalation.'

'There's no way! That's absolutely impossible!'

'What makes you say that?'

'Sara wouldn't harm a fly!'

He must have asked where I was and what I saw at least a dozen times. There are no holes in my story. It all matches up.

I get a kick out of lying to his face. It proves how easy it is to fool the authorities.

'Were there any problems between Sara and your parents?'

'No . . . I wouldn't say that. But Sara might have been a little misunderstood.'

With that, he's all ears.

'Oh? How so?'

'She was a little different, a little strange, and my parents couldn't always figure her out.'

'So she might have nursed a grudge against them because of it?'

I pretend to think for a long time, and he clears his throat to urge me to go on.

'It's possible,' I say. 'But Jesus, this is terrible!'

Now he looks pompous and self-satisfied. A complete idiot, like all cops.

'But now that you mention it,' I continue, 'there was that fire in the neighbours' chicken coop. Our closest neighbours weren't far, and there was a fire, and it was definitely arson. But we never would have suspected Sara . . .'

He nods eagerly, inviting me to keep talking with his sweaty little chin.

I don't say anything for a moment and pretend to be battling with my own thoughts.

'And there was that incident at school. Someone accused Sara of a knife attack. It sounded ridiculous then, but now that I think about it . . . this can't be true!'

I bury my head in my arms against his desk and let my back tremble a little.

It ends perfectly.

He shakes my hand and expresses his condolences, saying that I should seek help from a psychologist. That it's the best way to get over the shock and loss.

'Yes, I suppose I'd better,' I say.

I'm smirking on the inside.

42

The rain began as scattered sprinkles in the evening but later turned into a quiet drizzle that lasted for several hours. The downpour didn't set in until late at night. Anna was already standing at the window when Sofia woke up. The pounding of raindrops was almost deafening.

'Look at that! I've never seen anything like it!'

Sofia came to the window and tried to see though the curtain of water washing across the pane. A small pond had formed in front of the barn.

'We'd better go check and make sure nothing is flooding,' she told Anna.

They tried to wake Elin, but she snapped at them and pulled the covers over her head.

'Whatever,' Anna said. 'We'll go on our own.'

They pulled their raincoats and boots over their nightgowns. It was still pouring when they stepped into the yard, and it limited their view. They could hear a rushing sound by the annexes as if a river were roaring between the buildings. The rain had whipped the barbed wire until it set off the alarm, and the spotlight was sweeping the grounds. But there wasn't a soul in sight.

'Where is everyone?' Anna shouted.

'I'll send a message to Bosse,' Sofia said.

Just then they heard a motorcycle and Benny, who was on watch, came skidding across the yard.

'Look!' Anna cried, pointing at the annexes.

A large puddle had formed in the middle of the lawn, right in front of the house. The ground sloped down toward the other buildings, and water was cascading through the cracks under the doors.

'Go get everyone else!' Sofia called to Benny. 'The annexes are flooding!'

Anna waded into the water, which went past her knees.

'There has to be a drain here somewhere. It must be plugged.'

Sofia stepped down too and shivered as her boots filled with the cold, muddy water.

The staff began to arrive in the yard, but at first they only stood there in bewilderment as Anna and Sofia dug around in the pool. The crowd grew, but Oswald was nowhere to be seen.

'I found a grate!' Anna shouted. She reached down and started tugging. Sofia followed her lead and caught hold of the grate, which was blocked by grass, leaves, and trash. They pulled up big chunks of debris and soon the water began to drain in. Bosse, Benny, Sten, and Simon had jumped in to help. The water had stopped pouring into the annexes.

The rain let up as the clouds broke up and the sun peered over the horizon.

It was almost five in the morning.

Anna was the one to open the first door. Sofia was close on her heels. It looked like a hurricane had raged through the room; the floor was completely under water. The rug, which had once been the colour of coral, was soaked and dirty grey. The furniture was strewn all over.

The scene was the same in each of the fifteen rooms that had doors facing the lawn.

The first guests would arrive in ten days.

★

The veins on Oswald's forehead were bulging and spittle flew as he screamed. He had already thrown the paperweight, all his pens, and a notebook at them. At first, his rage had been directed at no one in particular. He just lashed out and called them idiots, incompetents, and a slew of other unpleasant insults. But now his eyes were nailed to Bosse, who had dared to open his mouth.

'We can remove the water with a shop vac,' he'd said. 'And then we just have to clean up the rooms.'

'"Just?"' Oswald roared. 'So you think this is a minor issue? Have you seen this shit? Have you even been inside all the rooms?'

'No, I mean . . . I've seen a few, and —'

That was all it took. Oswald walked over, grabbed Bosse by the collar, and pulled his face close. He braced his arms against Bosse's chest and knocked him backwards with one leg even as he let go. Bosse landed on his behind, then hit his head on the marble floor with a thud. At first he seemed to have lost consciousness; he lay perfectly still with his eyes closed for a few seconds. But then he came to, opened his eyes, and stared in terror at Oswald, who was standing over him, legs planted wide. Oswald sank to his knees and straddled Bosse's chest. He put him in a stranglehold and pressed hard. A horrid gurgle came from Bosse's throat, but Oswald didn't stop.

Have to put an end to this, have to . . .

'I have a suggestion!' Sofia called out.

453

Oswald was startled and loosened his grip on Bosse's throat. He hurriedly stood up; for a moment he looked confused. He adjusted his clothes while Bosse lay gasping for breath. But the confusion in Oswald's eyes quickly vanished and rage returned anew.

'Did you see how that bastard looked at me? Did you see that disgusting sneer?'

No one answered, but most of them nodded.

'Look at those fucking fish eyes. There's no life in him.'

Since no one had spoken yet, Bosse mumbled a faint 'I understand, sir' from the floor, which only made the mood more stressful and uncomfortable.

'What kind of suggestion?' Oswald asked, turning to Sofia, back to his usual arrogant self.

'We can divide up into different teams. One team can handle the shop vacs and —'

'Shut up! I don't even want to hear it. These idiots will have to fix it.'

He pointed at the small group in front of him: Anna, Corinne, Krister, and Joel, the unit in charge of the annexes.

It struck Sofia, as she stood there, that someone else was going to die. Someone was next in line after Benjamin. It might not happen that day or the next, but it would happen again. And then it occurred to her that perhaps that was exactly the way Oswald wanted it. That he got joy out of the chaos, the crises, and the moments he lashed out at them, took things out on them. It was a peculiar thought, but it stuck with her.

Bosse slowly got up off the floor. He tried to look unaffected, but his hair was pointing in all directions, his shirt had become untucked, and his eyes were red.

He's a wreck, Sofia thought. *I can't even look at him, because all I see is myself in a week, a month . . . because that is exactly what I'll look like if I don't get out of here soon.*

'Give me my Dictaphone!' Oswald directed Sofia. She fumbled through his desk drawer and found it. She turned it on and handed it to him, and he began to list the so-called Consequences for what had happened in the annexes.

'That goes for you too,' Oswald told Bosse when he was finished. 'You have no control over the staff around here.'

Sofia couldn't stop herself — the injustice was pounding in her head until it felt like her temples would burst.

'Sir, I don't want to contradict you, but Anna was the one who discovered the blockage. And the guests will be here soon, and Anna takes care of everything in the annexes: the organic food, the rooms, the gym — the whole program.'

Oswald's laugh was wild and shrill.

'The program? Are you really that stupid? Do you think this has anything to do with the program? The food, sleep, all of that crap? People just like that stuff. Don't you understand that the theses are the important thing here? The theses!'

His open palm struck the desk with a bang.

'Fine. Anna won't be punished. But she *will* clean up this shit, and you will help her, just for talking back.'

She noticed his pinkie finger trembling slightly and hoped he'd hurt it when he attacked Bosse.

'What the hell are you staring at?' he said, and she was startled to find that his eyes were fixed on her.

★

455

She stood observing the new punishment camp, watching the pale, half-naked bodies that had gathered around the garden hose. They used it to shower. Corinne was there with the guys, naked aside from her bra and panties. Those were the rules. Their shelter, a small military tent that sagged in the middle, swayed with the wind. While they showered, their clothes hung from a rope strung between two trees.

This was meant to be the living quarters for the absolute scum, the lowest ranks in Penance. It was the last step before you were simply dumped in the sound, gone forever. But of course that wasn't accurate. He would always find something worse, something more degrading. Their tent had been erected behind a grove of trees so no one would have to look at them. They weren't allowed food or water from the property. Only the garden hose. Oswald had said they had to do their business in chamber pots, because they weren't allowed to use the toilets in the manor house. If they wanted any food they had to beg and plead with Simon, and if they were given any vegetables they had to eat them raw, because under no circumstances were they allowed to set foot in the kitchen or light any fires. And if there weren't any vegetables, they could just eat the scraps from the staff meals.

Besides Corinne, the group was made up of Bosse, Joel, and Krister. Sten, their guard, hung around by a tree, staring at them. At Corinne's body especially. Their first job would be to transform the annexes back into a palace before the guests arrived. And they had to pay for the damages from their own funds. Those who had any funds, at least. The others found themselves in debt.

Her pager vibrated.

Report to the office immediately.

It was eight-thirty, and she didn't want to see Oswald again that evening. But there was no room for a misstep now. The slightest blunder, and she too would be showering in bra and panties under the garden hose.

★

When she opened the door, the office appeared to be empty. He wasn't at his desk, and the lights were out. She took a few steps in and suddenly he was on her. He had been standing behind the door. He flung himself at her, grabbing her shoulders and shoving her forward so hard she hit her head on the wall. His body flew at her from behind; he grabbed her wrists, pinned her arms to the wall above her head, and pressed so hard against her that at last she was stretched and flattened and helpless before him. Everything about him was hard; he was so insane with fury that his breathing came in sharp blasts. Something burned her neck and she realized he was biting and nibbling at her. One of his hands was under her blazer, and he yanked at her blouse until the buttons bounced off the marble floor. He grabbed her breast and squeezed so hard she cried out. Fear had nearly paralysed her and tears burned her eyes, but all she could think was that she had better not pee herself. She screamed — not a drawn-out call for help, but a short screech of frustration, and he let go.

Took a few steps back.

His voice was rough and hoarse.

'You are a cheeky, shameless slut, and you are going to beg forgiveness for talking back in front of those other idiots. Get down on your knees.'

There was a new, violent undertone to his voice.

It was like she was riveted to the wall; she couldn't move. The air was being sucked out of her, her lungs collapsing.

'I said, get down on your knees!'

She slowly turned around and sank to her knees before him. She couldn't bring herself to make eye contact, so she stared at the floor.

At that moment, there was nothing she wanted more than to tell him to go to hell.

Her lips formed the words, but no sound escaped.

Deep inside, a voice warned her that he would smash her to bits if she disobeyed him right now.

She swallowed the words and closed her mouth.

Aware that she had just crossed the line of his patience, she decided that she had to apologize.

'I'm sorry,' she whispered.

'Look me in the eye!' he shouted.

She looked up. His eyes were wild.

'I'm sorry,' she whispered again.

'Louder! I can't hear you.'

'I'm sorry!' she cried.

'Good. Now get out of here. Before I give you a real thrashing.'

She stood up, adjusted her skirt, which had slid up, pulled down her blazer, and did up a few of its buttons to hide her ruined shirt.

But he blocked her way as she started for the door.

'Come to work like an ordinary person tomorrow. Who is in charge around here?'

'You are, sir.'

'That's right. Now get out of here.'

She cried all the way down to her dormitory, but clenched her teeth so no one would hear.

The room was empty. She sat down on her bed and cried a while longer. Regret surged through her. She had been so close to making everything end differently, but she hadn't dared to take the chance. And she hated herself for it. Rage welled up in her chest — she pounded the bedspread with her fists, then got up and kicked the bureau until her toes hurt. She hated herself for giving in. Hated his hard body, his strong hands, his fucking mouth that spouted insults, his goddamn aftershave. Hate, hate, hate.

Pull yourself together, Bauman, fucking get it together.

She tore off her blazer and blouse and tossed them in the wastebasket.

Her chest still ached. The weight of his body seemed to linger against her back, and the marks left by his teeth burned on her neck. As she rooted around in a drawer to find a shirt, she noticed the pen and notebook she'd left there. Once dressed, she picked them up and sat down on the bed to sketch. She drew a stick figure, a horned devil with thick eyebrows and an evil smile.

She ripped the drawing from the pad, folded it, and stuck it in her pocket, then ran down the stairs and out to the lawn. No one was there, so she slipped around the corner of the house and into the garage.

She spotted his favourite motorcycle almost immediately. It was parked in one corner, freshly polished and gleaming. Taking the pocketknife out, she approached the bike. For a second she hesitated, but then she stabbed the blade right into the seat and made a long cut. The leather made a very satisfying sound as the knife sliced through it. She took out her sketch of the devil and stuffed it into the slit.

On her way back, she stopped at the greenhouse.

She stayed for a long time, concocting a plan with Simon.

*

As she stepped into the dormitory, her doubt returned. It rumbled into her head like a steamroller, squashing all the courage she had gathered during the evening. She wondered how anyone could be so certain of something and then begin to doubt again. *Benjamin is dead*, she thought. *Oswald is going to end up killing Elvira soon, he almost strangled Bosse today, and next time he gets angry he's going to rape me. What will happen if he discovers me with a backpack full of his secrets?*

Soon Elin and Anna would return and all she could do was turn out the lights and pretend everything was normal. She went to the bathroom and stared at her own reflection, trying to bring life into the frightened eyes that peered back at her. It was now or never — she had to escape, even if fear was to be her constant companion.

She sneaked out into the corridor and down the stairs and found the main electrical switch.

When she peeked out the small window in the corridor, she could see the ladder Simon had placed against the wall. She counted the steps from the switch to her room and from the door to her bed. She pulled out her backpack and wound a windproof jacket around it, then stuffed the bundle back under the bed. A pair of sneakers went next to the bundle, the slip-on kind — there would be no time to tie laces. The dull sound of voices came from outside the door, so she quickly crawled under the covers and closed her eyes.

Everything was in place.

A little over an hour left.

She began to count the seconds.

I peer over his shoulder and out the window.

The sun is setting. It's as though my entire future is bathing in the sunset.

I can't concentrate on all these numbers and all his blather.

*'It seems that the insurance company won't cover the loss of the villa,'
he says. 'After all, it was arson.'*

I nod. I don't care — I'll just sell the lot and get rid of the whole thing.

*'But even so, you'll have immense resources,' he continues. 'And
investments, of course. If you'd like me to explain —'*

I hold up my hand.

*'No, that's fine. I'm not going to remain here, as you can understand.
There's too much to remind me of . . .'*

He nods.

'So you'll go to Sweden?'

'Yes, I think so. I'm considering returning to my studies up there.'

He starts in again.

About investing money, how best to manage all the assets.

*But I only listen with half an ear. I'm thinking about how important
I am going to be for humanity.*

The only person who has discovered the truth all on his own.

The truth truth that I discovered under the water at Devil's Rock.

The truth about the darkness in the tiny closet on the ferry.

All these truths I have lived. I think of them and draw strength from them. That's right, the truth about strength — the most important of all.

The sun has almost vanished below the horizon. Yet my adventure only begins now. And there's one thing I know for certain.

Those who cross my path. Those I take on.

They will never be the same again.

43

A dog was barking nearby.

Back at the manor, the alarm was blaring.

I cannot pass out, I can't!

But her legs gave way, she was sapped of energy.

The man on the path in front of her stood perfectly still.

The din of the alarm blended with the pattering of the rain and the barking, which had grown more frantic. Spotlights swept the treetops. The cacophony of sounds and images faded as she nearly lost consciousness.

She sank into a crouch and pressed both hands to the path to steady herself.

Do not pass out.

The shower of sparks behind her eyelids died down.

Her vision began to return: the faint outlines of gravel on the path, her shoes.

Her pulse slowed and a mild wave of strength returned to her body.

Then came hands on her shoulders, supporting her, trying to hold her up.

'What's the matter?'

She looked up at him, but his face was too blurry.

A dog growled behind him.

'Sofia! It is Sofia, isn't it?'

The face came into focus. A kind face. Edwin Björk.

The words caught in her throat, and all that came from her mouth was a disturbing hacking sound.

He hooked his hands under her arms and helped her stand.

'What happened?'

Her tongue untied itself and the words came out in bursts.

'Please, help me, you have to help me! They're after me!'

Björk looked at her in astonishment.

'Of course I'll help you. Do you mean the cult? Are they chasing you?'

He didn't even wait for an answer — he just took her arm and led her down the path.

'Can you manage to walk a short way?'

She nodded.

'My house isn't far at all. I'm sorry I scared you. Just out with the dog.'

'Do you live here? In the middle of the woods?'

'Yep, in a lovely old cottage.'

Her heart was still beating so hard that she could hear the rush in her ears, and it was hard to hear what he said. She breathed through her mouth and each inhalation burned her lungs.

'You can explain when we get inside,' he said. 'We'll put on some coffee and have a chat.'

He led her down the narrowest of paths, and she caught sight of the little cottage, which was on a rise in a grove of trees. Warm light glowed from a single window.

On the way up the slope, she heard them — scattered voices and calls from back in the woods. Twigs snapping. And when she turned around, she saw beams of lights sweeping the trees.

'We have to hurry,' she said, running the last little bit. Björk kept up, but she reached the door before he did. She stumbled on the second to last step and grabbed for the door, but at the same time it opened from the inside and she almost fell straight into the arms of a surprised woman. Björk stepped in and pulled the door closed. The woman appeared to be in her sixties, with grey hair that fell to her waist, and she was wearing a nightgown. The small dog bounced around, jumping up at her as she studied Sofia curiously.

'This is my wife Elsa,' said Björk. 'Elsa, this is Sofia. She's escaped the devilry up at the manor, and now we need to help her.'

★

They drank coffee at the little kitchen table. She found herself in a peculiar rapture-like state.

The small cottage was like a temple, a sanctuary where she was safe and hidden from what had to be a thorough search for her outside. It was so warm in the room that she was sweating. Her rain-soaked clothes were in the dryer and Elsa Björk had given her a nightgown and robe to wear in the meantime.

'I'm sure they'll come looking for you on the ferry tomorrow,' Edwin said. 'But we'll go down around seven so you can hide in the wheelhouse.'

'Excuse me for asking,' Elsa said, 'but why can't you just tell them to get lost if they show up? Edwin will be there. They can't attack you, can they?'

Sofia thought for a moment. There was so much to consider. The contents of her backpack. Oswald and Östling. Elvira in the attic. Suddenly the cottage didn't feel as cosy anymore and she wondered how long it would take for Oswald to realize she had copied the files and stolen his Dictaphone.

'It's more complicated than that,' she said. 'Franz Oswald has contacts, and I'd really like to get a head start so no one can follow me.'

'But how will she get off the ferry without anyone seeing her?' Elsa asked Edwin.

'I'll have to keep an eye out,' he replied. 'Make sure that anyone who's tailing her gets off the boat before Sofia does. We'll work it out somehow. Do you think they'll get off on the mainland and search for you there, Sofia?'

'I'm not sure. But the ferry doesn't return to the island for hours, and I'm sure they won't just stay on the boat.'

'Good point. So I'll keep an eye on things, and when the coast is clear you can sneak out and disappear into the crowds on the quay. But for now, can't you tell us about what's been going on up at the manor?'

Sofia was hesitant. Björk would go crazy and call the police straight away if she mentioned Oswald and Elvira.

'Franz Oswald, the man who owns the place, has almost lost his mind,' she said. 'He deals out all sorts of punishment, and, well, maybe you've seen the electric fence he put up around the property.'

Björk nodded, encouraging her to go on.

'You've probably also heard about the death up at Devil's Rock. He was my boyfriend, the guy who jumped, and he was forced to do it. As punishment. That was the last straw for me.'

Björk lost his temper. 'Good heavens! This is ridiculous. I knew he was up to some sort of devilry up there.'

'Yes, but I'm going to report him to the police. I took some evidence with me.'

'So we just have to sit here and wait?'

'Yes, more or less. But I promise to contact you as soon as I can.'

'Well, there you have it,' Edwin said, turning to Elsa. 'I've always said that place is cursed, and now it's worse than ever. The whole bloody thing ought to be torn down. Levelled to the ground.'

Elsa shook her head.

'I don't believe in curses, but it certainly is odd. I mean, how he just *had* to have the manor for his ridiculous cult. He came here, this superior ass, and offered an indecent amount of money for the place. We've always thought there was something fishy about it.'

'But it was nice at first,' Sofia hurried to say. 'He put together a good operation with organic gardens and the farm and everything. It was really great, actually. But then —'

'It always starts out just fine,' Edwin interrupted her. 'That's how they lure you in. But then they get delusions of grandeur and it becomes hellish. I've read about it . . .'

'Stop that now,' Elsa said. 'Can't you see Sofia is already shaken? She needs to get some sleep.'

Edwin turned to Sofia. 'Yes, yes, but there's just one more thing I want to say. If we don't hear from you in a few days, we're going to the police. We will.'

'Okay, please do. It's nice to know you will. But I do promise to call.'

Elsa rose and left the kitchen. Sofia could hear her turning off the dryer and opening some cabinets in the next room. Edwin gazed out the window with a distant, anxious expression on his face.

'Sofia, come here!' Elsa called. 'You can sleep on our pull-out sofa. It's not much, but it's all we have.'

'It'll be perfect. I was planning to sleep under the tarp on the ferry.'

★

The house was so quiet once they had gone to bed. The rain had stopped and all she could hear was the rustle of the trees in the wind. The dog lay in a small bed on the floor beside her, whimpering now and then. It must have been dreaming.

She reached for the backpack, which she'd placed next to the sofa. Opening each compartment, she reassured herself that everything was there: the thumb drive, the Dictaphone, the phone numbers she'd received from various people on the island. She thought about hiding it all in the Björks' house, but then she would have nothing. It would be her word against that of fifty others at ViaTerra, and Wilgot Östling with his police allies.

Sleep was not in the cards for her that night, she knew it already. It wasn't the coffee keeping her awake, it was her mind. Mostly she was afraid that she would wake up and discover she was back in the dormitory. That her escape had been nothing but a dream. Then she thought of Elvira and prayed once more that Oswald wouldn't kill her. She fell into a light slumber just after her watch read 4:55. But when Elsa Björk woke her at six-thirty, she wasn't at all tired, only excited and nervous.

'Breakfast is ready,' said Elsa. 'And Edwin has been lying awake most of the night cursing the cult. We're so worried for your sake.'

'It's going to be okay,' Sofia said, mostly to reassure Elsa.

There was a tiny nook in the wheelhouse, just under the spot where Edwin stood when he piloted the ferry. He had brought a pile of blankets and a sleeping bag to make it more comfortable. Elsa had filled Sofia's thermos with coffee and made a heap of sandwiches to put in her backpack.

The morning was still and foggy. She had felt watched all the way down to the ferry, and found herself peering over her shoulder again and again. Her imagination told her there were shadows and figures behind the trees and bushes. Her initial sense of freedom had given way to fear, which had grown into mild paranoia.

'You can lie in here,' Edwin said. 'I'll have to keep you entertained with jokes and ghost stories.'

'I'd prefer jokes, and you'll have to keep a lookout too. They'll almost definitely be wearing their uniforms, grey suits. They're not allowed to go anywhere without them. So they should stick out.'

'Like Mormons, sort of?'

'Right, exactly.'

The little cubby was damp and smelled like diesel and seaweed, overlaid with a sour odour from a nearby pair of boots. She lay down on the sleeping bag with several blankets over her.

'Okay, the passengers are starting to arrive,' Edwin said.

She could hear and feel the faint thumps as cars drove onto the deck, and then came the sound of voices and stomping feet. Soon enough Edwin was busy steering the ferry, so he was silent. She could tell how tired she was — she'd hardly gotten a wink, and now that the tension had abated a little and the ferry engine was droning so soothingly, she felt drowsy. She sank into a warm torpor and almost fell asleep. But then Björk's voice broke through the fog.

He was speaking with someone. 'Can I help you?'

'Yes, perhaps. We're looking for a friend.'

She recognized the voice immediately, and suddenly she was wide awake. Her blood ran cold: it was Benny.

'We were supposed to meet here and take the ferry over,' came another familiar voice.

Sten! Benny and Sten are on the ferry, looking for me!

It couldn't get any worse — they were big and dumb and strong, and they wouldn't hesitate to use force if they thought it was necessary. Furthermore, they were standing dangerously close to her. She could hear their feet scraping against the steel floor. Their voices were suddenly perfectly clear.

'I see,' came Björk's voice. 'Who are you looking for?'

'A girl, short, thin, with long, dark hair. Frizzy, too. Probably wearing jeans and a hoodie.'

'I haven't seen her,' Björk said. 'But as you can see, I'm busy with the ferry.'

'It's pretty urgent that we get hold of her,' Benny said.

'I haven't seen her. She must have changed her mind. Now, if you'll excuse me . . . '

But they weren't about to give up.

'Is there any sort of hiding place on this ferry, I mean, somewhere where no one would see you?'

'No, there certainly isn't. It's a small ferry. Guys, it's too bad you can't find your friend, but I need to concentrate on piloting the ferry.'

She held her breath and lay still.

'Okay, but if you see her . . .'

'I'll tell her you're looking for her. But now you'll have to leave me alone.'

Steps died away across the steel floor. She still didn't dare move.

'They weren't wearing suits,' she heard Edwin's voice at last. 'Just normal clothes. What stubborn, pushy rascals.'

At first she was afraid to speak.

'They can't hear you. And I don't think they'll be back.'

'Thank you,' she said. 'Thanks for handling it so well.'

'No problem, but I'm going to try to keep my mouth shut for this last bit. So it doesn't look like I'm talking to myself.'

★

She lay in the darkness for nearly an hour, listening to the lapping waves, the ferry engine, and Edwin's persistent whistling. Reality was still sinking in: she really had made it over the wall. She really was close to freedom; it was within reach. She felt her lips turn up in a smile. At the same time she was tormented at the thought of what might happen when they reached the harbour. She tried to figure out why Oswald had sent Benny and Sten out in civilian clothes. It occurred to her that she had no real plan. She had planned the escape itself, but she had no idea how she would get home or what she would tell her parents or the police. The only thing that mattered was getting over that damn wall. She'd thought everything would just work itself out after that.

The ferry swayed and lurched as it docked, and she could hear a faint buzz from the harbour.

'I'll keep my eye on them,' Edwin said. 'Then we'll decide which way you should go. Oh, curse it! They're waiting for al the passengers to disembark, staring them up and down. As if you would suddenly show up there. What idiots!'

Sofia crawled out of the cubby and sat on the floor at Edwin's feet.

'They're moving now,' he reported. 'Yes indeed. They're heading for the cafés over by the guest marina. So you can run the other direction, toward the bus terminal. You can get up now.'

She stretched out her stiff, sore limbs and peered over Edwin's shoulder.

Two figures had separated from the crowd and were striding toward the cafés and outdoor seating. She couldn't imagine what they would do there — eat lunch maybe — but it didn't matter. This was her chance. She grabbed her backpack, hugged Edwin and thanked him, and ran down the pier and onto the quay.

She looked around one last time and vanished into the crowd.

44

She sank into her seat on the bus with a long sigh.

As soon as they began moving, a pleasant sense of calm spread through her body. The steel shell of the bus felt like protective armour. She was inside; they were on the outside somewhere and couldn't get at her. And now she had a head start.

A few women her own age were sitting in front of her and looking at something on their phones, talking so fast their words blended together, giggling and guffawing.

Suddenly she felt old, as if she had aged twenty years on that island. She imagined how those women had spent the past two years: guys and parties, clothes and fun trips. Meanwhile she had been running around saying 'Yes sir!' and 'No sir!' day in and day out. She had nearly turned into an old woman, who had to stop herself from telling the women to keep it down. *Unless you want three laps around the manor.* She suspected she would never feel that happy-go-lucky again.

*

By the time they reached Gothenburg Central Station, the stress had almost lifted. Perhaps this would be easy after all. The train straight to Lund, then the bus to her parents' place in Fjelie. It occurred to her that her parents might not be home and she considered calling, but it seemed like a bad idea. One evening she'd overheard Bosse mention something to Oswald about how they could trace mobile phone calls. It had been a breakthrough for them at the time. But how? Through Östling, maybe?

She turned off her phone and put it in her backpack to avoid temptation.

The station was full of people. She hadn't been in such a big crowd for a long time. For a while she just walked around, enjoying being jostled now and then and pretending that she too had an important life and somewhere to be. She purchased her ticket from an agent and put a timetable for the bus to Fjelie in her pocket. Her mom must have deposited the money, because her card was working.

The next train to Lund wouldn't leave for an hour. Her stomach began to grumble and she remembered Elsa's sandwiches in her pack. She bought sparkling water and a newspaper at Pressbyrån and sat down on a bench to eat the sandwiches. It almost felt nice, but only almost — something was still chafing at her. The feeling that there was something she hadn't thought of. An important piece of the puzzle that had gone missing in the chaos. But she couldn't figure out what it might be.

According to the paper, it was June 4. The past few days had been a muddle, but now she knew. Thursday, June 4. The news encompassed everything from a political scandal to a whole two-page spread forecasting unpredictable weather for Midsummer. Her skin crawled and she had trouble concentrating. She just wanted to get on the train and be on her way. Instead of reading, she people-watched. Everyone seemed to be running around like aged mice, stressed and with no time for reflection. An older man with a Pressbyrån bag sat down beside her, fished a pear out of his bag, and began to eat it. It smelled sweet and good, even though she was full after eating the sandwiches. She smiled at him and they began to chat.

'I come here every day,' he said. 'To sit and watch people. It feels less lonely that way.'

She grew warm inside from a moment of such simple and relaxed human contact. They continued to chat until her train was called over the loudspeakers.

Her seat was by the window and the early summer landscape spread out beyond the glass pane. Blue sky with small, airy clouds, birches, lakes, red cottages. Since she felt drowsy after her meal, she decided to try to get some sleep. *If I focus on the goal of coming home, and not on all the terrible stuff in my backpack, it will be just fine,* she thought before she dozed off.

*

When she woke up, the train was stopped in Landskrona. She wanted coffee, but hers had gone cold in the thermos and tasted bitter so she decided to head to the restaurant car. She threw the backpack over her shoulder, not wanting it out of sight for even a second.

There was a short line for the register and she floated in and out of dreamlike thoughts as she waited. *Simon.* What was he doing now? Had they made him help search for her? She wondered whether he had managed to keep up the façade or if he had given in to the pressure.

She was last in line, and it didn't seem to be moving at all.

A man turned around and left the register with a tray of food

Her whole body went stiff; all she could do was stand there gaping, trying to understand what she had just seen, because the man was Sten. His profile was facing her for a moment before he turned his back and headed into the next car, but it was definitely him. With a tray full of food. After him came Benny, with another tray. Her heart thudded against her ribs.

Shit! How did they find me?

The paralysis lifted and she hurried out of the restaurant car, waving her hands frantically at the glass motion-sensor doors, which took forever to open.

She headed for the nearest toilet, but it was occupied, so she pressed herself to the wall as she waited, trying to make herself invisible. *They're eating*, she thought. *It's fine. I have some time.*

The toilet flushed, but no one came out.

Hurry, dammit, get a move on!

At last the door opened and a tall bald man came out and gave her a friendly smile. She slipped in and closed the door, then sat on the lid of the toilet and attempted to organize her thoughts.

How long did it take to get from Landskrona to Lund? Twenty, maybe thirty minutes.

Staying in the bathroom was her only option; there was no avoiding it. *What are they doing here?* she wondered. *They couldn't have followed me, because they weren't on the bus. And they must not have been searching for me on the train, because I was asleep for at least an hour. But here they are. What on earth is going on?*

She tried to be logical, to keep from reacting without thinking things through. *Well, one thing's for sure*, she thought. *They may not know I'm on this train, but they're headed for Lund and it's me they're after. I have no choice. Half an hour in the bathroom until we arrive.*

Just as the train got up to speed, the rails thumping steadily, it slowed down again and stopped.

'We're waiting for an oncoming train,' came the voice on the loudspeaker.

Soon, people would want to use this bathroom. She made sure the door was locked — and just as she did, someone pulled on the handle, gently at first, but after a few minutes it became impatient. She pictured a queue forming. *No one can blame a person for having stomach issues*, she thought. Yet an annoyed voice spoke up outside.

'Have you locked this bathroom or something?'

The person must have asked a conductor, because the response was patient.

'No, there's probably someone in there, but there's another toilet after the next car.'

Shuffling steps grew fainter, thank goodness, and now she just had to wait out the rest of the trip.

The car jerked as the train started moving again. Memories from the island came back to her as she sat there swaying back and forth through the curves. They formed a slideshow, starting with her first day there. But there was no warmth to the images. *I feel like an escaped prisoner*, she thought. *I even feel guilty. Every damn day, he made me feel like this. Like I'm filthy and inadequate. But I'm not the one with issues here.*

After endless yanks at the door handle, the loudspeaker voice returned.

'We're approaching Lund Central Station. Lund, next station. Exit the train on the left side.'

The instant she opened the bathroom door, she saw them. Benny and Sten were by the nearest exit, at the front of a crowd waiting to disembark. They were chatting and laughing. It would be all she needed right now, for one of them to turn in her direction. A single glance, and everything would be ruined.

She turned around, pulled up her hood, and joined the queue for a different exit, trying to blend in with everyone else. She spied through a glass door and watched Benny and Sten disembark, but she lingered on board until the very last passenger was gone. She could see them, far ahead. They seemed to be in a hurry and were moving quickly toward the exit.

If they were on their way to her house, they would take the bus to Fjelie. It went once an hour, so she would let them get a head start; she could take the next bus. After all, her parents didn't know where she was. The kind of conversation the men were after would hardly take very long, so by the time she arrived home the coast would be clear.

When she unfolded the timetable, she found that the next bus to Fjelie left at four — in twenty minutes — so she would take the five o'clock.

To keep from running into them inside the station, she spent half an hour waiting on a bench by the tracks. Then she bought her ticket from a machine and wandered around for what seemed an eternity. Her body was restless, her mouth was dry as a bone, and she felt too antsy to sit down. There wasn't much to look at — a few posters, some tired travellers on their way home after a day of work. She glanced constantly at the wall clock, but it hands hardly seemed to move, and she was so early to the bus stop that she had to stand around waiting for a long time. When she finally got on, she was so relieved that the driver must have noticed; he laughed.

'In a rush to get home?'

'You can say that again.'

She had made this trip so many times before.

Eighteen minutes, and I'll be home, she thought. *The worst is almost over.*

The landscape was so familiar, so beautiful, that the tears began to flow as she gazed out the window. The open fields of rapeseed, already pale yellow. She recognized every house and every yard, and even a pair of horses grazing in a meadow.

Eighteen minutes, and everything will be okay.

Her house was visible even from the bus stop — only the roof and part of the eaves, but still. She hurried across the road and turned onto the beloved old street. She looked up toward the yard. Something was wrong.

Something was terribly wrong.

Two police cars were parked in front of her house. An officer was standing on the street with a German shepherd at his side, and another was speaking to her parents, who were standing on the lawn.

She turned around and saw the bus back to Lund approaching on the other side of the road. Instinct and adrenaline took over and she ran as fast as her legs could carry her toward the oncoming bus.

45

The bus was empty. Five-thirty, almost dinnertime, a little too early to head to Lund for an evening out. She thought the bus driver shot her an odd look as she boarded, so she sat at the back.

I have eighteen minutes to decide what to do, she thought. Either she could go back and find out what was going on, or she could hide and come up with a better plan. But first she had to try to think like Oswald, to understand why he had sent the police after her so quickly. And a K9 unit at that. *Why on earth would they have a dog?* she thought. *Dogs track drugs, corpses, and missing people.*

It struck her that it had to be that simple. He'd reported her missing, so they would search for her; he'd worked with Östling to get hold of her. And then what?

She squeezed her backpack and gazed out at the crops, which bent slightly in the breeze. Fog Island seemed so distant, like a tiny speck in outer space. But Oswald was sure to have a crafty plan and she had nearly walked right into his trap. She knew she had to stop acting like an escaped criminal, because that must be exactly what he wanted her to do. Then again, it was no surprise that he was so desperate. She was the only one who knew his terrible secrets.

That tiny burst of courage took hold of her again, and she knew exactly what to do.

Nothing. Not a single goddamn thing. Just let him agonize.

She got off the bus at Central Station and walked briskly toward Hotel Lundia. She'd seen their sign from the bus stop earlier that day.

The hotel seemed empty, cool, and sleepy when she stepped in. A great marble floor extended to the black reception desk, which was framed with reddish wood. No music. No people. Just her and the receptionist who was reading something on a computer screen. The young woman had dark red lips and pale, powdered skin that took on a bluish hue in the glow of the screen. She didn't notice Sofia until she was right up next to the desk.

'I'd like a room for the night.'

The young woman looked up with a practised smile.

'All right. May I see your credit card?'

'There's another thing.'

'What's that?'

'I'd like to remain anonymous. Is that possible?'

'What do you mean?'

'I'd like you to put me down as Annika Svensson.'

The young woman brightened up and winked at her.

'Oh no! Problems with your boyfriend?'

'Right, big problems,' Sofia said, raising her eyebrows meaningfully.

'Okay, that's fine . . . Annika. We start serving breakfast at six-thirty.'

★

The room was simple. Pale walls. A grey easy chair, a small oak desk, a double bed with a grey bedspread. Yet it felt like she had stepped into a luxury suite.

She put her backpack on the chair and threw herself onto the bed, where she gazed up at the ceiling for a while trying to find dots and patterns in all the white. She shoved away all her thoughts and let her body relax. After a while she gathered her courage and took her phone from her pack. She dialled her mother, who answered after the second ring. The words poured from her quickly — this wouldn't be a real conversation.

'Mom, it's me, I'm fine. It's not like you think. I'm going to be gone for a while, but I didn't do anything wrong. You have to believe me. And you can't tell anyone I called —'

Her mother cried out before Sofia had finished her sentence.

'Sofia? Where are you? The police were here, and they said —'

'You can't tell them I called,' she interrupted. 'I have to go now. I love you. I'll be home soon.'

Then she ended the call, her face wet with tears, and tried to send telepathic waves of hope to her parents. She knew they were on her side, but she didn't want them to worry.

Her stomach was grumbling angrily, so after she turned off her phone and put it back in her pack she went to the restaurant, where only a few guests were seated at the tables. She ordered the most expensive item on the menu, sole with asparagus and lemon sauce. And a glass of wine. She looked around as she waited for her food. A young couple was at the table next to hers, arguing over what to order. The woman thought the man's food was too expensive, so he was sulking and staring out the window. At another table was a lone man, busy with his phone. An older couple sat in the far corner, looking away from each other as they ate. The speakers were pouring out non-stop pop. She made believe about these people's lives for a while. Where they lived, what they did all day; eventually her thoughts turned to her parents, and she was overwhelmed with a piercing homesickness.

Her food arrived, and it was even more delicious than she'd imagined. She devoured it all, and ordered dessert and coffee. Suddenly she realized why Benny and Sten had looked so happy on the train, with their trays of food. They, too, had been eating rice and beans for months. Trailing her was probably just a big adventure for them. *It doesn't matter how much Oswald tries to clamp down on us*, she thought. *There will always be a little devil inside, ready to let loose.*

She went back up to her room, where she washed her clothes in the bathtub and hung them to dry in the bathroom. She turned on the TV and watched the news on two different channels.

Later she watched a movie, and opened the minibar to make a gin and tonic to enjoy with the entertainment. At last she was tired and fell asleep, warm, a little tipsy, and almost happy.

When she first woke up, she had no idea where she was. She thought she was in the dormitory bed and her heart sank, but then she saw the clock radio on the nightstand, which read 6:25. Her memories of the past twenty-four hours returned. She tried to fall back to sleep, but she was wide awake. Her head felt a little heavy from the alcohol, but she was otherwise alert and ready to put her plan into action. Although it wasn't much of a plan. She had only decided to go away for a while. To hide. She didn't know where she would go, but she had been so tired after the movie that she decided to sleep on it.

She got out of bed and opened the blinds. It was a beautiful summer day outside. Her clothes had dried. She took a long, hot bath and a cool shower, then realized she'd brought toothpaste but no toothbrush and rubbed her finger around her mouth until the taste of alcohol disappeared. Out of habit she made the bed and straightened up — it was unfathomable that someone would clean up after her. She decided not to come back to the room; instead she would take advantage of the early morning.

The dining room was almost empty and she had the breakfast buffet to herself. She loaded a plate with eggs, bacon, and toast and drank two cups of black coffee before she even touched the food.

A woman with a large roller suitcase came up to the buffet. The sight of her roused Sofia's desire to travel again. If only she could decide where she would go. She had no relatives to go to, and it would have been too risky anyway. The idea was to find a place so unlikely that no one would think to look there. And it had to be almost free, or she would run out of money.

She fetched a couple of newspapers, thinking they might show her some cheap travel destinations. But when she opened the first one, she didn't even manage to read the headlines, because she was staring at a picture of herself.

46

She remembered exactly when that photo was taken. They'd been sitting in the hammock in the yard at their house in Fjelie. Her mom was cropped out; only her shoulder was visible. Sofia hadn't wanted to have her picture taken, but her dad had pestered her until she agreed to look into the lens. There was a trace of a smile in her eyes. It was a decent shot, true to life somehow, and therefore stood in stark contrast to the article that followed.

YOUNG WOMAN MISSING

A twenty-two-year old woman has been reported missing from the organization ViaTerra on West Fog Island off the coast of Bohuslän. Sofia Bauman, originally from Lund, has worked for ViaTerra for two years but failed to show up to work on Tuesday. It is unknown whether she is still on the island or has come to the mainland, because she was not seen on the ferry that crosses the sound.

In addition, according to police, there was a theft just prior to Bauman's disappearance. Among the missing items are the first draft of a novel by the organization's leader, Franz Oswald. Bauman, who has studied literature in Lund, has hopes of becoming an author and is suspected of being involved in the theft. According to sources at ViaTerra, she is also mentally unstable as the result of a breakdown earlier this year. Th police are searching for Bauman and encourage the public to contact them if Bauman is seen or heard from.

She stood up so fast the coffee cup fell over, but it was empty.

That bastard!

Mentally unstable? Breakdown?

It sounded like Oswald had written that drivel himself and sent it to Östling, who forwarded it to the paper. How else could he have the police looking for her after such a short time?

She read the article again; she had become stuck on the word 'novel.' He hadn't been working on any novel. The thought was absurd. He was so sure he had the answer to life's every mystery. A nonfiction book about it, but a novel? It had to be a misunderstanding. Her thoughts turned to the Dictaphone in her backpack. She couldn't believe she'd forgotten to listen to it in the hotel, but it must be the dizzying feeling of freedom causing her absent-mindedness. She had to listen to what he had recorded. But not now — right now, she had to hurry.

She slung the backpack over her shoulder and hurried to the reception desk. A new, male receptionist was there, and she sent up a quick prayer that he hadn't read the morning paper. As she checked out, she turned away, letting her gaze wander, pretending to be interested in a painting on the wall. But the receptionist only invited her to come back soon and handed her a receipt.

They would surely be looking for her at the station, but probably not this early in the morning. There was an ATM across the road; she only took out five hundred kronor at first so she could check her balance. She had just over eight thousand left, so she drained the account and stuck the cash in one of the pockets on her backpack.

There. She had cleaned up the last of her trail. From now on she would be untraceable and invisible — but where on earth could she go?

A patrol car came zooming down the opposite side of the street, then stopped and turned toward downtown. Her heart pounded against her ribcage as panic gripped her again. The certainty that she was wanted caught up with her.

Go to the police, you little idiot! said a voice in the back of her head. *Give Oswald's belongings back. It's not smart to be running around like this.*

But her mind hit the brakes when she thought of the consequences. She pictured herself in a straitjacket, locked up in a mental hospital.

There on the sidewalk, she crouched down, desperate and exhausted. And then the image came to her. It had been there all along, but it was such a part of her that it had become invisible. It was an image of her grandmother's summer cottage on the island of Seskarö outside Haparanda — way up north, on the border with Finland. It was her most loved and hated place on earth. Loved, because she had been so happy there. Hated, because her grandmother had died in that cottage, alone and unable to call for help when she'd had a stroke almost seven years ago. Since that time, no one in the family had wanted to visit or even think about selling the cottage. Her aunt, who lived in Umeå, had promised to check on the place now and then, but Sofia doubted she went very often. Who would look for her there, way up in Norrland, in a place her family didn't even want to admit existed?

She hurried across the street to the station. The morning commuters had begun to stream in, so she pulled up her hood and stuffed her hair inside and stared at the ground as she walked to the ticket machine. She searched for the next train to Luleå but found that it didn't leave until 12:23. But the trip required her to change trains in Stockholm anyway, so she might as well take the first train there and wait for the train to Luleå and later, the bus to Haparanda. That was that. Everything seemed easy enough until it was time to pay — she took her card from her pocket, remembered that she had just taken out all the money, and besides, she didn't want to be traced.

There was no ticket counter at the station.

She looked around the waiting room. Most of the travellers were in motion, but there was one old woman reading a book on a bench. Sofia approached her cautiously and cleared her throat.

The woman glanced up at her and put her book down in her lap, mildly irritated to be interrupted in her reading.

'Excuse me, I wonder if you could do me a huge favour?'

'What is it?'

'Well, I left my debit card at home and I have to take the train to Stockholm that leaves in fifteen minutes. I wonder if I could give you cash . . .'

'Sure, I can buy the ticket for you.'

'Oh, thank you!'

'No problem. I was just sitting here waiting for my train anyway.'

When the woman handed Sofia the ticket and took the cash, there was a glimmer in her eyes.

'You look familiar. Aren't you on some TV show?'

'No, but people are always confusing me with, you know, that woman . . .'

'Right. Well, good luck with your trip!'

'Thanks, you too.'

She ran to the platform. The train was already there, so she hopped on and quickly found her seat, which was on the aisle. A man in a suit was sitting in the window seat, typing frantically on his laptop. He didn't even seem to notice her. She didn't think he looked like the type to read the local Lund paper.

Six hours to Stockholm, she thought. *Six hours I have to make pass quickly, or I'll lose my mind.* She picked up her backpack and set it in her lap, digging among shirts, jeans, and underwear to find the diary.

She decided to use the time to write down everything that had happened on the island, to resume where she'd left off so long ago.

Going back in time, she recalled more. Insults and degrading games. Nicknames he'd given to staff. She wrote and wrote and wasn't even aware when the train began to roll.

When she needed to use the bathroom, she took the opportunity to walk through the whole train and make sure Benny and Sten weren't on it. Most of the passengers paid no attention to her. Everything seemed calm and a little idle, as if the danger were only in her mind.

The trip went smoothly. She found a spot where she could sit alone and kept writing, looking up now and then to observe the other passengers in her car. She wondered what they would think if they knew what had gone on out on Fog Island.

When they reached Stockholm, almost the whole diary was full of writing.

At Central Station in Stockholm, she bought a crime novel and read half of it as she waited for the train to Luleå. Before she got on the night train, she went to McDonald's and had a Big Mac with extra toppings.

It was still light outside, and the forest grew taller and thicker the farther north they got. The sun found her face now and then through the thick branches, flickering like a glimmer of hope. She kept reading and paused to gaze out the window between chapters. Her eyelids grew heavy and the words flowed together — at last she put the book down.

Soon this will all be over, she thought before she dozed off.

She only woke up once that night, but knew where she was right away and fell asleep again.

★

In Luleå, the sun was shining.

It was six-thirty in the morning, and the platform was empty, but the air was fresh and smelled deliciously like fresh-baked bread.

The only other people on the bus were a couple of men in their thirties. They had crew cuts and wore jeans and sneakers and spoke in oddly loud voices. As if they were half deaf. She found them annoying — so much so, in the end, that she let their conversation turn into a dull hum. Maybe life out here in the real world wasn't always that much better after all. Yes, people had more freedom, but they mostly wasted it on stupid stuff.

★

Haparanda is the very edge of the world, she thought when she stepped off the bus. She remembered the town as a single, long street where the *raggare* gangs drove back and forth in their flashy cars, tossing beer bottles out the window now and then. But then she recalled the bright nights. The darkness could never quite get a full grip on the sky. She and her dad had spent nights down by the river, watching the blood-orange sun sink, only to rise again soon after.

She wasn't sure where to catch the bus to Seskarö, if there was even still a bus service there. But she knew the way there, because she had often biked from the cottage to Haparanda in the summer.

There wasn't a soul in sight. The whole city was asleep under a golden blanket of streaming sunshine.

Then she saw the bike. It was an old ladies' model with a basket, and it had been left leaning against a lamppost. She walked over and picked it up, finding it unlocked. There were some spider webs on the back wheel; she tested the tyres and there was still some air inside.

It was waiting for me, she thought. *No one will miss this old bike. Hell, this isn't even theft.*

She tossed her backpack in the basket, jumped on, and pedalled onto the road. There was a small shop on the way to the island; she would stop there and buy enough food to survive in the cottage for a while.

Gravel crunched under the tyres and the morning air was gentle and cool. It was as if this place had more air than Lund did. The sky seemed larger, wider, more open.

The shop was still there, but it wouldn't open for two more hours. She was just about to keep going and buy food on the island instead, when a man walked up carrying a huge pile of newspapers. He was tall and stocky and had a beard and moustache; he seemed familiar. Someone she must have met during her summers on the island.

'Are you opening now?' she asked.

'No, not yet, just bringing in the papers — but do you need something?'

His voice was rough and he had a Finnish accent.

'I need to buy a bunch of food.'

'I'm sure that can be arranged. I have to go inside anyway.'

She leaned the bike against the wall and hurried to help him with the door, then grabbed a basket and started tossing food in as fast as she could — anything that looked cheap and easy to make. Noodles, frozen pizza, eggs and potatoes, milk, cereal, bottles of water, and coffee. She noticed that he sold pay-as-you-go phone cards and took one, so her phone wouldn't be traceable.

'That's a big shop,' said the man, who was standing at the register.

'Yes, and I just need a few newspapers as well, and I'll be done.'

'No rush.'

She was just about to place a few morning papers in the basket when she noticed *Aftonbladet* on the same shelf. At first she thought she was seeing things, that she was so focused on Oswald that her mind was showing her images of him.

But the picture on the front page was perfectly real: a large photo of Oswald at a lecture, his hands high in the air. Like an all-powerful prophet.

47

She picked up the paper and read the headline.

Will Franz Oswald reveal celebrities' darkest secrets?

What dark secrets? But as soon as she read on, it became clear.

Is the stolen novel an exposé?

The article speculated that Oswald was going to spill all on ViaTerra's famous guests in his new book. That it wasn't a novel at all, but an autobiography full of remarkable details on the celebrities. There was even a list of actors and musicians who had gone through the ViaTerra program. She glanced through the text, which continued on the inside, and there was the picture of her again. Smaller than last time, but the same one. The mysterious woman who had stolen the book and vanished without a trace.

She began to tremble — only slightly, but the basket was no longer steady on her arm. Sweat broke on her forehead and palms, even though it was cool in the shop. The man at the register was unaware that anything was amiss; he was scratching his head as he worked on a crossword and waited for her. There was a shelf of summer supplies next to the register: sunblock, hats, and sunglasses. She stuck a sunhat and a pair of sunglasses in her basket as the trembling increased. Her whole body became bathed in sweat.

'I have everything I need,' she said, putting the basket down in front of him. She tried to look cheerful and untroubled.

'Well, this lovely weather is supposed to last,' said the man as he typed the sunglasses into the register. 'Do you need any sunblock?'

'No thanks. My skin can take the sun.'

Her legs were shaking now, and she felt vaguely dizzy. But the man just smiled kindly.

'Well, have a lovely vacation!'

She placed the bag of food in the bike basket, slung the backpack over her shoulder, and jumped on, pedalling fast down the road until she couldn't stand it any longer. She simply had to read the newspaper article. She stopped, fished the paper out of the basket, and read the whole thing.

Afterwards, all she wanted to do was sit down in the ditch and collect herself, but the damn bike didn't have a kickstand. So she just stood there breathing hard in the bright rays of the sun, which had already climbed quite high in the sky.

This has really blown up.

There's no way I'll manage.

The article was full of details on ViaTerra, the celebrities who had taken refuge there, speculations of what had gone on . . . maybe some sort of sex therapy? And in the middle of it all was the mysterious novel that might contain the answer to all the riddles. She stuffed her hair into the sunhat, which she had bought at least three sizes too large to hide her distinctive mane — it was the first thing people noticed when they saw her. Then she perched the sunglasses on her nose and got back on the bike. She sincerely hoped that the man in the shop didn't read *Aftonbladet* and wondered if anyone had noticed her on the train, but she thought she was safe on that count.

She couldn't wait to reach the cottage; she wanted to listen to the recording on the Dictaphone. As fast as she could, she pedalled across the bridge to Seskarö, hardly taking note of how beautiful the scenery was. She was so distracted that she nearly ran off the road a few times.

One hundred metres before she reached the cottage, she got a flat tyre and had to drag the bike the last bit down the gravel path. At first she couldn't see the building and was afraid it was no longer there, that perhaps her aunt had had it torn down. It turned out that the hedge had grown so tall it hid the house.

And there it was. A bit high on its foundation and with a large porch built to float over the garden. The white paint was flaking and moss grew enthusiastically on the roof, but otherwise it looked just the same.

She pulled the bike onto the lot, leaned it against an apple tree, and removed the grocery bag. Then she lay on the grass and let herself relax for a moment, disappearing into the endless blue sky until her energy returned.

The cottage was locked, but she went to the kitchen door in back and broke its window with a small shovel she found in a flowerbed. She cautiously stuck her arm in and opened the door from the inside. It smelled stale in there, but everything looked fine. The old stove, the rickety kitchen table, and the ugly green cabinet doors. The fridge was empty and the electricity was off. There were a few dead blowflies on the windowsill.

She cautiously tiptoed into the living room, feeling tense, because the silence and stillness were so palpable that she felt she had to fill them with something. An image of her grandmother on the couch intruded into her mind; she summoned her presence, giving herself such a fright that her heart began to race. But the living room was empty. The easy chairs and sofa were covered in sheets; the screen of the TV was covered in a thick layer of dust that the sun found through a gap in the curtains.

The beds in the two small bedrooms were made. It struck her how silly it was that no one ever came here anymore. Surely her grandmother would have wanted them to use the cottage. A person could live here — a thorough going-over with a dusting rag and a broom, and with the electricity and water on it would be truly comfortable.

She found the breaker, and turned on the water in the separate wash house. The food went in the fridge, and then she turned on the kitchen faucet, which spurted dirty yellow water that ran clear after a moment.

At first she had only planned to tidy up a little, but once she got started she couldn't stop cleaning. She dusted and swept, scrubbed the shower and toilet. It felt like making amends for the neglect the cottage had seen. In fact, it felt almost like her grandmother were standing right there, nodding, happy to see that someone was finally taking care of the place.

She ate only cereal and milk when she got hungry, and kept cleaning until she had made her way through all the rooms. Then she decided which bedroom to sleep in and placed her extra jeans and shirts in the wardrobe.

As she dug around in her backpack, her hand brushed the box with the Dictaphone in it. Her delight over the cottage fell away immediately and she dropped everything in her hands. She went to lie down on the sofa in the living room, propping her head on a pillow. Before she even began to listen, she shuddered. She didn't want to let Oswald into this lovely cottage. But she pressed *play* and there was his voice, the voice she had learned to obey, fear, and hate. It thundered against the walls of the cottage, serious and formal at first.

This is a draft of a novel I intend to write in the future. It is immaterial which parts are and are not based on my actual life.

Then the voice changed. It was almost as if he had put himself into a trance; he sounded a bit lax, as if he were drowsing.

I let the bumblebee fly around in the small aquarium for a while. It tries to get out, buzzing angrily, but all it can do is bounce off the walls. Then it gives up for a moment and lands on the cork mat at the bottom.

Her head was spinning.
What on earth is this? A novel about bumblebees?
There was a blanket on the couch and she wrapped it around her shoulders, because although it was still warm out it suddenly felt raw in the cottage. As the recording went on, she began to understand. The voice was painting a picture of a past that played out in familiar places.

That voice that just kept speaking, never stopping, never pausing, except for effect. That goddamn voice talking about killing people the way you might talk about making a cup of coffee. Yet she kept listening. She wondered where it was all going and shivered to think of how it would end.

After the recording, the words spilled out.

'Oh my god, oh my god, oh my god,' she said to herself.

She lay still for a moment, staring at the ceiling, and found that she was scared. It was a sort of fear she had never experienced before. A feeling that the windows of the cottage would shatter and he would suddenly be standing there and staring at her with the eyes of a killer.

She rose from the sofa and locked both doors. Then she rooted around under the sink until she found a piece of cardboard to tape over the broken window. To be on the safe side, she propped a chair against the door. Then she paced back and forth through the cottage, with no idea what to do next.

Something about the recording had caught her attention. At first it had seemed completely unimportant, and yet it stuck with her. She pressed her palms to her forehead, trying to get her brain to work. And the words returned to her.

Those rocks are way too deep down. You can't hit your head below that cliff.

The thought came to her like an icy tingle that started in her brain and spread down the back of her neck. It was absurd, idiotic, totally crazy. But even after she pushed it away, it came back. It was something that had been chafing at her subconscious. Facts that didn't add up. And Oswald's voice had brought them to life and made them flow together into an incredible whole. It wasn't just the comment about Devil's Rock; it was the manner in which Fredrik, or Oswald, or whoever he was, had fled the island.

The images grew clearer.

The body slicing through the surface so cleanly.

The waves rolling in from the sea, the head she just knew would pop up — but it never had.

The sounds of that day returned.

The roar of the sea and the wind and the silence echoing from the empty space on the cliff where he had stood.

And that voice on the phone, so completely lacking any hint of sadness.

She slowly let herself consider the idea that it might be true.

It moved in and out, like a slow inhalation you follow with your mind.

He was, after all, the type of person who could have done something like that.

In the end.

Closed off, reluctant, quick to withdraw when things didn't go his way.

He let others take the brunt.

It was the craziest thought she'd ever had.

Yet her certainty only grew the more she thought about it.

She dashed into the kitchen, yanked out the new SIM card, and switched out the old one. Then she took out her backpack and opened the pocket with all the notes. She found the one she was looking for and tried to dial the number, but her hand seemed paralyzed; she couldn't get her fingers to work.

Once she was able to move them, they trembled so hard that it took her three attempts to dial.

She hesitated for a moment when the warm voice answered, but she forced herself to speak.

'I know he's there. And I want to talk to him right now.'

48

There was a protracted silence.

'I'm sorry, who's calling?'

'You can tell him this is Sofia and I won't hang up until I speak with him.'

'Sofia, there must be some mistake, he —'

'There's no mistake. I know he's there. And I want to talk to him.'

Don't give up! Stand your ground!

'But you know he —'

'If he won't talk to me, I'll call Oswald and tell him he's alive. Tell him that.'

'Jesus Christ, give it up! That's enough.'

The mild voice had transformed, turning truly mean.

'But I won't give up, that's the thing,' she said, letting a bit of desperation into her voice. 'I need his help, okay?'

'Hold on!'

The line went silent again. For way too long. At first she thought Vanja had hung up on her, but then she heard a faint murmur in the background.

It seemed to take forever. An unpleasant bitter taste filled her mouth and her body was tingling.

'Sofia.'

It was his voice, but it sounded different on the phone — weak and thin. She thought her heart would stop. It really was his voice.

'Sofia, are you there?'

'Oh my god! You're alive!'

'It's not like you think —'

'No, this time it is exactly like I think! Let me talk, don't hang up. You betrayed me when we were going to run away, and you let everyone think . . . goddammit, you are such a lying bastard!'

He fell silent again, and cleared his throat.

'There was no other way out. I did what I had to do. It is my life after all, Sofia.'

'I liked you better when you were dead.'

'Don't say that.'

'It's true.'

Silence again. A long moment.

'I've read the papers. What did you do? Where are you?' he said at last.

'Okay, look, this time it's not what *you* think.'

'But you have to go to the police, give back Franz's things.'

'You and he can kiss my ass.'

'Don't be like that.'

'He's a murderer, Benjamin. He's been strangling Elvira with a belt in the attic.'

'What? You're hysterical.'

'No I'm not. There's so much . . . I can't tell you everything over the phone. You have to come here; I need help.'

'Where are you?'

'If you fail me one more time . . .'

'I won't.'

'When were you planning to stop playing dead?'

'Once everything on Fog Island was all figured out. I was just going to lay low until there was some sort of change there.'

'Why couldn't you just have left? You had the chance every single day.'

'I couldn't. He would have come after me. I know too much . . . it's kind of complicated, Sofia.'

'Don't say my name like that. Like we're friends.'

'Sorry. I can come and help you. Where are you? I'll rent a car.'

'How can you do that when you don't exist?'

'Oh fine, I'll take Vanja's. Sofia, I'll come, but promise me we won't argue. We're so different. I just take off when I can't handle something any more. You get angry and fight back.'

'Does Oswald know you're alive?'

'Hell no.'

'So he came to your funeral and everything?'

'He sure did.'

'A real funeral, with guests and everything?'

'No, not yet. He gave us money. Vanja was going to wait a while.'

Now she couldn't hold back a chuckle. She felt warm and weightless.

'A dead man and a wanted runaway. I'm sure we can work it out.'

He was laughing now too.

'Tell me where you are, and I'll hop in the car.'

'You're not going to like it.'

'Why not?'

'Because it's going to take like fifteen or twenty hours to drive here.'

'Sofia, I miss you so much.'

503

'Me too, until I realized you weren't dead.'

But she did miss him in that moment. So much that her chest ached. She didn't know how she would manage to wait for him to arrive. Just the thought of having him there, having someone to talk to, made her feel giddy.

'Your sister. She won't say anything, will she?'

'Never. But listen, I can't borrow her phone, so you'll just have to wait for me to get there.'

'You don't have a phone yet? What have you been doing all this time?'

'Lying low, although there's some stuff I have to tell you. But we'll deal with that when I get there.'

I really should hate him for what he did, she thought after they hung up. But there was no hate in her. Just the fact that he was alive was miraculous and sufficient, all on its own. That was all he had to do, keep living and come to her. She only wanted him to hurry. She'd never wanted anything so much.

Suddenly the little cottage was very quiet. Even the blackbird had stopped singing outside the open window. She wanted to take a walk on the island, go see the people at the campground. Talk to someone. Walk down to the beach and take an evening dip.

But she was no idiot, so she decided to turn on the TV instead. This was the only human contact she would get until Benjamin arrived. She pressed the button, but the screen remained dark. It turned out the appliance was unplugged; once it was on, she found a news channel.

The segment came on almost immediately. It started with a picture of her: the missing cult member who was assumed to be involved in some type of theft. Then came a clip from some

504

official building, and Oswald was suddenly being interviewed, as if he were simply on his way somewhere.

'We only want to find Sofia. We're so anxious for her. She's part of our big family, you know.'

He looked concerned. Honest. There was genuine worry in his eyes, and the worst part was that he was so handsome that all of Sweden would believe him right off the bat. He was wearing a suit and was tanned and clean-shaven. The camera zoomed in on his hands, which were folded and resting lightly over his jacket.

Liar! Bastard!

'And what is your novel about?'

'No comment,' he was quick to say. He gave a secretive smile, turned around, and walked off.

But then the picture changed to a studio sofa, and there sat Magnus Strid. He looked just as she remembered him, a bit flabby and dressed carelessly in a sweater and high-water pants that showed his socks and a decent amount of leg. The camera zoomed in on his face.

'So what do you think of all this, Magnus? You've been there, after all, to write about the cult,' said the woman interviewing him.

'I think something's not right. I met Sofia Bauman while I was there. She was ambitious and pleasant and seemed mentally stable. I believe she has good reason to be in hiding. Or perhaps she is even in danger out there on Fog Island. It's even possible that someone in the cult has made up the part about how she stole those things.'

'So it is a cult?'

'Definitely. It fulfils all the criteria.'

They discussed this for a while. Strid took the opportunity to mention that he was planning to write a book about ViaTerra, a nonfiction piece.

'So, Magnus, if Sofia were watching this program right now, what would you want to say to her?'

He looked straight into the camera.

'Contact me, Sofia, and we'll figure this out. I promise to help you.'

Her first impulse was to throw herself on her backpack, find Strid's card, and call him. But then she realized it was more complicated than that, because he didn't know anything about the Dictaphone, Elvira, or Östling. It would be Sofia and a journalist against the whole police force; what would happen? It was better to wait for Benjamin to arrive, but then it struck her that Benjamin might have set a trap. That he might come with Oswald and all the police in tow. She didn't know which way was up, and all she wanted to do was put an end to these racing thoughts.

You have to think like him. Feel the way he does.

There was something about the news segment. Oswald's hands! His pinkie finger was trembling, just a tiny bit, as it always did when he was upset and had to keep a lid on his anger. *He's agonizing*, she thought. *He's truly tormented by this.*

Frantically she searched for a different news channel and waited impatiently for the segment to come up again. And there it was. The close-up of his hands. His littlest finger dancing against the fabric of his jacket.

She wished she could send a telepathic message his way.

I hate you more than anyone else could.

The same words he said to Karin before he left the island so long ago.

There was only one thing to do now: settle in and wait for Benjamin. He would understand more of this.

She found a movie on TV, and watched it, and another after it. The cottage had grown chilly, so she pulled the blanket up to her chin. She found another movie and watched until she fell asleep.

In the middle of the night she woke up and thought her grandmother was standing over her, next to the sofa. She knew it was a dream, but she still thought she saw a shadow fade slowly as she opened her eyes. Then she heard a persistent scraping sound.

There was someone on the roof.

It sounded like someone was carving something into the roofing tiles or trying to dig their way in through the ceiling. She sat up and found that the window was still half open; she had no idea what was going on. She got up and slipped over to the window, trying to look up at the roof, but she couldn't see anything. The sound kept coming and even got louder. She stole into the kitchen and grabbed the largest knife hanging on the wall, then went to the door and opened it a crack so she could stick out her head and look up.

There sat a magpie, its beak shoved under a tile.

'God, you scared me!' she said loudly, shooing it away. She locked the door and dragged herself back to the sofa, her head still pounding. For a while, she lay still, letting her hands slip over her breasts and belly, under her shirt. Thinking about how it had felt when Benjamin stroked her there. She missed him so much it hurt.

★

When she woke up, the sun had found her feet through the

window and was warming them. *He'll be here soon!* was her first thought when she opened her eyes.

While she waited, she sunned herself in the yard. She was sure no one could see her through the hedge. It felt nice at first, but then the summer tourists began to pass by on their way to the beach, and every time she heard voices she thought it was Benjamin, Oswald, and a gang of police officers. At last she wrapped her towel around her shoulders and went back inside.

After a lunch of noodles she turned on the news, but there was nothing new on Oswald or Sofia herself. It was almost three o'clock — he ought to have arrived.

What if something happened? she wondered. *What if the police stop Benjamin and look him up in their database? Would it say he was dead?*

She went to the bathroom to peer in the mirror and found she looked terrible. She was still pale from the winter and her hair was going every which way. On a whim, she decided to make herself pretty for him. To smell good when he arrived. She hopped in the shower and began to sing as she washed up.

Just as she finished rinsing her hair and turned off the water, she heard a whistle in the yard. A gentle, melodic tone — at first she thought it was coming from some unusual bird.

She hurried to dry her thick, wet mane and wrapped the towel around her body. When she went out to the yard, she found Benjamin with two big grocery bags in hand and a big smile on his lips, as if nothing had happened.

49

Benjamin's smile faded and he shook his head in wonder, as if he couldn't quite believe she was really standing there before him. She, too, felt mildly shaken and stood there mutely for a moment before throwing her arms around his neck. He swayed and dropped the grocery bags; her towel slipped off and fell at their feet like a carpet.

After a while, he pushed her away to look at her face. She noticed that his eyes were brimming with tears and she found herself at a loss — she had never seen Benjamin cry. She took his arm and pulled him into the cottage, barely noticing that she was completely nude.

'You have to listen to this,' she said. 'Before we even think about discussing anything else, you have to listen.'

'Hold on,' he said, laughing. 'Can I put the food away first?'

He let his eyes rove over her naked body and smiled.

She took in his face again. Those lively eyes, even more freckles than before, and his bright red hair, which had grown long enough to reach his shoulders by now. She was so happy to see him that she began to cry, and then so did he, and they just stood there in the kitchen, holding each other and sobbing. Then they looked at each other and started laughing. She clung to him little longer, because it was so nice not to be alone anymore.

After a while she became aware of her nakedness against his clothes. Goosebumps rose on her skin and she felt a little fire kindle and spread through her body. She dragged him into the bedroom and lay down on the bed. It made her crazy to watch him taking off his clothes, so she pulled him close and wound her body around his, arms and legs holding tight until he entered her and they made love as frantically as they had the very first time. Taking back what was theirs. The feeling that had become so worn and broken by exhaustion and stress out on the island.

He grew heavy and limp and almost fell asleep on her afterwards. Gently, she rolled him away and gazed at his face, at his eyelids which fluttered like butterflies as he tried to stay awake. She ran a finger from the freckled bridge of his nose down to his mouth and let it rest on his lips.

'Listen, can't we start over?' he whispered.

'We'll see,' she said. 'Maybe if you're a good boy and you help me out of this bind.'

'Anything.'

They got dressed and she stood close to him as he put away all the food in the pantry and refrigerator.

'Now you have to listen to this recording,' she said impatiently. 'You won't believe your ears. Then we can make some food and talk.'

They got comfortable on the couch and she set the Dictaphone behind them, on the side table, so it was right next to their heads. And then they listened in silence as the sunlight found its way through the cottage window and danced across their linked hands.

When it was over, Benjamin didn't say anything at first. He just shook his head.

'Jesus Christ!'

'Now do you see?'

'Yes, but it also explains quite a bit.'

'What do you mean?'

'There're some things I need to tell you, Sofia. Please listen for a while, and you can weigh in later.'

'Okay, I'll try to keep my mouth shut.'

'I knew Franz from before,' he began. 'When he was Fredrik. We had a summer cottage on Fog Island, as you know, and I played with him sometimes when I was little. He taught me a ton of stuff, like how to build a fire and jump from Devil's Rock. And he was the one who showed me the cave. He even taught me how to hit on girls when I was, like, eleven. He was pretty cool at first, but then something happened.'

He paused as his eyes flicked around the room. Then he took a deep breath and went on.

'There was this girl I liked. I was only eleven, of course, so it wasn't anything serious, but Fredrik found out. He took her to the cave and made her take off her clothes. I don't know what all he did to her, but she said he, like, strangled her and tried to shove it inside her, but she fought him and then he made her walk home totally naked. There was a huge uproar about it, but he just denied everything and in the end it all blew over. He did an awful lot of strange things, too. He fed bees to frogs to see if it made them mean, weird stuff like that. I started to avoid him and found other friends. And eventually he spent most of his time with Lily, who had moved in at the manor. He lost interest in us other boys. When I found out he had jumped from Devil's Rock and died, I was actually super relieved. I guess I was afraid of him.'

He paused again, searching inside himself.

'Then what?'

'Then I ran into him, years later. When he came to Lund. At first I didn't recognize him, and when I realized who he was I was shaken up, because he was *dead*. But he made me promise not to tell anyone. He was calling himself Franz Oswald by then and said he'd inherited a ton of money and had chosen a name to suit a count. Things were rough for me back then. I owned a small carrier company that was about to go bankrupt. He helped me out, gave me money to get my business back on its feet again. Later, when he offered me a position out on the island, there was no way I could refuse. And you know the rest.'

'But why the hell didn't you say anything? All the shit he did to the staff — how could you?'

'I don't actually know. But listen, I had no idea about what he did to Lily in the barn, or to his family in France. If I'd known, obviously I would have gone to the police.'

'Is there anything else I should know?'

'Yes — about when you and I were going to run away.'

She let him tell the tale, even though she already knew it.

'He had cameras in our room, videotaping us. He sent a message in the middle of the night telling me to come to his office early the next morning. And Bosse and his gang were already there, so it was like I had no choice.'

'You could have come to Penance with me.'

'He said he was going to split us up. It only would have been worse that way.'

'So everything he says in his tale is true?'

'As far as I know. But again, I didn't know about Lily and all that. And that family in Antibes. Shit, it's so disgusting!'

'But why would he call it a novel?'

512

'No idea. Although if it's a novel, there's no way it can be used as evidence, right?'

'But why would he have recorded it in the first place?'

'Don't you get it?' said Benjamin. 'He's doing thesis number two on himself. Taking power from his own evilness. I think he's proud of it. Can't you hear it in his voice?'

'I wonder how he turned out the way he did. What they did to him down in that cellar. But it must be in that family history.'

'Forget it. Just because you have a difficult childhood doesn't give you the right to rape and kill other people.'

That was true. Benjamin knew what he was talking about.

'Every second you spend thinking about him is a waste,' he added.

'Not if I can learn something from it.'

'Listen, I'll give you something better to think about. What the hell are we going to do now?'

'I don't know yet. Why did you stay for so long?'

'I suppose I felt like I owed him something. He was so nice when we met up in Lund. He seemed to care. And later on, *you* were there.'

'He's such a creep. I just don't get it. His mom is perfectly normal; she's really nice. How can a person like that give birth to such a monster?'

'What a weird question. Can't you just accept that he is the way he is? That there might not be any reason for it?'

'There's always a reason.'

'Hmm. Come on, let's eat. I'm so hungry I think I'm about to pass out.'

She didn't know he could cook. In fact, they didn't know much at all about each other — there had hardly ever been time to talk. But he made salmon with new potatoes and wine, and made it look easy as pie.

The wine made her drowsy, and after the meal they relaxed on the sofa for a while.

'What happened, that night when you jumped?' she asked.

'I just swam underwater for a long time. I would come up for air now and then. It was so windy I was worried I wouldn't make it, but I made it to an outcropping on the other side of the bay and ran through the forest to the cottage. I spent the night there and dried my clothes. In the morning I walked over the rocks to the harbour and hid under the tarp on the ferry.'

'Almost exactly like he did.'

'Yeah. Weird, right?'

'And exactly as we had planned.'

'Right.'

'So I could have found you if I'd only thought about it.'

'Would you have wanted to?'

She considered this for a moment.

'No, not really. But I guess I would have wanted to you to be free from that hell.'

'Now it's your turn,' he said.

She told him everything that had happened, starting on the day he disappeared. He only interrupted her once, when she told him about Elvira.

'Jesus, that's crazy!'

When she was finished, it felt like they had finally sorted out a tangled ball of yarn. All the thoughts that had been so mixed up were suddenly in a straight line, and it became crystal clear what they had to do. She found her backpack and opened the pocket with all the business cards.

'I'm going to make a call,' she said. 'To a contact.'

'A contact?'

'Yes, Magnus Strid. What time is it?'

He looked at his watch.

'Eight-thirty.'

'And what day is it?'

'Friday. Didn't you know?'

'It's a little late, but it can't be helped.'

She took out her phone and dialled the number. All she got was his voicemail, so she left a message.

'Hi, this is Sofia — I'm ready to talk.'

Her phone rang almost immediately.

'Hey there, Sofia Bauman, where are you holed up?'

'I need some help.'

'You can say that again.'

When she finished her tale, there was a brief moment of silence and then Magnus chuckled.

'Well, damn.'

'Will you help me?'

'Of course I will. I'll take care of it. But you'll have to give me some time, since it's the weekend and all that. But I'll be as fast as I possibly can.'

'And you won't drag the cops into it?'

'No. At least not *that* cop.'

'And until then?'

'Stay inside and wait.'

Benjamin gave her a curious look when she ended the call.

'What do we do now?'

'Now we wait,' she said.

50

They all sat around the kitchen table, which they'd moved to the centre of the living room. Magnus Strid, Benjamin, Chief Inspector Hildur Roos, and Sofia herself. Ellis was in the corner, trying to crack the password to Oswald's folders. She still felt a shock of surprise each time she looked his way; she couldn't believe he was there.

Hildur Roos was a tall, bony woman with snow-white skin and grey hair in a sloppy bun. Aside from her eyes, she was very plain, but her gaze penetrated like a laser, turning you inside out. Sofia hadn't seen her blink yet.

Strid had contacted Roos and Ellis, and they simply showed up after the weekend.

The mood around the table was tense. They had just listened to Oswald's recording and watched Sofia's video clip of Oswald and Elvira.

Benjamin looked anxious, he was gnawing on his lower lip and avoiding Hildur Roos's stern eyes. He shot angry glances at Ellis now and then. Benjamin had turned rather brown in the past few days; they'd been sunning themselves in the yard. His freckles had grown to a clump at the bridge of his nose. Sofia thought he looked like a schoolboy and wondered if he would ever grow up.

'You're not going to like what I have to say,' Roos began. 'But that recording is completely worthless.'

'What?' Magnus Strid couldn't believe his ears.

'Just as I said,' Roos went on. 'Oswald says it's a novel, so he can basically say whatever he wants and we can't do a thing about it.'

'But he confessed to terrible crimes!'

'Do you remember the man who confessed to eight murders and then went free?' Roos asked.

'Wallberg?'

'Right. This is more or less the same situation. There's no proof to link Oswald to the deaths or the fires. I did some research before coming up. Both cases are closed. His half-sister set the fire in Antibes, and the poor little girl in the barn on Fog Island was so badly burned that it was impossible to determine the cause of death.'

'So the events he talks about really happened?'

Roos nodded.

'But that doesn't mean everything he says is true. As I'm sure you can appreciate, we must have tangible, irrefutable evidence to lock him up.'

All the air went out of Sofia.

'Furthermore, Sofia joined the cult of her own free will,' Roos went on. 'And as far as I know she made no attempt to leave before she ran away.'

Hildur Roos spoke as if Sofia weren't present, looking past er to Magnus Strid. Sofia's temper flared before she had time o think.

'Are you some sort of cult expert?'

'I'm sorry?'

'You make it sound like you are when you talk, but you have

no idea what it's like. You think it's so simple, do you? You just walk up to the gate and say "Bye, I'm leaving now!" and boom, they let you right out? But that's not how it works. There's a huge wall and an electric fence, and guards who will use force to stop you if you try to escape. And you have to perform slave labour on the property and eat nothing but rice and beans for months. Right now they've got people in a prison camp washing themselves with a garden hose and doing their business in chamber pots. Just because there was a flood in the guest quarters. Do you get it now? Because then maybe you can stop talking about me like I'm not here.'

'Sofia . . .' This was Benjamin, trying to calm her down.

'You can just shut up. You won't say anything anyway.'

Hildur Roos's expression hadn't changed in the least, but now she raised her eyebrows. Sofia glanced at Magnus Strid and saw an amused smile on his lips.

'And now that we mention it, it's not at all like you think when you arrive either,' Sofia went on. 'Everything is beautiful and super modern and everyone is so damn friendly, but then slowly everything changes. So slowly you hardly notice.'

Roos's eyebrows returned to their normal position. 'Are you finished?'

'Sure, as long as you don't tell me I need psychiatric help.'

'No, that's up to you to decide, but I was just going to say think there is something we can do. If we manage to convic Oswald of child pornography and raping a minor, he'll get hefty prison sentence, and that's what matters in the end, right

They waited for her to go on.

'If Mr Hacker in the corner over there can open those folde and there's child pornography in them, we'll apprehend hi

Although even that isn't watertight, because you did in fact steal the contents of his computer, Sofia, and he could claim that you downloaded the images from elsewhere. So there's really only one sure-fire way to put him away.'

'What's that?' Strid asked eagerly.

'To catch him red-handed. We'll have to hope that poor girl is still up in the attic. If we find her, we've got him. And we have your video clip, of course, Sofia. And you also said there are cameras in the staff members' private rooms. That's illegal, of course. So there will have to be a raid.'

'What do we do about the Dictaphone?' Benjamin asked.

'You'll send it back to him.'

'What?'

'Yes. Mail it back with a note of apology from Sofia.'

'Not on your life!' Sofia said.

'Okay, send it without a note then, but it has to go back, and soon. It will make things easier for us. I'll send it from Stockholm so the package isn't postmarked from here.'

'So it was totally pointless for me to take it?' Sofia asked, disappointed.

'Not at all!' Roos said. 'At least now we know what a pig he is.'

'I've got the folders open!' Ellis cried.

They'd almost given up hope when Ellis first tackled the folders, mumbling that the files might be corrupt, but now he had made it in.

Everyone sprang from the table to stand behind Ellis and stare over his shoulder at the screen.

Images flashed by. Photos of a naked Elvira in various positions and degrees of exposure. And in these photos, her face was visible.

The pictures made Sofia feel dizzy and nauseated. She found

519

herself back in the attic for a moment, suffering alongside Elvira. Benjamin groaned and covered his face with his hands. Magnus Strid shook his head and grimaced. Ellis just looked stupidly proud.

'There you go,' Roos said. 'So we've got a plan. Are you all prepared to testify against him in court?'

Sofia and Benjamin nodded.

'So what do we do now?' Strid asked. 'I assume you'll inform me when you raid the place?'

'Hardly. But there's nothing to keep you from hanging out on Fog Island for a few days. We'll be hard to miss when we come on the ferry.'

Strid nodded, satisfied.

'What about Sofia and Benjamin?'

'They can wait here. I'll be in touch. But now I have to jump in the car and get back to Stockholm to deal with all of this.'

Benjamin cleared his throat.

'Listen . . . It so happens that I've been declared dead. And now I'm wondering —'

Roos laughed.

'You can rise from the dead once we've completed the raid. Magnus can write an article about it: "Dead man returns from the depths of the sea."'

Was Benjamin blushing? Yes, a faint pink glow had spread across his cheeks and up to his forehead.

'There's one more thing,' Sofia said. 'Oswald's mom still owns that cottage on the island. I don't think she actually knows he's alive.'

'That has no bearing on this investigation,' Roos said. 'Whether or not he has a mother is immaterial. But if you war to contact her when this is all over, you're free to do so. Although she'll probably read about it in the media.'

'What about my parents?' Sofia asked. 'When can I call them?'

'I'll contact them so they don't have to worry. But for now, you two are only to do one thing.'

She aimed her X-ray eyes at Sofia and then Benjamin.

'What's that?'

'Nothing. You are not to move a muscle until you hear from me.'

Roos began to gather her belongings. She handed Sofia an envelope; Sofia reluctantly put the Dictaphone inside and wrote the address of the manor on the front. Roos took the SIM card from Sofia and the thumb drive from Ellis.

'Are you riding back with me?' she asked Strid. He nodded, then approached Sofia and placed his hands on her shoulders.

'You can be sure we will see each other again,' he said with a wink. 'You can always call —'

'No!' Roos interrupted. 'No phone calls.'

Sofia noticed Ellis looking at her. She knew he wanted to stick around and talk. To make everything right.

'You can stay the night if you want,' she told him. 'You can sleep on the sofa.'

'That's nice of you.'

'Hardly. But without your help —'

'It was nothing,' he cut in. 'After . . . Oh, let's not talk about it.'

Roos was already on her way out, but she turned around to nail Ellis with her gaze.

'And you — control yourself! No blogging or tweeting about this, do you understand?'

Ellis nodded and swallowed. Even he was reduced to nothing in her presence.

As Sofia watched Magnus Strid's frame cross the lawn, she thought of their evening chat by the pond on Fog Island. It had been the loveliest summer night ever — not just the weather, but the mood among the group. Yet Strid had known even then that something was horribly wrong. She wondered how it felt to have such a nose for the truth.

51

Ellis went home the next morning. When he was gone, the cottage felt empty and it began to make Sofia jumpy and anxious.

'Calm down,' Benjamin said — he had sensed her mood straight away. 'Strid and Roos will have only just made it back. We'll have to find some way to pass the time.'

It was sticky and warm but overcast that day. Heavy, oppressive clouds hung in a granite-coloured sky, and now and then they could hear a dull rumble of thunder in the distance. They spent the morning sitting in the yard and talking. Going through everything that had happened on the island with a fine-tooth comb. The catastrophes and Oswald's outbursts and whims. They tried to work out why they had stayed so long.

'I wonder what it's like now,' she said. 'What they're doing.'

'I'm sure they're toiling nonstop, as usual. I think you overestimate Franz. He thinks far too highly of himself to panic. He's probably sitting there, puffed up with pride because he has the whole police force after you.'

'Maybe. But then again, he never figured out you were alive. What happened when he came to your house?'

'Suddenly he was just there, standing at the door. We had no idea he would show up. I had to hide in my sister's closet. He fawned over her until she was totally charmed.'

Just talking about Oswald made Sofia anxious. The certainty that he was somewhere out there, his brain working nonstop to think of a way to find her, was really getting to her. She had the sudden urge to do some yard work to pass the time. She found an old lawnmower in a shed and shoved it into Benjamin's hands; meanwhile she began to rake up last year's leaves. When it was time to make lunch, they discovered that the fridge was empty and the garbage was starting to smell.

'Can't you go to town to get some food, and bring the trash with you?' she said. 'No one will recognize you there.'

'But Roos said —'

'Oh, she's just afraid someone will spot me.'

He let himself be convinced and they wrote a list of items they needed. She felt a stab of pain in her chest when she heard the car start and drive off; she wasn't used to Benjamin's constant appearing and disappearing in her life.

The thunder was closer, and the yard was bathed in a strange, pale light. A cool gust of wind came in ahead of the rain, and a nervous murmur went through the treetops.

Only ten or fifteen minutes passed before she heard a car stop on the gravel drive. *That's weird*, she thought. *It should have taken him longer than that.* She wondered if Benjamin had changed his mind. A car door slammed and the voices that reached her through the hedge were shrill and irritating. There was something familiar about them. Something that made her prick up her ears and stop raking.

'Here it is! Behind the hedge here.'

'What a place.'

'Shut up, we don't want her to hear us.'

Benny and Sten.

She didn't even have time to be afraid. Or maybe she just didn't feel it, because the instinct to hide was so sudden and violent that it took over all her senses. The cottage door was open, but she was around the corner and would never make it there before they were on the property. But she recalled seeing a small opening that led to the crawlspace under the foundation. There it was — a few metres behind her. She tossed the rake on the ground, got down on all fours, and crawled to the hole. She wiggled her way in — her hips barely fit, but with a shove she slid inside. The crawlspace was full of junk: boxes, old gardening tools, and a couple of car tyres. She had to crouch down, her back bent under the floor of the house.

They were on the property now.

She couldn't see them, only hear them.

'Look, the door's open!' she heard Sten.

'Call the boss. He said we should get in touch before we go in.'

'Yeah, but what if she hears —'

'Then quiet down! Whisper, dammit.'

For a long time, there was no sound. She was breathing so hard that she was afraid they would hear it. Her pulse thundered in her ears.

'Sir, we found the place!' came Sten's voice.

Hissing static from the phone. They were being chewed out; she could feel the vibes even from her hiding spot.

'Yes sir, sorry it took so long, but we found the cottage. The door is even open.'

Silence again.

'Yes sir, I promise. Yes, we'll bring her with us. Yes, sir. Okay, sir.'

'What did he say?' This was Benny's voice.

'That we have to bring her back with us. And the Dictaphone.'

'Yeah, I figured that much. Let's go in.'

And suddenly they were inside. She could hear their shuffling steps on the floor above her. She felt in her jeans pocket for her phone, although she knew it was in the living room. Steps clomped from room to room, and she considered dashing through the gate and down to the beach. But they would spot her through the window.

Then they were back in the yard. A phone jangled.

'No sir, she's not here. Although it seems like her stuff is.'

Static hissing again. Worse this time.

'Yes sir. I understand. Okay.'

'What did he say?'

'That she's hiding. And a bunch of other stuff.'

She could see their feet now, stupid uniform shoes trampling around in the grass. As if they hadn't had time to change into proper clothes before they took off to search for her.

It all happened in an instant: shoes coming closer, creaking joints as he squatted down, and Sten's eyes staring into hers. She had the idiotic impulse to remain perfectly still, to become one with the junk, an object he wouldn't notice.

They stared at each other for a moment. His eyes were bloodshot as if he hadn't slept in a very long time or had had a hell of a lot to drink.

'I found her!'

She caught a whiff of his bad breath.

'Come out, Sofia. We only want to talk to you.'

'Go to hell! You have no right to be here. Go away!'

'Franz just wants to talk to you. There's been a misunderstanding.'

'The hell there has. Go!'

His hands moved so fast she had no time to withdraw her own. One grabbed her wrist and the other her arm.

'Come out now, Sofia. We only want to have a chat.' Benny's voice came from above while Sten began to tug and yank at her. She resisted, but he was stronger and dragged her out onto the grass on her stomach. She let out a long, enraged screech. Then came a string of curse words and she bit his arm so hard he yelped and let go of her. But Benny was there, grabbing her from behind and dragging her up, locking her arms and pulling them above her head. It hurt so much that she whimpered and almost started crying. Sten stood in front of her, furious about the bite, which he was rubbing with the other hand.

'You're coming back with us. Franz wants to talk to you. Either you come along willingly, or we'll just take you. Even if we have to tie you up.'

He was shouting right in her face. And there it was again, that sour breath, a mixture of beer, cheap hamburgers, and unbrushed teeth.

This was no joke. This was truly serious, and if she didn't react now, if she didn't do something — anything — they would drag her off. There were so many things she wanted to scream at them: that Oswald would be locked up soon. That this was kidnapping, and they were brainwashed. But there was no time. Instead she kicked Sten in the crotch with all her might. His roar was so loud she didn't even hear the car stopping down on the road.

Sten sank onto the grass, mewling and whimpering. Benny tugged at her arms harder, but suddenly he lost his grip as someone shouted behind them, and there stood Benjamin, swinging the rake in the air. It looked perfectly ridiculous, but Benny, who must have thought he was seeing a ghost, just stood there staring. His jaw dropped, but nothing came out of his mouth.

'Let her go!' Benjamin cried, although Benny already had.

She would never find out what happened to Benny in that moment. Maybe it was the fact that Sten was lying on the lawn, or his shock at seeing Benjamin, or some realization that everything had gotten out of control, but whatever it was, the fight went out of him. He grabbed Sten, who was still whimpering on the ground, and helped him to his feet.

'Come on, let's get out of here!' he yelled, leading the staggering Sten toward the gate.

Sofia sank to the ground; the pain in her arms was nearly unbearable.

Benjamin followed Sten and Benny, still waving the rake in the air — it was a crazy sight. She just lay there, unable to comprehend what had just happened. She tried to get up, but her whole body was shaking and she felt ice cold yet sticky with sweat. Their voices were still echoing beyond the hedge. Benjamin was going on about something and Sten was howling: 'Shit, shit, I think I'm seriously wounded, that fucking bitch.'

The car door slammed, the engine started, and the tyres skidded on the gravel. Big, heavy raindrops had started to fall, and in some strange way each drop that struck her face felt freeing. Benjamin came rushing back to the yard.

'Are you okay, Sofia? What the heck were they doing here?'

'Those bastards came here to kidnap me. For real. They were on the phone with Oswald. Benjamin, what's going on?'

He didn't respond. He just walked over and picked her up, carried her inside, and placed her on the sofa.

'I *can* walk, you know,' she snapped, although it felt nice to be in his arms.

★

She called Strid as Benjamin locked all the doors and windows. Strid's voice sounded surreally happy, as if it were coming from a different universe.

'Well, damn,' he said once she'd updated him. 'I'll call Hildur and make sure she sends someone over right away.'

'But what if Oswald calls Östling and he sends someone before that?'

'Östling's out of the picture,' said Strid. 'That's probably why Oswald sent those baboons. Lock everything. I'll call you tomorrow. It's almost over now; tomorrow's showtime. You'll see.'

They didn't hear anything more from him that day.

No one showed up.

The rain roared against the cottage roof, and it felt like they had been abandoned way out in the middle of nowhere.

But she didn't want to call Strid again. She just wanted to trust him, because he was the only link to reality they had at the moment.

Neither of them could fall asleep that night. Benjamin tossed and turned until she sent him to sleep on the sofa, while she couldn't stop thinking about what would happen the next day. At last she slept, but uneasily — she woke in the middle of the night and saw Oswald's face on the pillow next to her, his eyes staring. She screeched and sat up in bed. Frantically she patted the pillow to make sure it wasn't real. She went to the living room and crawled into Benjamin's arms.

The phone call from Magnus came the next afternoon.

'Do you have a TV out there?'

'Sure.'

'Watch the channel one news at six. I have to hang up now.'

There was hope. Something was up.

They spent all afternoon waiting for the news, bringing out blankets and pillows, setting out wine, cheese, and grapes. It was as though they were preparing for an important visitor.

The news began with a report on deficiencies in school cafeteria food. But then the announcer reappeared in the frame.

'We turn now to West Fog Island off the coast of Bohuslän, where our reporter on assignment, Magnus Strid, will tell us about a police raid that's underway on the property of the cult ViaTerra. Magnus, what is actually going on out there?'

Strid was standing some distance from the gate. A bunch of people were visible in the background, including police in uniform, a couple of patrol cars, and an ambulance. They could hear agitated voices and barking dogs, as well as the alarm. She saw someone she recognized — was it Bosse or Ulf? She couldn't tell, but then the camera zoomed in on Strid.

'Well, a police raid is well underway here. The police suspect the cult leader, Franz Oswald, of being involved in the rape of a minor. And there are also suspicions of child pornography. The only mystery is that he himself seems to have disappeared. And no one here knows, or wants to say, where he is.'

'Does it seem that they've found anything else there?'

'Yes, a girl was led away from the manor house, wrapped in a blanket. She looked quite shaken, but she's in a patrol car now. It seems that they are putting the focus on the search for the cult leader.'

Sofia pounded the coffee table with her fist and shook Benjamin, who was just staring at the TV.

'Did you hear that? The bastard got away!'

The segment was over. She hadn't even heard the end. All she wanted to do was smack Benjamin for just sitting there and gaping at the TV.

'It's not so bad, really,' he said at last. 'After all, it seems like they found Elvira. Isn't that the most important thing?'

Her phone rang again. Strid was panting on the other end like an eager bloodhound.

'Sofia, do you have any idea where Oswald might have hidden?'

'Could he have taken the ferry?'

'No, the ferryman is positive he didn't. He saw Oswald on his way to the island a few days ago, and he's been checking the ferry carefully ever since. Do you know him?'

'Björk? Yes, I do. He's a good man. He helped me escape.'

'Besides, there's no way Oswald could have known about the raid. There's no chance he had any advance warning. Maybe from the guard, when the police arrived . . .'

'Did they check the cabin?'

'Yes, not a trace of him there. They even called his mother and she became hysterical; she had a breakdown on the spot. She had seen pictures of him in the paper and thought he looked familiar, but she hadn't put it together. She didn't take it very well when they told her. I think they had to take her to a psychiatric ward.'

Poor Karin. What a way to find out.

'What about the cellar?'

'They looked there too.'

'I know where he is,' came Benjamin's voice from the sofa.

'Huh? One second, Magnus.'

'in the cave,' Benjamin said, perfectly calm. 'I'm one hundred percent sure of it.'

'How can you be so certain?'

'He feels safe there. The cave is like his special place. It's like a literal man-cave. Tell them to look there.'

'Benjamin thinks he's in the cave,' she told Strid.

'The cave? Where's that?'

Sofia described the path as best she could — how it looked, where to climb down.

'I'll call you back,' Strid said before he hung up.

She shot Benjamin a look of reproach.

'The cave? No way he's in there. What would he be doing there?'

'Think about it. The guard calls and says the cops are there. Where is he supposed to go? He uses his key to exit through the gate behind the annexes and runs to the nearest hiding place. The cave, of course. He, you, and I are the only ones who know about it.'

'We'll see, I guess,' she muttered. 'What do we do now?'

'Eat. And wait.'

They shuffled into the kitchen. She made spaghetti while Benjamin put out two plates and poured water into glasses. They ate in front of the TV, channel surfing to keep from missing any news segment about the raid.

Benjamin seemed restless and vaguely distant.

'What's the deal with you and Oswald?' she asked.

'What do you mean?'

'I can just tell there's something there. You seem so sure you know how he thinks. Are you still friends?'

'Definitely not. But he did confide in me a few times. We wer to the cave together now and then, to sit and talk about how it used to be on the island. That's all.'

'What? I didn't know that.'

She sneaked a glance at him; something seemed to be hanging in the air between them. A tension that hadn't been there before.

'There's something you're not telling me.'

He turned and looked her straight in the eye.

'He had big plans for you, Sofia.'

'Me?'

'Yeah. The day we tried to run away he was so furious. I've never seen him so angry. He said that your future was clearly laid out. That he would rather kill you than let you get away. And that by God, he had dealt with people like you before. I was so scared.'

A cold wind stole through the living room window and found its way under her shirt, where it struck a chill in her heart.

'Did he really say that?'

Benjamin nodded.

She looked down at her arms and found that they were covered in gooseflesh. It was spreading toward her shoulders.

Just then, the phone rang.

'They've got him!' Strid shouted. 'Benjamin was right. Watch the news at seven. I'll call later.'

As soon as Benjamin understood, he jumped up and down on the sofa like a little kid.

'Stop!' she cried. 'Quit that nonsense. I want to see it with my own two eyes.'

He sat down on the sofa and glared at her. 'Oh, give it up. Strid *said* —'

'I still want to see it for myself.'

They watched in silence, waiting.

It was the first segment on the news. There was Strid again, but this time he was on the heath right next to Devil's Rock. The cliffs, the sea, and the lighthouse were visible in the background.

She didn't even hear what Strid was saying; all she could take in were the figures behind him. They were blurry at first, but they were approaching the camera and soon came into focus. A policeman on either side of him, holding his arms. His hair had come loose from its ponytail and was fluttering in the breeze. His face was turned away, looking at the ground.

Then, for a split second, he pivoted toward the camera. It was so brief, but she was sure of what she had seen. Her body flooded with warmth.

For the first time, she had seen fear in his eyes.

She stared at the TV.

Oswald was still in the frame.

Never again, she thought. *Never again will I have to see your lying face. I hope the rest of your life is miserable and you burn in hell for what you've done. And that a huge, nasty bad guy rapes you in prison.*

Then she cried for a while, for everything that had been so nice in the beginning, for the walls that had finally fallen, and for the evil that had run so rampant on the lovely island.

52

'Do you know what?' said Edwin Björk. 'In the end it was like you all didn't even exist.'

They were drinking coffee in the Björks' cottage.

'What do you mean?' Benjamin asked.

'Well, at first we were rather pissed off when you all showed up and took over the manor. No one in the village wanted a cult on the island. But later on it was so quiet up there. And with the fog and the walls, it was hard to see the estate. So it felt like you had disappeared. Like you no longer existed.'

'So anything could have happened?'

'More or less. To be honest, we wouldn't have noticed if he had killed every soul up there. Life just went on as usual out here on the island.'

'Are you going to go see the place again?' Elsa asked.

'Yes, we're going to take one last look,' said Sofia.

'What do you think will happen to the manor now?'

'I don't actually know,' said Sofia. 'But I heard everyone left, because the whole property has to be cordoned off — it's a crime scene.'

'He does still own the place,' said Edwin. 'I'm sure he'll sell it to some other idiot. Some poor fellow who doesn't know about the curse. And then the Countess will pay a visit some dark night...'

'There is no curse,' Sofia interrupted. 'That was Oswald and his girlfriend, scaring you that day out on the heath. She was wearing the Countess's cape. They had found it in the attic.'

'I'll be damned!'

Björk gazed near-sightedly into his coffee cup, and when he looked up his eyes had taken on a sheen of dreamy amazement. It was still there when they left the cottage not long after.

★

They took the path through the woods and up to the manor. She showed Benjamin the path she'd run that rainy, dark night. Everything looked different in the daylight — there were no dangers lurking behind trees, no steps echoing in front of them on the path, and when an owl hooted in the forest it just sounded like home. The setting sun shot golden rays between the trees, and the pine shadows grew long, stretching over the moss and the narrow path. They scared a crow, which flapped away above their heads with a hoarse caw.

When they reached the gravel path that led to the estate, the sun glinted off the gravel, bright enough to blind her, so she looked up and saw the façade of the manor house towering up against the sky. It stood there like a mountain, a landmark, completely untouched by everything that had happened. The breeze carried a faint scent of the sea and for an instant time stood still. Then she felt the urge to turn around, forget this bloody place, and just move on with her life.

'I suppose it's all closed and locked up here,' she said to Benjamin.

'I doubt it. If it is, we'll just go over the wall.'

She squinted, because she saw a shape just inside the gate. Sure enough, someone was standing there, a figure leaning against the iron bars.

'There's someone here,' she said, poking Benjamin in the side.

'You're imagining things!' he said at first, but then he, too, spotted the figure. 'Wait, that's —'

He was dressed in his usual get-up, a coverall and large gardening gloves. He was hanging around the gate lazily, standing so still that he might have been an illusion. She wondered if her desire to see him was so strong that she'd manufactured a vision.

But then he started laughing and she set off for the gate as fast as she could. She threw her arms around him, laughing herself.

'Simon! What are you doing here?'

'Björk said the two of you were coming. And I didn't want to miss out on the chance to see you.'

'But why are you still here?'

'It's a long story. I was about to leave with everyone else, but then the woman who owns the guest house in the village called. They want to start serving organic, local food, so I'm going to work there. I just have to move all my plants and tools and everything, and it's a tough job. Who would think that a few tiny plants could be such trouble?'

'Damn, it's good to see you again, Simon,' Benjamin said, thumping him on the back.

'You too,' he replied. 'Just think, you made the walls fall at last.'

As they walked through the gate, the sky paled, no longer the clear blue it had been that afternoon. The sun shone weakly through thin clouds, striking the manor house and making it sparkle like crystal. It was still the same beautiful place, even though the property was deserted. The wide-open space still made her head spin. Then she thought of how it had looked when the fog had enveloped the buildings, when the storms whipped at the trees and twigs chased each other across the courtyard, and when the snow had been the only bright point of the coldest, harshest part of winter. Yet her memories were beautiful in a strange, surreal way.

They walked through all the buildings on the property. In only a few weeks, their magnificence had started to fade. The lawn was soft and springy, overgrown with moss. The flowerbeds were brown and full of weeds. Dust had begun to gather in thick layers on indoor surfaces. How well she knew these rooms, their moods and light, how the shadows fell on the walls. Yet it wasn't the rooms themselves that sparked the most memories, but the objects that had been left behind in them.

Boxes of letters in the tiny mailroom, so painstakingly addressed — a couple of spiders were creeping over them now. A few plates in the kitchen sink, still covered in bits of rice and beans. The paperweight on Oswald's desk, the one he had thrown at them on that awful day. A cigarette butt in a flowerbed from someone's illicit smoke break. A hair-band and a pen pocked with bite marks from Sofia's teeth lay on her old desk.

It wasn't painful at first; it wasn't even uncomfortable to walk around there. She just thought of how things might have been if it hadn't all gone so wrong. She recalled the winter in the stable, how she had felt more at home there, with Simon, than in Oswald's office.

'Where are the animals?' she asked Simon.

'A farmer on the island is taking care of them. They're all fine,' he assured her.

'Even the pigs?'

'Yes, even the pigs.'

She walked over to the wall where she had been standing when Oswald attacked her. An icy tingle spread down her spine and the hand she had rested on the wall began to tremble.

'Let's skip the attic,' she said. 'I don't want to see it. Let's go out to Devil's Rock instead.'

'Tell me what happened after I ran away,' she requested as they came out to the yard.

Simon scratched his head.

'Well, nothing, really.'

'Nothing at all?'

'Oh, that first night there was a hell of a fuss. After the alarm sounded. Bosse and his gang dashed around asking if we had seen you and made us comb the forest for you. We were up all night. But afterwards, everything went back to normal again.' He thought back for a moment. 'Wait, there was one thing. The day after you escaped.'

'What was it?'

'Oswald came to the assembly and sent around a sheet of paper. It was a drawing. He said that if any of us had drawn it we had to confess before the night was over.'

'So what was it?' Benjamin asked.

'It was a drawing of a little devil with horns and an evil smile.'

★

They were sitting on the very edge of Devil's Rock, dangling their legs over the water. The gentle curve of the inlet lay before them. A few grey clouds had parked on the horizon, blocking the sun, but the sky around the clouds glowed red. The sea was high, reaching for them, sparkling and billowing. Further out the fog had begun to rise off the water and only the very tip of the lighthouse was visible, like a little knob. A flock of birds soared across the sky, circling and darting back and forth like a single, coordinated being.

It seemed like you could see the whole world from up there.

She wondered how much of what had happened would end up affecting her. She wasn't sure if the worst memories were lying in wait somewhere deep down inside, only to force their way up to the surface one day and surprise her. But at that particular moment, all she felt was relief. She tried to decide how much she regretted the moment when she had accepted Oswald's offer and started working for him. She had lost two years of her life. Could she get them back? But she didn't find any regret there. If she'd said no, she would never have learned how to put together a library, how to save animals from an inferno, how to hack a computer or climb over an electric fence. And she never would have met Benjamin and Simon. And what would have happened to Elvira? Besides, she never would have experienced the joy of seeing Oswald apprehended in the end.

It felt like a whole lifetime had passed since the first day she saw him at that lecture. And now everything had come full circle; this whole moment had begun when she had gotten sidetracked two years ago. Because here she was again, with no plans for the future, no vision for her life. She had no idea what she would do, no idea where she would live or how she would earn money. She didn't even know what would happen with Benjamin. And that was just the way she wanted it.

'There's just one thing that irks me,' she said aloud. 'The family history. Oswald's got it now, and there's nothing I can to do get my hands on it. What if —'

'Don't go getting any ideas,' Benjamin cut her off.

A lone gull cried out at sea as the darkness spread; the night would soon swallow the bay.

Benjamin tugged teasingly at her earlobe. 'Hey, you can stop worrying now.'

He said it like it was as easy as flipping a switch.

Epilogue

On the other side of the sound, the lights begin to come on in the city. Here and there, they pop up through the pale light of dusk.

The night is almost cloudless, but the air is still heavy and damp.

Anna-Maria Callini is sitting in her car, thinking about her headache, a persistent pounding at her temples. She wonders if it might be the change in the weather, but she knows exactly when it began: that morning, as she read the documents on her new case.

There's something that's not quite right. She has defended murderers and paedophiles before, but it's never affected her this way. They have every right to a good defence, and that's all there is to it. But there's something about this case. Something she can't put her finger on.

She thinks that what Oswald did out on the island was awful and that it's probably all true. But there are always loopholes and extenuating circumstances, and if anyone can find them, it's her.

No, it isn't what he did that's bothering her. Maybe it's his tenacity. How he insisted that *she* had to take his case. No one else. He doesn't even know her. She doesn't understand why he picked her, and maybe that's the question that's pounding so violently in her head right now.

The darkness has stolen in. She can see the prison towering against the sky at the end of the road, a black shadow with cold, illuminated windows. There aren't many cars on the street, and the asphalt gleams in the spotlights. High above the road, the occasional light glows in an office or apartment. She has a melancholy feeling that life is sliding out of her firm grasp, but chides herself for being so gloomy. She decides to get this over with quickly, sleep off her headache, and tomorrow everything will be back to normal.

She presents her ID to the prison guard in the booth and states her business. The massive iron gates creak and glide open. The parking lot is nearly empty so late in the evening. She parks the car, steps out, and looks up at the creepy building. The iron bars over the windows sneer down at her like bared teeth. So this is where they're holding him.

A guard follows her in and walks beside her at a polite distance, but she can still hear him breathing through his mouth; his lungs are rattling as if he has a cold. The corridor is dark and draughty and the lighting is low and greenish. One fluorescent tube isn't working; it flickers over their heads.

The only sound that can be heard is the echo of her ten-centimetre stilettos clacking against the stone floor. She may not be all that pretty, but she's got style and that's what matters in this business.

The presence of the guard bothers her. He seems nervous and his rattling breaths are getting on her nerves. There's that tingle in her stomach again, and the sweat breaking out on her palms. She is not a woman who sweats.

They reach the door, and the guard clears his throat, hesitating for a moment before inserting the key into the hole.

'You've got one hour,' he says. 'I'll be right here outside. Knock if you need anything. Although he's not violent at all, just so you know.'

She has seen pictures of him in the paper. His image is on the front of every rag in the country these days. He is damn attractive in each photo, from every angle — in close-ups and full-body shots. She knows this already and has prepared herself for it.

And still, all the air goes out of her when she opens the door.

He's sitting in the centre of the bare room, his hands folded on the desk, his long legs stretched out in front of him, his hair shiny and black. He is tan, dressed in a tight T-shirt that shows off his muscles. Almost immediately, his scent hits her — a mysterious, pleasant aroma. She's been to hundreds of conferences and events, and she has never encountered a man who smells like this.

His eyes lock onto hers, reeling her in like a fish flopping on a line. Then his gaze moves up and down her body, and up again, setting her on fire.

She can't help the gasp that escapes her as she steps into the room so she takes hold of the chair in front of him, suddenly shaky and weak.

'I'm so glad you're finally here,' he says, gesturing at the chair.

She hangs her purse on the back and sits down, noticing that her legs are trembling. Almost imperceptibly, but still.

He hasn't taken her eyes off her since she walked into the room. A spark flashes in his eyes and he smiles, open and warm, as if they've known each other forever.

'This is going to be good,' he says. 'This is going to be really good.'

About the events and characters in this book

All people and events in this book are fictional. I have taken certain liberties in my descriptions of Fjelie, Haparanda, and Hotel Lundia and I hope no one takes offence. West Fog Island and ViaTerra are products of my imagination.

I hope my story can bring a deeper understanding of what it's like to get caught up in a cult. It's easy to be drawn in, but almost impossible to get out. It can be done, however, and it is never too late to create a new and better life.

Thanks!

Thanks to everyone who helped me write this book: My wonderful family in Sweden, Los Angeles, and San Francisco. My husband Dan, who has toiled alongside me since the story took its very first breath.

Ann-Catrin Sköld Pilback, who read it so many times, editing, polishing, and correcting. There never would have been a book without your help.

Those who read and shared your opinions: Andrea Lindblom, Helena Braggins, and Emmie Ellman.

Håkan Järvå and Magnus Utvik, who fight so hard to help others who have suffered abuse and oppression in cults.

Lawrence Wright, who gave me the courage to speak out.

And thank you to Kate Mills and all of HarperCollins UK for believing in this book, and to Rachel Willson-Broyles, my fantastic English translator.

And last but not least, thanks to my editor, Frida Arwen Rosesund.

ONE PLACE. MANY STORIES

Bold, innovative and
empowering publishing.

FOLLOW US ON:

@HQStories